Mighty One Series:

Their children will be mighty in the land; the generation of the upright will be blessed. Psalm 112:2

Burgundy Gloves
Broken Chain
Black Coat

Escape to an era bere true love prevails.

Release dates and extras at juliadwrites.com

Burgundy Gloves

A novel by

JULIA DAVID

Field Runner Press

ISBN 9780999113400

Published by Field Runner Press

Redding, Ca.

Printed in the United States of America

I dedicate this love story to my husband, Larry, who believes in truth, healing, and prevailing love.

To my beta readers, Jeannine Dwyer, Ann Vallotton, Renee Hanks, Colleen Berry, and Lisa Steen. Without your prayers, time, energy, gifting, and encouragement, I would never have stepped out on the water. My life is rich and overflowing just to call you friends.

And to my sweet parents, Hal and Judy Berry, who would still post my work on the fridge if they could.

Neither height nor depth, nor
anything else in all creation, will
be able to separate us from the love
of God that is in Christ Jesus our Lord.
Romans 8:39

1

Outside of Chicago
May, 1880

Allison Kent gazed out the third story window of her room at Webster's School for Young Women. Green grass laid like a thick blanket over a bumpy bed. The school was delightful in the spring. With the long, cold winter passed, the temperature was inviting for an afternoon of flower picking—just right for coaxing her out of her melancholy. She turned as Yvette appeared, returning to help her pack.

"There you are," Allison whined. "I guess I won't have to put up with your incompetence much longer." A small pang of guilt stirred in Allison's heart for speaking unkindly, and for how she often mistreated the third-floor maid. "Have you or have you not seen my burgundy gloves?"

"No, Miss Kent. I've looked through the layers of your trunk, in between the tissue paper, and in your hat boxes. I can't seem to find them."

Allison pursed her lips to contain the sharp words. "You're sure that you didn't pack them with Suzanne's things?"

"Yes, ma'am, quite sure. Could you have left them at the seniors' graduation party?"

"Very possibly, if I had worn them there. But since I didn't, they have to be here somewhere." Allison looked up from the contents of her carpetbag, splayed all over her bed. "They're just not here." She took a deep breath and clamped down her jaw. *Could this day get any more frustrating?* Once and for all, she was leaving the boarding school that had been her home since she was six years old. Before her roommate, Suzanne, had left, they had talked about their futures, and she felt hopeful. But when Suzanne and her family drove away in their carriage, Allison waved goodbye with a familiar pain in her deserted heart.

"Hello, ladies." Mrs. Webster's entrance into the dorm room caused Allison to straighten up.

"Mrs. Webster, I hate to feel this frustration in these last moments. My burgundy gloves are missing, and according to Yvette, they have simply disappeared."

"Oh, dear. But Allison, to have commotion in your last moments here doesn't seem too unusual, now does it?"

"Why, Mrs. Webster, it sounds as if you're going to miss me."

"Ahh." Mrs. Webster's voice was firm, but caring. "Just when we thought we were going to say goodbye to your confidence and passion, you were kind enough to stay two more years to teach. It has been our pleasure to watch you blossom into the beautiful young woman that you are."

"How wonderfully kind of you to say that, Mrs. Webster. Freshman French was the class no one else wanted to teach."

"Yes, dear. So many things about you I will never forget."

"Hmmph," Allison knew Mrs. Webster was trying to divert her with pleasantness. "Those burgundy gloves have priceless sentimental value to me. Will you promise to send them to me when found?" She shot Yvette a glare.

"Why, of course, my dear. I just wanted to say goodbye. It will be a little sleepy here without you and Suzanne. Please give your grandmother my best."

"Thank you for everything, Mrs. Webster. I will give my grandmother your regards." She met the older woman's gray eyes and leaned in to hug her.

Mrs. Webster patted her back. "Good luck, dear." She placed a soft kiss on Allison's cheek.

Allison looked down, her eyes unexpectedly filling with tears. *I need to find those gloves.* Turning away to find her hanky on the bed, she dabbed the corners of her eyes before anyone could see. Quickly packing the remaining items back in her carpetbag, she slipped her reticule onto her wrist. Mrs. Webster was gone when she looked up.

Allison scanned the room. Fighting the painful truth, she put a hand to her heart to quell the grief of having to leave without those gloves. "You can be thankful, Yvette, that at least I have my cream gloves to go with my suit today." Letting out an exaggerated huff, she wedged the gloves between her fingers.

"I'm ready to go." Taking a deep breath, she glanced for the last time over at Suzanne's bed, remembering the countless nights of talking and laughing, sharing dreams, making up stories about the young men they were going to meet.

"What else, miss?" Yvette's voice broke in.

"That's all." She flung her hand toward the door. "Send Mr. Stewart to get my things."

Allison turned around in the small dorm room that had been home for so many years. The lace curtains outlining the window drew her again. She popped the window latch and pulled it up from the sill. A group of girls were laughing below while they waited their turn to be picked up. Birds chirped in the nearby trees, happy for the new season. *I should feel happy*, she mused. *What's wrong with me? I used to hate this school. I used to hate the cold winters. I've longed for the day when I could be a bird, flying from this cage. And now the door is wide open, so why do I feel so forlorn?*

Knowing most of the students were gone and the others wouldn't come out to say goodbye to her, Allison quietly entered the carriage as the driver shut the door. She straightened her back and pulled on the hem of her linen jacket. With her reticule placed carefully in the center of her lap, she nodded at the driver.

She had taken many of these drives to the Chicago train station. It seemed strange, though, that this was going to be the last. Allison shook her head, amused at her fancies. It wasn't as if she was a captain going to sea, never to see land again.

Oh dear. To get to France, it would be by sea. For the last six months, Suzanne had given her every hope that she would be joining her family on their trip to Paris. With every month, her hopes and dreams had built. The only drawback for Allison was seasickness; the rocking of the boat just might do her in. She had a terribly weak stomach when it came to anything swaying back and forth. *I'm not going to think about it. I'd rather think about Suzanne's two older brothers.* Her perfect fantasy was for them all to travel together, seeing museums and art exhibits, picnicking by the Louvre.

Leaning her head back, she rehearsed for the hundredth time how to approach her Uncle Simon. Certainly, she could get her grandmother's permission, but her uncle held the family purse strings, and he was never charitable toward her. Her grandmother had promised at Christmas that she would persuade him to have an open mind—and pocketbook.

The carriage hit a rut, and Allison grabbed the small window. She leaned out and found she could no longer see the school. *Why can't I feel some joy in this day? Why was Mrs. Webster's goodbye so emotional? Going to miss my confidence and passion?* Mrs. Webster would never speak a harsh word. *How many times over the years did my teachers suspend me from class for causing trouble? Only Mrs. Webster could smooth things over. I spent many an hour swinging my heels from that silly hard bench outside of her office. I suppose my teachers just didn't know what to do with me.*

When Allison was a child, her outbursts came and went, seemingly without reason. She gazed out to the rolling countryside and remembered…

It was Mrs. Covington who did not want her back in class. Mrs. Webster had not closed her office door all the way that day. They didn't know Allison could hear every word of their discussion.

"That girl is prideful and unrepentant!" said Mrs. Covington. "What's more, she is rebellious and contentious!"

"I don't believe our Allison is a bad child," said Mrs. Webster. "I believe she is a sad child, since the loss of her parents. As educators, we must look at the grief and loss she has suffered and pray for God's help to reach her."

Seated on the bench, Allison listened. She didn't want to be rebellious. She didn't want to cause any difficulties. Somewhere deep inside, she wanted to please her teachers.

Upon returning from Christmas break, Mrs. Webster had called her into her office. She had a smile on her face instead of a frown, and she complimented

*Allison on her recent good behavior. "I'd like you to be a friend to a new girl,
Allison. Her name is Suzanne, and you are to room together." Mrs. Webster's
kind smile told Allison that she was being entrusted with an important task…*

Allison straightened her back into the carriage seat. Those were
her best memories. Those times with Suzanne were moments of
true happiness in her life. Soon the countryside faded behind her,
and the noise and bustle of the city took its place.

Late that afternoon, the train pulled into Madison, where
Grandmother's handyman, Burch, stood waving from the landing
as he did every time he picked her up.

"Miss Alli, Miss Alli! You're home," he said, patting her on the
shoulder.

"Yes, Burch, it's me. Who else would it be?"

"Well, now, Miss, it's not every day you're home for good."

"Let's hope I'm not home for good." He looked more bent
over than usual. "Are you going to find someone to help with my
trunks?"

"Oh, Miss, your grandmother gave me strict orders to bring you
straight home. I'm to come back with the flatbed to pick up all
your things."

"Fine, then." Allison walked to the family carriage. Thankfully,
Burch rattled on about Grandmother's health and the garden and
the weather. Lacking the nerve to ask if Uncle Simon was at home,
she let her mind wander. She needed him to be gone on business,
or away with any of his usual excuses. She wanted time alone with
Grandmother to talk about the lovely trip to Paris being offered to
her.

The family's pale yellow Victorian house was a beautiful home
where crocuses and daffodils bloomed in the flowerbeds. Burch
was getting old, but he never let his duty slip in keeping the home
clean and tidy. Allison ran her hands down her jacket and skirt to
straighten out any wrinkles and tightened the pins in her hair,
wanting to appear independent and mature.

She entered the side door to an empty kitchen.
"Grandmother?" The house was silent.

"Hello? Mrs. Clark?" She walked into the open hallway, looking for the housekeeper.

"Oh, Miss Allison, you're home," Mrs. Clark said as she rushed down the staircase. "How was your trip, dear?"

"Fine, as usual. The house is so quiet—where is Grandmother?"

"In bed."

"In bed at this hour? Is she ill? Or did she just have a bad day?"

"Probably a combination of both," Mrs. Clark said.

Allison set down her reticule and began to climb the stairs, then stopped short, turning back to Mrs. Clark. "Is my Uncle Simon at home?"

"That's hard to say, dear. Sometimes he comes in so late at night, I can only guess his comings and goings based on the bed being made or unmade."

"Well, has his bed been slept in?"

"No dear, not the last two nights."

Allison continued to her room and opened the heavy brown curtains. The sun had not yet set, and a soft glow filled the room. The floors and furniture were all polished. Resting on her cream and brown bedspread was her companion, Freddy. She picked up the stuffed animal and touched his tattered fur. "Please forgive me, friend, but you must enjoy my company from the rocking chair from now on." She placed him on the chair next to the embroidered pillow.

"Dearest, is that you?" The faint voice of her grandmother came from the next room.

"Yes, I'm home." She crossed the hall. "I see you've taken to bed early."

"Child, I haven't left this bed in two days."

She pulled a chair next to her grandmother's bed. "What is it?"

"Dr. Green was here yesterday. He used the word *failing*. I'm failing. What do you suppose that means? Every day I find a new ache. Of course my knees buckle when I try to take those stairs. I'm getting old. What am I to do? Mrs. Clark certainly can't catch me if I fall." Grandmother grimaced.

"The first thing we need to do is get you settled in a downstairs room."

"Don't you think I thought of that?" her grandmother fussed. "Simon can certainly take this room, and I can move into his room downstairs. The two minutes I've had to talk to him, he says he doesn't have time to help me. He probably won't find the time to get my corpse out of here, either."

"Please, Grandmother." Allison sighed.

"Your uncle has no conscience, Allison. Believe me, if you weren't here, no one would care if I lived or died. Lord knows, I tried not to favor your father, but Simon was always stepping on toes, arguing over everything."

Allison stretched, rubbing out the ache from a long day of travel. Unfortunately, this was not the time to bring up Paris.

2

Northern Michigan

Levi Graham was a driven young man, but he wore a cloak of calm and peace. Dominance over the land and the elements beat in him like his own heartbeat. His goal was never money or man's approval; it was the kill. Nothing made him feel more alive than the release of his bow and the satisfaction of the arrow penetrating the target. This morning was no different. The beauty of the upper Michigan landscape covered with a light frost energized him with every step. After an hour of following a deer trail, he thought he saw movement. He came down on one knee, pulled his dog to sit and positioned his bow. The sun broke through the trees. He strained to see if what he thought appeared to be a buck could also be the leaves slightly moving. He had mastered his ability to relax his breathing and this was when he became calculating, evaluating, and ready. He had a grand respect for this buck. He would not wound it; only a clean kill was acceptable.

Birds chattered relentlessly, shattering the serenity of the woods. He waited—and his patience paid off. His prey presented itself, reaching up to nibble at a tall leaf. The decision made, his bow and arrow in place, Levi aimed with confidence, felt the exact tension he needed in his fingers, released the arrow, and pierced the target. The deer bolted, as expected. Levi's muscles filled with adrenaline and swiftly carried him through the brush. He was agile and young, and could track for many hours, if necessary. The buck leaped from left to right, but hesitated when two large boulders blocked him. It was the only hesitation Levi needed, and in a split second, another arrow met its target, and the buck fell to the ground.

The first purple shade of dusk illuminated the sky when Levi finished dressing the deer. The hide and meat were securely bagged, tied, and lifted onto his back. Awakening his beloved dog Patch, he trudged onward for an hour before he caught sight of Sault Creek. Even though his legs were burning, it would be another hour or so until he reached his cabin. He smiled at the furry companion that never left his side. *The only thing better than Patch's company would be to have someone waiting for me at home.* He remembered what it was like to have his ma waiting at their family home—her warm meals after a long day. Hot stew, fresh soft buns, a glass of buttermilk—all he had to do was sit down. Those were the days.

Levi realized the pain shooting through his back was covering up his empty stomach. But hunting meant food, and food meant hunting. Unlike his younger brother, Ben, once he'd left home, he knew would never choose to live there again. He could never do what Ben did. *Ben likes to ramble from place to place. He thrives on people and attention. I like my solitude too much. God dwells in my solitude. I never could hear God in the midst of a bunch of chattering people.*

As soon as Levi caught sight of the cabin, Patch ran ahead.

Reaching the fence, he squatted, letting the pack slide down his shoulders.

Patch jumped up on him. "Feels good to be home, huh, boy?" Levi dug his fingers into the dog's thick tan fur. Patch went instinctively to sniff his heavy pack, then back to Levi for more attention, and then back to the smell of fresh meat.

"I know, I know, I'm hungry, too. Give me half an hour and we'll eat."

Sometime later, Levi burped. "That wasn't bad." He wiped his chin, smiling at Patch for approval. Then wandering out the door, he looked up into a star filled night. Patch ran ahead.

Levi released the tense muscles in his back while Patch ran from bush to bush along the creek, looking for a hidden varmint to come out to play. He stretched his neck, observing the billions of stars. A familiar song rose in his throat:

For the beauty of the earth,
For the beauty of the skies,
For the Love which from our birth
Over and around us lies:
Christ, our God, to Thee we raise
This our Sacrifice of Praise

For the beauty of...

Levi couldn't remember the second verse. He sat on a large flat rock by the creek, and Patch came over to nudge his leg. "Did you want to hear me sing, Patch? I hate it when I forget the words." He leaned back on his elbows, praying out loud.

"Dear Father, thank you for your goodness in this day. Thank you for the buck and the provision it will bring. Thank you that you forgive me when I don't remember the songs we used to sing in church. Watch over my ma and pa. Please keep your eye on my brothers. Help me with my desires. You answered my prayers when you got me off the docks. I don't want to seem ungrateful for what you've given me now. Give me the grace to accept this life, I pray in Jesus' name, Amen."

Opening his eyes, he saw that his faithful friend held a stick in his mouth, ready to play. "Patch, it's too dark, old boy. You'd run head-on into a tree, trying to find that stick." Levi wrestled the stick from his mouth, which ended up being a game in itself.

"Okay, okay, I see how it can be. You can have that one. I'll gather my own kindling."

He walked into the woods, picking up sticks here and there and trying the song again:

For the beauty of the earth
Of the day and of the night
Hill and hum and hum hum hum
Sun and moon and stars of light.

3
&ৎ৽

Allison opened one eye to confirm it was indeed morning. Her grandmother's steady snoring was audible through the walls, so she rolled over and pulled the covers tighter under her chin, enjoying the privacy of her old room. While contemplating how long she could stay in bed, she heard a knock at the door.

"Miss Allison, are you awake, dear? Can you open the door for me?"

Allison jumped up, opened the door, and climbed back into bed.

"Thank you, dear." Mrs. Clark entered, carrying a silver tray with a steamy cup of coffee and a biscuit.

Allison stacked the pillows behind her back and smiled. "Mrs. Clark, this is very sweet of you."

"This is a special morning, my dear. It's not every day our girl comes home for good." She placed the tray carefully on Allison's lap. "Coffee with lots of cream and sugar, right?"

"Mmm, my favorite." Allison reached for the warm biscuit covered with butter and strawberry jam.

"Some mornings your grandmother doesn't even wake up till ten. It's worked out better just to prepare her something light to get her through until lunch. Now that you're home, let me know when you want to sit down and go over the daily schedule. We'll find a new way of doing things that will work out for both of you." Mrs. Clark gave her a motherly nod.

Allison sipped her hot coffee. "Please, I don't want to make too much of a schedule. I really don't plan to stay long."

Mrs. Clark looked up. "Oh, your grandmother never said anything about your plans. What are you looking to do?"

Allison swallowed a bite of biscuit and cleared her throat. She desperately wanted to relay her plans as if they were solid, but she knew that everything was dependent on Uncle Simon's good will.

"You know of my friend Suzanne? Her family has offered to take me to Paris with them in one month's time. I spoke to Grandmother about it at our last holiday. I just haven't had the opportunity to speak to Uncle Simon yet. I'll need your help going through my dresses. After I talk to Grandmother, I'll need two more gowns bought or made. Is your daughter still a seamstress?"

"Oh, my! One month isn't much time. What a lovely opportunity for you, Allison. Yes, Katie still is doing dressmaking. She had her fourth little one, you know. Beautiful baby boy, big blue eyes, and sweetest smile you ever saw." Mrs. Clark's voice trailed off. "She's very busy, but maybe I can ask for a special favor."

"Your daughter does lovely work, but I can't imagine her having much time for sewing with four young children. I might just have to purchase store-bought." Allison handed the tray back to Mrs. Clark.

"Whatever you think, dear. Would you like me to prepare a bath for you, or help wash your hair?"

Allison hoped for an opportunity to run into Uncle Simon. "Yes, a bath would be lovely. I assume Burch brought all my trunks in. Maybe we could organize my things before Grandmother wakes up and needs you."

"Good thinking, dear." Mrs. Clark left the room and quietly closed the door.

Bright streams of sunshine shone across the dining room table where Allison worked on sorting out her papers from school. The morning felt productive and surprisingly uninterrupted by her grandmother's calls. After several quiet and busy hours, Mrs. Clark met Allison in the hallway. "Your grandmother would like you to come up in about ten minutes, dear. She's almost ready."

"Ready for what?"

"Oh, it's her surprise."

Returning to the dining room, Allison picked up some remaining school papers that she wanted to keep, then wandered into the parlor. What a disaster—Grandmother's beautiful cherry wood desk was now covered with paper, ashtrays, and Uncle Simon's clutter. The sideboard was covered with decanters of bourbon and whiskey. Stepping to the desk, she scanned it, searching for...what? A ledger, maybe. What if she could find something with the evidence that they had the necessary money? Riffling through a few papers, she heard Mrs. Clark call her from the hallway.

"Coming." She sucked in a breath and took the stairs, stopping in front of her grandmother's door. "Grandmother, may I come in?"

"Yes, dear." Grandmother was sitting, fully dressed, in the corner chair.

Allison bent to kiss her grandmother's cheek. "Nice to see that you've risen from your bed today."

Her grandmother shook her head, squinting. "Sometimes you look so much like your mother. But other times, like now, I see Jonathan in you." These recollections were rare; Allison didn't want to breathe.

"You have your mother's beautiful figure. But I see Jonathan in your eyes and in your manner. You have his honey colored hair, with just a shimmer of red when you stand by the light."

Allison wanted to beg her to keep speaking of her parents. "Tell me more. I love to hear about them," she said softly.

"No, dear, it only brings back more pain." Grandmother pressed her hands against the chair's arms in an attempt to stand.

Allison stiffened, Grandmother always closed off the conversation. *Maybe it would do my heart good if I knew more about them than my father's hair and my mother's hourglass figure.*

"Let me assist you." Allison wrapped her arms around her grandmother to steady her.

"Just go get Burch, he's the only one I trust getting me down those stairs."

19

"Yes, ma'am. You'll be fine to stand here while I go find him?"

"Yes, ninny girl, I can stand and walk. I'm just not ready yet to break my neck on those stairs. Tell Mrs. Clark to have tea ready in the parlor."

Allison gave her grandmother a curious look.

"No, make it the dining room. At least your uncle hasn't abused that room yet."

Allison sat across from Grandmother at the dining room table and sipped her tea. It was getting harder and harder to sit and listen to Grandmother ramble about neighborhood gossip, while her Paris proposal hung by a thread.

"I did tell you Mrs. McLaren's broken toe healed up fine, didn't I? She should be hostess at the hotel tomorrow. We'll plan on having lunch there around one o'clock."

Allison wondered what kind of burst of energy would get her grandmother out of the door by that time tomorrow. "Are you sure you're up to it? We can certainly pick another day." She breathed in the courage to interrupt the boring chat. "You remember the Goudes have asked me to go to Paris with them." She could only pray that her grandmother understood the importance of this.

"I talked to you a bit about it over the holiday. They would like me to meet them in New York City in four weeks. I know I need to speak to Uncle Simon about the details." She remembered her girlhood days, when rambling had been the best way to sway her grandmother. "I would be traveling with Suzanne's family the entire time. They have a home there, you know. Suzanne and I have made plans for sightseeing. So many things I've read about in books, and now I'll be able to see them in person. I can't believe how fortunate I am to get this invitation. The Goudes have been so generous. My only responsibilities are getting to New York and paying my fare. Then, with just a little spending money, everything else will be taken care of. I am so very excited; you can't imagine how much I've looked forward to this trip." She stopped, breathless.

"For how long did you say they would be taking this holiday?" Grandmother asked sharply.

"They usually stay about three months, depending on Mr. Goude's business."

"Well! It seems you're barely here, and your plan is to leave." Grandmother huffed, rubbing her hand against the lace tablecloth. "You may have forgotten that I was a young woman once. My older sister was already married at your age. Times were different back then. Schooling and marriage were the only options. I realize that your years in an all women's school have made it difficult for you to meet young men. But society here in Madison is becoming quite varied. I do have some connections. Even if you were to start courting now, it would take a year to procure an engagement. You realize that gallivanting off in Europe, though it may it be exciting, will delay this next season in your life." Grandmother shook her head. "It sounds as if you're willing to give up security and a good home for another girlish adventure."

"Adventure?" Allison's cheeks flushed. "I've had no adventure, Grandmother. Everything I know about the world is from Suzanne's eyes. What adventure do you think happens, sitting year after year in an all girls' school?"

Allison's nerves were fraying, so desperate was her desire for her grandmother's approval. "Seeing historical sites in Europe will only help to broaden my mind and perspectives. The modern man wants a woman who knows a bit more than how to fold napkins and set proper silver settings. This trip will be to my advantage. It will help me to be more interesting."

"*Pfft*, you make us sound like bumpkins. At least you have napkins to fold and silver to set out properly." Grandmother pressed her lips in a frown. "You seem a bit ungrateful, Allison. Really."

Allison took a deep breath and planned her words carefully. "Please…I promise you, I am grateful. When you say that you see my mother in me, my heart overflows. But my memories of her are vague. I'm thankful to you for seeing that I was raised properly. Telling you how badly I yearn to go on this trip is not a reflection of something amiss. I would just like a real voyage to other places. Is that so wrong?"

"No, of course it's not wrong. But I have to tell you, it's a bit unrealistic."

Allison felt the air leave her lungs. "Grandmother, what are you saying?"

"The only news your Uncle Simon can seem to relate to me is our lack of finances. I've asked him just what investments have gone bad, but all I get are excuses. It's quite frightening. I lay awake at night, wondering if the bank will come and take our furnishings, for heaven's sake." She grimaced. "I wish your father had put aside a trust fund for you. But you were only six; who knew what tragedy was ahead? Such is this fearful life. Uncle Simon has had no children, and I've told him year after year that it is his responsibility to care for you. But he always seems to resist the notion, like most things I bring to him. However, now you are an educated woman. Talk to him as such. Try your best to reason with him. I would imagine that he is your only hope."

Allison rose from the table, full of all the bad news she could take.

Grandmother struggled to rise. "I'm tired of bothering Burch. See if you can help me up those stairs. I need a nap."

4

"Mrs. Clark, may I have a word with you?"

The housekeeper stopped chopping the vegetables.

"It's going on a week, and my Uncle Simon has not been here. Does he live here or not? Is this typical for him?"

"Well… there doesn't seem to be anything typical about your Uncle Simon. But you know it's not my place to speak ill of your family."

Allison closed her eyes and took a deep breath. "I give you permission. Please, tell me what you know."

"Well, I know I don't like how he treats your grandmother. We know she's not the easiest woman, but no son should ever talk to a mother like he does. It's because he drinks too much."

Allison nodded. "Thank you for telling me. I'm sorry. It must be difficult for you to work here."

"I've often thought… but I know it's not my place. Maybe Mr. Mackenzie could come here and talk to your grandmother."

"Mr. Mackenzie?" The name sounded familiar.

"His mother and your grandmother were friends, years ago. He's a lawyer. Maybe as a favor, he would look into your grandmother's affairs and bring her some peace in these last years of her life."

"A good idea, thank you." Allison would love for her grandmother to have some peace of mind—and to take a slice of it for herself, too.

"Grandmother, are you finished with your plate? I'll take it for you."

"No, no, I'd like to be able to finish these carrots."

Both women turned their heads when they heard the front door open and close. They stared at each other in silence as they listened to the clomping of feet, the dropping of a bag, and the clinking of glass decanters.

Uncle Simon entered the dining room. "And there sits Allison, back at the family table." His tone was cheerless.

Allison straightened in her chair. "Yes, it's me."

"How wonderful for you, Mother, a reason to come to the dinner table. Mrs. Clark!" he yelled. "Oh, forget it." He went to the sideboard and grabbed a plate.

Allison noted that his hair was thinner and grayer. He hadn't shaved, and he looked as if he'd slept in his clothes.

"Simon, you could take a minute to freshen up. This is not the saloon, it is a dining room," Grandmother said.

"So sorry not to meet your standards for this fine dining room, but I'm starving and you'll just have to put up with me."

Allison wondered if anything she could say would save this conversation.

Simon lifted the lid from the tureen and flopped a piece of meat onto his plate. "And Mother, you should be so happy," he said, chewing noisily. "Allison is home now. You'll have a companion, and someone else to take care of you. She'll always dress properly I'm sure, all prim and tidy. We should see something for all that money," he mumbled, reaching for his glass of whiskey. "Am I correct, Allison?" He looked at her with droopy eyes. "You ladies can have tea every day, gossip about the neighbors, plan your parties..."

That was just the spur Allison needed. "Not exactly," she said, straightening up.

"Oh, excuse me." Simon wiped his shirtsleeve across his face. "What have I missed?"

Allison took a deep breath. "I have plans to go to France in three weeks."

"*Oo la la* for you." Simon teetered in his chair as he reached for more food. "Some school trip, I suppose?"

"My roommate, Suzanne. Her family is traveling and has offered to take me with them for a holiday."

"Holiday? What do you need a holiday from? Your whole life has been a holiday. If anybody needs a trip to France, it's me. I know you, Mother, I'm sure you don't approve. No guarantee of chaperones. Who knows what kind of trouble she could get into there?"

"Uncle Simon, please! There's no need to be rude." Allison glared.

"You were trouble when you were little. I don't know how many times I had to go to that school and talk them into keeping you. And now look at you." He slapped his back against the chair. "You're all fancy, just a grownup version of trouble. I tell you, Mother, nothing good can come of this."

"Stop it, Simon," Grandmother barked. "You're the trouble. You wouldn't know a proper young lady if you met one. Don't you think I hear of the scandalous women you associate with? You're a disgrace."

"Here we go." Simon took another drink.

"Uncle Simon, I need your help," Allison told herself to speak as an adult. "I know the amount needed, and I have Mr. and Mrs. Goude's address. We need to wire the money as soon as possible. They will purchase my ticket with theirs. Then I will need to meet them in New York City."

"Really? Is that all? New York City! You sure you don't want me to row the boat to France, too?" Simon rubbed his eyebrows.

"If you can't help me, then tell me who I need to speak to."

Simon closed his eyes and rested his head on the back of the chair. "This is why I don't come home. I have the most demanding relations. You wonder why I find the company of others more gratifying, Mother."

Allison clutched her hands in her lap. "Grandmother and I can make an appointment with Mr. Mackenzie tomorrow, if you wish."

Simon sat up, leaning so close to her that she could smell his foul breath. "That lawyer? You think you can waltz your little bustle in there and ... do what?"

Allison felt her heart beating rapidly. She hated that he was able to intimidate her. "I guess Grandmother and I will figure it out when we get there." Scooting her chair out, she reached for the plates.

"Sit down!" he yelled.

Allison swallowed the knot forming in her throat and sat.

"I'll make your arrangements," he said. "Give me your information, and I'll take care of it in the morning. Is that soon enough for you?"

She did not trust his insolent demeanor. "Yes, tomorrow morning would be fine, but I would like to come with you."

Uncle Simon got up. "It's not necessary. I paid for and made arrangements for all your schooling and all those pretty little frills you had to have. Your grandmother made me responsible for you so you could be the spoiled brat that you are. I'm sure I can handle this myself." He walked away with glass in hand.

"Help me to bed, Allison." Grandmother reached her arm up for assistance.

"I'll see you at breakfast, Allison, but not too early," Uncle Simon called from the hallway. You can thank me then."

Looking out at the black night from her bedroom window, Allison restlessly listened to Grandmother's snoring. This would be a sleepless night. She tried pacing. What were her choices? Sitting on the edge of her bed, she dropped her face in her hands. Her smooth voyage was losing its appeal. Deep in her gut, she did not trust Uncle Simon. But what could she do? If he said he would make the arrangements, maybe he would. Tonight, he had been drinking. Maybe in the morning, he would have a different temperament. In truth, he was the one who had paid for her schooling; asking for two new gowns from him, though, was out of the question.

Walking to her wardrobe, she opened the cupboard doors. *Bustles may soon go out of style. Uncle Simon is so ignorant.* She fingered through her dresses and tried to evaluate the best ones. The tulle under her purple crêpe had stuck to the hem of her peach lace dress. When she pulled them apart, something fell to the floor of the wardrobe. She looked down and picked up the missing burgundy gloves. Grateful, she slipped them on her hands and held them to her chest. How often she had felt her mother's love and kindness through them. She regretted the provoking tone she had taken with Yvette. *Uncle Simon was right. I have been a spoiled brat. I want to be my mother's daughter. I want to leave that petty girl behind. When I'm overseas, I want to find a brighter outlook and kinder conduct. Please, oh please, Uncle Simon, help get me there.*

5

~~

Allison rubbed her eyes. *Did I even sleep an hour?* While she dressed, she listened for any movement in the house and thought she heard Mrs. Clark coming up the stairs. She lifted her bedroom window for fresh air as Mrs. Clark came in with a tray. "My stomach is a bit in knots this morning, but I desperately need your help with my hair."

A few minutes later, Allison reached back and touched the smooth bun Mrs. Clark had just pinned into place. "Please, I need this chignon to be just right. I think it's too low. Could you try it again?"

"Why, yes." The housekeeper pulled several pins out.

"I guess I sat in one too many deportment classes. I am truly convinced that presentation is everything." She peered at the paper she held in her hand. The Goude's information, the pier in New York, the date and the address for wiring the money—all still there from the last time she looked. *This should be all Uncle Simon needs to book the trip.* She nibbled on her bottom lip. *What if there is insufficient time to wire me back? It's a risk I'm willing to take.*

"And, Mrs. Clark, if I happen to be in conversation with Uncle Simon, maybe you could delay my grandmother just for a few minutes. She tends to set his temper off, and I'm desperate for his cooperation this morning."

"I'll try my best, dear."

Allison sat in the dining room for an hour by herself. She pulled out her original note in Suzanne's handwriting. She wanted to keep the original, so she checked for the hundredth time to be sure her note was copied perfectly.

As she refolded the paper, Uncle Simon walked in. "Well, well, who should I find but little Miss Allison, waiting with her stubborn chin out."

Allison clenched her hands. "Is this your usual breakfast hour?" She regretted the words as soon as they left her mouth. *Why do I intentionally provoke him?*

He poured himself a cup of coffee, standing uncomfortably close to her chair.

Allison felt every muscle in her body tense as Uncle Simon rested his free hand on the back of her neck. He slowly ran his thumb up and down. "You never were much of an innocent child, Allison. Always trying to manipulate your way into something."

"I'm not manipulating." Jerking away from his touch, she threw her napkin on the table. "This is the information you'll need to send the wire." She held out her note.

Ignoring her outstretched hand, Simon went to touch her cheek. "You look so very pale."

Allison swerved from his touch. "Uncle Simon, this is not a joke to me."

Simon took a sip of coffee. "Oh dear, Allison, if looks could kill, I would be dead right now. This family only wants me for what I can provide. Thanks to my dead brother, I am saddled with an expensive child who isn't even mine." He snatched the paper out of her hand and glanced down at it with a smirk.

Allison bit her tongue so hard she thought she had drawn blood. *How dare he taunt me? How dare he treat my life so lightly? How dare he hold all the power for my future?*

"Well, I'm waiting." He tilted his head to the side.

"Waiting for what?"

He set down his coffee cup. "*Tsk, tsk.* I'm going to have to write Mrs. Webster. One of her students left her fancy girls' school without one ounce of manners. I may just have to ask for a refund." He turned to walk out of the dining room.

"Wait." A surge of panic overwhelmed her. "You have given me no assurance you will see to the details of this trip." She followed him as he rounded the corner to the parlor.

He thumbed through the piles of paper on his desk.

"Are you going to help me?"

Uncle Simon raised her note in his hand and waved it at her, never making eye contact.

"Thank you, Uncle Simon." Allison wished for a hot washcloth to remove his touch from the back of her neck.

Later in the week, Allison made plans with Burch to go into town. Grandmother had made it to lunch with her a few days earlier at the hotel, but there had been no time for her to shop for her trip. Suzanne would have a completely new collection of the latest gowns. What possible kind of fashion could she get at this short notice in this uncivilized territory?

As Allison walked into the kitchen, the smell of freshly baked bread beckoned her.

"Burch said he'd pull around for you right after lunch." Mrs. Clark set the bread to cool.

"Wonderful," Allison said, somber.

"You don't sound too pleased, dear."

"You have no idea the pressure I'm under. I have less than a week to prepare and pack. Uncle Simon is so...I'm not complaining, precisely. He upsets Grandmother; for that matter, he upsets me. But I'd like him to keep me abreast of our travel plans. I asked Grandmother about seeing Mr. Mackenzie, as you suggested. Then the worst of all is my wardrobe; it's in shambles."

"Oh, my."

"My pride is at stake." Allison paced the kitchen. "Can you imagine the horror I'll feel when the first dinner served on board will feature beautiful starched linen and spotless china, and here I come in my day dress from my teaching position? It's humiliating."

"What's wrong with your peach lace? Oh, and I love the purple taffeta," Mrs. Clark said.

"I've had the peach lace for two years! All of Suzanne's family has seen me in it. They will know how old it is. Wearing it would probably diminish their goodwill toward me."

"Oh, I see." Mrs. Clark nodded.

Allison heard something and looked through the kitchen window. "Good Lord! It's Uncle Simon." Her heart pounded. "I'm sure it's bad news."

"Calm down, child. I can tell by that satchel, he's here to drop off his laundry." Mrs. Clark patted her back. "Just ask him for the money for a store-bought gown. My Katie will take it in or hem it for you."

Allison groaned. "Right now, I want to find a place to hide."

Simon swung the door open and dropped the laundry on the floor. He ignored Allison and looked over at Mrs. Clark. "I'll take a slice of that bread. Cover it in butter, and the meat…do you have any gravy?"

"No, the last drop went out at dinner last night."

"And none for me." He started to exit the kitchen.

"Uncle Simon!" Allison spoke more loudly than she intended. "What is the plan for next week? Are all the arrangements for the trip completed?" She followed him to the dining room. "You did get a confirmation, I assume. You haven't been here in days, so…I need time and some money to prepare."

"Here are the rules," he said in a low growl. "I made the arrangements. I paid for the trip."

Something inside her jumped at those words.

"I don't want to answer any more questions. Don't bother me. Don't follow me. We're leaving next Thursday morning at eight. I expect you to be ready. Do you understand me?" he mocked. "Just be ready."

She froze, trying to assure herself of what he'd said.

Simon grabbed her by the chin. "Good. This is how I like it."

6

At tea a few days later, Allison heard Grandmother let out another long sigh. "You know, it does seem as if you just got here, and now you're packing to leave again. I hate to think an old grandmother can't ask for what she wants, but when you return, I would hope we could make a plan for you settling down."

"I understand, Grandmother. After this trip, you and I will talk, I promise."

Allison felt the lie deep in her heart. Her dream was to settle down with someone rich and secure, the farther away from this place, the better. Neither of Suzanne's older brothers had found wives yet. She would never tell her grandmother, but she hoped one of them might be in her future.

"You've had Mrs. Clark carefully go through your trunk?" Grandmother said. "Traveling to Europe is a bit different from going to school."

"Yes, Grandmother. I've been in such a tizzy over packing that Mrs. Clark is going to relish the quiet once I'm gone."

"What has your uncle given you for your pocket money?"

"Nothing yet." Her grandmother scowled, and Allison said, "He made it very clear he doesn't want me asking questions, so I'm assuming he'll give me what I need before I leave the United States."

"*Pfft.* He may have his reasons, but I'm not so sure I agree with him. In my day, it was improper for women to handle money. But it doesn't seem right for Mr. Goude to be your bank while you're traveling. You tell Simon you have my permission to keep track of a bit of your own pocket money."

"Yes, ma'am." She knew she would never mention it to Uncle Simon. Money was one of his sorest spots.

Allison had been up since dawn, sorting and checking all her belongings. The new day was quiet and peaceful. *This is what I've been waiting for. How long have Suzanne and I talked about this? Today's the day my adventure begins.* She thought about Mrs. Clark providing some nourishing breakfast, in hopes it would settle the churning in her stomach. Checking over her things one more time, she kissed Freddy goodbye and headed down the stairs.

"Your grandmother seems understandably melancholy this morning, Allison. She'd like you to come up to see her," said Mrs. Clark.

"Yes, of course." She headed to her grandmother's room.

"Take my tray, dear, and have a seat here next to me," Grandmother said, as soon as she entered.

Allison set the tray on the side table. "Just think of this as one of the many times you said goodbye to me as I left for school." She sat next to her grandmother on the bed.

"It's different, dear. I expect more letters with details of the places you are seeing."

"Yes, of course." She squeezed her grandmother's hand and felt some paper inside.

Grandmother released her hand and Allison held up a tight roll of cash.

"This, my child, is between you and me. Do you understand that? Do not say anything to your Uncle Simon. In fact, I have a special place I want you to keep it." Grandmother had a mischievous grin on her face.

Allison tilted her head with a playful smile. "Hmmm… inside my shoe?"

"Keep it right in here." Grandmother tapped on Allison's corset.

She laughed out loud. "Oh, Grandmother, you never cease to amaze me."

"Go in your room and do it now. Quickly, before your Uncle Simon gets here."

"Yes, ma'am. I can assure you, it will be our little secret." Allison placed a quick kiss on her Grandmother's cheek.

Burch had already loaded her trunk onto the back of the buggy, and Mrs. Clark wrapped some lunch and snacks in a canvas bag. When Uncle Simon finally rode up, Allison exhaled. She thanked Mrs. Clark for all her assistance, and Burch helped her up into the buggy. She tapped her foot on the floorboard, thinking, *trunk, umbrella, bonnet, brown velvet jacket, burgundy gloves.* Finally, Uncle Simon emerged from the house.

"Mrs. Clark, tell my mother I'll be in touch soon." Simon boarded the buggy and slapped the reins, and they were off. Allison gripped the seat, trying to convince herself she could make this trip without talking.

Two days of rocking and jolting back and forth, and of dirt and heat, left Allison parched and panting. "Uncle Simon, I need to get some water."

"I'll give you some water. There … is that enough for you?"

She blinked at the sight before her. It was indeed a lot of water. "We're taking a ferry across Lake Michigan?"

"Does this look like a train station to you?" he snapped.

"I don't do well with the rocking motion. Can't we please take a train?" she asked.

"This is why you were not invited to any discussions. I knew you'd disapprove of every one of my plans." Uncle Simon pulled the buggy to a stop.

Allison chewed on her fingernail. The day didn't seem too windy. She looked around. The ferry was quite large; she tried to distract herself by watching the people bustle around.

Uncle Simon found a dockhand to unload her things. With his usual lack of consideration, he left her standing at the dock while he made arrangements for the horse and buggy down at the livery. She followed her things onto the ferry and stood, gripping the railing. After what felt like an eternity, she sought a bench with some shade and sat down. Finally, Uncle Simon appeared, just as the ferry was about to leave.

He walked toward her, and she could not help herself. "Where have you been?" She shielded her eyes against the sun. "Grandmother would be furious that you left me on this ferry without an escort." The ferry rocked, adding to her discomfort.

"And yet, somehow you survived." He pulled a flask from his pocket and took a swig.

She couldn't tolerate another minute of her uncle's sour manners. Gathering her belongings, she stood.

"Leave the food." He grabbed the canvas bag and plopped down in her shade.

The ferry stabilized quite a bit after leaving the dock, and Allison tried walking along the deck. The insufferable heat had cooled, with a breeze coming up from the lake. *This is the worst of the trip. Surely the next leg will be by train.* She looked around at the people enjoying the boat ride. Seeing a refreshment stand, she asked for a glass of water. Standing at the rail, she sipped it slowly, taking in the vast blue water. The land grew farther and farther away, and her stomach started to churn. *Oh, no, please no. No one else seems to be afflicted. I will be fine*, she thought, tucking some stray hair behind her ear. Drawing in a calming breath, she remembering that Mrs. Clark gave her crackers when she was young and felt queasy. *I don't want to go ask for food from Uncle Simon, and I won't be digging out my pocket money.* She went back to the refreshment stand and bought a bag of peanuts with a coin from her reticule. Finding a bench, she nibbled them cautiously, then closed her eyes and lifted her face to the sun, hoping she could escape the queasiness with rest.

Sometime later, she woke to find Uncle Simon leaning on the rail, smoking. "I told you I don't do well on boats. I don't feel at all well." Ignoring her, he blew out a stream of smoke.

Turning away from the foul smoke, Allison made an angry choking sound. This whole travel arrangement was simply unacceptable. For pity sakes, she was starting to sweat and tremble. Spying the man at the refreshment counter, she approached him. "Where is the ladies' water closet?"

"Go down this corridor, it's the last door on the right."

Assaulted by the foul smell of the water closet, she closed the door quickly, trying to steady herself against the rocking of the ferry. The pain in her stomach grew in intensity; the smell could not be ignored, and she could take it no longer.

Please, someone get me off this boat. Allison wiped her chin, praying that no one had heard her vomiting.

After she had leaned against the wall with her eyes closed for several minutes, the rocking seemed to stabilize. *Please, God! Get me off this boat!* She rolled her head back against the wall.

Grabbing the hanky out of her reticule, she dabbed sweat off her face. Although the day was hot, her body alternated between chills and sweat, and she wished for someplace private she could just lie down. Finally, when her stomach could be trusted, she left the water closet. The fresh air coming through the corridor helped. Making her way back to her bench, she dozed, still feeling weak and shaky.

The late afternoon air became cooler, and Allison looked up, making out a town. Thank God—the ferry was about to dock. Uncle Simon came and sat next to her, "We don't get off till the next stop."

She huffed and held her hands against her churning belly. Most of the people who had gotten on with them departed, while rougher, backwoods people jumped on. Two men conversed to her right, holding long rifles over their shoulders. Looking over the departing town, she decided that the train station must be at the next stop. After what seemed like hours, the ferry finally came to rest. She elbowed Simon, and he nearly fell off the bench. She clenched her hands, watching him struggle to stand. He was drunk.

Taking the hand offered by the porter, Allison stepped gratefully onto solid ground. She stood to the side, waiting for Uncle Simon. Glancing at her surroundings, she saw no evidence of a train station. Finally, Uncle Simon came toward her with a horse and buggy. Offering a deckhand some change, he was obviously too drunk to load her trunk by himself, so she wearily stepped into the buggy on her own. It had no cover, so she popped open her parasol. Uncle Simon unsteadily sank into the seat, seeming to be in no hurry, as they took a dusty road out of the small port town. The road curved higher and higher into the trees and forest. *How can this possibly be right?*

"Uncle Simon," she asked, "where could this road be leading? It's going to be dark soon."

"Shortcut," he yawned, eyes shutting down.

"Uncle Simon! You can't even stay awake. Where is this shortcut leading?" Having long collapsed her parasol, she bent forward to miss a low-lying branch coming toward her. "I think we're lost! The forest is getting denser and denser. We haven't passed anyone else. How do you know where this road goes?"

Unable to keep his eyes open, Uncle Simon grunted and his head lolled. The buggy rocked in a rutted spot of the road.

"Give me the reins." She went to pull them from his hands.

"I know where I'm going!" He pulled away from her, swinging the horse to the right, completely veering off the road. He whipped the horse forward as Allison clung to the seat, the buggy rocking unsteadily over the rough terrain.

After what seemed like forever, she could not take it anymore. Grabbing at the reins to try to the pull the horse to a stop, she screamed, "Uncle Simon, stop this horse at once! You are so drunk you can't see, and this can't possibly be the way." She pulled against his tight grip. "There's a dangerous ravine on the right. Stop this horse, I say! Give me the reins now!" Allison pulled on the reins, but Simon elbowed her back into the seat. Everything within her wanted to jump off her side of the buggy, but all she could see were rocks. The buggy tilted, and she yelled, "Get away from the edge!" Throwing all her weight against Uncle Simon, she grabbed the reins and pulled to the left. He let go and jerked her up by the neck, shaking her and roaring, "Where is the money! I know she gave it to you!"

Allison tried to fight and twist away from his grip, but Simon pulled at her hair and brought her up to his evil, twisted face. "Give it to me, now!" He bared his yellow teeth and grabbed at her reticule with one hand.

Allison screamed as the horse reared. Uncle Simon pushed against her as he tore at her purse.

With no way to catch her footing, she fell backward. There were seconds of nothing but clawing at the air. A small scrub tree caught her back and arms and tossed her like a feather down into the rocks below.

✌︎

Simon flopped down on the seat and dug his hand inside her small purse. Finding only a few coins, he flung it away. Stepping down on the other side, he lost his balance and fell into the brush. He looked around blearily, but Allison was nowhere to be seen. "You finally disappeared," he mumbled, pulling up on the back of the buggy to stand. "Ha! You were never going on any fancy holiday, because I told your snooty friends you weren't available." He fumbled with the trunk until it popped open. "So you never needed any of this." He rammed his hands through the neatly packed items, opening the small drawers of the trunk and dumping them out, kicking the contents. "But I need that money worse than you, you spoiled brat." He unzipped every zipper and found nothing. Falling on his backside, he stopped and listened. Nothing. He tried to think, but couldn't.

Swaying and dizzy, he rose, grabbed the horse by the bridle and left.

7

"Patch! Get back here," Levi yelled. "We're not chasing squirrels today. And please tell me you're not after a skunk."

He thought the dog would have learned a lesson after the last skunk that got him. Patch wasn't pure hound dog, but no one would ever know. Chockfull of instinct and tenacity, he could track better than Levi could. He yelled again after the missing dog, but wasn't really worried; he could be miles away and always find his way back.

Levi looked up to the sky and caught the noonday sun beating down through the trees. There were some hawks circling a mile or so away. *Oh, Patch.* He shook his head. *That's probably where you've gone.*

He removed his hat and ran his hand through his thick, wavy hair. *There's something dead by the creek,* he thought, plopping his hat back on his head.

He walked toward the circling hawks, his curiosity as avid as his dog's. Whatever it was, he could take the hide and leave the raw meat for the birds. He hadn't quite made it to the creek when Patch ran up to him with something dark red in his mouth.

"Oh, Patch, what'd you do? Did you rip a foot off for yourself?"

As the dog got closer, however, he realized it wasn't a blood-covered animal part. Levi held out his hand, and Patch obediently dropped the wet object.

"What is this?" Levi held it up by the corner. "It's a woman's glove." He glanced again at the circling hawks. "What do you make of this, Patch?" He let out a sigh. The dog had already headed back. "Did you find a dead coon wearing gloves?" he yelled after his dog.

Patch stopped and barked, then headed for the creek.

Levi followed, glancing down at the glove. It looked somewhat new. Who would've dropped it out here in the middle of nowhere?

He climbed over a few small boulders and noticed something white against the ravine wall. Dropping his pack to the ground, he climbed up the steep incline. Snatching at the white fabric, he shook it loose; it was maybe a nightgown, something his ma might wear. He threw it over his shoulder and noticed more clothing strewn around the ledge. He plucked a few more items before his head shot up in a startling realization. A hawk's screeches confirmed his fears—what if a carriage had flown off the edge?

"Patch!" He knew his dog could find them before he could scramble down the ledge. "Patch, what do you see?" He tossed the garments to the dog, "Where are they?" Heart beating rapidly, he scanned the area.

Patch ran a few feet away to a stretch of tall grass. Levi pulled his hunting knife from its sheath. Suddenly jumping back, he saw a large mass of light blue and brown fabric in front of him. "Oh, Lord," he gasped.

Patch began to bark. "Shut up, Patch, I know it's bad." He bent down to the woman's side and carefully rolled her over. Blood and dirt smeared her face. Blood had never affected him before, but he felt his stomach roll up into his throat. Patch pushed his way in to sniff at the woman's face.

"Get back, Patch." He pushed the dog away, then looked closer. The woman moved her head. "Oh, Jesus. She's alive."

He pulled the blood-caked hair away from her face, and she let out a small moan.

Levi jumped up to retrieve his pack and his canteen. Soaking his bandana, he held it gently against the side of her face. There was a large purple knot protruding from her forehead, and her eyes were puffy and swollen shut. The water washed away the blood, revealing gashes and bruises. He began to pray.

"Help me," she murmured, as he knelt next to her.

"I'm here, miss, don't worry. I'll help you." Levi tried to sound reassuring. He poured water into his small tin cup and lifted her head, pressing the cup to her lips.

She swallowed. "My head hurts so badly. Everything hurts," she said, sounding dazed.

Levi gently lowered her head, looking for broken bones. "Miss, can you tell me is anything else hurting besides your head? When I push on your arm, does this hurt?"

"Yes…everything hurts," she whimpered.

"Can you move your legs, your feet?"

She touched the toes of her boots together.

"Yes, I saw that. That's good."

Patch sat obediently. "What are you doing, boy?" Levi tried to keep the panic out of his voice. "Where are the others? Go find them." He flung his hand out to get the dog to move. Patch made a quick circle and came back to sit by the woman.

"Miss, who else is with you?"

"I… don't… know."

"Can you tell me your name?"

"Allison K…Kent."

Levi paced, unable to get his heart to stop racing.

Please, Lord, I don't know what to do. Please, Lord, help this girl. He turned again and walked back to the spot he had prepared for her. He laid his blanket on some soft pine needles. The afternoon sun set lower, and tree shade was as far as he could move her. Searching the area, he could find no tracks; the ground was dry and covered with leaves. No carriage, no horse with a broken leg. She must have run off by herself. Maybe she got thrown off a horse from the ledge above. He even climbed to the top and searched around, finding some of her personal belongings, but it still made no sense. Likely, she would be the only source of information. He came back to where she rested and knelt on the blanket. "Miss Kent, can you hear me?"

"Yes...but I'm so tired... I just want to sleep. Only when I'm asleep... my head... won't... hurt." Her voice trailed off.

"Why are you out here alone?" He asked.

Allison let out a moan. She covered her face with a shaking hand, and her breathing thickened.

As Allison slept, Levi started a small fire close to where she lay. Maybe someone who was looking for her would see the smoke. He made a pile of her personal items, gathered from the surrounding area. Obviously, she wasn't just out on a day trip. A woman who was going somewhere would want all these things. Maybe she was running away from home? But from the quality of her clothing, she had come from a nice home. That didn't make sense. Maybe she and her husband had a falling out, and she decided to leave him? No wedding ring, though, and why would she be out in the middle of the woods? She had to have gotten lost. That was the only thing that made sense, but where would she be going? There was nothing for miles around.

Levi skewered some of the meat he'd trapped earlier and cooked it over the fire, then dropped the sizzling pieces into his tin bowl. As they cooled, he threw a handful of pieces out to Patch. The sun was setting, and he went back to the blanket.

"Miss." He tapped her hand. "I've cooked up some food. You should try a bite or two."

Allison slid her hand away from his touch. "Not hungry. Sleepy," she whispered.

Levi tossed his hat to the ground and scratched his head. "Can you try to sit up for a minute, ma'am?"

She shook her head. "I can't."

"I'll help you. I don't know how long you've gone without any food. So we need to try." He gently slid his hands and arms under her shoulders. "There's a big, strong tree right here, and I'm going to help you lean against it." Patch came around from the other side of the tree to observe.

Levi grabbed the loose fabric of her velvet jacket and slid her back up against the tree. Both of her eyes cracked open.

"Okay, okay, you're doing well. Do you know where you're at?" He held her steady.

"No," she whined. Her head wobbled.

"That's okay, we'll do harder questions later. For now, could you just try to take a bite of food?"

Blinking, she reached up to take the meat from his hand. Carefully taking a small bite, she chewed and swallowed.

"Good, that's good. One more bite," he offered.

Allison warily chewed and swallowed a second piece of meat.

Levi wiped his brow. This was a good sign. "How about trying some more?"

"I don't know... I feel dizzy." She stilled for a few moments before she began to whimper, her face turning ashen.

"What's the matter?"

She started to topple, and he had to grab the back of her jacket to keep her from falling over. Holding her stomach, she vomited the few bites she had just eaten. He helped her lean back again against the tree.

"No more food." She held up her hand.

He wet his handkerchief and gently wiped her face. She tilted her head back and closed her eyes.

"I have a younger brother..." Levi couldn't tell if she was falling back asleep or still awake. "When he was a kid, he fell out of a pine tree. He had the biggest knot on the back of his head." He grimaced at the large bump on her forehead. "He acted like you, nothing could seem to keep him awake. He kept throwing up most of the day."

Allison lifted a finger. "Don't talk."

Raking his hands through his long hair, he moved to the fire and put a few bigger pieces on the coals. Realizing how dark it was, he glanced back at the young woman sitting against the tree. *Oh, Lord, what do I make of this? She looks as if she could fall any minute.* Making his way back to the tree, he sat against it, making sure their shoulders did not touch. Beholding the beauty of the stars, he breathed in the peace of the deep woods. Patch stretched out, sound asleep after such an eventful day. Succumbing to the heaviness in his eyes, Levi leaned his head against the tree and let them close for a few minutes.

He didn't know how long he'd been asleep. The fire still crackled a few feet away, but something pressed against his shoulder. It was the young woman. Uncomfortable, he carefully moved his shoulder, but before he could get away, her head slipped down and rested on his chest. He sucked in his alarm as her head dropped further and came to rest on his lap. She drew her hands under her chin and nestled in.

"Glory be, girl." His body froze. "I'm not your pillow." He looked into the woods as if some answer was just going to appear for this predicament. Knowing she was dead asleep, he still had to remind himself to breathe. He swallowed and looked down. Her light hair was a mass of tangles and pins. Carefully touching a protruding pin, he easily pulled it free. *Surely it doesn't help to have these sticking in her head.* Soon he had pulled nine or ten pins and dropped them into his shirt pocket. She hadn't moved a muscle, so he pulled out some leaves and twigs, also.

Thine head upon thee is like Carmel, and the hair of thine head like purple, the king is held captive by your tresses...

Levi ran his hand over his stubble, remembering Sister Vicker telling the junior boys' Sunday School class that the Song of Solomon was only for the married. Which, of course, only made them want to read it more.

Even with the bruises and scratches, Allison Kent appeared to be a beautiful young woman. It's not as if he'd never seen a beautiful woman before, but he had never had an opportunity to touch one. He pulled a few more strands of hair away from her face. His fingers enjoyed the texture of the soft tresses, a golden hue highlighted by the faint firelight. Her face was puffy, but he would guess she couldn't be more than twenty or so. He cautiously touched the cameo peeking from her collar. *Take away all the dirt, and these are still fancy clothes. Surely someone is out looking for her. And when they do find her, I shouldn't be caught like this.* He lifted her head and placed it on the blanket, then covered her and moved to a spot near the fire. Sleep finally came, but he woke often through the night to look at her, to make sure she was still alive. Over and over, dozing, awake...thinking this was some crazy dream.

8

Levi woke up cold and uncomfortable, remembering why he didn't have his blanket. He knelt close to the coals and gently blew them alive, adding a few twigs and branches. Soon, he was warming his hands. He walked to the creek's edge and got water to make coffee, then approached the sleeping young woman. She was so still that something akin to panic rose up in him. He nudged her boot with his foot. Pulling her foot in closer, she curled up tight. He didn't want to wake her; he was just thankful she was still alive.

Lord, he prayed, *what do you have for this day? I know how to tend to a wounded animal, but I have no idea what to do with her. I know I can't just leave her here.*

He began to make the coffee. *I just can't dawdle out here too long. If Ben had showed up like I thought he would, I wouldn't have to worry about my place. I don't care if the garden dries up, but somebody's got to feed my mule. What if some squatters take over?* He realized he'd gone from praying to worrying.

Lord, he tried again, *I'll take all the wisdom You got for this one.*

Allison moved into a more comfortable position. Her neck was stiff, and her head pounded like a drum. One eye opened, the other barely would. The crisp, woodsy smell suggested she was outside, under a tree—but why? Pulling the blanket tighter under her chin, she thought, *wasn't there a man helping me last night? Is this his blanket?* She inched her shoulder forward until she could see the man kneeling by the fire, next to a big tan dog. Emotions were rising within her that she did not like. It was painful, but she tried to open her eyes wider and look around. *I know I'm hurt, but don't I know where I am. Why can't I remember what happened to me?* A lump in her throat made it hard to swallow. *Maybe he knows.* She drew her knees up under the blanket and wrapped her arms around them.

The dog lifted its head and sauntered over. Allison winced as a tear ran down her open cuts and scratches. The dog stopped close to her, and she put her hand out to halt his progress. It sniffed around her and licked her palm.

"Patch, come here, boy." Levi walked near. "I'm sorry, miss, did he wake you up?"

Feeling overwhelmed, all Allison could do was to slightly shake her head. This scruffy young man did not look dangerous, but she felt incredibly exposed, lying on the ground curled up with a blanket.

"Would you like to try some coffee?" The fellow headed back to the fire before she could answer. She took the opportunity to push herself up. Her head felt as if a hundred bricks had landed on it. She debated lying back down, but took a deep breath and sat up against the tree.

He walked toward her with a mug of hot coffee. Dropping to one knee, he held it out.

"Wait, let me see." He took a sip from the cup, then offered it again. "Just wanted to make sure it didn't burn you. I think it should be fine."

Allison's hand emerged from her tightly-gripped blanket. Her knuckles were raw and scratched and her nails broken and jagged, caked with dirt. Her hand shook so badly that she quickly tucked it back inside the blanket. "Thank you. Maybe you could just put it down until I'm ready."

He nodded. "You told me your name last night. Allison Kent? Is that right?"

"Yes," Allison whispered, watching him tip his hat at her.

"I'm Levi, Levi Graham."

❧

Despite the lack of sleep, Levi found his mind racing: his pelts, his need to get home, even her injuries were hard to look at—why had he allowed her head to rest on his lap last night? He almost missed it when she spoke quietly.

"Do we know each other, Mr. Graham?"

"No, ma'am, I've never seen you before." A surge of guilt hit him for touching her last night, but he quickly pushed it away. "Can you remember where you're from?"

Allison raised a shaky hand to the swelling on her forehead. "I can't seem to remember much at all."

"You know something bad happened to you, though?" She stilled, and he wished he had said that better. Tears welled up in her eyes as she regarded her surroundings.

"Don't cry, Miss, I'm going to help you. We can figure this out. I've lived in the woods most of my life." Levi stopped short. He didn't want to sound like he was the savior.

Tears streamed down her face, and she swallowed hard. "Then you'll see me to the nearest doctor?"

"Umm… nearest doctor?" He rubbed his knuckles against his chin, picturing Ready Springs. "There's no doctor anywhere near here."

"I need to get to a doctor," she sniffled.

"Okay." Levi stood and started to pace. "I was hoping maybe to get you back to where you came from. Your people could see you to a doctor, I'm sure."

Allison took a sip of coffee, trying to steady the shaking in her body.

"Here…" Walking over to the pile of her things, he grabbed a few articles of clothing. "You must've been traveling somewhere. Do you remember packing these things?" He held them close to her.

"Yes, of course, they're mine." She reached out and crumpled up the personal items. "Where did you find them?"

"All over the ravine," Levi said. "They were just scattered here and there. Can you think of how that happened?"

She pulled her knees closer, tightly wrapping her skirt around her legs, and rested her chin on them. "My mind feels like a thick fog."

"Tell me anything you remember. Were you on a horse?"

"No…that doesn't sound right, I just can't seem to remember anything."

"Your parents—are they Mr. and Mrs. Kent? Your father's name is…" He searched her puffy eyes.

Her mouth opened, shut, and then opened again. "I don't know. There's something terribly wrong with me. That's why you need to get me to a doctor. My mother…I can't think of her name."

Levi poured a cup of coffee. He took a swallow and dug out a biscuit from his bag. His stomach growled, but he held the biscuit out to Allison. "Here, try to eat this. I'm sure as you rest and get better, things will start to come back to you."

❧

Allison took the biscuit and ate a few bites, watching Levi as he walked away. *He seems like a decent young man. I seem to have no other choice but to trust in his care. Oh, for pity sakes. Why can't I remember anything?* She closed her eyes and touched the tender scratches on her face. Opening her eyes, she watched him again. *He doesn't look familiar. Where is his family? Does he live out here alone?* Her eyelids would not cooperate. They were so heavy, and she was so sleepy. She considered the soft pine needles, and decided to lie down before she fell over. Pulling the blanket up close, she laid down and rested her head on her forearm. The pounding subsided; the bed of pine needles was a welcome relief.

Levi spent the morning tracking around the area, hoping for a clue as to what had happened to Allison. He didn't want to go off too far, although he trusted Patch to watch her. He found himself back along the creek bed, struggling with the turmoil in his mind. *Lord,* he prayed again, *what do you want me to do?* He squatted and washed his hands. *Have faith,* he thought he heard. *Have faith.* He let the words roll around in his mind. *Have faith, even when you can't see.* He nodded with assurance. *It makes sense. I'm always confident when I know what to do. So Lord, give me the faith to trust you when there's no map and nothing I can see.* Levi splashed cold water on his face. Patch left his post and walked into the middle of the creek. The dog's long tail hairs floated on top of the water, and something occurred to Levi. *I know I can't carry both my pack and her. But what if we floated? It just might work.*

Allison fought sleep, willing her eyes to open, and taking a deep breath. She let the blanket drop from her sweat-covered body, then pushed herself back up against the tree. For the first time, she realized her hair was down and spilling over her shoulders. Self-conscious, she ran her hand over the knots in her hair. *A rat could nest in this.* She unbuttoned her soft velvet jacket, but her hands were still shaking, her heart pounding rapidly. Finally, she slid the jacket off and leaned her head back, breathing deeply. How could one act leave her so exhausted? After resting, she evaluated the rest of her clothing. Her white cotton blouse was intact, but dirt-smudged around the lace cuffs. Her blue skirt had some small tears, but not too much damage.

Levi and his dog came up from behind, startling her.

"I'm glad you got to sleep most of the morning. How do you feel?" he asked.

Allison swallowed hard, her heart still beating too fast. She took a long look at the young man standing before her. His hat was off, and she could see for the first time that he had long, wavy brown hair tucked behind his ears. His face was strong and serious, with a scruffy beard. His eyes were deep brown with dark eyelashes. Handsome. She stared, mesmerized. He was quite handsome.

"Are you okay?" He ran his hand over his beard.

" Oh, I was just thinking, is… there anyone else with you besides your dog?"

He shook his head.

"How is it you found me out here?" Embarrassed, she tried to smooth her hair back.

"I trap and hunt, mostly." He nodded at a pile of animal skins. "I saw some hawks circling over you. Of course, I didn't know it was a person." An awkward silence hung in the air. "And so…what I need to say is…" He rubbed his finger against his bottom lip and glanced away. "I gotta get back to my place. If I knew my brother had shown up, I could sit around with you until you got better. But knowing him, he probably hasn't. So this all…" He circled his arm around the camp area, not making eye contact with her. "I need to get going, so I think you're just going to have to come with me." He rattled the last part off.

"I don't think I could make it to the next tree," she said.

"I have an idea for that," he mumbled.

"Besides..." Allison found her courage. "I will only agree to go to someplace with a doctor."

He stiffened and rubbed his neck. "I know you said your memory is foggy. Do you remember me saying there aren't any doctors around here?"

"Yes," she sighed. "I remember that. Where you live, the town, someone must know a doctor."

She wanted to wait for an answer, but her eyes betrayed her; she was falling asleep again. Kneeling, Levi gathered up her jacket and carefully placed it under her head.

"Please, don't...take me...anywhere. I just want to sleep," she whispered.

"Patch, come here, boy. Stay right here and keep an eye on her. I have a project to work on."

Levi stripped his shirt off in the afternoon heat. He was just about done with the simple raft he had made. After tying the last of the knots, he shoved the raft out into the creek water. It floated well enough. No one was going to stay dry, but in the heat of the day, it wouldn't matter. He pulled the raft to shore and walked a few feet back. It was too late in the day to start now, and he knew in his gut it was going to be hard to win Allison Kent's cooperation. He threw his shirt back on and headed over to where she slept.

The sunlight streamed through the branches onto her face. He gently put his hand under her jacket and head and moved her into the shade.

"Don't touch me!" She cowered away. "Please...leave me..."

"Okay, okay." Levi stood away from her. "I wasn't taking you anywhere. The sun was on your face."

Shaking, she pulled herself up. "Can you get me some water?"

"Yes, hold on." He grabbed his canteen. "Here you go."

Allison pulled away from the canteen. "Where is the cup? I need a cup."

He walked back with his tin cup and poured the liquid inside, then offered it to her.

She took small sips of water while he rehearsed his words. *What if she won't come with me?*

"I can't imagine how dreadful I must look."

Levi tilted his head and looked at her, hoping she wasn't going to start crying again. "No, not dreadful. You have some cuts and bruises. Nothing that won't clear up someday."

She groaned, her countenance falling. "You must know that this...this is the worst thing that's ever happened to me. Not remembering anything," she huffed. "I can't decide which is worse, my mental or physical debilitations. I won't be able to travel. I'm sorry you feel burdened with my care. I hate being an encumbrance."

"I need you to trust me," he said calmly.

She took a long look at him.

Levi breathed deeply and plunged in. "We'll stay here tonight. Get more food and water in you. But in the morning, we're going to head out. I have a pack full of pelts, and I made a raft..."

"A raft? What are you talking about?" Her voice cracked.

He cleared his throat. "A raft." He paused, waiting for her to understand. "It'll hold you and my pack. It'll float. I'll be next to it the entire time. The water's so low that you could stand in it. You won't need to swim, you won't drown."

"Swim! Drown! This is nonsense. Is this your only idea? It'll never work. You're increasing the pounding in my skull. Do you know that?" Her swollen eyes blazed.

Levi clenched his teeth. He had a feeling this would be her reaction. "Listen, I told you I can't leave you here. And I told you I have to get going in the morning. Unless God suggests another plan, you're going with me, and you're going on that raft."

"Absolutely not. I have no reason to trust you."

Levi stood and slapped the dirt off his pants. He needed some time to breathe so he wouldn't say or do the wrong thing. He grew up with brothers, but wrestling this woman into submission didn't seem like a good idea.

Allison fought to stay awake till dusk, wanting to watch Levi, but with increasingly heavy eyes. *What if he packs up his things and leaves me here?* Earlier, when he was out of sight, she had tried to stand up on her own. She had leaned heavily against the tree, but even gripping it with her arms, the dizziness and nausea were too great.

"What did you mean earlier?" she called out. "When you said unless God suggests another idea?"

"All God's ideas are better than mine." He didn't look up; he was cooking something over the fire. "But unless he gives me another one…I'm sorry, but we're rafting in the morning."

After a few minutes, he came over and sat beside her with the intention of sharing the meat from his tin plate.

"God put a baby in a basket and sent it down a river. Do you know that story?" he asked.

She looked at the food and then at him. "Moses."

"Good. You remember some things, then."

Allison noticed for the first time that he had a pleasant smile and straight teeth. A comforting warmth shone in his brown eyes.

"If you can remember your Bible stories, your other memories are probably just around the corner."

Sitting there quietly and sharing his food was the strangest feeling—she couldn't put a name to it.

"You need to believe me, the water is not fast. It's as slow as it gets the whole season. I will never let go of the raft, I promise. You don't need to be afraid."

"You haven't told me where you live." Allison picked at another piece of meat, not yet ready to comply.

"I live in the northeastern section of this county. I have my own place, close to Sault Creek."

"You keep saying your own place. Where does your family live?"

"They live fifteen miles on the other side of Ready Springs."

"Will that be the town you take me for help?"

Straightening up, Levi rolled his shoulders. "I'll take you to any town or area that will help you get back to where you belong. But Ready Springs might well be in the wrong direction."

9

While the bright moon cast shadows from the trees, Levi watched Allison sleep. She rolled over, whimpering, a few times; she'd probably never slept on the ground before. The conversation over dinner had eased his mind a bit. When a man says *absolutely not*, a knife or a gun is the only thing that will change his mind. Yet she seemed willing to listen to reason. *I'm certain it'll be only a week or so until the knot on her head goes away*, he consoled himself. *By then she'll surely remember her people and where she's from. At least now she's talking—but she also looks at me funny.* He rolled to his back and laid an arm over his forehead. It was strange having a woman stare at him. *Sometimes she makes me feel downright nervous*, Levi admitted.

He remembered watching his brothers chase the girls around the schoolyard. Throwing rocks, doing anything to get their attention. He would laugh at them trying their best, but he was never the type to chase after girls. He liked being alone. Well, that wasn't completely true. Sometimes he liked to picture the wife God would bring him. She'd be warm and caring like his ma. Of course, she'd have to love God with all her heart, like he did. Wouldn't hurt if she was pretty, but her character and virtue were more important. It would be nice to have someone to talk to in the evening. Talking with Patch was always a one-sided conversation.

Levi watched her through the shadows. *Some women have a mind of their own. That won't work for me.* He shook his head and turned again, trying to get comfortable. *A gentle and quiet spirit, that's what the Bible talks about.*

The chill was already off the early morning, and Levi had done everything he could do while Allison slept. He shoved as many of her things as he could into his pack. He secured the pack and pelts to the raft, hoping this morning wouldn't end up in a battle of wills. They would have to travel slowly, and they needed to get going soon. He'd paced around long enough; he knew what he had to do.

"Allison, wake up. It's time to go." He kneeled before her.

She sluggishly pushed her way up and held her head. "What?" Her eyes were cloudy and pained.

"We need to go," he said, keeping his voice light.

"Mr. Graham..." She sighed. "I don't think..."

He moved in close. "Put your arm around my neck," he said.

Before she could argue, he swept her up into his arms, as if she weighed nothing at all. She started to squirm loose, but his arms were tight, pressing her close. Trying to keep his face forward, he walked with her down to the edge of the creek. "I've already got the raft out into the deepest part." She tensed as the water came up around his legs.

"Oh, no...right now? We're going on this...this...little..." He could feel her body stiffen. "Plank of wood."

"No, not us. Just you." He began to lower her.

"Oh, no." She gasped, gripping his shirt.

"Listen, I'm not going to let it take you away. I'll be alongside you the whole time."

"Please, Levi." She clung to his shoulders. "I'm scared."

The use of his name stopped him, but he lowered her anyway. The raft sank a bit under her weight, and the water soaked her skirt.

"For pity sakes! It's cold! I'm getting all wet!"

He pulled her hands free. "Lean against my pack." He pushed the raft forward.

"Mr. Graham! It feels like it's going to tip. It's not big enough, I can tell. I can't do this. Please...take me back."

"Be still, miss. It won't tip if you can be still. Come on, Patch! We're going home." Giving the raft a push, he set it afloat in the flowing water.

Hours later, his feet and legs ached from his bright idea. It was the heat of the day, but still, the water was very cold. Allison had finally curled into a ball, gripping his pack. Only half her clothes were wet, but Levi was going numb. He saw a sandy spot downstream and guided the raft to a stop.

"Oh, thank God, I thought we'd never arrive." She shielded her eyes from the bright sun.

"This isn't where we're going. We just have to take a break for some food." *And to get the feeling back in my feet.*

Patch growled, and Levi froze. "Just stay put for a minute," he whispered. Two men on horseback loomed up on the grassy bank. Instinctively, he swung his rifle from his back to his front. "Gentlemen." Levi tipped his hat. "How's everyone doing today?"

"We's about to get a whole lot better. You got any booze in that hefty pack?" A man with a red checkered shirt spat out a stream of tobacco juice.

"No booze," Levi said.

"Well...what ya got there for trading?" The other man gripped the gun resting on his saddle.

"Not interested in trading today, boys," Levi snapped.

"Boys! Who you callin' boys? You some dirty river rat. Who's that hidin' behind ya'?"

Allison gripped the back of his wet trousers. "This here's my new bride," Levi lied confidently.

The men busted out a laugh. "Well, you are the stupid boy. Who would bring a woman out here?"

"Maybe it's their honeymoon," the short man said, taunting.

"Actually, she's one of those city girls." Levi tried to distract them. "You've probably heard about them. Too many unmarried women in the cities now. All the good men out trapping or mining. For a fair price, you can go to the city and get one." They looked interested.

"So how much d'ya have to pay for one like that?"

"Well, she's young and doesn't eat much, so her daddy let her go for my horse. That's why we're traveling by river." Allison leaned closer.

"So, what if you be wantin' one older, fatter. How much'd that be?"

"Oh, for fine trappers like yourselves, probably a half dozen beaver pelts and a couple deer hides."

The short man spat and shifted in his saddle. "I got a good trade. You toss over those pelts I see there, and we'll let you go on y'all's honeymoon."

The smooth talk was over. "Not in my lifetime."

"Well, then," the other one said, "we'll take the woman."

Allison whimpered and clasped him tighter.

The men nodded to each other and raised their guns.

"Wait!" Levi's finger gripped the trigger.

"The pelts." The man held out his free hand.

Levi untied the leather strap holding his pelts to his pack. Without taking his eyes off them, he heaved over his livelihood. It landed with a *thud* close to them. Patch began to growl as the shorter man dismounted and picked up the furs.

"Get your dog back!"

Levi yelled to Patch.

"Put your rifle down, boy. We're just going to be on our way. You won't have time to shoot both of us before one of us finishes you off. And then where would your wet city gal be?" They pulled their horses back and moved away.

Levi fumed until they were out of sight. "Miss." He turned and grabbed her by the shoulders. She fell forward against him. "I think we'll be okay. But we have to move fast." Holding her with one arm, he reached and threaded his pack onto his back. Wrapping his arm under her, he pulled her up, catching her legs before she could argue.

She let out a moan as her head dropped back.

"Miss…miss." He gave her a small shake. "Here, drink some water." Levi held out the cup, supporting her head.

"What happened?" She tried to sit up.

"It's my fault," he said, still supporting her weight. "I pushed you too hard, and then a robbery didn't help."

Allison sat further up. "Those men, are they coming back?" she asked, wide eyed.

"No, I carried you over enough rock that a lizard couldn't track us." His hair and clothes were wet from sweat and the labor of carrying her.

"I've been such a burden to you, but I thank you from the bottom of my heart for not…trading me."

Levi smiled at the ground; she obviously remembered the tall tale he had weaved.

"I valued those pelts." His jaw twitched. "But you are one of God's children in need, so I value you more." She squinted at him. Was she in pain? Was she going to cry? But a small, sad smile appeared on her scratched and bruised face. Something warm washed over his being.

"Did you mean that?" she whispered.

The air escaped his lungs. "Yes," he finally managed to say. They were sitting close; her doleful blue eyes mesmerized him.

Levi scooted back. Dagnabbit, she was gawking again. *What's that about? Of course, I wasn't going to trade her off.*

"I'm sorry, I've made you uncomfortable." She leaned back on the flat rock. "I would like to pay you back. I mean…for the value of those pelts and the food and…"

"No thanks, I don't need your money. When your family comes for you, I won't be taking anything." He pulled out some jerky and handed it to her.

"But certainly we can do something. Your generosity is above and beyond."

"No, do you understand that? No." He glared at her.

"Why does my offer offend you so?" She straightened her twisted skirt.

"You didn't offend me." He shrugged. "You do confuse me, though." Enough talking—he tossed the cup in the pack and loaded it on his back. He reached for her hand and wrapped her arm around his neck.

"Wait," she said, as he easily hoisted her upward. "Please, put me down."

He pulled his arm out from under her legs, which left her dangling by her other arm against him. "This…" she grunted, pushing away from his body, "is not acceptable. I cannot have you…touching me. I can't have it." Her feet found the ground.

"Carrying you and this pack and half the river on your skirt isn't pleasant, you know. Go ahead and walk. Just let me know when you're going to pass out again. One more knot like that one," he nodded toward her injury, "and you may not remember your name."

She gasped.

"Come on, Patch." Levi headed out, knowing full well he was being unruly. Why did she upset him? Pay him? For doing what any upright man would do? *Lord, how can I deal with this? I try to help her, and she thinks I'm just trying to get my hands on her. First, she attacks my character, and then my honor.*

Offended, said a still, small voice.

Oh, Lord, you were misunderstood, and yet without sin. Levi stopped suddenly. He'd been marching instead of walking. He turned around to see Allison, walking with Patch. *My dog has more manners than I do.*

༺❧༻

Allison wondered if this man had any proper upbringing at all. She knew it was unfitting for him to carry her, although his strength was appreciated—to a point. He had a strange effect on her. Calling her confusing…*hmmph. Doesn't he know how vulnerable I feel? Well, I certainly do*, she thought. *One of us should know right from wrong.*

Walking a fair bit ahead of her, Levi kept turning around, probably watching for when she would drop to the ground. She trudged along, longing to ask if they could stop and make camp for the night. He paused ahead and kicked a few rocks around, then gathered some pine needles. She could only pray they were stopping here.

"Will this be okay?" he said as she approached. "Is this a good place for you to stop?"

Allison barely nodded. She was beyond exhausted, amazed she hadn't collapsed miles ago.

"Could I borrow your blanket again?"

"Go ahead." He nodded at the dropped pack.

Dragging herself over, she moved his rifle from atop the pack.

"Here, let me." He took the gun from her. "It's loaded." Yanking the blanket free, he handed it to her.

"Thank you." Their eyes met; Allison thought he didn't look cross.

"That pile of pine needles will help." He nodded to the ground, and she gave him a small smile of thanks. *How peculiar this is this young man, these feelings. Those brown eyes, so full of warmth.* She snuck one more peek. He stared at her as she wrapped the blanket around her body and laid down. *So strange...*she yawned, remembering to cover her mouth.

10

Levi rose from the hard ground and surveyed the new morning. He had a strong inclination to do something before he got up. He stretched the taut muscles aching in his back, lowered his face into his hands, and began to pray. *Lord, each new day is a gift from you. Help me to see your goodness today. Help me to watch my tongue. Help me to trust you with my cabin. Everything you have given me is yours.*

He stretched his back as Patch sniffed around the sleeping woman. *And help heal Miss Kent. Give her memory back soon.*

Tell her you're sorry. The words came as an interruption to his prayer.

He knew, just as he knew he had ten toes, those quiet words were from the Lord. He focused on the expanse of sky. *Okay.*

When the coffee was ready and he had gathered some blackberries, he brought the items like a peace offering and laid them near her. "Miss, can you wake up?" He gently touched her shoulder.

"Oh…what…for pity sakes, why isn't this a bad dream?" she mumbled, rubbing her temples.

"Here, I brought you some breakfast."

"Ugh." Pulling herself up, she stared down at the simple fare. "Breakfast should be eggs, ham or sausage, and scones." She rolled her swollen eyes. "Why do I remember that?"

Levi bristled. She was clearly rejecting his attempts at kindness.

Tell her.

He shook his head. *You never let me get away with anything, Lord.*

"I wanted to say something to you." He chewed on his bottom lip, waiting for the words, then plopped a few berries into his mouth. "I just wanted to say I'm sorry for the way I treated you." *There, Lord, I said it.*

More.

He bowed his head. "I probably let those guys stealing my pelts get to me." He knew that wasn't it. "I'm usually very patient." *Not hard when you live alone.* "I guess I didn't know what to do." He finally met her eyes.

"You seem confident enough to me. Are we not going to your place?" Her eyes narrowed.

"Yes, I clearly know where I'm going. I just don't know about you." He looked down, shuffling his feet. "I want to help you, but I guess I'm doing something wrong. I don't want to make excuses. I'm just sorry for yesterday."

"I forgive you," Allison whispered. She pulled on her mass of tangled hair and shyly pushed a strand behind her ear. Carefully standing, she began to fold the blanket.

Every move seemed to exhaust her, and Levi took the blanket from her hands. "Just take your time, eat and drink a bit, and then we'll move on."

❧

"Mr. Graham. I don't seem to have my bearings yet. I don't need you to carry me," she said, eyeing him as he loaded his pack, "but would you mind if I tucked my hand in the crook of your arm? I feel so unsteady this morning."

"Of course." Levi lifted his elbow to her.

Allison carefully wrapped her arm under his and laid her palm on his rolled-up shirt sleeve. As they stepped forward, her fingers rolled inside his cuff, against his skin.

Trying to watch for the easiest steps through these woods he had hunted a hundred times, Levi slowed. There was a steeper, more direct trail over the ridge to Sault Creek, but he was incredibly aware that he wasn't alone. Her arm was warm against his sleeve. Good Lord, her fingers were touching him. He tried to understand what was happening. *If I grab her and carry her, that's improper? If she touches me, that's okay? As long as it's her idea?* He glanced to the side; she was watching her every step. It was plain as day that she wasn't affected the way he was.

After walking most of the morning, they finally approached a large fallen tree to sit on.

"Let's rest here," Levi said, offering her a drink from the cup. She took a few small sips between labored breaths.

"I'm too warm." She handed the water back and unbuttoned her jacket.

Levi looked away, an uncomfortable feeling on the back of his neck. "Patch, open up, boy." He poured the water into his dog's mouth, while Allison billowed her blouse.

"I wish I had a fan...a parasol...a bonnet." Her face sank. "How many days have I been without a bonnet? Mr. Graham, was there a bonnet in my things?"

Levi shook his head.

"What things did you bring? I don't remember gathering them."

He had a feeling this wasn't going to sit well. "I only grabbed what I could stuff in my pack."

"Such as...?"

"Well, I don't know what they're all called. Soft girly things."

Allison ran her hand down her face. "Ouch." She touched her scrapes. "This is very embarrassing, Mr. Graham. I probably look and smell like one of your dead animals. Do you have someone who does your wash?"

"No," he sighed. "I live alone, in a cabin, miles from anyone. Why do you always worry about how you look? I know you've been hurt. I don't expect you to be all pretty and flowery. But— there's a great hole in the creek for bathing." As soon as he said it, he knew it was unlikely. "Also, I have a tub that can be used." *Don't say the water for the mule is in that.*

She stood and brushed off some invading ants. "I'm only speaking of my appearance for my own decorum. Not because of you."

"Okay, since I don't even know what decorum is, I'll just take your word for it." He swiped a few ants off her sleeve. "Should I bow before I offer you my arm?" He risked teasing her with a small bow and an extended arm. She squinted, clutching her hands together in front of her.

"Would you like to wear my hat?" He pulled it up, and the sun hit his face.

"Heavens, no." She grimaced.

Levi let his hat drop back on his head. "Let's go."

The thick fog encompassed her again. Allison needed to wake up, but kept drifting back into sleep. The air was stuffy, and her damp blouse stuck to her skin. She lifted her heavy lids and ran her hand under her wet neck, willing her mind awake. Turning to the side, she tried to focus. *Where am I? A shed? A barn? Another bad dream? Someone has put me in an outbuilding.* Her boots were off and lying below a rough cot. *This is all wrong.* Sunlight peered through a dirty glass window, and more streamed through the half-open door. A table with three chairs sat only a few feet from her; farther past that were a bookshelf, a trunk, and a rusted potbelly stove. A rock fireplace loomed from one wall. *Where am I?*

❦

Levi hauled water, trying to calm down. His brother Ben could be such an idiot. He'd talked to him a month ago, and he knew about this short summer expedition. He had said he would come and watch over the place while Levi was gone, but nothing had been watered. Even though he'd pulled about everything he could from the ground, the garden was dry weeds. What about the cabin? Squatters could have come, thinking that the old cabin was there for the taking. His mule looked okay, but anyone could have come and taken him. It's a miracle there was straw and water left.

The word *miracle* reminded Levi of the prayer he had said over his things when he left. *I guess I should thank God instead of cursing my brother.* He raked his hand through his hair. The cool water of the creek called out to his hot and aching body, but he looked over to the cabin, puzzled. How could he wash himself and his clothes with her only a few feet away? She had walked the last couple of miles like a sleepwalker. By the time he picked her up and laid her on his bed, she was incapable of making a sound. Why did he feel inclined to take her fancy boots off? A mixture of the most awkward feelings surfaced, seeing her asleep in his cabin. Something in him wanted to help and protect her. Something else didn't want to risk her reaction to his chosen life. Dropping his boots to the side, he tossed everything but his pants into the sandy water of the creek. Swishing everything around, he wadded his things into a pile and went to fetch the soap from the cabin. He figured while he was there, he could just check to make sure she was still asleep.

✌♥✎

Allison yawned, tired and dizzy, but desperately wanting to drink the cup of water left sitting on the table. She took a step toward the water when the cabin door moved, and someone large and looming stood outlined in the low, setting sun.

She screamed and fell back against the table, knocking the water and closest chair over. Levi jumped to grab her arms before she hit the floor.

"Whoa, girl!"

"Don't touch me! Let go!" she yelled, pulling away.

"Allison! It's me, Levi! I'm not going to hurt you!" He pulled her up.

Shuffling backward, she clutched the rock fireplace, blinking hard. "Oh, my lands," she said, panting. "I didn't...I couldn't see you." Her eyes grew wide. "Mr. Graham! Where are your clothes?"

"I'm sorry," he said, backing away. "I was about to go swimming, but I wanted to check on you."

Allison fell in a heap onto the closest chair and dropped her head on the table. "Please, don't ever come in to check on me without being fully dressed."

"Well, of course...I know that. I thought you were sleeping."

"And what is this...this...outbuilding?" She shielded her eyes and swung her other hand in a circle. "You're leaving me in here while you sleep in your home?"

"What are you talking about? This is my home, my cabin." She followed his hand, pointing at the cot she just left. "That's my bed."

Frozen, she stared, making sure he was serious. "I'm so sorry, Mr. Graham. Every time I open my mouth, I offend you. Your home is quite…quaint." Her eyes dropped. She'd never seen such a large bare chest and square shoulders. He was incredibly intimidating.

༄ঌ৯

Why does she do that? He turned to leave. "Don't come out. I lied to you!" He stalked away. "I'm not swimming, I'm bathing. And I'm not about to do it with my clothes on." He jogged to the creek and jumped in.

Levi scrubbed himself and his clothes spotless. He threw what he could over the bushes and the rest he put on and sat on a flat rock in the sun. He pulled his hands through his wet hair as Patch came up to greet him.

"Hey, friend. You still like me, right?" Patch nuzzled him. "That's good, 'cause that girl in there is crazy," Patch looked to the cabin and rested his chin on his master's leg.

Scratching behind his dog's ears, Levi huffed. "She's lost the good sense God gave her." As soon as the words left his mouth, he regretted them. "All right, Patch." He remembered that Allison's appearance was important to her. "Let's try again to be helpful."

He went to the fence and pulled the large mule trough free and hauled it down to the creek. He scrubbed it with sand and water until it shone like new. He purposely grabbed his drying shirt and buttoned it up, then lugged the mule trough up to the cabin door and knocked. *This feels strange. Knocking on my own door.* "Hey, are you awake?"

"Yes, come in." She sounded as if she'd been asleep.

Levi lugged the big tub inside and set it between the bookshelf and the table.

Allison sat up from the cot and rubbed her eyes.

"I'll bring the water, then you can put the bar over the door." He tried to think of what else she would want. "If you toss your stuff out first, I can wash it for you, and it should dry before nightfall. I'll leave my pack in here, and you can see what there was to bring." So far she seemed to follow, except now, she was staring at his bare feet. *Feet, too?*

"Why don't you…" Levi remembered the small trunk under his bed and crossed the room to where she sat. "Put all your personal belongings in here."

66

"I won't be staying long."

"Oh, I know. It's just because I need my pack for other stuff, and I don't know where else..." He scanned the small cabin.

"This trunk will work fine," she sighed.

"Good. I'll bring in four or five buckets of water, and you can wash. Sorry, but it's going to be cold." He left with the bucket. After several trips, he poured in the last bucket and looked at Allison apologetically. "If you want it warm, I'd have to build a fire."

"No, no, this will work fine." She nodded as he dropped the soap in the water.

Looking around, he grabbed a dishrag and draped it on the tub. "Got some of your things for you." He pushed the pack onto the table. "Here's a comb, and these pins from your hair." He pulled the flap up from his shirt pocket and pulled them out, laying them carefully on the table, sure she would question how he got them. But she stayed silent.

"Anything else?" He headed toward the door.

"Wait," she called after him. Levi stopped but didn't turn.

"I'll wash my own clothes. Thank you for the offer, though.

11

✥

Just as she had closed the door securely, Allison heard Levi's voice from out front.

"I'm going fishing. Patch will stay by the cabin. Be back soon." His voice trailed off.

She hooked the large piece of wood across the door and stood back, scratching her head. With the window covered, this was as private as it was going to get. Pulling her belongings from Levi's pack, she laid them out on the table. A clean pair of drawers, a chemise, a petticoat, another blouse, and the burgundy gloves were all there was. Her one skirt and jacket would have to suffice. Sighing, she glanced around the small cabin one more time. Pulling off her outer clothes, drawers, and stockings, and untying her corset, she took a deep breath and felt something fall to the floor. Bending down, she picked up a roll of money. Holding it out in front of her, she stared down to where her corset lay. Why was there money tucked in her unmentionables? Something about this seemed familiar. What was it? Maybe the money held a clue? She pulled the stiff bills apart and gasped when she counted out five twenty dollar bills. Good Lord, one hundred dollars.

For pity sakes. Allison dropped the money on the table and stepped back. *Did I rob a bank? Is this money mine? Why did I keep it tucked in my corset?* It was quite an interesting hiding place, she thought, gently rubbing her never-ending headache. *What can I do to remember?* She checked the floor. *What else might have fallen out of my clothing?*

The water was cold. As badly as Allison wanted to linger, she washed her body and hair quickly. She couldn't help but look at the money as she got dressed. Should she tell Mr. Graham about it? *It doesn't really matter. As soon as my memory returns, I'll need it to get to wherever it is I'm going.* She picked up the wide-toothed comb and carefully pulled the knots and tangles out of her hair. The small cabin was hot and stuffy, so she lifted off the wood plank that secured the door. She opened it halfway to see Patch sitting in the direct sun, panting.

"You must be hot. Come on inside." Patch entered, and so did a summer afternoon breeze. Allison wondered if it was safe to leave the door open.

She washed and rinsed her dirty items and stepped outside the cabin. To her left was a large woodpile. The area had been cleared, with mostly dead grass surrounding it, and beyond lay the tree line. To her right, there was a pen, a fence, and a lean-to, with a mule who didn't bother to look up at her.

Searching the area outside the cabin, she wondered where would be the best place to dry out her things when she noticed the creek, with its grassy banks and tall brush. She wasn't sure how far she should go from the cabin, but looking both ways, she didn't see Levi anywhere. Carefully setting her undergarments on the fence, she scanned the area one more time. How unfamiliarly humble and rustic it all was.

Her hair was down and loose around her shoulders, blowing softly in the afternoon breeze. It felt freeing, but also somewhat improper. Walking back into the cabin, she stared at the comb and her hair pins. *I should know how to do this.* She peered in the glass window, straining to see her reflection. Her fingers worked a bun at the back of her head, and she inserted the pins, relieved to achieve a sort of loose, low bundle.

Sighing, she looked around and noticed a large crate by the bookshelf. She stood over it, hesitating. It could be anything, she supposed, as she lifted the lid. It contained the obvious things belonging to Mr. Graham: a heavy buckskin jacket, trousers, shirts, a holster, and black suspenders. Kneeling on the floor, she moved some things aside and grabbed a few faded photographs. One showed a stoic father and mother and four little boys. The oldest boy had a square face and chubby cheeks. The next child had an angelic face with large dark eyes. The third was a toddler standing on a stool, with bright eyes and a cowlick sticking up from his forehead. Finally, there was a baby boy sitting tall on his mother's lap. Brothers—Mr. Graham had said something about having brothers. Allison brought the photo in closer. The second boy had to be Levi. She had seen those same eyes up close—except in a man's face.

The door creaked, and she jumped back as Levi entered. "I'm sorry," she said, quickly covering the crate and patting her loosening hair.

Silently, he laid a string with two small fish on a wood platter. "It's okay." He glanced to the floor and back at her. "I'm just surprised, is all. You're all… clean." He shook his head, a red flush rising up his neck.

"Yes, that was the plan." Looking down, she tucked several uncooperative strands back behind an ear.

"Let me get the water out, and we'll cook up the fish," Levi said, breaking the awkward moment.

"Umm…okay." Allison knew there was something else he wanted to say. She realized she was still holding the picture. "Is this your family?"

"Yes."

"I shouldn't have snooped. I'm sorry."

"I guess I should've knocked, but the door was open. I'm not used to knocking, you know." He dipped the water bucket into the tub, tossing the bathwater out the door.

Allison watched him, chewing on her bottom lip. She wanted to ask him about the picture, about his family, but he seemed reserved. Carefully, she set the picture on the table.

"Oh, for pity sakes," she mumbled to herself. Stepping out the door, she snatched all her unmentionables off the fence.

∾೮✺

Levi set the galvanized tub on its side and pulled it through the door, then hauled it back into the pen. Picking up the bucket, he looked at the mule. "This is going to be interesting," he murmured. On the third bucket of water, he still hadn't found his composure. He took a handful of the cold water and splashed it on his face. It helped a little, but Allison was certainly having a strange effect on him. Blowing out a long breath, he gazed out to the tree line. *I judged her for her vanity, and yet her soft appearance is unnerving me. She looks so different.* He shook his head. *She looks younger—more innocent.*

Like a sister, said the still voice.

Like a sister? That sounds like You, Lord. Plastering his damp hair behind his ears, he chuckled at himself.

Allison stared at the fish on the table, surrounded by buzzing flies. *How would you cook something like this? Why don't I know such a simple thing?* Levi walked in, opened the stove, and loaded it with wood, lighting a match. Moving around his cabin with ease, he grabbed the things he needed. Feeling in the way, she sat down at the table, watching him. Soon the fish were sizzling in a pan, and he finally turned to her.

"It'll be just a few more minutes." The family picture still sat on the table.

"Tell me about them," she said.

"Ahh, okay." Levi took the photo. "My father's name is James. This is my older brother, and he's also James. That's me. Then Daniel. Then Ben. My ma is Laura." An awkward silence filled the cabin as he went to flip the fish.

Allison placed the picture back into the wooden crate. Picking up a cloth from the shelf, she unfolded it over the table. "Tablecloth or napkin, which would you like?"

More silence, with that now-familiar creased brow.

Allison folded it and put it back. "You told me their names...but what else about them?"

Levi slid the fish onto two plates. "It's hot in here. Do you mind if I eat outside?"

"No, of course not. I'm guessing you want to be alone?"

"No." He nodded at the chairs. "Grab one."

Allison took her plate and reached for the chair.

"Here, I'll get it for you." Levi carried the chair a few feet from the cabin and set it down in the shade. "For you."

"Thank you. And thank you for dinner." The sun was setting, glistening through the trees, and she drew in a deep breath of evening air. As they ate in silence, she wondered if he, too, felt this new calm.

Levi cleared his throat. "My father and oldest brother work in the copper mines south of Sault Creek. That's where I grew up. I worked on the docks, loading the copper for almost two years. I was able to save enough money to buy this place. Ben, my younger brother, is a vagabond. He would never admit it, but he likes to travel around and never commit to anything."

Allison nodded, even though she wasn't sure what she was agreeing with.

"James—we call him Junior—is married to Frieda. They have a little girl named Miranda."

"Ahh...so you're an uncle." She smiled.

"Yes, I am." His face lightened. "She's a cute girl. Thankfully, she looks nothing like my brother."

Patch came up, nosing around the fish bones lying on the ground.

"And then there's this guy." Levi rubbed the dog's back.

'Please tell me how you and Patch came to be." Hearing about his family was endearing—almost comforting.

"Well, now. My pa doesn't allow us to own anything that doesn't have a use. Patch was a stray pup I found. I knew better than to try and bring him home." Levi scratched under Patch's chin. "My pa didn't take to him. Said he looked sickly, no good for hunting, so he made me take him in the woods to shoot him."

"That's terrible," Allison frowned.

"I tried for weeks to shoot him, but I just couldn't do it. So I left him tied to a tree and brought him scraps. But I knew if I left him tied up, one day I was going to approach that tree and find him torn to pieces. So I took him as deep in the woods as I could and..." Levi eyed her, snickering.

"Why are you laughing at me?"

"You're about to chew your knuckle off, and the dog is lying right here, safe and sound."

"Oh. Well, true, but you're a riveting storyteller." She relaxed, laughing at herself.

"So he followed me home, where I received a whipping for not killing him. Then my pa mumbled something about being able to track that far from the woods to our homestead. Saw some good in Patch, and let me keep him."

Allison looked from dog to owner. "Oh, my."

"He was worth the whipping." Leaning forward with his elbows on his knees, he grabbed a stick and drew some circles in the dirt. He turned his head toward her, squinting. "Do you think we're worth the whipping Jesus took?"

"Oh. I…I don't know." She shrugged.

Levi leaned back in the chair until the front legs came off the ground, and grasped his hands behind his head. "God must have thought we were. Jesus was a man who had to take our punishment. He was wounded for our transgressions. He was bruised for our iniquities. The chastisement of our peace was upon him. And for all that pain we get life, freedom, healing." His chair came forward and landed on the ground.

"That's…remarkable." She didn't know if she was referring to Jesus or Levi.

12

❧

"Mr. Graham, my memory is lacking, but I don't think I've ever been around dogs. And as I watched you cook, it sparked no recognition for me. What do you think?"

"Could well be." Levi took her hands. "When I first found you, your hands were scratched up and such." He rubbed his thumbs along her fingers. "But they were soft." He flipped them over and traced his thumbs across her palms. "Soft hands." He placed them back on her knees. "They haven't seen a day of real work."

"Oh." Allison felt rattled by his touch.

"I want you to call me Levi. All this *Mr. Graham* reminds me of my pa too much."

"I suppose it would be acceptable, as long as there's no one else who would question our imprudence."

He shook his head. "I don't know what imprudence is. Just call me Levi, and can I call you Allison?"

"Yes, you may, Mr. Graham."

He dropped his head into his hands.

"Don't look so forlorn. I was trying to use humor. It's probably left me, along with my memory." Her voice trailed off.

Smiling, he bit his bottom lip and nodded at her.

Allison felt her spirits lift a bit, but it couldn't cover the pounding in her head. "I'd like to retire. Earlier, I napped on your cot."

"Bed," he corrected.

"Well, as for tonight, I don't want to displace you. Where would be an appropriate place for me to sleep?"

"You can have the cabin, Allison. And the bed."

A moment of staring ensued, each wondering who would win.

"Where will you be?"

"There's a wide shelf in the lean-to." He nodded to where the mule was.

"I see. Is there anything you need before I close the door?" She picked up their plates. Levi followed her in, carrying the chairs.

"Here's the oil lamp." He lit it, then grabbed a quilt off the shelf and gathered the dirty dishes. "I'll do these down at the water. Bar the door."

"Thank you…" She almost said *Levi*, but it felt far too familiar, as they stood together in the soft light.

"All right, then," He nodded, walking out.

✑❧

Allison dropped the plank over the door. The cabin was still hot and stuffy, but she couldn't imagine leaving the door open. Her awareness of her surroundings had come into perspective. *To think I slept two nights in the woods! How absurd. Who knows what creatures could have got to me in the night?*

She laid her skirt and blouse over the back of a chair. With all distractions gone, she lay down and fell instantly asleep.

Hours into the night, she dreamed of Patch as a little puppy. His fat little paws, his big brown eyes. He jumped on her and began licking her hands. She leaned down to pick him up, and he licked her face. She dreamed that her hand came up to move him away, but something startled her out of sleep. It seemed so real that she thought her hand had actually touched the dog. Her eyes flew open, and she realized that someone or something was on her bed—on top of her. She screamed and swung hard at the dark shadow above her. Her arm made contact with something real. This was no dream.

"Good night!" It was a man's voice.

Allison swung again until her attacker captured her arms and pinned them above her head. She screamed, trying to kick her legs

75

free, but his weight and strength were crushing her. In one last attempt, she pushed off with her feet, and they both rolled onto the floor. She sat up on top of him and twisted her arms free with everything she had.

The door suddenly slammed open, and Allison could feel someone grabbing her around the waist and pulling her back. Levi set her behind him and grabbed the man off the floor.

"Ben! What are you doing!" Levi had him by the shirt, jerking him back and forth.

"Lord Almighty, Levi! Who is that sleeping in your bed? She just about knocked me into next week!"

"I swear, Ben…" Levi pulled his fist back.

"Don't hit me!" Ben tensed. "She already cracked me a good one. My lip is bleeding."

"No mercy for you," Levi growled.

Allison could feel Levi's body pulsing—or maybe it was her own heart beating. She wrapped her hands around his extended arm. It was hard as a rock.

"Please, Levi, don't hit him." She tugged on his arm again. "Maybe you should introduce me to your brother."

The oil lamp was lit, and Allison suddenly realized she was standing there in her underclothes, in the presence of two men. She quickly grabbed the blanket off the floor and wrapped it around her. It was obvious Levi had enough anger for both of them, and she surprised herself by being the calm one.

"I think your brother thought it was you."

"I know, Allison, but there's no excuse for his behavior." His eyes were still locked on Ben.

"See…" Ben reluctantly smiled, touching his painful lip. "The dog lick thing was something we used to do to each other when we were kids."

"You licked her face?" Levi took a step closer as Ben moved to the other side of the table.

Ben held his hand out. "I'm very sorry, miss. Believe me, a pretty young woman was the last thing I thought I'd find in Levi's bed." He snickered and moved swiftly as Levi lunged after him.

"Wait!" Allison stopped Levi's advancement. "Everyone calm down." She put her hand on his shirt, feeling the pounding of his heart.

He grabbed her hand and brushed it away.

She turned to Ben. "I don't think Levi wants to do the introductions, so I will. I'm Allison Kent."

"Nice to meet you, Allison Kent. I'm Benjamin Graham." Ben reached out his hand, and she took it.

"Sorry about the bloody lip. Please forgive me for hitting you." She shook Ben's hand.

"Of course. If you'll forgive me for the... intrusion."

Levi growled and grabbed Allison's wrist, pulling it free from Ben's hand. "Enough with the niceties. You should not be easily forgiven." He poked a hard finger against Ben's chest. "Outside. Now." Grasping his brother by the shoulder, he pushed him through the door.

"Levi." Allison started to touch his arm and changed her mind. "I bolted the door like you said. I didn't leave it..."

"I know." He cut her off. "I know."

Allison took a few minutes to set the cabin right, listening to the quiet night interrupted by Levi's angry voice. He rambled on about responsibilities and something about the mule and water. She blew out the lamp and lay back down. Thankfully, the arguing voices got lower. Feeling as if she were eavesdropping on some family business, she thought she heard Levi talking about her. She wondered how he would explain her being here.

Covering her ears the next morning, Allison wished someone would quiet the squawking birds. She knew she could easily fall back asleep, but her mind was wide awake from what had occurred last night. Pulling on her clothes, she tried to smooth the wrinkles, with little success. Maybe she should be thankful there was no mirror. She tried again to secure something decent for her hair;

leaving it down was too indiscreet. Finally, she managed a loose bun; it was better than nothing. She jumped when she heard Levi and Ben talking outside. One young man was nerve-racking enough. For pity sakes, now there were two.

Allison opened the door and saw them before they saw her. Levi was pointing to something, shaking his head. She could hear Ben saying that Levi was wrong about something, and Levi said, "No, Ben, you're wrong," and gave him a shove. Suddenly, Ben jumped on Levi's back. Clutching her throat, she hid behind the door as the brothers rolled around in a ball of dust. When he saw her, though, Levi stilled, pushed Ben away, and straightened up.

"Good morning." Levi pulled his hair back behind his ears.

"Hello, Miss Kent." Ben purposely cut in front of Levi to get to the cabin. "You look very well this morning. I like your hair like that," Ben said with a quick wink. "And your own clothes do so much more for you than an old blanket."

Allison blushed. Ben was attractive. He was a bit taller than Levi, and slenderer. He had a twinkle in his eye when he talked, and she fought the smile she felt coming on. Last night had seemed like some indecent attack, but in the morning light, it was almost comical.

"If you two are done, I'd like to start something for breakfast," Levi said, walking between them.

Ben and Allison followed him into the cabin. Suddenly it felt smaller, and she wondered if they felt as uncomfortable as she did.

"Levi, would you like me to get some water?" she asked.

"No, Ben can do it." He pushed the pitcher toward his brother.

Thirty minutes later, Levi set the hot coffee on the table. He slid out pan of biscuits and a bowl with some kind of meat and gravy. Ben quickly came over to pull out Allison's chair, and Levi rolled his eyes.

"Let's pray." Levi and Ben grasped hands, then reached out to Allison. She timidly took each man's free hand in one of hers.

Levi spoke out. "Father, thank you for the life you've given us. Thank you for the food you've given us. Forgive us for our many sins. Help us to bring glory to you. Amen."

She stared as both brothers dug into the food as if they hadn't eaten in a week.

"I was shocked to hear about your mishap," Ben said, chewing. "It does seem as if God was watching over you."

Allison nodded. "If Levi hadn't come along, I suppose I'd be dead." Levi stopped eating for a minute and watched her.

"Ahh, the Good Samaritan. How biblical." Ben gave Levi a slap on the back, and he jerked away.

"So even now, you don't remember anything? Not even your family?" Ben squinted.

"Manners, Ben, manners." Levi shot Ben a warning.

"Certain things, like my own name. I know what a train is. I know there's a proper way I would have set this table." She stirred the unusual gravy with her fork.

"Oh, yeah? Well, that's good." Ben gulped some coffee. "I'm sure it'll all come back soon, and when it does, we'll all be thankful not to rely on Levi's cooking." Ben reached for another biscuit and hit the burned side against the table.

"We're not relying on Allison to do *the* cooking, either way, Ben." Levi shot him an annoyed look.

"That's right. You said she couldn't cook." He looked over at her. "Was it because you don't remember, or you never learned how?"

Allison bristled, knowing Levi had been telling Ben about her limitations. What else had he said?

"I don't know the answer to that; I just said it felt very unfamiliar." She shifted in her seat. *How long am I going to feel impaired?* The food was almost certainly something she had ever eaten before—that she could remember. Getting up, she pushed her chair in and walked out the door.

The brothers looked at each other. "I'm not sure what I said, but I think I upset her." Ben scratched his head. "I'll go apologize."

Levi put his hand on Ben's arm. "No, just give her a few minutes. I've found it helps." He cleared the breakfast mess and glanced out the door. "I'll be back," he said. Looking up and down Sault Creek, he spotted her trying to get rid of Patch. He approached them and told Patch to go on.

"I'd like to be alone, thank you." She walked ahead.

"Allison, please, stop for a minute. Ben isn't real smart. He doesn't think."

"I'm not upset with Ben," she frowned. "I just wanted to be alone a moment."

"Okay, then you're upset with me. Just stop and tell me why. I can't help without knowing what or why."

"Remember? I'm confusing. So just stay confused." She walked on.

No problem with her memory from the last couple days, he thought. "Allison, please." The frustration built again. "Maybe I need to say I'm sorry, but I can't when your back is to me."

"You don't even know what you're sorry for." She shot him a glare. "Go ahead, let's see what you're sorry for." She placed her hands on her hips, waiting.

Levi stretched his neck from side to side, wondering about the tension that suddenly came on when he had to talk to her. "Listen. Ben and I don't care about your ability to cook. Ben just says that because he'd look forward to Patch's cooking over mine." He moved a few steps closer.

She started to open her mouth and shut it quickly, then took in a deep breath and stepped away from him. "It wasn't just about the cooking. I know you've told him things about me. And when I don't know what's been said, I feel as if you two have…have…oh, forget it."

Levi reached out and took her hand as she turned away.

She stared down at his hand holding hers, and he braced himself for her rebuff.

"Okay." He let go. "I shouldn't have said anything. Truth is, Allison…" He kicked a pinecone. "Ben and I shouldn't even be allowed around women. We're just left-footed brothers from the hills, which you are clearly not. We never had sisters. I don't know anything about women. I know it must be miserable being you, far away from all you know." He rubbed his temples. "So I'm sorry if we hurt your feelings. We both are. If you could just tell us when we're being stupid, that might help, too."

She let out a sigh. "You can be incredibly endearing when you want. But yet incredibly rough. My goodness, your arms are like…"

"One other thing." He cleared his throat. "I'm going to leave for a few days, maybe a week." He hoped she was following him.

"What? Leaving for where?"

"You remember the pelts I lost to those two men?"

She nodded.

"Well, those pelts were what I relied on for my winter provisions. No pelts to sell, no provisions. Summer isn't the best time to trap, so I'm going to head southeast to an area I don't usually trap in and see what I can do. When I have enough, I'll come home, and by then we can head to Ready Springs. I usually trade there. And we can see to getting you back to where it is you need to go."

Allison rubbed her temples. Several days to a week?

"It actually worked out, because Ben was supposed to be here last week and watch the place while I was gone. But he can stay here now and make sure you're safe." Levi took a closer look at her. "You seem to be feeling better. The swelling has gone down on that knot. Your face is very beautiful." *How in the world did that just come straight from my mouth?* He ran his hand across his scraggly beard. "What I'm trying to say is, I believe Ben will be a perfect gentleman. I wouldn't go unless I was confident that he would be honorable. He can be absentminded, but he's somewhat house trained." He tried to read her expression. "Is that okay?"

"I don't seem to have any choice, do I?"

"No." He grinned.

Levi took Allison's empty dinner plate from her hand.

"You look like you're going to drop. Go ahead and go to bed." He nodded toward the cabin.

"I think I will."

Stepping inside, she put the bar over the door. How had Ben got past it? She was too tired to care. Draping her clothes over the chair, she laid down. What an entertaining day. It was the first day she hadn't taken a nap. She wanted to, but she didn't want to leave the brothers. They had spent the afternoon digging out rocks from their swimming area and creating log platforms for diving. The brothers had jumped and dived, then Ben ran and sprang off the platform with his hands, flipping into the creek. Afraid they would try something more dangerous, she had fought the impulse to applaud. When Levi had come over to her, sopping wet and winded, she had to ask how many years the boys had belonged to the circus.

He had stared at her, puzzled. Another failed attempt at humor.

Allison snuggled down into the mattress. This was the time of night she wanted to clear every thought, in hopes that something familiar would find its way home to her. But she had to suppress a giggle. The brothers were so terribly competitive. She wondered how much was for her benefit. Their antics were all so dangerous that it was a wonder one of them hadn't broken a bone. She doubted she would ever be free enough to have such abandonment. Certainly not to the level of their behavior—but something still ladylike might be fun.

13

❧❧

Allison opened the door to Levi's soft knocking the following morning. "Good day." She felt lighter, refreshed.

He gave her a smile. "Do you remember anything?"

"No, I guess I just slept well. No interruptions, anyway."

Ben walked in, and she shot him a smile. He waggled his eyebrows and grinned.

"Ben, I need you to clean the old shotgun. I've got to work on some of the damaged traps this morning," Levi said.

"I'll file the hatchet and knife, too. Are you trying for beaver?" Ben asked.

"Yeah, unless you've heard the market has dwindled down again."

"I haven't heard anything new." Ben checked to see if the coffee was ready.

"Last year some guys were bragging about getting top dollar. Trading with the Chippewa was getting unpredictable, so maybe it's true, maybe not." Ben glanced at Allison. "Trappers aren't known for the pure and blameless lifestyle our beloved

saint Levi has."

Levi bopped Ben on his head.

"Ouch! Overlooking his love of violence toward me." Ben rubbed the back of his head.

"I'm going to be at the mercy of Rolf Crocker at this point." Levi added more kindling to the little stove.

"Crocker's is the Mercantile and Dry Goods Store in Ready Springs," Ben explained. Allison nodded, wondering if that would be her first encounter with civilization since her accident.

Ben sat down and scratched under his chin. "I'm thinking that when you get back, I might head up to Von Keller's dairy farm. He said I could make some money working the dairy—something about trains having box cars now that are kept cold?"

"Refrigeration."

Both brothers stopped and stared at her.

"I've been on trains. I remember, they make me sick sometimes." She stopped to concentrate any specific memories tied to trains. The brothers watched her expectantly.

"And, yes, a dairy would use refrigeration cars. Their products wouldn't spoil so fast," she added.

"This is good." Ben circled a finger at her forehead as if he could stir up her thoughts. "Picture yourself on a train. Where is it going? What do you see outside? A town or a lake or...."

"Ben! Let her think," Levi said.

The brothers watched her drift in thought, but after a few moments, her face dropped. "I just know certain things...and other things are not there."

"Was she lost or did she lose her mind?" Ben asked Levi.

"I haven't lost my mind, Ben! For goodness sake!"

"Don't get angry, Allison. Try to ask him politely not to be so stupid." Levi set a steaming pan down on the table.

"Porridge, how perfect, " Ben said with wide eyes.

Later in the day, the brothers repaired the fence.

"Ben, do you have cheese for brains? I went out of my way to tell her what a fine upstanding gentleman you'd be while I'm gone."

"That's so nice of you, fur face." Ben held the fence board in place. "It's just when I think a girl likes me, I say dumb things."

Levi's arm froze, gripping the hammer in midair. "What? You think she likes you?"

The hammer shook, and Ben moved back. "Did you see the way she smiled at me this morning? Levi, your nostrils are flaring."

"You think every girl likes you." He finally struck the nail. "If you weren't so busy trying to be charming, you could see she doesn't."

"Maybe she does. And maybe you're jealous."

"Do you think if I was worried, I'd be leaving her in your care?"

"Do think she has feelings for *you*?"

"The only feelings I know about involve a headache and being tired."

"That's what's wrong with you, Levi. You never try. Constance Bing would have licked your boots to get your attention. All the girls in school would swoon to have you speak one word their way."

"I don't even know why we're having this conversation. She's going to get her memory back and be on the first stage or train out of here."

"What if she's faking this memory loss?" Ben said. "What if she did something really bad? Maybe she's a runaway."

"Well, cheese head, if you'd seen her half dead with a knot the size of your fist on her forehead, or the way she vomited all over herself…doesn't seem likely she'd fake all that, do ya' think?"

Ben pulled back. "Ick, you can have her." He quickly licked Levi's face and took off running.

At supper, Allison cut and sawed, but couldn't seem to get anywhere with the meat on her tin plate. She put her fork and knife down and sat back in her chair.

"Levi, you so eloquently pray over the food. Maybe you could pray for the strength to cut it."

His brows narrowed as he tried to figure out if she was serious. They hadn't talked much today. "Would you like me to cut it for you?"

"And how will I possibly manage this next week without your cutting skills every night?" She grabbed the knife and stabbed it hard into the meat. Both brothers jumped, but Ben snatched her upright knife away from the punctured meat. Grinning, he held it behind his chair. Allison covered a giggle.

She eyed them both, then impulsively grabbed at the knife resting on Levi's plate. Rising quickly, he captured her wrist without difficulty.

"Now, now," he said, gripping her firmly. "What kind of table manners are these?" He held her tight as she tried to pull free.

"I need a knife for my meat is all." She couldn't glare at him without smiling. For a split second, he wanted to jerk her forward across the table and into his arms. He let go suddenly as he felt heat rising to his face.

"Allison, you would fit right in at the Graham table," Ben joked. "We'll turn you into a scrapper yet."

"Oh, dear." She smiled at Ben while she massaged her wrists.

Levi cleared his throat. "I'm sorry for grabbing you like that. There is no excuse." He pulled his chair in and sat.

"No need to be so contrite. I think I started it." She sat down, fighting a silly smile.

"I started it," Ben broke in. "As the baby of the family, I just accept blame for everything. Do you have any memories of maybe a sister or brother?" he asked. "I know Levi could never forget me, no matter how hard he tried." He reached over to pat Levi's head as his brother pushed him away.

"No… no memories." Allison shook her head.

Later, Levi rose from the table and explained that he'd be leaving as soon as he got a few things done tomorrow. If Allison wanted anything, he needed to know.

She shrugged. "Could we walk for a moment?"

"Go ahead, you two want to be alone. I'm not offended, I'll have her to myself soon." Ben raised his eyebrows, and Allison shot him a weary look.

As Allison and Levi walked toward the creek, the air became lighter and cooler.

She took a deep breath, "When I barred the door the other night, how did Ben get in?"

"There's a crack in the door. You can slide a knife up between the slats and push the bar up."

"Could you repair that before you leave?"

"Not really."

"What do you mean? No, you really can't fix it, or no, you don't want to fix it?"

"Both. There are only four people who know that trick. Five, counting you."

"Certainly this isn't my home, and soon enough I'll be leaving." She hesitated, choosing her words carefully. "So I have no right to demand anything of you. But…"

"Ray Cox built the cabin forty years ago, when he was my age. He was a free trapper. He married late in life, a woman named Thelma," he said, kicking a rock. "What are you worried about?" He faced her.

Allison swatted a mosquito hovering near her ear. "I'm not worried, just a little nervous in these surroundings. No neighbors, no town…I don't know how you do it."

"I worked on the docks loading copper for almost two years. I feared for my life nearly every day. The city felt like a prison. The more people crammed in, the more desperation I saw."

"And so, with only five people that know how to unbar the door, I should feel safe?"

"Safety, protection—those are things only God can give you."

Allison shook her head. "You and Ben talk about God in a very personal way. Yet you carry guns and bar doors. Why do all that, if protection is only from God?"

Levi was equally annoyed and impressed at her question. "People in the Bible protected themselves. Swords, slingshots, David hid in caves. I think we all do what we must to survive. I just meant you either trust God for your life and death, or you don't. I don't think I can talk you into feeling safe, especially after whatever happened to you. Some experiences just take a long time to get over. As long as you're here, I'll do anything in my power to make sure you're safe."

It just happened again. She was staring at him as if he had just confessed his eternal love.

"Do you believe that?" he asked, unnerved by her silent stare.

"I do," she said locking her eyes with his. "I remember those men by the river asking for me or your pelts. You didn't hesitate to make sure I was safe. You gave up your income for me. You carried me when I didn't have the strength. I know that you're a man of character, and I do believe you'll help me, as you've said."

Levi was struck dumb at the depth of her words. Every day she seemed kinder, and tonight, when her playful side had come out, he'd been struck by her beautiful, mischievous smile.

"One other thing beyond safety. I have some money I can give you for all the care I've received. And I know…" She held up her palm to stop his interruption. "You have to do what you need to do this week, but it doesn't change anything. I want to help you with your supplies. I've eaten your food…"

"Not much," he cut in.

"I want to reimburse you, so you won't be without what you need this winter."

Levi felt as if someone had just dropped a large rock on his toe. "Stop, Allison, please. Let's get back." He touched her elbow to lead her in the dark.

She pulled up her skirts a bit so that she could see where to step. "I can tell you didn't receive any of my offers." They walked up to the soft light of the cabin.

"You know me pretty well." He winked, letting go of her elbow. "Goodnight."

14

Levi smiled as he jumped over a dry creek bed. Why do I enjoy unnerving her? I shouldn't take pleasure in that. Her face was white as a sheet the day Ben and I dove in the water. Maybe it was too childish? But then when she stabbed a knife clear through the tin plate to the wooden table…Lord, have mercy. She was laughing. One minute upset, the next minute laughing. It's a good thing she has such a sweet smile. Pulling a branch away, he ambled through the brush. He'd hiked for hours, but his mind was stuck in one place. *Oh, Lord, I can't quit thinking about her. This isn't like me. It's like an itch that won't go away until I scratch it.*

Allison bent over to straighten the blankets and decided they needed to be washed. Who knows how long Levi had slept here without clean blankets? The sun peeked through fluffy white clouds; surely there was enough time to wash and dry the bedding. She headed out the front door in search of her bathing tub and saw Ben heading her way. "Levi gave me a large tub earlier for bathing and washing. Do you know where he keeps it?

"The only thing big enough for bathing is the mule trough." Ben pointed over to the pen.

"Oh, my." Allison scrutinized the dirty tub with flies buzzing around it.

"We just wash in the creek, unless…do you need the water warmed?"

"No, not necessarily." She looked at the sandy bank of the creek. "I just want to learn to do a few things. I think it will help me not to feel so idle."

Ben took a giant step forward and bowed gallantly, hat in hand. "I am at your service, a master teacher of many things. You name it, I will show you the Benjamin Graham method…"

"Of washing in a creek?" She cut him off.

"Yes." He plopped his hat back on. "Let's start with the wash." He bowed again, extending his hand. "And by tonight, you'll be taking warm pie out of the oven."

"Such faith in your teaching." She smiled.

"Oh no, dear lady. All my faith is in you."

Allison shook her head, laughing. "Working that primitive stove may have to be a later lesson."

Ben dropped his boots and rolled up his pants. "So you take the blanket, soak it…" He held the blanket under the water. "Scrub a bit of soap here and there. Then plunge and rub. Like this." He demonstrated his technique.

Allison was already discouraged, seeing how wet Ben was getting. She couldn't picture herself repeating this task. She chewed on her lip, wondering if the mule trough was a better way.

"Now, here's the hard part. You carry the wet item over to a nice flat rock." He plopped it down. "And beginning at the top, squeeze all the water from top to bottom. Squeeze and roll, until the water is mostly out." He stepped back. "Now, you try."

"I don't know. This is my only skirt. I don't want to get wet."

"Well, here's another way." He grabbed the wet blanket and walked it up to the fence. Allison couldn't help but grimace at the mud and grass clinging to his feet.

"Hang it over like this, and squeeze it out here."

She pulled some fabric free and began to twist it.

"Good, that's right," Ben said encouragingly.

She felt like a child who could finally tie her own shoes.

"Then just spread it out facing the sun, and you can do the next one."

"Maybe that's enough wash for today."

"Of course, you rest or nap or whatever you need to do," Ben said.

Allison bristled. Levi would have challenged her. Ben was nothing but accommodating. One made her stronger, one made her feel frailer.

After avoiding the afternoon heat with a nap, she rose and peered out the door for any sign of Ben. Her attempt at wash billowed in the afternoon breeze, and she lifted it and turned it over. It was almost dry. Ben sat on a stump in the shade, working on something.

"How was your rest?" he called.

"Good." She walked closer, trying to figure out what he was doing.

"This is going to be a porch swing." Ben strained to tie a knot in a rope at the end of some wood.

"For whose porch, may I ask?"

"Yours," he said.

"Mine?" she said, looking around. "Ben, I am a woman without a porch."

"Well, true, so it will be a tree swing." He got up and set it aside. "Now, about those sugar cookies you're going to bake for me." He placed his hand on her shoulder and started walking toward the cabin.

A couple of hours later, Allison realized he was teasing about the cookies, but he had taken the time to show her the dugout cellar. It wasn't wide enough for two people, but it was dry and cool enough to store some meat and vegetables. He showed her which pot to use and gave detailed instructions for cutting meat and vegetables into cubes for cooking. He even took the time to show her how to light a fire. It seemed like something everyone should know, but she wasn't aware of ever having built a fire before.

"You make everything look so easy." She added water to the pot.

"What will Levi think when he comes home to find you the mistress of his one-man cabin?"

She frowned, shoulders sagging.

"But this will be our secret," he said, leaning down to meet her eye to eye. "He'll accuse me of having only a stomach for brains. You must promise, this was all your idea."

"Of course." Allison found the bowls sitting on the shelf. "I don't know how Levi does it." She set the spoons in their place. "Living here alone. Just thinking about him out in the woods tonight...I..." She shook her head, unable to find the right words.

"He's not alone," Ben said.

"What do you mean?"

"I will never leave you or forsake you...do you know who said that?"

She shook her head, confused, crazily wondering for a moment if Levi was with a girl.

"The One who never takes His eyes from us. The One who holds this planet in His care," Ben said.

Allison hesitated. "You're speaking of God? You believe God knows right this minute where Levi is? Of all the people in the world?"

"Without a doubt. When we ask the Lord into our lives, He comes in and lives in us. So where we go, He goes."

She squinted, dumbfounded. "For the first time, you sound just like Levi."

Allison stretched the corner of the fresh smelling blanket over her shoulders. It was dark, and time to let her mind slow down. She had wanted to question Ben about why God, who was supposed to have His eye on everyone at the same time, hadn't kept her safe. Why did she have to spend this last week in confusion and pain? Why hadn't He rescued her from her terrible fall? Levi and Ben had such strange ideas about God. What backwoods preacher had taught them to see God as a friend? Everyone knows God is holy, invisible, and revered. God certainly didn't watch out for...she stilled. She was alive. Levi *had* found her in the middle of the woods. She wasn't well, yet she was feeling better every day. If God was as close as Levi and Ben believed, was this part of His will for her? She let out a long breath and turned to her side. *Oh, memories, please come back,* she thought, closing her eyes.

The next morning, Allison clasped her hands together in victory. The little fire burned well, and the coffee was on. All from her own two hands. What would Levi think when he got home to find her useful? She tapped her finger on her bottom lip. Part of her wanted to prove something to him. Helplessness was a terrible feeling. But this was not her life. What if it became too cozy? What if it looked as if she was trying to make her place here?

"Honey! I'm ready to teach you biscuit baking," came a voice through the cabin door.

Oh, Ben. She opened the door, smiling. If he only knew what she was thinking.

"Timberrrr," Ben yelled out to the empty woods. The small dead tree needed no warning, but he was in a mischievous mood. "I just like the sound of my own voice," he said out loud. He came around and attacked the branches with a saw. Soon the small tree was chopped into stackable pieces.

"George, I'm not taking any pigheadedness from you, being you are a mule." He pulled the mule closer to his woodpile. "You're pulling this load." Ben stacked the wood on the simple pallet. "We aren't going to take all day, and I need a swim before supper."

Allison tapped her chin. Ben said something about the soup or stew, or whatever it is, being good for days. She lifted the lid and stirred the sticky contents. Something in her stomach would not agree. Would it help to add water? She grabbed the pitcher and headed out as Ben came through the woods with the mule.

"You've been working hard," she said as he came closer.

"I have. What a good pioneer woman you are, fetching me some water."

"Oh," Allison looked down at the empty pitcher. "Yes, I can get you some water."

Down at the creek, she filled the pitcher. For a moment, she caught her reflection, and her stomach lurched. Who was this girl with soft hair flowing around her shoulders? She set the pitcher aside and dampened her hands in the water. Carefully, she swept her hair back. Glancing back at the woodpile to make sure Ben was occupied, she pulled and twisted her hair into a tight ball at the nape of her neck. Her new appearance produced mixed emotions. She looked older, yet still confused. *I recognize this woman.* She let go of her hair. *Why can't I remember her life?*

Ben ate the last scoop of supper from his bowl. "Where's the pie, missy?"

"Probably out growing on some plant or tree?" Allison couldn't keep a straight face.

"Well then, let's go find my pie!"

"Ben," she laughed. "It's going to be dark soon."

"Do you have other plans for tonight?" he asked. "Do you need me to ask your pa if I can take you out berry pickin' in the woods?" He smiled, then caught her frown. "Sorry about that. I didn't think before I spoke."

"I'm more worried about you taking me out into the woods." She poked his arm.

"Miss Kent!" He stood from the table. "My intentions are nothing but upright."

"Yes, of course. Those intentions for finding something for a pie."

"You caught me. It's not you I want to stroll with, I just need you to hold back the stickers while I pick the berries."

"Oh, Ben..." She sighed.

The sun set low in the trees when they grabbed the bucket and headed out.

"It's going to get dark soon." Allison trailed after Ben.

"Not to worry, my dear, I know right where the berry bushes are."

"But then how long does it take to cook a pie? Won't the cabin be hot and stuffy? I don't sleep well when it's too hot." She marched through the woods, talking to his back.

Ben's long legs carried him swiftly, and her short steps were having trouble keeping up. Just when she wanted to tell him to slow down, he turned and pointed to the blackberries.

"These look perfect." He set the bucket down between them. "You get started on that side, and we'll have this bucket full in no time."

Ben pulled the sticker vines toward him, plucking the berries off. Allison carefully reached in, only to have her cotton blouse catch on a thorn. She tried to jerk herself free and noticed Ben had already dropped handfuls into the bucket. She followed the vines until she discovered some berries exposed and easily accessible. They came off effortlessly, and soon she was proud of learning another new skill, even if it was a skill common to all humans but herself.

Something flew through the air and hit her in the face. She swatted at it and turned to see Ben laughing. "Don't pick the small ones. The bigger, the sweeter," he teased.

"Like this one?" Allison reached for a giant berry and showed it to Ben. She brought it up close to his face, but just as he opened his lips, she quickly popped it into her mouth.

"That was a big berry, but you should have taken the spider off before you ate it," he said.

"What?" She gagged, shaking her head, spitting on the ground.

Ben burst out laughing. "I was just joking," he said, holding his belly. "Nice stream of black spit off your chin."

Allison wiped her chin and reached into the bucket. In an instant, she smashed a handful of berries against his cheek. "Now that is funny!" she said in triumph.

Ben shook them off and smirked. "Miss Kent, you forget that I grew up the youngest of nothing but brothers." His voice was steady. "Now you're going to get what was done to me every day of my life." He rubbed his hands together.

A bolt of fear shot through her. Hiking her skirt, she screamed and took off running.

"Run as far as you want, I'll hunt you down!" he yelled through the woods. She darted back and forth, running as fast as her legs would allow. Searching for a large tree to hide behind, she panicked, not knowing the way to the cabin. Her chest was burning as she found a tree and ducked quickly behind it, breathing so hard she thought she might pass out. Unable to stay still, she peered around the tree—and Ben grabbed her from behind.

"Ben!" She screamed as he lifted her, swinging her in a circle. "Please put me down!"

Finally, he dropped her to her feet. "Are you okay, Allison?" His face was flushed.

"I am not..." she could barely catch her breath, "one of your brothers."

"No, of course not. That's why I'm going to go easy on you." Before she could anticipate his move, he grabbed her around her hips and threw her over his shoulder.

"Put me down!"

Ben took long strides down a small dirt bank, toward the edge of the creek.

"Stop!" She pushed off his back. "What are you doing?"

He sloshed into the creek, dangling her above the water.

Allison clung to his shirt for dear life, whimpering. "Don't get me wet. Please."

"Please what?"

"Please don't get me wet...and I'll bake you a pie?" She tried to pull herself up.

"You can't bargain with pie. You can't even cook."

The ends of her hair dangled near the creek as Ben lowered her closer and closer. Allison could feel the crown of her head in the water. "Please don't make me beg. These are all the clothes I have." She struggled against his hold.

"That's so sad," he taunted her.

"When I get scared, I can get mad, Ben. Don't forget I had to teach you a lesson once already."

"Now you've hurt my pride." He quickly dunked her face under and pulled her out.

The water ran into Allison's nose, and she came up snorting and choking. Snarling mad, she slapped his arm. "I can't believe you did that!" she choked out.

Ben took two steps backward and deposited her on her feet. He pointed, laughing at her wet hair sticking off her head.

"I hate you!" she shouted, stomping off. "You're very childish!"

He followed her as she zigzagged looking for the cabin. "All right, I know I'm in big trouble, and I'm certainly going without pie tonight," he said, getting no response.

❧

Allison squeezed the water out of her hair. Attempting to pull a comb through the snarls, she felt a leaf and pulled it out. The problem was, she couldn't get her heart to slow down. *I can't believe he picked me up and treated me like a sack of potatoes. No man should ever be that assertive with a woman. Under no circumstances. No manners at all. And to think I thought him so sweet. He comes across so helpful, funny, and even considerate. And Levi said he would be a gentleman.*

"Allison." Ben's voice made her jump. "Please, can I say I'm sorry to you? Not through the door."

She chewed her lip in stony silence.

"Please open the door." He sounded sad. "I understand why you don't want to talk to me. I was wrong. For everything." She heard a small *thud,* as if he had thumped his head against the door. "Please."

She huffed. He did sound sorry, but just a few minutes ago, she was ready to have him beheaded. Now she realized she was a full partner to the shenanigans, had maybe even led him on. She stood and let out a long breath, putting her hand on the bar of the door. First, it was trying to learn about Levi, and now she had turmoil with Ben.

"Okay," came a quiet voice from the other side of the door. "I'm going to get up at dawn and go hunting." She could hear him shuffle away. She looked down at her hand on the bar and her pile of wet clothes, then took her hand away.

Worn out from setting traps all day, Levi stared, half asleep, at the dying fire. He didn't want to relive the last night at Sault Creek, but

97

his mind would not cooperate. Walking next to her at the creek, feeling her hand on the crook of his arm,

the way her soft blue eyes crinkled up when she laughed. *Why did I go and say she was beautiful? I didn't want her to hear that. Oh, Lord, you know what I'm thinking.* He clenched his jaw. *And it doesn't feel like sisterly affection. But I can't stand to think of having feelings for her when I'll only be alone again when she leaves. Please, Lord, help me to keep a guard over my heart. Can I have a brotherly love that will help her and not hurt me?*

What about My love?

Levi felt the question roll around in his heart. *Your love, Lord, knows no limits. Your love is the sacrificial kind. You love past rejection. Your love doesn't wait for us to be good. With all lowliness and meekness, with longsuffering, forbearing one another.*

15

∾ঞ

Allison thought she heard a dog barking and stepped out of the cabin. Taking a long look around, all she could see were the leaves blowing lightly through the trees. Ben had been gone when she woke up, and as the hours ticked on, she felt more restless. Earlier, she had ventured into the mule pen. The mule didn't look as if it would attack, so she stepped carefully around the animal deposits and peeked into the lean-to. It had a roof and a large shelf the size of a bed. One bale of hay was intact, and another had been broken up and tossed around the shelf, with blankets over it. How could two large brothers sleep together there? Looking back at the cabin, she let out a long sigh. She was the reason they were displaced. This wasn't working. They hadn't asked to be her caregivers. Unfortunately, she didn't understand them—but she couldn't survive without them. She stepped out of the pen and went to find a place in the shade.

I need to do something to regain my memory. Restless, she picked up some rocks and threw them into the creek. *But what? It's a bit hard to find help when you're stranded in the middle of the woods. Are there hospitals for people like me?* A shudder ran down her back. She had money, probably enough to travel to a town, maybe to post an advertisement. *Lost woman, come and get me if you know who I am. Oh, how ridiculous. Maybe I should find a home and just start over.* She pictured meeting the neighbors. *Nice to meet you, Allison. Where are you from?* She sulked, rubbing her tender forehead in despair. *At least when Levi and Ben are here, I'm distracted from my condition.*

Back at the cabin, Allison nibbled on some dried meat and flipped open Levi's Bible. *How funny*, she thought, *he's marked up so many passages. He even writes in the margins. 'My prayer' or 'My hope.' Poor man, nothing to read but a Bible.* She tensed her lips, trying to think of books she had read, squeezing her eyes to evoke a memory—but the harder she tried, the more her head hurt. She fluffed a blanket and lay down on the bed.

Her eyes flew open at a sudden sound. How long had she been asleep? The voice was definitely Ben. Standing, she straightened her skirt and redid her hairpins. She started to step out the door, but remembered they had had words last night. Should she wait for him to check on her? Allison couldn't help herself, and peeked out the door. Ben stood in the creek, covered in blood.

"Ben!" She ran toward him. "What happened?"

"Oh, don't worry. This isn't my blood." He undid the first few buttons of his shirt and pulled it over his head. He dropped it in the creek and began to rinse himself off.

"Whose blood is it?" She averted her eyes.

'His." He pointed toward a tree.

"Oh! Oh, my." Allison put her hand over her mouth. A deer hung from the tree by its back feet. Its eyes were open. "Is it dead?"

"Yes, it's very dead. I shot it."

"Of course." She realized how stupid she sounded. "I'll go back to the cabin and let you bathe." She ducked her chin and walked away.

"Wait," he said, stepping out of the water. "All day I've tried to think of a really good apology."

She stilled, staring at the ground.

"Something that would be right for a gal like you. But that's just my trouble. How does a three-legged dog know what to say to a kitten?"

Allison smiled at his analogy.

"For you, Allison Kent, I'm really sorry for dunking you in the creek. For me, it would get this rock from my stomach—if you would forgive me?"

She scanned this rail-thin young man, ribs sticking out, dripping wet—yet adorable.

"Yes, Ben. I forgive you." She smiled.

"Thank you." He gripped his bare belly. "The rock is gone."

Allison stayed clear of the butchering. She snuck a peek every now and then, but the sight of that poor deer being sliced into pieces was too much. Ben had come into the cabin and grabbed a grill from the fireplace. He built a fire near where he worked and then shoved a large piece of meat onto the center pole, roasting it slowly.

She used the little stove for a pan of biscuits. It seemed to be warm enough.

"Allison, would you hand me a bowl? I need something for the brains." Ben leaned into the cabin door, splattered with blood.

Her stomach lurched as she searched the wooden shelves. "Will this one do?" She held up a bowl. "What are you doing with the brains? You're not going to bring them in here, are you?"

"No, the brains are for tanning. Can you hand me that bag of salt?" He nodded toward a bag on the floor.

It was heavy, but handing him the salt was the only way she was going to help with any of this.

He took it from her and winked. "Thanks."

Ben skinned the deer and boned out the tail. He carefully scraped every particle of fat and flesh from the hide with his knife, ready now to cure the hide with salt. He was proud of a good kill, but the truth was, this was all for his brother. *Levi has always been a serious loner who thinks everything I do is wasteful and reckless. I like to have fun, sure. But I can set my mind to things, too. Besides that, I can have resolve and commitment. I want to find a nice girl. I want to provide for her, and have our own place. I need Levi to see there's more to me than he thinks.*

An hour later, Ben carried the sizzling meat into the cabin and let it slide onto a plate. "Allison, could you grab a can of butter beans?" She set the can on the table. "Pan." He motioned to the shelf.

"Okay." She set the pan next to the can.

"Tin opener." Ben held the can up.

She looked around, flustered.

"I'm just joking with you." He pulled his knife from its sheath and punched it into the can. "This works."

❧

When everything was ready, Allison proudly pulled a cloth from the biscuits and placed them on the table. They sat down and prayed. Taking a small bite of her biscuit, Allison realized that something was very wrong. For pity sakes, what had she forgotten? An uncomfortable silence hung in the air until Ben snatched a biscuit.

"Wait!" She tried to swipe it from his hand. "They didn't turn out right. I'm afraid you'll chip a tooth."

"Well, thanks for the warning," he laughed, tapping the hard biscuit. "These will be good with some cream. Or maybe with runny gravy—or maybe to kill small animals." He raised his arm and chucked his biscuit out the open door.

Allison covered her face with her hands.

"Hey." Ben shook her arm. "The cabin looks really good. I can see you picked up and straightened things. It looks really nice." He touched a little cup holding small purple flowers. "As long as I've ever been here, I've never seen it so fancy."

Allison lifted her head. "Do you think it'll make Levi mad? I wasn't trying to move his things, I just got homesick or something, sitting inside all day." She wondered if she should remove the flowers, but they brought an unaccustomed cheer to her melancholy.

"No, no. Levi loves the outdoors. Why would he object to flowers coming inside? He lets Patch inside. Our ma would never let our critters in the house. She said it was enough to have to pick up after all us kids."

"Do you think he'll return tomorrow? He's been gone quite a while." She looked out the open door.

"Why? Do you miss him?"

"No," she bristled. "I just wondered." She grimaced, chewing a piece of venison.

"It's okay if you miss him. He's the one who saved your life. I can understand that you would feel…"

"Don't try to guess what I'm feeling," she snapped.

"Okay, I won't." Ben's stare was unnerving. "Then tell me."

"What do you want me to say?" She shrugged. "I don't know Levi very well. I don't know you very well, and the person I really don't know is myself. You remember your mother didn't allow animals in the house." Her voice cracked. "What I would give to have some memory like that. Not to be able to remember your own mother or father? I wondered today if I need to go to some kind of institution for insane people." She pushed her chair back and rubbed her temples.

Ben looked around the cabin and cleared his throat. "So what you're saying is… you want to hear all about me?" He gave her a dramatic smile. "Well, I was born on a beautiful summer morn."

Allison relaxed, giving way to his gracious change of subject.

"The most gorgeous baby my mother had ever seen. My name came to my parents just like the patriarch Jacob and his beloved Rachel. The child of promise, the last son, the light of the tribe. Benjamin."

Allison enjoyed the lighter moment. "Now, really?"

"Yep." He scratched behind his ear. "Something like that. What do you want to know about the Graham household?"

"Tell me about your mother and father."

"Let's see." Ben leaned his chair back, just like Levi. "Our father is strict. He didn't take kindly to his boys joking around or being unruly. He was sure the rod of correction would beat it out of us. Must have worked on Levi—but not me." His face darkened.

"We mostly learned to stay clear of him. Levi did a better job of that, too. He would have lived outdoors every minute if our ma didn't make him come in. By the time Levi was eight or nine, he did most of the hunting for the family. My father worked off and on in the copper mines."

"Did you go to school?"

"Oh, yeah. The school was in the church building. But the snow would be so bad, sometimes we were home for months. Our ma kept us up on all the schoolwork."

"Your mother could read and write?"

"Oh, sure. She knew her figures and read us the Bible from when we were babies. Then she made sure we could read the Good Book for ourselves." He pulled his chair forward and rubbed his chin. "We didn't mind our schoolwork. It was the only time we got to stay away from chores."

"Levi said you never went to the doctor as kids. Your mother would just pray?"

"Yeah, that's true."

Allison wondered about this family's strange beliefs. "She really expected that she could pray to God and something miraculous would happen?"

"Maybe not instantly. Don't all mothers pray for their kids?"

"I wouldn't know." She frowned, gathering the empty dishes.

"She was a good ma." Ben laughed. "Still is. She has great faith, I guess you could say. Maybe she had no choice, but she believed God would always take care of us. And He did...I guess." Ben's voice faded.

Allison looked back at him and sat down. His face was blotchy.

"Why do you say you guess?" she asked softly.

Ben looked away and shook his head. Unsure what was wrong, she put her hand on his arm. He looked at it; she wanted to pull away, but didn't want to hurt his feelings. He carefully rested his other hand on her fingers. Gently, finger on finger. His hand was so warm that hers felt frozen. Ben let his fingers intertwine with hers. Her throat clenched; his touch was far too personal. She pulled her hand free, and the room was suddenly void of air.

Ben rubbed his hands over his chin. "I'm not good at all this. Just ask Levi what you want to know."

She swallowed, searching for her voice. "Ben, I'm sorry. I shouldn't have..."

He reached across the table, touching her upper arm. She leaned forward, avoiding his eyes. Only inches from her ear, he whispered, "Levi and I have things to be sorry about, but you...you have nothing." He let go. "Goodnight, Allison."

Levi had been gone for a week, but she wasn't really sure what day it was. She pulled her jacket on, noting the drop in temperature. Ben had stayed busy with tanning and stretching the deerskin. He was kind and cordial, but something was missing. His teasing and joking had gone away. Allison didn't want to ask any more personal questions. She felt as if she had allowed too much familiarity, and wondered if she'd lost her common sense along with her memory. Ben had taken the time to add corn muffins and flapjacks to her tutoring. She still could not remember what the missing ingredient was on the rock-hard biscuits. This morning, Ben had pointed out a canister that held some tea leaves. Allison brewed a cup and added a bit of sugar. Halfway through the morning, alone in the cold cabin, she placed her hands around the warm mug, a faint tea scent coming up with the steam. Closing her eyes, she let her mind drift. Was it her imagination, a small recollection? Was there a long table in a large, wood-paneled room? She thought she saw a soft, cream-colored tablecloth...her eyes flew open when she heard an unfamiliar sound. Frustrated, she looked out the door to see Ben flying back and forth on his new swing.

Setting down her mug, Allison ventured out to watch.

"Come on, your swing awaits you!" He let go of the ropes and flew through the air, landing with a thud.

"No, thank you. That's better left for the free-spirited, like yourself."

"It's perfectly safe. Everything held me just fine." He nodded toward the wooden swing.

She regretted coming outside. Ever since the handholding incident, she wondered if Ben's quieter demeanor was from feeling rejected.

"Okay, I'll sit on it. But you have to promise not to push me. I want to do it." She inspected the knots, then sat straight and alert on the wooden seat. She gripped the ropes, keeping a toe on the ground for safety.

Ben leaned a shoulder against the tree and crossed one relaxed leg in front of the other. "I promise." His expression mimicked self-restraint, though she knew everything in him wanted to give her a huge push. "You're a mix of many things, Miss Allison." He leaned his back into the tree. "Sweet but guarded, genuine but mysterious."

"Mysterious? Hmmph." She pushed off with her big toe and allowed the swing to move a few inches.

"Just let me know if you need help getting off. We wouldn't want you to break a toe, as fast as you're swinging."

She scrunched up her face.

Ben grabbed the rope.

"You promised!"

"I did promise—not to swing you." He began to twirl her in a circle, and the swing spun faster and faster.

"Stop! I'm getting dizzy."

He abruptly brought the swing to a halt. "Yes, ma'am." Her swinging feet caught him in the shins, and he let go.

Allison had no way to jump off as the twisted rope flung her in the opposite direction. When the ropes came apart, it whipped her back and forth like a rag doll.

She stood quickly; the forest was still spinning. "For pity sakes, you are completely incorrigible." Trying to steady herself, she gripped the rope. "I'll see to your flapjacks. Or maybe not," she mumbled, looking toward the cabin. Darn it, if her eyes and her steps weren't crossing.

16

ల౨౦

Levi bundled the pelts together and hoisted his pack on his back. He knew he could carry more, hunt more, but something in him longed for home. Would Allison have remembered her past? He prepared himself for that conversation as he pounded through the woods. How long before she would insist that he take her to Ready Springs? How long was he willing to be gone again from his place? Hiking on the trail, he poured out his agitated thoughts. *Oh, Lord, why can't I be thankful her memory might have returned? I told her I would take her wherever she needed. Of course, she would be in a hurry to get back to her people. Maybe she's already asked Ben to take her.* The fastmoving clouds resembled his churning insides. *Forgive me, Lord. All I can think about is what's best for myself.*

The next morning, Allison shivered as she moved about the cabin. She had never felt such wind, at least not that she could remember. Some of the gusts actually shook the cabin. *If it doesn't rain, it would be a perfect day to hang out clothes.* She looked around, feeling inspired. *After I clean up the breakfast mess, I'll heat some water on the stove and wash a few things.*

Ben peeked in the door. "I think it's going to stay cool today. I'll build a fire in the fireplace. A large log or two will keep you warm and toasty."

"I have the little stove going. I wanted to put some water on to heat."

"That's good. It just takes so many small sticks to fit in the little door. The fireplace will burn a log or two all day."

"All right." She nodded.

Ben walked in a few moments later, his arms heavy with wood. "I filled the barrel next to the cabin this morning, too. It's easier to fetch water from it."

"Thank you," she said as he struck the flint to the pine needles. "Does it often get windy like this?" The rattling walls were starting to unnerve her.

"Just a storm coming, or maybe just wind." Ben blew lightly as the flames ignited.

"The cabin won't fall down, will it?"

Ben shook his head. "No, you'll be fine. This cabin has held up through worse."

"Like what?" Allison grabbed the bucket and kettle and headed to the door.

Ben held it open so it wouldn't slam on her. "Like tons and tons of snow. Heavy wet snow is harder on a cabin than the wind is."

As soon as they stepped out, they were both whipped by the gusts of wind.

"Here, you can have the bucket." She handed it to him, struggling to pull her hair off her face. "I'll use the coffee kettle to heat my water." They both approached the creek and dipped their vessels for what they needed.

Allison steadied her steps as the wind whipped her skirt in every direction. Back at the cabin, she leaned into the door, closing it behind her. Ben's log was burning nicely and had already cut the cold from the air. She placed the kettle on the small stove and added a few more pieces of kindling. Gathering her underthings, she piled them on the table to wash, but the breakfast items were still there, in her way. She grabbed the skillet from the table and the wooden spoon, caked with batter, hit the floor.

"Oh dear. At least no one saw that." She took a cloth and bent to clean up the sticky batter. *Well, at least the flapjacks were edible.* Ben must have eaten ten, maybe twelve.

Allison thought she smelled smoke, and rose to check the little stove. It looked fine. No, something was definitely burning. She whipped around to view the fireplace, where nothing looked wrong. Suddenly a sharp pain touched the back of her legs, and she looked back to see flames coming up her skirt.

She cried out, trying to swing the cloth in her hands at the flames. "Ben!" The pain seared her skin as she fought to make it to the door. "Ben! Help!"

He looked up, wide eyed, as Allison cried out again, running toward him and swatting the back of her skirt with the towel.

Ben quickly grabbed her off her feet and knocked her to the ground, crushing her with his weight. Rolling back and forth, she tried not to fight him, but his weight intensified the burning pain.

"Hold still! The fire is out!" Ben pushed off her body.

She rolled to her belly, clawing at the dirt, trying to get away from the excruciating pain. The rag she had been holding was burning and rolling in the wind. She gasped as it hit a particularly weedy area. Like five long skinny fingers, the fire took off in five different directions.

"I'll get the shovel!" Ben jumped to his feet and raced behind the cabin.

Fingers of fire spread as the wind carried them rapidly, looking for fuel. Icy shivers ran up and down Allison's shaking body.

Ben raced back around to see the flames now tripled in size. "Help me! Get a wet blanket!" he yelled over the wind, running toward the dancing flames.

She froze, and her heart rose in her throat, choking her. She wondered how long it would be until she fainted.

"Allison! Please do something!" Ben ran to fill the bucket from the water barrel and raced back to the flames.

*Water...water...*She ran on shaking legs into the cabin and grabbed her blanket. She turned the corner outside the cabin, dunked it in the barrel, and pulled it out, dripping. Ben snatched the blanket and yelled for her to fill the bucket. "The fence! Throw the water on the fence and open the gate!" The flames were devouring the dry wood, and she filled the bucket and pulled back to let loose a disappointing toss. Groaning, she dunked the bucket again and tried another toss at the burning fence.

"Woodpile! Allison, throw water on the woodpile!" Ben yelled as he ran back and forth. She quickly dipped the bucket and ran to douse the woodpile. The bucket was woefully inadequate, and she ran back for another. Smoke was everywhere; it was too hard to see which way the wind was taking it next. Ben slapped the blanket into the tree line as a small bush by the creek exploded in flames. "Ben! Down here!" She pointed to the flames.

"Don't worry about the creek! It's the forest!" Ben raced back to dunk the blanket. "Bring water!"

Allison ran inside for another blanket and shoved it into the bottom of the barrel. It was wet and heavy, and she slapped it against the crackling pine.

"We can't let the forest catch fire in this wind! Hit everything with the blanket!"

Allison swung the wet blanket over and over until her aching arms would no longer cooperate, while Ben raced back and forth from the creek, continuing to beat he ground. Bending over, she grasped her knees, trying to find air.

"Stop. I can do the rest." Ben wrapped his arm around her, steadying her from falling over. "I think it's just smoke now, but I'll have to watch it for hours." Covered in soot and sweat, he let go of her and surveyed the area. "Thank you, God!" He threw his hands up in the air. "The creek made a natural fire break." He panted. The wind whipped wildly around them. "But if the forest had caught fire…" He dropped to his knees. "We'd be dead."

Levi dipped his hands in the Sault Creek, just five miles downstream from his cabin. By tonight he'd be home. He wanted to drop his pack for a few minutes, but something assaulted his senses. Was it smoke? The wind had pushed him every direction today, and watching the clouds, he thought some thunder could be likely. He listened. No, he was sure he would have heard thunder. That smell was definitely smoke. He stepped up his pace.

A mile or so out, a sudden urgency hit him. Something was wrong. It was almost dark, but he knew this last stretch like he knew his name. It wasn't because of her, he told himself, but he decided to drop his pack and run. He may look foolish in front of Ben, but he didn't care. He'd come back for it later.

As he neared the cabin, he saw his brother in a dead run, coming closer.

"Ben… Oh, Lord…" Levi sucked in the night air. "Are you all right?" He grabbed his younger brother by the nape of his neck and pulled him in. "You're okay?" Levi pulled away to look him over. Ben's jaw twitched as he tried to hold back his emotions.

"I'm so sorry, Levi." He blinked. "We had a fire."

"I can see that. But the cabin is standing. And you…and Allison…is Allison okay?" Levi fought his pounding heartbeat.

Ben dropped his chin. Anytime Ben couldn't look him in the face, it wasn't good. "Look at me." Levi jerked on his brother's arms. "Is she all right?" Ben's expression twisted and fell, and he let out a painful groan. "She got burned."

Levi dashed to the door, trying to suppress the panic overcoming him.

"Allison, it's Levi. I'm coming in." He couldn't tolerate waiting for a reply—he had to see.

She stood at the end of the bed, hiding in the corner. The light was dim, and he turned the lantern knob to illuminate the small cabin. His breathing finally slowed, and he was able to see that her face and clothes were dirty. But there she stood, in one piece. His eyes roamed over her. "Ben said you got burned. Where are you hurt?"

Her eyes pooled with tears that flowed over her cheeks, but she seemed frozen in place. Her skin was odd shades of white and red, and his gut twisted.

"You look like you're about to faint." He pulled out a chair. "Please, come sit down." She shook her head. Ben entered and came around the other side of the table.

"Allison." Ben's voice was so soft when he held his hand out for her that Levi wondered what had passed between them while he was gone.

"Somebody please tell me what happened," he said, looking back and forth between them.

"It was my fault." Allison finally spoke. "I…" Her voice faded in and out. "I was cleaning the floor. And my skirt…went into…and the rag in my hand…" She shook her head, searching for words. "When Ben tried to…" A sob escaped. "The rag was on fire and…caught the woods on fire."

Levi twisted his knuckles and threw his hat on the table.

"The back of your legs are burnt? Is that why you won't come sit down?"

Allison nodded.

"I should have helped her. But I asked her to help me…and she saved the mule and the wood pile." Ben never took his eyes from her. "I'm so sorry, Allison. I didn't realize you were hurt when I yelled at you to help."

Levi squinted. The way they were looking at each other was too much to handle.

Ben finally turned to face him. "I've been praying you would return. I knew you'd know what to do."

Levi swallowed hard. "Allison, what do the burns look like? Are they red, or like blisters?"

She tightened her lips. "I can't tell. The fabric of my…" She let out a sigh. "My undergarment…is stuck to my skin."

"Are you in pain?" He chided himself. Obviously, she was.

She shook her head.

"She's not telling the truth," Ben huffed.

Eyes red and puffy, she shot daggers at Ben.

"Allison, let me see your legs," Levi said firmly.

"Absolutely not. I said I was fine." She backed further into the corner. "My skirt is completely gone in the back. I…I don't have another to wear."

Levi wasn't alarmed by her absolute refusal; he'd seen it before. "We'll figure something out for clothes. I need to see how bad your burns are."

She clenched her jaw and took a deep breath. "Why don't you boys just pray? Your mother didn't need anything but prayer." Her voice cracked with sarcasm.

Levi glanced at Ben, wondering why her words were so bitter. She must be ready to pass out.

"Allison." He took a step closer. "I want you to lie down on your stomach." He nodded to the bed. "You can do it on your own, or I'm going to have Ben hold you down."

"Levi, stop it." Her chin quivered. She put her hand up to stop the discussion, but her whole arm was shaking, and she quickly pulled it down. "I put some cold compresses on earlier. That's all I need."

The brothers looked at each other and took a step toward her.

"Wait!" She threw both her hands up. "Give me the towel." Ben handed it to her. "I'd rather drown than do this," she growled, pulling the towel taut behind her hips. "I'd rather..." Wincing, she put both knees on the mattress. "I'd rather live in a cave by myself." She cried out as she lowered her face and arms into the pillow.

"I'll be very careful, I promise." Levi pulled the damp white fabric back from her calves. It shredded in half up the back of her legs.

"I hate both of you!" she wailed into her pillow.

"Ben, there's some salve in my trunk. Get it." He examined her bright red skin. He touched her shoulder, and she jerked away. "The left leg isn't too bad. You have some blisters on the right leg, but they should heal up. I'm sorry. I know it hurts." Ben handed Levi the salve. "I'm going to put some of this on. It might sting." As he applied the salve, her cries were so loud that he doubted she heard his comforting words. Ben came around and gently held her boots to the bed.

"I just want to go home!" Her cries went on and on until finally, they subsided. She had fallen asleep.

Ben staggered as if he was about to drop. "The wind has died down," he said, "but I'm going to keep watch outside. We can't have one little ember start up again." Levi nodded, and Ben headed for the door.

"The thing is, Levi," Ben said, amazed, "I just filled the water barrel this morning. She wouldn't have to go to the creek for water that way. But God knew how fast those flames would reach the tree line. He knew." Ben drew his hand over his ragged face. "He knew."

Allison tried to crane her head, but her neck was stiff, and pain shot through her shoulders and down her back. She turned to her side and cried out from her stinging legs. *Oh. It wasn't a bad dream.* She pulled her pillow over her face. *I'm trapped in this absurd cabin with these backward brothers.* Looking up, she saw a plate of food with a cloth over it. A blanket covered her below the waist. She exhaled. This was the blanket from the mule pen. They had slept outside with nothing. The cabin was cold, and whatever was under that cloth hadn't been cooked in here. *Oh, that stupid fireplace. Well, my skirt catching fire started it.* She rubbed her hipbone. Ben knocking her to the ground accounted for this discomfort. *Maybe if I had faith like Levi, tribulation wouldn't follow me so close.* Tossing the hay-smelling blanket off, she undid the small buttons of her skirt and wriggled free of the damaged garment. The lovely pale blue skirt had been through hell and back. The small tears, the black soot—and now the entire back was missing. Something came up from her rib cage and bubbled out—pathetic laughter. The skirt looked so ridiculous. Her life was so ridiculous that all she could do was laugh.

Levi had retrieved his pack earlier that morning. After last night, he realized that he didn't have to worry about how soon Allison wanted to get away from the cabin. He now knew for a fact she was finished with anything with the last name of Graham.

The brothers worked on the hides side by side, with little to say. Levi seesawed from wanting to pound every unknown detail from Ben to praying he never had to see the way he and Allison stared at each other again. Sure, Ben was sorry. But Levi saw the unspoken words pass between them; it had to have meant something. Something he prayed he'd never have to hear about. *Oh, God. I have no doubt You are good. I hate that this has shown me how jealous and selfish I am.*

Allison shuffled around the cabin like an elderly woman, then stopped. Something about the cold food on the table triggered a memory. She closed her eyes, but the stinging of her legs pushed to the front of her consciousness, so she took a towel and tried to clean her face and arms instead. The cabin smelled like smoke. She remembered the belt she had seen in Levi's crate; she took it and cinched a blanket around her waist.

"This will have to do."

Ben handed Levi the salt. "It's after supper—think one of us should check on her?"

She's all yours came from an ill-tempered place, and Levi was glad it didn't leave his mouth. "Go ahead. I think it's going to be a blue moon before she wants to talk to me."

"She needed the help, willing or not. You were only trying to help her," Ben said.

Levi considered asking Ben if Allison had remembered anything, but really, he wanted to keep the question between just the two of them. Maybe she had already gotten over last night. Maybe by today or tomorrow, she would have let it go. She had screamed some pretty angry things.

Out of the abundance of the heart the mouth speaks. He took a deep breath and tried to focus on what he was doing.

17

The next morning, Levi was refilling the barrel by the door when Allison stepped outside.

"Oh!" She clutched her chest. "I didn't see you."

"How are your legs today?" he asked, looking away and scratching his nose.

Shrugging one shoulder, she said, "Better, I guess."

Levi noticed the blanket around her waist, cinched up with his belt. "Will you come in with me for a minute?" He nodded toward the door. She didn't answer, but stepped back into the cabin. He closed the door behind him; their eyes met and quickly shot elsewhere. She appeared pale and shaky, her silence speaking volumes. He bent down to his crate of personal things and pulled out some brown denim trousers.

"These are clean. You can wear them." He held them out to her, but she stared at the floor.

"No, thank you."

Levi folded the trousers and dropped them back into the crate. "We understand you have nothing else. We don't care if you're wearing trousers."

"I know you don't care."

This time her eyes and words punched him like a fist. He glanced at the door, but something told him to stay put. He scratched the side of his head. "Allison, you know what I mean. We understand a beautiful woman doesn't want to wear a man's clothing. I meant we don't care about…" He struggled to find the words.

"Civility? Propriety? Good manners?" Her eyes were wide.

Levi groaned. "Yes, those things are important. But it's just the three of us and so…" He held his hands up in surrender. "Do whatever you want."

Allison stood still, pressing her lips together. He knew she wanted to give him a piece of her mind. She raised her chin and brushed her hands down the blanket skirt. "Yesterday I laughed about this. Today, though…" her voice cracked. "It's just not that funny." She held her hand against her face to swipe away the uninvited tears. "The injury to my head is just barely healed, and now my legs are burned, and I have nothing suitable to wear." She tugged on the blanket. "Oh, forgive me for complaining, I do still have a hankie." Reaching for her reticule, she pulled the hankie out, then took out her burgundy gloves. "And my mother's gloves. At least they didn't burn up."

"Your mother's gloves? Are you remembering things?"

She looked away, sniffing and dabbing her eyes. "No."

"I've never heard you say those were your mother's gloves. Is that hankie your mother's, too?"

Allison looked it over. "I don't think so."

"But you know those gloves belonged to your mother?"

She wrinkled her brow. "It's just the way it just came out of my mouth. I believe it's true." She dropped the gloves on the table. "Oh, I don't know. Levi. Please tell me, when will my memories come back?" Her soft blue eyes pleaded with him. "I try to calm my thoughts, but it's just one thing after another. Sometimes I laugh and then the next minute I'm crying. One minute I'm happy, the next second I'm falling apart."

Levi picked up the gloves. "Patch brought me one of these before I found you. The other one was on a rock." He hesitated, then spoke again. "Do you have feelings for Ben?"

Allison straightened up. "What are you talking about?"

He moved past her to the window, making sure Ben wasn't right outside listening. "I don't know what they say where you are from. Romantic feelings, that's what I'm asking."

"You haven't been listening to me at all."

"I've heard every word you said. You're still without your memory. You're tired of so many unfortunate things happening, one after another. You don't think we care. But that's what I'm getting to." He swallowed. "We really do care about you."

"We?" Her jaw went slack.

Levi thought she looked another shade of pale.

Ben's afternoon string of fish turned into a man-pleasing dinner. The brothers made each meal the highlight of their day. Allison felt like a china cup sitting at the table with two hungry bears. Her thoughts were still in turmoil over Levi's earlier question. Romantic feelings? What kind of question was that? Both of them had endearing qualities. Both of them could make her madder than a hornet. *And why does Levi need to know? What would he say if I asked him that? Nothing about my feelings matters to these two. I'm not staying. This is not my life and never will be. So why does it matter?*

"Allison, where are you?" Ben waved his hand in front of her face. "The beans are good."

"Soak them all day and boil them for an hour. Not one of the harder things to handle." She moved them around with her fork, trying to get comfortable on the hard chair.

"Have you ever smelled burned beans?" Ben asked. "You'd wish for a skunk to visit to improve the atmosphere." He gulped down some water. "Besides the little mishap with the fire, you were, I mean *are* doing really good with cooking." Ben looked flustered and changed the subject. "Our ma is a great cook."

"I think we've said that already, Ben." Levi cleared his empty plate.

"Speaking of your family," Allison said, "there are four brothers in the photograph. Levi spoke of James, but you've never spoken of the other one. Just in case he shows up here, I'd like a fair warning. Two of you are as much as I think I can take." Levi and Ben looked away, and she wondered if she had spoken too rudely. "Just a fair warning," she said in a lighter tone.

Levi sat back down. "Daniel will never show up here." The once lively conversation came to a standstill. "He drowned when we were little." He clenched his jaw.

"I'm sorry. Truly sorry."

Levi stared out into the uncomfortable silence, chewing on a faraway thought.

"I remember being cooped up that winter." He breathed in, shaking his head. "The snow had been up to the roof, but after just one week of spring sunshine, everything was melting and muddy. We wanted out so bad." He laughed bitterly, staring at the table. "Junior and I had permission, but Daniel started crying when Ma said he had to stay in. He was never trouble, he was usually so happy. I felt bad for him, so I promised Ma I'd watch him close. He wasn't quite four. You were still in diapers." Levi glanced up as Ben winced, then looked back down at the table.

"How did he drown?" Allison asked gently.

"We went down by the creek." Levi rubbed his hand back and forth over the rough wood of the table. "The water was churning and flowing hard over the banks. I...I...had him by the hand."

His voice struggled, and Allison wished she had not asked. Red blotches appeared on Levi's neck and face.

He cleared his throat. "Junior was only a few feet away, and he showed me a puddle full of worms. We started to grab them and put them in our pockets for fishing later. It was only a minute or two...but when I turned around, Daniel was gone." Levi swallowed hard. "Just gone. I looked every direction. I thought maybe he'd climbed a tree or something. I ran to the water's edge. Nothing." He rocked back in his chair, lifting the front legs, then set them back and put his elbows on the table. "The mud was giving way, and I pulled my boots off and started running up and down the creek. I screamed and screamed his name. The water was so loud..." He rubbed his hands over his face. "Junior ran for help, but I knew I had to find him. Maybe he got hung up on a branch somewhere. See, I..." Levi shook his head. "I promised my ma I would...watch him."

Ben dropped his face into his hands.

Levi sucked in a deep breath. "First my father came, and then a few neighbor men. My pa hollered at me to go home. I didn't want to, but I had some hope maybe they could find him. I walked into our cabin and Ben was standing on a chair, crying his lungs out. And my ma was pacing back and forth, mumbling prayers. Ben's face was beet red, bawling, holding his arms out, so I went over to pick him up, and my ma spun around and yelled at me, 'Don't take him anywhere!'"

Levi paused. The silence filling the cabin pained Allison's ears.

He wiped his eyes with his fingers, stopping the overflowing tears. "I held Ben in the corner, and we sat there for a long time. My ma just paced back and forth until they brought Daniel's body in and laid him on the table. He was white as a sheet, but his lips were purple. He had a big gash above his eye. His jacket was gone, and he only had one shoe. I don't know why I remember that…maybe because they were once mine." Levi strained to speak. "She just held his body and cried, 'Jesus, no, Jesus,' over and over. I remember her holding his chin, begging him to come back to her. But there was no life in him."

Allison felt hot tears rolling down her cheeks. "Oh, your poor mother."

Levi sat, unmoving. "Neighbors came. The Von Keller's lived close back then. They had lost a son to influenza. That was part of the reason they wanted to move on. I remember Mrs. Von Keller holding my ma as she cried. I hated that I made her cry. The next day, after the burial, Pa took Junior and me out to the barn for a whipping."

"No!" The word escaped before she realized it. She touched his arm, but he didn't seem to feel it.

"It reminded me of skinning an animal before you kill it. Can you imagine that?" Levi said, despondent. "Pulling skin off a live animal? That's what it felt like."

Ben passed his hand over his mouth.

"I left the barn and walked deep into the woods. I laid on the ground, thinking of never seeing his face again…never having him following me around and saying my name." He spoke so slow that it felt like something sacred was happening. "I begged God to take me. I was too young to know how to kill myself. I just imagined if I lay there long enough, I would stop breathing and the pain would be over. That's all I wanted. For it all to be over."

Nobody moved at the weight of his words. "I remember pushing my face against the ground, and I heard a voice say, *Rise up, my child, your brother is with me. Only I control the first and last breath, not you.*

Allison sucked in a silent gasp.

"Levi." Ben shook his head. "You've never told me this before."

He gave a small shrug. "I've never wanted to tell anyone before." He gazed into Allison's eyes, communicating something fierce and powerful.

A few days later, the warmth of summer was back, and the itching of her healing skin next to a scratchy woolen blanket was driving Allison crazy. She decided to tell the brothers of her plan to go swimming at dark. They could stay in the cabin. She was so matter of fact that they both looked at her and just nodded in agreement, then covered the window with a dishtowel.

"There are lots of good spots down from the cabin. Deep enough to take a bath, but covered with brush," Ben said.

"I thought of that, but I just don't want to be somewhere unfamiliar. I've watched you use the deep spot out front..."

She stopped when she heard Ben snickering.

"What? What did I say?" Ben shook his head.

"Levi, what did I say?"

Levi just widened his eyes, smirking.

"Levi," she said sternly.

"You said you watched us bathe." He shook his head. "Ben is still twelve and had to laugh. Even though we both know we weren't naked or anything."

Allison gasped at the implication, making Ben snicker harder.

"To think I looked forward to this all day! Oh, just forget it." She opened the door to let them out, but only Patch left. Levi grabbed the door. "Get your things and go. We're sitting at this table and not moving until we hear you say you're done." They stared at each other. "Go." He nodded outside. Allison dared not look at Ben, but gathered her things and reluctantly stepped out.

"Sit down, Ben," Levi barked. "We're reading the Bible until you repent of your waywardness."

Allison walked toward the water, flustered. Patch crisscrossed in front of her as if she was coming out to play.

"Really, Patch, I don't want you out here, either," she said as she laid her things on a flat rock. It was dark, with a few shards of moonlight breaking through the trees. Glancing back at the silent cabin, she saw light flowing through the old dishtowel in the window. She really did trust Levi and Ben. They would not compromise her plan. Her own fears would do her in first. Sitting carefully on the bank, she slipped off her boots and stockings, peering to the left and right to make sure no other observers were looking her way, then undid the belt and let the blanket fall loose. The heat and irritation immediately left, and she let out a short breath. *Oh, so wonderful.* Glancing back at the unchanged cabin, she called for Patch. "Just stay right here and guard my things. Don't let any little critters near my bath." She scratched behind his ears. "You'll guard me, right, boy?"

With one last look for good measure, she slipped off her blouse and chemise and tiptoed into the creek. The water was cool at first, but she took her time to step deeper and deeper. The most sensational feeling traveled up her body as the cool water hit her. Arms over her chest, she turned and faced the cabin. Just like a queen about to sit back on her throne, she leaned back and went completely under. Every inch of her body was awakened by the cool water. She felt her hair float above her head and tilted her face upward just to grab a small breath and then sink back down into bliss. When her body refused to stay down, she floated, feeling like a feather. For the first time in weeks, nothing hurt, nothing throbbed. Finally, she surfaced to see Patch, loyal and true. "I'm sorry for not liking you. You really are the best dog." She wiped water from her eyes. Patch's tail thumped twice on the sandy bank as he headed in to greet his admirer.

"Oh, no. I want to be alone a few more moments." She shooed him away.

After several minutes, she came out and sat on the edge of the rock, allowing the quiet forest into her senses. She pulled her knees up, resting her chin. Just when she thought the tranquility couldn't get more hallowed, a mosquito buzzed in her ear and landed on her shoulder. She swatted it away and reached for her clean undergarments, sighing with distain at the wool blanket. "Right now, I'd take my old chambray uniform," she said to Patch. Suddenly she sat up. "Did I just say chambray uniform? Yes, I did." Allison jumped up and threw on her blouse, attacking the buttons. "Chambray uniform...chambray uniform." Cinching the blanket around her waist and reaching for her boots and stockings, she raced to the cabin door.

"Levi, open up!"

"Okay, okay! Was Patch bothering you?" He opened the door, staring at her bare feet. "Good Lord, Allison, what's wrong that you can't finish dressing?"

"Oh, who cares?" She dropped her boots and stockings on the cabin floor.

Ben stood quickly, admiring her bare feet. "She does have a problem with getting wet in the creek."

"Stop!" She knew between the two of them they could have her completely flustered. "I remembered something. I used to wear a uniform. When I was in school. It was blue chambray." Both brothers looked wide-eyed, waiting for the rest of the revelation.

"And..." Ben leaned forward on the table. "What was the name of your school? The town?"

"Don't say anything. Just let me think. It seems like something with a W maybe in the name."

"West!" Ben piped up. "Or western?"

She tapped a fingertip against her lip. "Maybe."

"Or maybe 'women's'?" Levi joined in. "If you wore a uniform, it was probably a girls' school, so maybe it had women in the title."

"Possibly..." she said, *W* words rolling around in her mouth.

"Women's western school for girls," Ben tried. "Or Western Michigan school for girls?"

"No." Her shoulders sagged. "That doesn't sound right."

"Winnipeg!" Ben said excitedly.

"Ben, really. You think she just happened to travel from Winnipeg and then fall off a cliff into our backyard?" Levi shook his head.

"Please, just let me think." She rubbed her forehead.

"She could be from Canada. How do you know which way she was traveling from?" Ben said.

"I don't. That's the problem. I couldn't just leave her to go off tracking where she came from. Someone had to stay with her."

"Oh really, Levi. Are you sure that's how it went?"

"Ben, just shut up. You're the reason she can't think."

"Maybe you saw her from afar and knocked her on the head and dragged her off. Maybe you know where she's from. Maybe you kidnapped her from the Western Wild Women Academy," Ben snorted, laughing at his suggestion.

Levi wrapped an arm around his neck and pulled him to the ground.

"Please! What are you doing now?" Allison stood back, not wanting to get knocked over by the wrestling brothers. "Stop!" She felt her heart pounding as the mass of arms and legs flipped around the floor. Grabbing a pan, she held it up, her arm shaking. "Oh, please stop!" she tried again, louder.

Levi let go and popped up from the tangled pile of limbs.

"Sorry Allison." He panted hard. "He's all yours," he said as he stalked out.

"Oh no, he's not," she said as he walked away. "Ben." He lay flat on his back, trying to catch his breath. "Ben." His head never came off the floor. "Please get out."

"Okay, I will. Just give me two minutes to let him have the lead. You're my only protection." Breathing hard, he held out his hand for help up. Allison took it and pulled. He stood and put her hand to his lips, kissing her soft skin, "Even with wet hair, your blanket, and bare feet, we turn into dragons in the presence of a fair princess." She took a step back and pulled her hand free.

"Time to go." She surrendered a small smile as she nodded at the door.

18

~~~~~

Levi dug his fingers through the loose soil of the garden. The season was never long enough to grow much—sometimes just long enough for the small animals to have a meal on him. Restless and distracted, he watched Allison out of the corner of his eye, making little circles on Ben's swing. She was so refined; she must think them ridiculous. *How many times have I fought the loneliness of a long, cold winter—but now God is surely testing me. Why can't I help Allison without getting into a scrape? I need to be a better example. Her memory will return soon, and her legs seem to be healing. Ben could stay here and I should take her to Ready Springs. It might be the only answer to keep my little brother in my good graces.*

He stood, brushing the dirt off his trousers, when he heard Patch barking, then broke out in a wide smile. Ray and Thelma Cox were leading their mule toward the cabin. Ben came around the corner, waving at them, and there were handshakes and embraces all around.

Ray slapped Levi's back. "Up for a social call from these old folks?"

"I was just talking to the Lord about that very thing. We're happy to have you." He grinned at Thelma. "You're looking well."

"We're too old to drag through the snow anymore," Thelma said, "and you never come to see us. So we won't stay long—just wanted to see how the old place was doing."

Levi gestured toward the cabin. "It's still standing, still stays warm in the winter." He shuffled his feet. "And we even have a guest in it right now."

"Really?" Thelma said, peering past the brother to the woman standing near a tree. "She stays in it with who?" She gave both brothers a stern look.

"No, no, by herself," Levi clarified. "Ben and I have taken up residence in the lean-to."

There was a silence as Ray and Thelma waited for more information. Finally, Ray spoke. "Levi, let me see your pelts. Wondering if you remember anything I taught you."

"I do," he said. "But first, let me introduce you to Allison." Ben had started toward her, but Levi wanted to do the introductions. He didn't trust Ben's version of how she came to be here. "Ben!" he called. "Take care of the mule, will you?" Ben shrugged and took the animal's reins, while Levi and the older couple approached the cabin.

"Looks like you had a fire," Ray said.

"I'm just glad we caught it before it got too far. We had some high winds."

"It's a good thing you did," said Ray.

"Allison." Levi beckoned to her. "I want you to meet Ray and Thelma Cox. Ray built this cabin."

She nodded shyly, wrapping her arms around her middle to cover the blanket.

Levi scratched his temple. "You're probably wondering why she's here." They nodded, waiting. "Well, I was trapping over the west arm off Sault Creek." He glanced to Ray, knowing the older man knew the area. "I saw some buzzards, so I followed them and found her. She'd been in an accident. We don't know exactly what happened, because she can't remember much of anything. She knows her name, though. Allison Kent. Do you know any Kents?"

They both shook their heads. "Not that I can recall," Ray said.

"Well, I don't know which way to take her. And then we had the fire…" Levi realized that his excuses must sound lame. "So we've been hoping her memory will return, so we can get her back to where she came from."

"Oh, you poor thing." Thelma wrapped an arm around Allison. "Your folks must be worried sick."

"Don't recall your pa's name or where he worked?" Ray asked.

Allison shook her head. "Today, Levi and Ben are the only people I know."

"So…" Levi ran his fingers through his hair. "We're doing our best here. Soon I'll take my pelts to Ready Springs and ask around there."

Allison stepped away from Thelma's embrace. "Levi's forgetting his manners. Come in and sit for a while." She motioned to the door of the cabin.

"What did I forget?" Levi sulked as Ben walked in with the Coxes.

By the next day, Allison would describe Thelma as a godsend. They had chopped herbs and vegetables and prepared supper together. Thelma never made her feel inadequate, but took time to explain things, making light of how the Graham men cooked. The breakfast they prepared that morning was the best food Allison had eaten yet. Maybe it was just the way Thelma laughed—maybe gravy needed a happy cook to taste good.

"Do you and Ray have children?" Allison asked while cleaning up.

"No, we never did." Thelma sat, watching Allison. "See, I was the youngest of five brothers and two sisters. My mama had me doing most of the cooking and cleaning—I think she just got worn out by all the older kids, and so she let me take care of her. And then with all my nieces and nephews, it felt like I had my own brood. God brought Ray into my path when I was in my late thirties." She tapped her chin, where a few stray whiskers sprouted. "I was long past marrying age, and Ray wasn't no great fish to catch." She cackled. "He'd lived a hard life, trapping. Oh, the stories he could tell about trappers and Indians, drinking, horse racing, gambling…"

"How did you meet?"

"He'd come to town, needing his shirts sewn. My sister passed it off to me. I can't think why, but I just felt a fondness for him.

My ma said, 'He's a wanderer. He'll never give ya nothing.' But I thought I was always going to be an old maid, so I didn't have all those dreams packed in a hope chest. I just took him for who he was, and when he said 'I do,' he had to take me for who I was, too."

Allison touched her shoulder. "That seems right."

"So no, we never had any children of our own. We did move around a lot, so that's how we know the Grahams. Those boys were the cutest little ankle biters." She smiled.

"It's wonderful to see how you care for Ben and Levi," Allison said.

"They've always been special to us. Is one of them special to you?" Thelma looked straight into Allison's eyes.

She laughed. "No. They're both kind, in their own way." She looked away, shyly. "They're both handsome, too."

Thelma slapped the table, making her jump. "I'm glad you noticed that! How those boys live so rough, but still keep those beautiful teeth and pure skin! It's a surprise to me one of them don't got a backside of buckshot. That Ben—he could make a mean old grizzly laugh, a prank up every sleeve. And Levi—he must have been born with an old soul. Ray took to him straightaway, probably wished he was born to him. Levi would sit for hours, listening to Ray's trapping stories. He's a smart one, that boy, learns quick and can do anything he sets his mind to."

"I wish he knew how to make women's clothes." Allison grimaced at her odd apparel. "My only skirt was destroyed in the fire."

"Do you have any of the fabric left?" Thelma asked.

Allison pulled out the half-burned skirt.

"Where there's a will, there's a way." Thelma spread the fabric on the table.

A few hours later, Levi opened the door and leaned in. "Allison, can I talk to you?"

She felt the strangest shy feeling. "Sure."

"I wondered if you were feeling trapped in there." A small grin rose from the corner of his mouth.

"Not exactly." She smiled back, waiting for him to notice her transformation.

"I just wondered if you wanted to go for a walk with me."

She didn't answer, but looked pointedly downward.

"What are you doing? Do you want me to see something?" He squinted.

She spread her hands down the soft blue fabric of her newly-fashioned skirt.

He stepped back. "Your skirt!"

Clapping her hands, she beamed.

"You're not wearing the blanket!"

"Thelma took my burned skirt apart. She's a miracle worker!" She twirled, enjoying the moment of goodwill between them. "She took off the waistband, pulled the gathers and the bustle apart, patched here and there, and…it fits!"

"That was kind of her."

"And she has some fabric left over, too. I'm going to get a new blouse!"

"Then…do you want to go for a walk?"

"Thank you for the invitation, but I'm fine here. You wouldn't believe the things Thelma knows how to cook. Maybe after supper." She turned toward the table, and then back to Levi. "At least now I can go to town without a blanket around my waist."

There's nothing like the smell of bread baking. Allison closed her eyes, and for a moment, she saw a short woman with gray hair, pulling fresh bread out of the oven. It felt so familiar; she could see the kitchen…

"Darlin', you understand about the coals?"

"Oh. Yes." She came back to what Thelma was doing.

"Go tell the men thirty minutes. That helps keep their stomachs from talking back."

❧

Levi had carried in two tall rounds of wood for Ben and himself to sit on. The women placed the food before the men, and Levi prayed for the meal, and for blessings for the travelers.

"Today, Miss Allison got me thinking about the grace of God," Thelma said, as the men reached for their food.

Allison wondered what Thelma could possibly be talking about.

"The grace He gives us is really just for this day. This sweet girl has no recollection of her past, and she doesn't know what tomorrow will hold. She just has the grace of God for today. Isn't that a lesson for all of us?"

"Amen, Thelma. Keep going. I've missed your Sunday School teachings," Ben said.

"We need to trust Him for these precious moments. What use will it do to worry about what happened yesterday?"

Levi swallowed hard. He remembered Allison's head on his lap while he touched her hair, and all the other things he'd done wrong.

"God doesn't work in our yesterdays," Thelma went on. "All the love and provision and forgiveness are loaded up for today. And we should rejoice and be glad in it." She lifted her cup.

"Amen." The men all touched their cups in the air.

Levi held his cup out to Allison. "To good food and a skirt repaired." He waited. "Yes?"

"And endearing friends around the table." She touched her cup to his.

His smile lingered on her, and his warm eyes seemed to be saying something personal.

"Ben, knock it off," Levi whispered in the dark, so the Coxes wouldn't hear. "You keep tossing back and forth, landing on my arm. You got an itch or something?" He bumped his brother hard, almost tossing Ben from the lean-to shelf.

"Levi!" Ben tried to pull back from the edge. "You don't have to push me off."

"I've spent my whole life sleeping next to brothers, or in a bunkhouse with filthy dock workers," he growled. "Now I have my own place, and I'm stuck out here, smelling mule droppings, next to you." Levi stuffed some hay under his shoulder.

"I know," Ben said, excited. "You can have your bed back, and Allison can sleep out here with me."

"Are you asking for a black eye? Right now, I'd like to wrap your legs around that dumb tree swing you made and hang you from it."

"I made the swing for Allison. I don't care what you think about it." Ben shoved Levi, harder than necessary. "She likes it."

Levi shoved back, causing Ben to fly over the edge of the makeshift bed.

There was a solid *thunk* as Ben hit the ground. Levi couldn't contain his laughter as his brother stalked away.

19

➰➱

"**O**h, no." Allison covered her mouth. "Are they fighting?"

Levi and Ben danced around each other, stirring up dirt. One moment they were taunting and smiling, the next, swinging with full force.

"Why don't they have their shirts on?" She flinched as Levi caught Ben in the jaw with a solid punch.

"Blood," Thelma said. "Why ruin a good shirt?"

Sure enough, Ben wiped his bloody lip with the back of his hand. He wasn't smiling as he lurched at Levi.

"I don't think they're playing around. Do you think you could get Ray to make them stop?"

"Ray's been around men fighting his whole life." Thelma shook her head. "He's been in enough of his own. Best to just let them wear each other out."

"Oh, for pity sakes. What are they fighting about? Did you see what happened?" Allison grimaced as Levi took a blow to the gut.

"I heard a bit of a ruckus last night. Sounded like Ben had fallen out of a tree. But I think it was just them blowing off some steam."

Suddenly, Levi kicked Ben's legs out from under him and sent him flying through the dirt. Ben came up like a bear, ready to attack. "Is that all you got?" he taunted.

"Thelma, this makes my stomach hurt. Somehow I know I didn't grow up around this!" Allison turned her head into Thelma's shoulder when Ben rammed Levi, knocking them both to the ground.

"Well, I say we get started repairing that blouse." Thelma patted her arm and turned to the cabin. "I'll grab my sewing things."

"Ben...you know...you can't...take me..." Levi bent over, trying to catch his breath.

Ben's nostrils flared. "Maybe I can't...but...maybe I can." Charging, he ran and knocked Levi through the air and into the creek.

Levi came up in a flurry of water and arms, grabbing Ben by the neck. Something in him wanted to push Ben's face under and hold him there. He was shocked by his own evil rage. He stepped back as Ben's fist slammed into his cheek, sending him flying backward into the cold water. Now Ben was on top of him, gripping him by the neck. He finally got his feet underneath him and pushed up with everything he had. He turned his body, dragging Ben over his back, pulling him by his head until he flipped over, smacking the water. Levi let go and moved back up to the bank. Ben tried to stand up, but pure exhaustion made his legs buckle, and he fell back, slapping the water with both arms and letting out a loud growl.

Levi was panting, desperate for air. He watched Ben, soaked and fuming, hoping he was done. He knew for the sake of birth order that Ben had to give up first, but then decided he would be the one to save Ben's pride. "Enough," Levi choked out, "we're done."

Thelma glanced at the window. "As long as one of those boys don't need any stitches, then we have the cabin to ourselves."

Allison peered outside to see Levi and Ben, wet and worn out, stalking away. She began to unbutton her blouse. "I wish I knew what happened between them." The blouse slipped off her shoulders. "Somehow I think I'm causing the tension." Putting her hand protectively across her corset, she handed Thelma her blouse. The older woman examined the small tears fraying the white cotton. Like the repair of the skirt had, this felt vaguely familiar.

She reached to retrieve her jacket from its peg when the door swung open.

Allison squealed.

"Sorry. I should have knocked," Ray said, backing out quickly.

She clenched the jacket in front of her, red-faced.

"Don't worry, dear," Thelma smiled. "His eyesight is going."

"Let's take a break," Thelma finally said after an hour of stitching. Allison nodded in agreement and leaned back against the door, removing her velvet jacket. "Ahhh… that's better. I would only admit this to you, but the other evening, I took a dip in the creek."

"You did?" Thelma glanced up.

"It was one of the most glorious moments I've had. That I can remember."

Thelma scrunched her lips together. "Then you could very well be the reason those brothers are fighting."

Allison straightened up. "No! Ben and Levi were inside the cabin, and Patch was my guard." She slipped her arms back into the hot jacket. "I feel certain they wouldn't have watched me."

"I don't think they would. But they are both young men. What do you know of young men?" Thelma poured herself some water.

Allison sat down and rested her chin on her hand. "Nothing."

Thelma spoke gently, "Are you sure you're not married? Or maybe you were running from an undesirable suitor?"

"I just don't think so." She chewed on her thumbnail. "I don't feel like anyone has loved me. For pity sakes. Why hasn't anyone been searching? If someone wanted to find me, why haven't they by now?" Allison stomped on the dingy cabin floor, fighting tears.

Thelma came to her side. "Child." She wrapped her arms around Allison's stiff shoulders. "I can't imagine what you've been through, not to remember the things of your life."

Allison pulled back and wiped the tears off her face. "What if I can't remember because it was so awful?"

"Maybe it was." Thelma ran her hand over Allison's hair. "Maybe God wants to give you a new day for that darkness. Beauty for ashes."

"You mean just start my life over? Here in the woods? Oh, Thelma, I don't know how you do it."

Thelma gazed into Allison's eyes. "Love. You can bear all things because of love."

Allison shook her head. "I don't understand."

"Because you haven't got the bearings on your past, you can't see much of your future. But those young men—well, there are a few things you might want to know about them." Thelma moved away and took Levi's comb. She pulled out the pins and combed through Allison's hair. Her gentle touch caused a wave of new tears to appear. Someone doing her hair felt familiar, and Thelma's touch was calming to Allison's fragmented emotions.

"Those young men have needs. But they would never tell. So sometimes they act strange or even get in fights. Are you following me, dear?" Thelma asked.

"Not really."

Thelma twisted Allison's hair and pulled it together at the nape of her neck. "They want to be married. They want to find their own beauty to battle for." She secured another pin. "They want someone to share their evenings with. And they don't want to share that beauty with each other."

Realizing Thelma was talking about her, Allison blushed.

"Ben is still a bit of a wanderer," Thelma said. "He has yet to reach the stability a woman needs. But Levi is older. I think he knows what he wants." Thelma looked at her, an extra message in her words.

Suddenly uncomfortable, Allison stood. "Thank you for doing my hair. Should we pick up the sewing before supper?"

For supper, they sat on stumps and chairs out front. Earlier, Ray had brought in a string of fish, and Thelma took the time to explain how to cook them. Allison wondered what had kept Ben and Levi occupied all day, but when Levi came in the cabin, she froze.

"Your eye is all swollen and purple," she said, concerned.

"I know." He held out his tin plate, and Thelma laid a fish on it. "Thank you, Miss Thelma," he said as he grabbed a fork and walked out.

Allison frowned. He hadn't noticed her hair.

ఞ

Levi didn't want to talk. Allison was a worrywart. He knew she had seen him and Ben fighting. For that, he was embarrassed. But he didn't want to answer her questions. It wasn't his first scrape, and it wouldn't be his last. Her fretting somehow made it worse. He took a bite of fish as Ben approached the cabin. They hadn't spoken all day. Ben nodded to Ray and walked past him into the cabin. Levi tried not to watch through the open door. Would she fret over Ben's split lip? He forked another piece of fish and swatted a fly away.

"Sorry about walking in on your gal today," Ray said.

"She's not my gal, and you're welcome to walk in that cabin, day or night."

"She let out a good scream, so I thought maybe you heard and wondered what was going on," Ray said.

"Why would she scream?" he asked.

"Changing her clothes, I believe." Ray cleared his throat and changed the subject. "Thelma takes to anything with a broken wing."

Levi nodded. "Thanks for catching supper." He stood and called for Patch.

Late that night, Levi entered the lean-to where Ben sat on the edge, long legs dangling. Jumping up, he sat in the dark next to his brother.

"I'm glad you're here. I need to say something to you. I've been wrestling with God, and I took it out on you. I want to say I'm sorry, 'cause I shouldn't have turned my turmoil into a fight between you and me. What I got wrong isn't your fault. You've always had a lighter outlook on life than me. That's one of the things I love about you. I don't want to make excuses." Levi scratched the back of his neck. "I just want to know if you'll forgive me."

Ben pushed the hay around and finally laid down. "I forgive you, Levi, but I'm leaving with Ray and Thelma tomorrow."

20

Allison tossed and turned on the bed, her mind circling in conflict. Thelma and Ray were leaving soon to visit other friends; maybe she should just ask them to take her with them? At times, she wanted to ask more about how Ray and Thelma lived, but she held back, feeling as if she might be fishing for an invitation. And as much as Thelma seemed to like her, she never once hinted at her going with them. Had they made the suggestion to Levi? Did he assure them he would take her away from the cabin soon?

Of all the unknowns in Allison's life, this little cabin and Ben and Levi were the only security she had. Could she possibly risk leaving here just to go to another unknown? Levi had promised to take her anywhere she wanted to go. How long would Ray and Thelma want to put up with her? Would they be willing to take her home when her memory returned? She sighed, threading her hands through her hair. How long would her memory elude her? If she could get away from the chaos of this cabin, would she regain her memory?

Feeling more restless, she sat up and leaned against the cabin wall. Levi and Patch had never returned. It was so strange to see Levi and Ben ignore each other. Ray and Thelma took it all in stride, but to think of the brothers at odds still made her stomach hurt. Taking a deep breath, she rested her head back against the cabin wall. Maybe she should ask the Coxes to take her with them. Then the brothers would have nothing to divide them.

"Ben, no," Levi said, resting on the hay-lined shelf. "Please don't go." He turned to face his brother. "I've been hard on you, but you said you would forgive me."

"I do forgive you," Ben yawned.

"Then you don't need to go." Levi tried to keep his voice down.

"I've worn out my welcome." Ben rubbed his bruised lip. "Ray and I talked quite a while tonight. I'm going to help him the rest of the summer and then head up to the Von Keller's dairy farm. I guess Pa promised Mr. Von Keller one of his sons would help him out one day. I don't really see myself as a dairy farmer, but Pa would say that's my problem, I don't see myself doing anything much."

"Don't listen to Pa… ah, you know what I mean. Just listen to God. You're good at many things. You can build anything you set your mind to." Levi elbowed him. "You're not in the way here. Everything's been upside down because of Allison. As soon as she's gone, we could make it here hunting and trapping. Enough to get us through the winter."

"I couldn't do it. I'd go nuts with just you and Patch to talk to. I like being around people, probably as much as you don't."

"What if Allison doesn't get her memory back soon? What am I supposed to do with her?"

"Well, I could think of a few things," Ben snorted.

Levi shot an elbow into his brother's ribs.

"I was just joking. You take everything with her way too serious. You act like you got a tick in your ear over her."

Levi let out a groan. "I haven't been myself since the day I found her. I feel like she's come between me and God."

"What?" Ben said. "What are you talking about?"

"I can't read my Bible, I can't pray."

"Why not?" Ben said sarcastically.

"Because I'm always thinking about her. Something I said, something I should have said. The way she looks at me, the way she talks, the way she laughs. Sometimes she's sweet as honey, and sometimes she's just a…bear."

"So you never know where you stand with her?" Ben said.

"Exactly. She's completely baffling."

"I think God knows exactly what He's doing." Ben bumped Levi's shoulder. "You can't control or fix this one. You have to trust God, but you don't like doing that. You said yourself you've been wrestling with God."

Levi stared over at the pitch-black woods. He wished Ben wasn't right, but he knew he was. *Lord, help me.*

Thelma watched Allison stir the oatmeal. "Looks good. I'm going to miss having another woman to cook with."

"Why?"

"Ray's got an itching to get on. We never stay too long."

"It hasn't been long at all." Allison's heart dropped. "Can you ask him for a few more days? Please?"

"I'd love to stay and help you here, dear one, but the men are going to finish chinking the logs, and then we'll head out."

Allison chewed on her knuckles. If only Thelma would offer to take her. "I don't want you to stay for your help. It's just that I've so enjoyed your company," she said.

Thelma came to rub Allison's back. "I have also loved being part of what God has for your life. You said yesterday you didn't think you were ever loved. I believe He sent me here to tell you of the great love He has for you. And before you say anything, it's not the kind of love that's marked by everything going just so. It's the kind of love that sees how your heart can break and be lost and it comes and finds you in a place no man or circumstance can fix. That's the perfect love God has just for you, Miss Allison. You. Your fair-haired, seven freckles on your nose, petite hands and feet…you. Will you let Him love you that way?"

Allison looked away, and Thelma gently pulled her chin. "He loves you," she whispered. "Believe it, dear one."

Allison gave her a weak nod as Thelma wrapped her arms around her. "I know God is doing something," Allison said into her shoulder. "I don't think I even like being touched, and that's completely changed."

"Yes! Amen." Thelma moved back to give her a bright smile.

The men had finished breakfast and were all talking when Allison and Thelma finally came outside and sat down. Ben and Levi were back to their old selves. The brothers both rose and nodded in her direction as they took their leave. *Something still feels strange,* she thought. Out of the corner of her eye, she watched them prepare the chinking mixture and plaster the sides of the cabin. She realized the Coxes had lent their time and effort to see Levi and Ben succeed. It really was remarkable that these two people, old enough to be their grandparents, yet not related in any way, would share all their knowledge. Not only that, but go out of their way to come alongside these young men—and enjoy it. Allison caught Ray flicking a bit of mud on Ben. Ben quickly smeared it into a muddy mustache. Thelma had spent her time, not in leisure, but graciously teaching as much as she could. What an admiration she felt for them! Her mind drifted for a moment—she felt sure that she knew someone else of this caliber. Someone else who believed in her, who encouraged her...

"Mrs. Webster!" Allison jumped up so fast that she dumped her empty tin on the ground. "Mrs. Webster!" She ran over to Ben and Levi. "The W, I remembered! It's for Mrs. Webster!"

Levi and Ben eyed her.

"What W?" Levi returned to daubing the mud into place.

"The school! The school I went to! Mrs. Webster was a teacher! No...she was...the headmistress!" She clapped her hands with joy.

Ben stepped away from the cabin, mud and straw hanging from his hands. "What was the town, Allison? Don't get upset, just think slowly and calmly."

"I'm not upset. I'm happy."

"All right. What town was your school in? Were you there as a girl?"

Swallowing hard, she took a deep breath, ready to produce the name of the town. She squeezed her clasped hands together in some attempt to squeeze the name out.

"Calm down. Your face is getting all red. You're trying too hard," Ben said.

She closed her eyes and gritted her teeth. Nothing. One small ray of hope, then nothing. Her shoulders drooped as she walked away.

Allison stood quietly as Thelma wrapped up leftovers for their trip. She didn't feel like being friendly. Frowning, she watched while Ray loaded the last of their gear on their mule. Ben stood nearby with his pack and gun around his shoulder. She walked out of the cabin toward him. "Are you going hunting? Right now?"

Ben shuffled his feet. "No, I'm going on with Ray and Thelma."

"What?" She thought she must have heard wrong. "Going where?"

He nodded toward the tree line, silent.

"How long till you return?"

"I...um." He popped his hat on his head. "I'm going to stay with them a while and then head over toward Wisconsin."

"Wisconsin!" *Why didn't he tell me sooner?* Levi stared at his feet; it felt as if they all had a secret she wasn't in on. The feeling of betrayal squeezed her chest. Ray stepped forward, blocking the stares between Ben and Allison. "Levi." Ray stuck his hand forward. "You do the old owner proud."

"Thank you for all your help," he said.

Allison stared at Ben as he mouthed *I'm sorry.* Thelma came up and hugged her, breaking the bitter moment. She stepped back from the hug and nodded goodbye to Ray. *Be polite, be cordial* was ringing in her head. *Not today*, rang louder, and she turned and walked away.

21

In an emotional daze, Allison walked circles in the woods. Losing sight of the creek, she sat on a fallen log, indifferent, as the sun dipped behind the trees. *I thought Ben was my friend. Why couldn't he have told me he was leaving? Probably too worried I'd get upset. But why didn't Thelma or Levi tell me? If Ben could tag along, why couldn't I? They all betrayed me.* She rubbed the bridge of her nose. *Ben said he was sorry. But why didn't he speak to me privately? Did Levi warn him against it?* What hurt the most was that Allison knew she'd grown attached to Ben. He was so unpredictable and yet so endearing, always the first one to jump to help her. *But did I ever show my appreciation? Probably not.* She dropped her elbows onto her knees, cupping her chin. Tears of disappointment trickled around her fingers. Hearing a branch snap, she sat up quickly, wiping her face.

"Patch, you scared me. Have you been missing me?" She scratched behind his ears, then looked out into the woods. Levi leaned against a large tree, expressionless, watching her. He bent down and pulled out a piece of dry grass and chewed on the end of it. Without a word, he nodded. He wanted her to follow him. She hesitated, but knew she didn't want to stay out here all night. She sighed and brushed off her skirt, then followed him back to the cabin.

They walked in silence, and he pushed open the cabin door for her to go first. He dropped his hat on the table and looked around a bit nervously.

"I saved a bowl of stew for you." He took the cloth off the bowl. "I can heat it up for you if you'd like."

"No, thank you." Allison stood, stoically.

"No to the food? Or no to heating it up?"

She gripped the back of her chair. "Why? For pity sakes, could no one tell me Ben was leaving? Can you answer me that, Levi?"

Levi dropped the cloth on the table. "He just told me late last night. I asked him to stay."

"Did he say why he was leaving?" She brushed her loose hair behind her ear.

"Just what he told you."

"I don't believe you." She hoped her words bothered him. "I know you were fighting. I know there's more to this."

A muscle flexed in his jaw. "Do you remember when I asked you if you had feelings for Ben? You never really answered. Is this why you're so upset?"

"Two can play this game." She braced her hands on the table. "What's the real reason Ben left?"

Levi paced in the small cabin. "He said something that made me mad, so I threw him out on his ear. I can't even remember who started it. But this is just what we do." He shook his head. "I know you don't understand," he mumbled. "I would never really hurt him."

"Was it me, then? Did I hurt him?" Tears pooled in her eyes.

"No." Levi pressed his temples. "Please don't cry."

"He tried to be helpful," she got out between gulps. "And I never was very appreciative. I wasn't very nice when he teased me."

"Really, Allison, you can't blame yourself for the way our family works. Ben is resting next to a fire somewhere, and he knows I love him. He knows I'd die in his place if I could. He knows he's welcome here day or night. He changes his mind like the wind, and he's been here before and left before. I understand you're going to miss him. I understand why you're sad."

"I just wasn't prepared." She dabbed her wet nose. "I was already unhappy about Thelma leaving. She was a great comfort to me." She hiccupped. "I thought she might take me with them, but she never offered."

"I told them I'd take you." His voice was strained. "I just assumed you'd remember everything, and I could take you to your home."

Allison hiccupped again.

"Are you hungry? Do you want something different?" He looked at the cold bowl.

"No." She shook her head. "I'm tired. I need to go to sleep."

Levi nodded but didn't move. "I'm sorry for keeping you up. The Coxes set me back a day or so, but when you're up to it, we'll head to Ready Springs."

His eyes radiated sincerity and care. *Why did it just get so warm in here? Why isn't he moving for the door?* "I'm sorry you had to come find me." She was suddenly very aware of him. She knew the strength in those arms, the warmth of his hand on hers, the way his little wink made her belly twist. And now, here they were, completely alone.

"I didn't have to. I wanted to." He raised a small smile.

"Thank you for talking to me. I feel a little better."

Levi took a few steps, and stood inches from her.

She froze, trembling at his closeness.

"Good." He pulled her in, and gently kissed her cheek.

Late that night, remembering the softness of her cheek, Levi made a decision. *Being alone with her will overcome the good sense God gave me. Her beauty has power, but she belongs to herself, not to me. She's a person who needs help, and with God's grace, I'll help her. Lord help me, when she's sweet and humble, it takes everything in me not to pull her in and…well, I'm a patient man. I'll apply that patience to helping her. She's just a lost friend. That's all.*

The next morning, Allison peered out to a gray day. Touching her cheek, she remembered Levi's kiss. She wasn't fearful of being alone with him—he'd always been a gentleman. But she was fearful of her feelings toward him. How many days had she been in this little cabin? Yet it had been a place of healing, and the brothers and the Coxes had been like family. She shook her head—was she starting to think of this as *home?*

Rain began to pelt the dust around the cabin. Levi had said they would leave soon—would they travel in these conditions? Thunder rumbled in the sky, and Patch came racing around the front of the cabin. When she opened the door, he plowed past her legs, wet and muddy.

"Oh, Patch! You're a mess." He came to rub a greeting against her skirt. "No!" She stepped away, groaning at the smeared paw prints all over the clean floor.

"Just stay in one place." She pushed on his back to get him to lie down. "Stay. Where did you leave Levi?" Turning around, she jumped; Levi stood just outside the cabin in the pouring rain.

"You scared me. Why are you standing out there?"

He came up to the threshold. "I'm just a bit soaked." The thunder crashed again, and she grabbed his shirt and pulled him inside.

Levi laughed. "I guess I just decided to come in."

"I don't want you to be hit by lightning."

"That's good," he said. "I don't want to, either." He pulled his hat off and held it over her head, and rainwater trickled over her hair.

"Ahh…you're as bad as Patch." She pushed his chest, returning his playful smile. There was something charming about him—the way his damp hair looked more untamed. He was even more handsome when he was wet. She hoped it would rain all day.

"Turn around. I need to change my shirt." He started undoing his buttons.

"Of course." She cleared her dry throat, hoping to clear her mind. *I've already seen him without a shirt. Oh, for pity sakes, that just makes it worse.* Allison touched her cheeks—they were burning. What was this effect he was having on her? Her foot tapped nervously on the floor.

"Is that your foot?" he asked.

She froze. "Not anymore."

The lightning struck in perfect harmony to her nerves, and she rolled her eyes.

"I'm done," he said.

Allison turned around to see him in his trousers with just a long johns shirt on. He pushed up his sleeves and bent to pick up his wet shirt.

"Do you want a fire?"

"No, I'm overly warm," she said. "I think the lightning is just making me flustered." *And maybe you standing there in your undergarment.*

"I have an idea. It'll get your mind off the storm." He reached for something in a basket on the shelf. "My parents think playing cards is a sin, but it helped me survive working out on the docks. I think it was a sin how much money the guys would lose, but cards themselves are harmless."

"Allison!" A few hours later, Levi laughed good-naturedly. "You can't show any excitement when you get a good hand. Haven't you ever heard of a poker face?" He stacked the cards together in a pile.

She shook her head. "I'll try. Really, I can do it. No expression. I promise." Squinting over her new cards, she scratched her head. "Just one quick question. If the numbers go in order, but they all have different colors…is that anything?"

Levi closed his eyes and let his cards fall from his hand. "I think that's enough for today. For certain the storm has long gone past us." He got up and stretched.

Allison was still studying her cards. "I thought you said this was something."

"Straight. You have a straight. But it doesn't work if I know about it." He pulled the front door open to see only a few drops running off the roof. "I'm going to go see how the new chinking held up." He pulled on his boots. Patch jumped up, and they both headed out.

Allison put the cards on the shelf. *That was fun.* She grabbed Levi's shirt off the back of the chair to see if it was dry, then held it to her nose. It smelled like him, like wood right after it had been split. Like fresh rain.

"What are you doing?" His voice made her jump.

"Nothing." She pulled his shirt quickly away from her face, and every shade of red rose up her cheeks.

Levi nodded. "Do you want anything from the cellar?" he finally said.

"Yes, some tomatoes would be nice," she said with a timid smile. *Now I have to think fast, what should I do with them?*

❧❦

Levi climbed down the ladder leading to the cellar. As he reached for the jar of tomatoes, his foot sank a few inches into mud and water. He remembered his ma canning those tomatoes last year. What would she say to him, living here alone with Allison? She wouldn't abide by it, not for a minute. The rainy day felt homelike. It felt good just being together. *She's lost some of her crossness. It seems that time with Thelma gave her something Ben and I couldn't. But why did she smell my shirt? She had her eyes closed.* Something in his gut did a flip. *Like she was enjoying it.*

Levi climbed back up the ladder. He rounded the corner and stopped outside the door. "I don't want you to think you have to do all the cooking. I can cook a fair bit."

Her faced dropped. "Why? I thought I was doing better."

"You are. But you've taken it all on, and you don't have to."

"Well, this is your cabin, Levi. I thought it was the least I could do for all you've done for me. And having Thelma show me some things—well, it helps me have something to do. My days are too idle." She looked around the cabin. "You have yet to tell me your plan to take me to Ready Springs." She rubbed her hand over the rough table.

Levi could feel the vein in his neck pulsing, and he tried to stop clenching his teeth. "I can take you tomorrow." She was obviously desperate to get away from him. "Too much rain today."

Allison frowned. "It doesn't have to be tomorrow. I just wondered what you were thinking about it."

"I was thinking that you would regain your memory. Then I was thinking that I would take you wherever you wanted to go. That's what I was thinking."

"Are you angry I can't remember anything helpful?" Her eyes narrowed.

148

"No." He shook his head. *I'm angry when I think of living here without your voice, your laugh, your gentle ways.* "But your poker is poor." He took a step closer, eyes flashing playfully.

She smiled nervously, taking a small step back.

"My cabin has never been so clean." Taking another step forward, he smiled at the mud tracks he had just made. "If you never regained your memory, it wouldn't make me angry." He reached out and took her elbow, then slowly brought his hand up the back of her arm.

He felt her waver ever so slightly. His eyes were holding her captive, and he wished she would just fall right into his arms. The force of being alone with her pushed him past his vow, and his pulse quickened as he held her arm.

Her entire face tensed up, and she pulled away from him. "Please let go. I feel you were about to…"

Levi stepped back and held up both hands. "I believe I was." How could she care about him one moment, and the next, think him a snake? "Allison, just be ready in the morning. It takes a couple of days to get to Ready Springs." He turned to leave. "By then, you can decide where you're going next."

22

Allison stood still in the early morning light, scanning the little cabin. It only took a minute to get her things together. She spied the little cup with sagging wildflowers she had picked before the rain. The towels were all clean and hanging neatly. This little cabin had become a home. She sighed, the reoccurring lump rising in her throat. Levi would walk in at any minute, and she desperately didn't want to be found crying, mourning the loss of this place. But it was special, she sniffed, as the tears flowed over. She would never again sit around the table and laugh with Ben and Levi. She would never hold hands and pray as they had prayed. She stomped her foot. *If I could just remember my own life, I wouldn't have to cling to this. And maybe I wouldn't have hurt Levi.* Blowing her nose, she pulled on her burgundy gloves and straightened her posture.

Levi walked in and briefly held her eyes. "You look ready," he said as he poured a cup of coffee. He pulled out a canvas bag and loaded a few kitchen items. He took a few more sips as his eyes took in the cabin. "You'll need your blanket." He gestured toward the bed. Allison nodded, remembering the blankets lost in the fire. She carefully folded it and tucked it under her arm. "Give me the blanket and the bag—I'll tie them to the mule."

She felt her chin begin to quiver as she handed him the items. "Levi, I barely slept last night. I just wanted to say…"

"No need," he said, stepping through the door. She shook her head and followed him out. He turned and secured her items, put a lock on the cabin, and grabbed the reins, jerking the mule forward.

"We'll stop here for lunch," Levi said.

Allison's feet were throbbing, and it only took her a minute to find a tree to sit against. Those were the first words they had spoken since leaving Sault Creek. Many times, she had wanted to comment on the beauty of the day. The sun was warm, but the air was cool. Giant white clouds floated brilliantly against the vivid blue sky. But something had changed since she had pulled away from his touch. It was no wonder he was in a hurry to drop her off and get on with his life.

"Here you go," he said.

She put her hands out to receive a napkin containing jerky and cornbread. "Thank you."

They ate their lunch in silence. Only the sound of a crow far overhead could be heard echoing through the forest. Levi finished and held the canteen out to her.

"I need a cup," she said, trying to get her weary body up.

"It's next to the coffee pot," he said, gesturing toward the mule.

Ben would have been happy to serve me. She returned with the cup, and he poured the water. Their eyes met, challenging. "Thank you," Allison said, staring at him.

He watched her until she was done. "Ready to keep moving?"

Tucking the cup back in its place, she didn't answer.

"Come on, Patch!" She jumped at Levi's raised voice, and Patch ran back through the woods. *This feels familiar. This I can remember.*

The afternoon turned warm, and Allison had to remove her jacket. She'd fallen back, and knew she was just about to drop. Finally, they stopped to rest and get water. Finding a large rock, she flopped down, wondering for a moment if Levi was punishing her. She dropped her head to her knees, worrying that she might fall asleep and hit the ground. Patch picked the wrong time to come up and sniff her face. "Stop it." She pushed at the dog, but he kept trying. "Get away!" Patch gave her a lick. "Levi! Please get your dog away from me!" She glared at him.

"What are you trying to do? Wake the dead? I'm right here."

"Your dog won't leave me alone."

"You could have told me sooner this was too much for you. You don't have to take it out on Patch."

"You turn everything into my problem. Your dog is being a pest." She continued to glare.

Levi growled. "Come here," He gestured to her as he walked over to the mule. "You can ride."

Allison crossed her arms. "You never listen! Don't call me to come as if I'm your dog!"

Levi started to answer, then his head perked straight up. In a swift step, he grabbed her wrist and pulled her up. "Hush," he said as he moved her behind him. With his other hand, he tugged his rifle free.

"What...what is it?" she said, clinging to the back of his shirt. They turned in unison to see a man holding a rifle at them.

"What are you two up to?" the man said.

"Well, mostly just having an argument." Levi relaxed his shoulders. The old man seemed harmless enough.

"Well, I don't get many visitors, and when I heard a girly voice through the woods, I had to come myself and see who it belonged to." The old man's crooked grin showed yellowing teeth.

Levi swung his rifle over his shoulder, avoiding Allison, who was still plastered to his back.

"I'm Levi Graham." He stepped forward. "And the voice belongs to Allison."

The man dropped his hat and nodded at her. "I'm Clemet Summers. How do you do?"

"Clemet Summers." Levi shook his hand. "I've heard of you. Are you the one who mixes the white willow bark and meadowsweet for some kinda medicine?"

"That'd be me." More yellow teeth. "I used to be a trapper like you." He pointed to the pelts hanging off the mule. "But I had a blood brother that taught me what the Indians have known from the beginning. So folks come around, and I help them when I can. You know, there's a feller in Ready Springs that pulls teeth. He's been want'n me to move closer to town. But I never will...and he still comes a day's ride to get pouches of my powder. I like it out here. Old men need a peaceful place."

"I can agree with that." Levi nodded.

Allison huffed.

"Now you two only have a couple more hours of daylight, might as well come and bunk down in my place. Most of this ground is still wet from the storm come through."

"Why, thank you, Mr. Summers." Levi nodded at him.

"Just call me Clemet. You, too, Mrs. Graham." He turned to grab the mule's reins.

"Levi, you need to tell him we're not married," Allison murmured to his back. "We don't even know him! Levi!"

As Allison listened to the men talk for the next few miles, she was more than upset. One minute Levi wanted her favor, maybe even a kiss, the next minute he wouldn't give her the time of day. She tapped her foot as Levi unloaded the mule and flung her bag and blanket on the ground. *Fine*, she thought. *I'll just sleep out here.* Mr. Summers had some shanty or dugout that looked like an animal's den. *Another bachelor mountain man.*

"Come in, come in," Clemet motioned to her. Allison took a deep breath. He looked like a kind man, and she didn't want to be rude. She followed him inside. It was dusk, and it was quite dark in his little one-room den. It smelled musty and pungent.

Clemet lit the lantern and pulled out a chair for her. She looked at the table and didn't move. He grabbed some old newspapers and dusted off the dirt and grime. "Don't get many visitors, especially not as pretty as you. Here ya' go, Mrs. Graham." He held out the chair, and she sat, glowering at Levi as he entered. "Please, call me Allison."

"I shot me a couple of rabbits this mornin'." He bent over and blew the small coals of the fire to life. "We'll have them roasting up in no time." He shot Allison a weathered grin as he grabbed a flimsy rabbit by its neck. He laid it on the table, and before she could move, he dropped his cleaver and chopped its head off. She turned her head while he skinned it. By the time she could get her stomach to go down, he had threaded both poor rabbits on a spit, and the smell of burning meat filled the room.

"I need air." She pushed past Levi and moved outside to breathe in the cool air of the night. Sitting on a small log to ease her aching feet, she dropped her chin into her hands. *Levi's cabin wasn't so bad. Would he really take me only so far and leave me? If we hadn't scuffled, would I be warm and asleep in my own bed?*

"Allison, here." Levi held out a tin plate of rabbit meat and fried potatoes. 'It's good, really." He bumped the plate against her arm.

She took it and tried a few bites. "I'm just tired, and I'm sorry for how I made you mad," she whispered.

A vein pulsed in his neck as he stared long into the darkness. Reaching for her empty plate, he sighed. "Let's just go in. We can talk when we're not tired."

"I'm turning in," Clemet said from his doorway. "You two can take the buckskin."

Levi raised a hand to him. "Thanks." He laid a reassuring hand on her arm. "This will be fine, and it's just for tonight."

She followed him back into the small cabin where Clemet lay on his cot. The only other space in the cabin was right next to the table and chairs. It was on the other side of Clemet's cot, but the buckskin was small. Too small.

'I can't lie here with you." she groaned, looking down. "Didn't you tell him we aren't married?"

"Shhh," he said, close to her ear. "Don't question his charity. It'll be fine for one night." Levi sat down on the buckskin and untied his boots.

"Where am I to sleep?" she whispered with clenched teeth.

"Right here." He took her wrist and pulled her down next to him. "You face that way." He nodded to the mud wall. "I'll face this way." Their shoulders were squished against each other.

Allison moved closer to the wall. "Levi, there are spider webs. I can't sleep with my nose in spider webs."

"Sleep here with me or over there with him."

"You are a rogue. Now I know it," she said.

"Goodnight, Allison." He turned his back to her and lay down.

She sat on the buckskin, pulling her knees close. *I'd rather go sleep with Patch.* Glaring at Levi's shoulders, she decided to inch her way down and face his back. As long as they didn't touch, she might be fine. She wrapped her skirt around her legs as tightly as possible. Easing down, she rested her head on her arm and felt her eyes begin to droop—when Clemet began to snore.

"Oh, for pity sakes," she whimpered. She pulled her other arm up and clamped her ears. She could see Levi's back moving—he was snickering. *He thinks this is funny?* She shot her elbow into his back.

He arched forward. "Ow, that hurt." He rolled over.

"This is torture." She rose up on one elbow.

He snickered, and she clamped a hand over his mouth. Pulling her hand away, he twisted her down, pinning her wrists next to her ears. "No, this is torture, thinking I was going to get any sleep next to you."

"Let me go," she growled. "Ben…" Immediately, she caught her mistake. "I mean, Levi…" A gray shadow overtook his face, and her wrists began to burn. "You're hurting me."

He slid his hands off her wrists and intertwined his fingers with hers, his face inches above her.

A whimper caught in her throat. "I'm not one of your animals, caught in a trap."

"What happened," he said, cold and raspy, "between you and Ben?"

His chest rose and fell quickly on hers, and she struggled to speak. "There was some horseplay, and… he picked me up and dunked me in the creek. I smacked him and went home." She squinted. "But I don't really have a home, do I?"

❧

Releasing her hands, he rolled on his back, crossing his arms over his face. He didn't feel better by forcing her to talk, even knowing Ben was only being a schoolboy. He felt worse. Worse than he ever had about himself.

Sometime in the night, Levi pulled a blanket over both of them. In the pitch black, he could hear her soft breathing. He lay there in the ironic pleasure and pain of sleeping next to her. She moved slowly from her back to her side and flung her arm out so that it rested on his chest. It was a bitter chastisement, to be so physically close and yet so far away. Obviously, she was in a dead sleep; otherwise, she never would have touched him. She leaned into his side, her face against his shoulder, her knee resting on his leg. It was excruciatingly tender, knowing he ranked only somewhere above the spiders.

A rising stream of sunlight entered the old cabin. Levi gently rubbed Allison's hand, lying unaware on his chest. "Wake up, Allison." He gave her hand a squeeze. Taking one last gaze at her peaceful sleeping form, he let out a slow breath. He could hear that Clemet was up and around. "Allison."

"What?" She grabbed at the blanket.

Levi sat up. "We need to get going." He began to fold the blanket. Sitting up, Allison started vainly to straighten her hair, when he offered her his hand. She took it as he pulled her to her feet, holding it a bit longer than necessary.

"I hope you two are hungry." Clemet's voice broke the tender moment. "I've been saving these eggs for company." He cracked them into a bowl. "And you two fit the bill."

"Please, Clemet. Don't use your supplies up on us."

"No, no, I got folks coming out here trading all the time for my powders. You able to keep chickens over Sault Creek way?"

"No," Levi ran his hand over the days' worth of stubble on his jaw. "The foxes always get 'em." He went to stoke the fire.

The breakfast was long eaten, and Levi squirmed, wanting to get going.

"Did I tell you about the boys that are planting corn?" Clemet said. "Corn in the wilderness! Have you ever heard that? I think they must be desperate for some moonshine."

"Could be." Levi had to stand up and take his leave before one more story started. "Clemet, thank you for all your hospitality. We need to get moving."

"Oh sure, good day for travel. What did you all think about that lightning storm?"

Levi kept moving for the door. "If you ever get near Sault Creek, you find me. You're welcome at my place any day." He stuck his hand out for a handshake.

"Yes, thank you." Allison nodded politely.

They both headed for the door. Allison slipped on her gloves and waved goodbye.

They walked for half a day. The clouds would only let the sun in once in a while, and a soft wind kept the air cool. The grades weren't even that bad, but the backs of Allison's legs were cramping. In a clearing, she saw a cabin with a barn and animals in a corral. Her heart skipped a beat. *We must be getting closer.* As they passed by, she noticed a few other dirt roads that ended with homes pushed back among the trees. As their trail met a road, a wagon with men coming toward them made her insides jump. Dizziness washed over her, making her skin cold.

"Levi, please." Her voice wobbled.

He took his eyes off the approaching wagon and saw her clutching her jacket. He grabbed her elbow. "What's wrong? Are you hurt?"

"What if people recognize me?" She swallowed the lump in her throat. "What if someone knows me and I don't know who they are?"

Levi turned from her as the approaching wagon slowed. He raised his hand to greet the men. One of them pulled the horses to a stop. "Levi! Good to see ya'."

"Ethan, Leon. You look like you're faring well."

"We are," one of the men said.

"Coming in to do some trading, it looks like."

"Yes." Both men nodded at Allison.

"Saw your folks come into town today," one of them said.

"Is that so?" Pushing his hat back, Levi let out a low groan.

"I saw them outside of Crocker's. He's built a hotel next to the general store and trading post."

"Is that so?" Levi repeated.

"We best be getting back." The men nodded, and the wagon jerked forward. Levi tipped his hat to them as they left. He shot a side glance at her. "This is a fine mess." He kicked a rock as he pulled the mule forward.

Allison felt petrified and joyful at the same time. The word *hotel* did something no other word had in these last months, but the thought of seeing Levi's parents brought dread to every part of her being. Her mind battled. Running her fingers through her hair, she wondered how bedraggled she looked. As buildings started to appear before her, another bout of panic hit. *I look like something Patch dragged in from the woods. Oh, for pity sakes, I am something Patch dragged in from the woods.* Her thankfulness for her remade skirt now highlighted her disarray. She froze and called to Levi.

Scowling, he tied the mule to a tree and took her by the arm, leading her off the road. His jaw was locked, and she knew her appearance was the last of his concerns.

"Your town has a hotel." She lightened her voice.

"I am in perdition." He paced next to her.

She looked at him, shocked. What did he have to be in agony about? Nervous, she pulled out a few hairpins and fumbled to put them back in place.

He glared at her and shook his head. "What is your plan, Allison? Something besides doing your hair?"

"My plan is to get to the town. See if anyone has been looking for me." She jammed in the last pin.

"And when you get over crying about how small and backward Ready Springs is, and there's no clue to where you're from, then what?"

"I don't know—but you said you'd help me."

He stalked away, muttering and growling, then returned to her. "Here's how I'll help you." He strained to keep his voice even. "We're going to walk into Ready Springs. We'll check at Crocker's for any notices. When we don't see anything, I'm going to introduce you to my parents. My ma is a lot like Thelma." He took in a deep breath. "When they hear your story, they'll take you in, and you can live with them until you get your memory back."

"Absolutely not!" Allison shook her head. "You said you would take me!"

"All right." He stared back at her. "Which way are we going? North? East? Maybe across Lake Michigan? Lake Superior? Would you like to head to Canada? Which way?"

She stomped her foot. "You're the reason I can't remember anything! One minute you're charming and kind, the next I can't get through a conversation with you without wanting to scream!"

His face contorted. He started to open his mouth, but she cut in.

"I tried to talk to you outside of Mr. Summers' cabin, but you just wanted to let him assume we're married!" she spat out. "That lie is more important than talking friend to friend. For heaven's sakes, let's not offend Mr. Summers' genteel hospitality!"

Levi appeared to ignore Allison's ranting. "I have an idea."

She grabbed her head in frustration. "I knew you weren't listening."

"Marry me." He pulled her hands off her head.

"Oh, Levi…" She dropped her head back in defeat.

"Only as an agreement. You agree to make me miserable. I agree to give you shelter and food. And I promise I will listen to you. I promise before God that when you know where you belong, I'll take you."

"We don't have to be married to have that as an agreement," she sighed.

Levi pressed her hands between his. "When we walk into this town, we will run into my folks." He took a deep breath. "I will not lie to them. I won't do it. Yes, I needed to help you, but you've been with me too long, and that's my fault. I can't dishonor who they raised me to be. I'm willing to…I want to take care of you." His voice held a certain determination. "Either you go with them, or we have to be married."

Allison took a long look into Levi's intense brown eyes. Oh, how he could melt her resolve. She knew firsthand the security she had felt sleeping next to him last night. It was the best night of sleep she'd known since her accident. Her belly flipped. "If I agree, what else will you expect?"

Levi let go of her hands. "I'm just so tired of the low image you have of me." He pulled back and walked around her. "It was a stupid solution." He grabbed the mule's reins. "I'm heading to Crocker's," he said, walking away.

Twisting her hands, she took a deep breath. "All right, I agree to your plan. I'll marry you."

23

✦✦

Approaching Ready Springs, Allison noticed a strange smell—a smoky odor lingering somewhere between burned meat and something else she couldn't identify. Levi slowed his steps and glanced back at her. She wondered if at any moment he was going to change his mind.

"The blacksmith." Levi pointed to the right. "Crocker's." He pointed ahead.

Allison swallowed a lump in her throat. They walked on; he seemed determined to go through with his idea of them getting married. Maybe he was thinking about how to make it happen in this small town. Maybe he was waiting for her to change her mind.

"Why don't you stay here with the mule and Patch, and I'll go check Crocker's for notices or mail."

Allison nodded in agreement. She felt ragged in appearance and soul.

From the outskirts of town, she noticed people walking among the buildings. Was anything familiar? The buckskins, the way the men carried their guns, the women in homespun dresses…

"Allison." Levi's voice made her jump.

Frowning, he reached out and touched her arm. "I'm sorry. There were no notices or mail or bulletins about you."

She opened her mouth and closed it again.

"Follow me, back behind this building." They came up behind a whitewashed wood building, and Levi tied the mule to a post. He stepped up into the building and Allison followed. A gray-haired woman was rubbing oil over some dark wooden pews. She looked up at them and stared.

"Is the reverend in, ma'am?" Levi said, taking his hat off.

"He's not far," she said, returning to her work.

"We'd like to get married." His voice faltered.

"And you probably want to get married right this minute?" she said, shaking her head.

"Yes, ma'am."

"It'll be two bits," she said rudely, and moved out from the pews.

"Yes, ma'am." He swallowed hard.

"Just give me a minute. Heaven forbid you young people have to wait for something." She waddled down the center aisle.

Allison hung back, and Levi turned to her, likely checking she wasn't already out the door.

She bit the skin of her dried and chapped lips. *Why, oh why, did I agree to this?* Levi's eyes were closed; he was most likely praying for deliverance.

He scratched his neck. It looked red and patchy. "I was thinking about you agreeing to make me miserable," he said, facing her, attempting a smile.

"I know," she said, breathlessly. "Levi, I…"

"Hello, young people." A tall man wearing a threadbare jacket came toward them. "Wanting to get hitched, I hear. Well, that's a fine thing, it is. Marriage, ya' know. No need to explain your reasons. Lots of folks get married and live through it…ha!" He slapped Levi on the back. "Did the missus tell you it would be two bits?" He stuck his hand out, and Levi dropped the coin in. "Come right up, and stand here." The reverend grabbed his Bible and opened it up. Allison removed her burgundy gloves and held them tight. *Oh, Mama…*the words brought comfort. *Forgive me.*

Confused as to why the minister held his Bible open but never read from it, she couldn't concentrate on one thing he said. The words *I do* floated out when he posed the question to her, and she heard Levi faintly say the same thing.

"I have no ring," Levi said in response to the minister's prompting.

"We're getting it tomorrow." The words flew out of her mouth.

The reverend shrugged, pronouncing them man and wife and wiping beads of sweat from his brow. "Good luck, son." He slapped Levi on the back again. As they turned to walk out, Allison heard him say, "You're going to need it." The gray-haired woman shook her head as they passed.

Once outside, Allison took a deep breath. Searching up and down the boardwalks of Ready Springs, she felt disappointed. Each storefront looked like something from an Indian village. She was afraid to ask which one was the hotel. "Levi." Trying to keep her voice steady, she asked, "Is this all of the town?"

"This is it." He turned to untie the mule. "Let's find out about this hotel. I can get you a room and then I can find my parents."

"I would love to freshen up." *And be alone when the tears start.*

They walked across the empty dirt road, retied the mule, and walked to Crocker's. A mixture of smells overcame Allison—cinnamon and every other kind of spice. The old wood floor creaked at their steps. There was a large counter with jars and bins of every kind, and rows and rows of shelves behind it. In a corner, women's clothes hung from a rack. Tables of folded shirts and trousers and bolts of fabric and burlap occupied one wall.

"Here's the notice board." Levi interrupted Allison's thoughts. "You might want to look for yourself."

"Thank you." She studied the notices: the date each month the law would be in town…someone selling a buckboard…a widows' meeting at the church on Tuesdays. Levi was right. This little town was not the answer. She wandered over to the corner, drawn to touch and handle the different fabrics. Levi was looking around in another area filled with skins and pelts. A small counter there held a scale.

Allison overheard the storekeeper speaking condescendingly to a man trying to return an ax. The man was pointing to the ax, trying to communicate in French and broken English. The storekeeper kept putting his hand up and shaking his head. How unfortunate that they couldn't communicate. Walking away from the fabric, she approached a few steps closer.

"He's saying he never had a chance to use it," she interrupted. "*Monsieur, puisje peut vous aider?*" Allison said to the agitated man.

"*Merci, merci! Cet sscrot. Je veux que vous me rendez mon argent. Cette hache… c'est defecteuse!*" The man's eyes were wide.

She nodded her understanding, and turned to the man behind the counter. "This man deserves his money back. He's been trying to tell you he never got to use the ax. It fell apart. You look like an honest storekeeper—can't you tell by looking at it that it's not used?"

"*Preferzvous vote argent, ou une nouvelle hache??*" Allison said to the man with the ax.

"*Rendezvous mon argent, s'il vous plait.*" he said.

"He would like you to please refund him the money he paid. You can have the ax back." She waited, looking expectantly at the storekeeper.

"I don't know where you just waltzed in from, lady, but this is my store, and I decide."

"Well, I can assure you I would never aid a man who was trying to do you or your business harm. It seems a satisfied customer would refer his family and friends to your store. And I note a bit of German in your voice. Surely you must have some compassion for those who are not as eloquent in English as you are."

Angrily, Rolf Crocker pulled a lever on his cash register and handed the man his money back.

"*Merci, Merci de votre aide.*" The happy man bowed to Allison.

Levi gestured for her to come his way. They stepped out onto the wooden sidewalk.

"You speak French?" he asked.

"I do." Allison chewed on her fingernail. "It just came out naturally. It seems that I know certain things, but I don't know any important things."

"That was Rolf Crocker you were challenging. He doesn't budge for anyone. You had him spinning." He chuckled. "Just like me." Levi pulled off his hat and scratched his long hair. "I think this day has contained about as much as I can take. I'll go back in and get your room…oh, Lord." Levi reached out and gripped her by the arm. "My parents."

24

As soon as Mr. Graham saw them, he smiled and waved. Allison immediately saw the resemblance to Ben. He was tall and lanky, an older, more worn version of his youngest son. Their mother came up quickly and wrapped her arms around Levi.

"I can't believe you're in town! Bless my soul!" She pulled him back, gawking. "Your hair is so long!" She ruffled his curls, once carefully tucked behind his ears.

"All right, all right." Levi smoothed his hair back. "I'll get it cut before I leave. Pa." He stuck out his hand, and the men shook.

"You look good, son. Healthy enough."

"Yes, sir, I'm doing all right."

"Your ma was about to make me take her to Sault Creek if you didn't show up soon. You saved me a trip."

"Oh, James." His mother pulled on his arm. "I knew we'd see him before the snow flies."

Levi took a deep breath and moved to reveal the hiding Allison.

"Ma, Pa, I want to introduce you to Allison…my… wife."

Allison looked up just in time to see the very thing she dreaded with all her being. This sweet mother had just been injured by her own son.

"What? Did you say *wife?*" Mrs. Graham looked confused.

"No wonder you've been hiding." His father smiled. "Hello, Allison. Please call me James. This is Mrs. Graham."

"Please call me Laura, dear." She squeezed Allison's hand.

Allison wanted to apologize a thousand ways. No wonder Levi didn't want to dishonor his parents—but why would he risk hurting them?

"I take it the Coxes and Ben didn't cross paths with you," Levi said.

"No, why?" Laura said, brows creasing.

"Well, they had all met Allison, and I thought maybe they had told you about her."

"This is the first we'd heard. You can understand how it's a bit shocking, can't you?" Laura said, half smiling.

"Yes, of course. Levi has spoken so highly of you both. It's a pleasure to finally meet you."

"How long have you two known each other?" James asked.

"Just a month or so," Levi said. "It's an interesting—well, unfortunate—but happy story." Allison understood why he was fumbling. "Maybe we could meet for supper and talk more. I promised Allison a chance to clean up."

"James, the key!" Laura bumped James' arm. "We want to give you our room. Crocker built some rooms back behind the store. He calls it Crocker Hotel. We'd already had an invitation to stay at the Nelsons. You take our room, and we'll meet you for supper. The café at six."

"No, no, Ma." He pushed the key back. "We don't want to take your room. We'll get another one."

"We got the last room for tonight, though. Rolf told us Ready Spring is excited to have a hotel." Laura said, smiling.

"How many rooms does he have?" Allison asked.

"Four." James nodded toward Laura. "We insist. Your mother hadn't given our regrets to the Nelsons yet, so the ladies will be happy."

Allison held her breath, hoping to have the room.

"It's our wedding present to you." Laura took her son's hand and placed the key into it.

"Thank you so much." Allison beamed at her before Levi could refuse.

Patch picked the perfect time to beg for attention.

"Hey, Patch." James knelt and greeted the dog.

"God's been at work in other ways, too." Laura winked at Levi and gestured at James.

"Allison," Levi said, "would you like to go on to the room, and I'll take a few minutes here with my pelts?"

"Yes, thank you." Laura walked Allison to the edge of the storefront and pointed out a long rectangular building with four doors.

"Number four."

At Crocker's, Levi let out a relieved breath, thankful to do his trading without Allison. An hour later, he looked down at the ledger of credit Rolf had given him. He hid his disappointment as his father came near.

"How did the trading go?" James asked.

"Well enough for now." He didn't want to tell his father about the stolen furs.

"Your mother insisted on getting a few things for Allison." He handed Levi a string wrapped brown paper package.

"Ma," Levi turned to her. "You didn't have to do this. First the room and now presents."

"Levi, just say thank you." She tilted her head and corrected him with her eyes. "You never let anyone do anything for you. That's why I didn't bother to ask what she would like."

Levi knew she was right to put him in his place. "Thank you, Ma."

Allison saw a young man waiting to take horses or luggage for the hotel guests. *Rooms* would be a better word than *hotel*, not to mislead folks like herself. She approached him and asked about getting warm water for a bath. In room four, there was a lovely old brass bed with a simple pink and blue quilt. In one corner sat a small woodstove; in the other, a bench and a rocking chair. Lacy curtains hung over the window. It was just a small room, but it was clean, and it smelled like new-cut wood. The young man brought in a tub and placed it beside the bed. Within a few minutes, he had it filled. She locked the door and dropped her clothes. Like pure heaven, the hot water caressed her weary skin. Sinking in as low as possible, she leaned her head back. Within minutes, she had drifted asleep.

❧❧

"Allison." Levi knocked a bit harder. He wondered for a split second if she had left him. There didn't seem to be anyone inside. He stepped back, swallowing his rising fear. She may not be in there—but then he heard the lock turn and the door opened a small crack. He started to enter the room.

"No, wait." She pushed back on the door. "I was in the tub."

Levi breathed out in relief. "Alright. But take this—it's from my mother." Hiding herself behind the door, she stuck her hand out and grabbed the package. She closed the door quickly, and he turned to find some shade.

The door creaked open another crack. "Levi! These are for me?"

"Yes," he said, not knowing what was in the package. The door closed again. He waited and finally went to check on Patch, who was asleep under a tree.

"You may come in," she said the next time he knocked. As he stepped in, his stomach flipped. She looked completely different. His jaw moved back and forth, but no words formed. Why was the room so muggy?

"Look at this dress!" She stepped closer, raising her arms. "It fits me perfectly. Your mother was so kind to think of me. And for someone who only raised boys, she has such exquisite taste." Levi noticed that the blue flowers on the dress brought out the softness in her eyes.

"And this! For pity sakes!" She lifted a bonnet off the bed. "Being without a bonnet has been like you being without a hat. It's just so kind of her."

Levi wished he'd thought of it first. The more citified she looked, the less likely she'd want anything to do with him. *Who am I kidding? Married or not, she won't agree to come back to Sault Creek with me.*

"Levi, what's wrong?" She dropped the bonnet on the bed. "You're mad about something."

"No, I'm not mad." He shuffled his feet. "I just wish I had done all this for you."

"I'm glad you didn't." She walked over and picked up another piece of something. "This is from your mother." She held up a soft white gown with pink satin ribbons gathered at the top. He realized it was a nightgown and looked away.

"This purchase, coming from you, would be completely unbefitting of our agreement." She smiled at him. Heat began to rise through his body, getting stuck in his throat.

"And it smells splendid." She held it up to her face and took another breath. "Not like the woods. It's store-bought. It smells store-bought." She stepped forward and held it out to him. "Smell it. Really, it's wonderful."

He stared at her, unmoving.

"All right." She turned back to the bed. "You wouldn't understand, anyway."

Levi sat on the rocker. "You're right," he said in a low voice, leaning forward with his face in his hands. "I don't understand how we're going to do this." He shook his head, running his hands through his hair.

Allison sat on the edge of the bed. "It's your parents. I can see how they love you so. I felt your discomfort in trying to explain me. Are you going to tell them everything? Have they asked yet how long we've been married?"

"Not yet," he mumbled to the floor.

"What do you want to do?" she asked softly.

"I want to get my peace back," he huffed.

"What does that mean? The way things were before I interrupted your harmonious life?"

He couldn't lie, she was on to something.

"I can move on, Levi. I don't have to go back with you. Is there a stage or boat or something from here?" She began to pace, talking faster. "You were the one who said we should get married. You said in the church you were joking about me agreeing to make you miserable. I knew you hadn't thought it out. You were trying to do the right thing, but it doesn't sound like it was the right thing for you. No one wants to live a life without peace. And I for sure don't want"

Levi grabbed her hand as she walked by. He pulled her in front of him, reaching for her other hand.

"Allison," he said softly, looking up. "It's not you. I don't get my peace from you. God is my only source of peace. He just puts me in situations that force me to turn to Him and Him alone. And this feels like one of those situations. God's peace didn't go anywhere. I've been distracted." He let go of her hands and touched the satin cream ribbon at the waist of her new dress. Allison stilled as he fingered the fabric. He had promised himself this was just a convenient agreement. *Lord help me, what a mess.* He dropped his hands. "I've just been distracted," Levi repeated, sucking in a deep breath. Leaning back in the rocker, he raked his hands again through his scraggly locks. "That's my problem."

25

~~~

Levi stood at the door of Crocker's Hotel, room four, and glanced back at Allison. "I'm going for a haircut and shave. I'll be back in about an hour, and we'll meet up with my folks."

Allison nodded a silent agreement and began to straighten up their things lying around the room. Their things, their room. This was craziness. Sitting on the edge of the bed, she picked up the new bonnet and let out a long sigh. Where was Levi sleeping tonight? Why hadn't he said anything? After what just happened in the rocking chair, for pity sakes—he made her insides go to mush. *I'm not really a married woman. I certainly don't feel like a married woman.* She flopped back on the bed and pulled out a hairbrush that was poking her back. *This bed is wonderful. And Levi is going to sleep on the hard floor? Or with the mule?* She flashed back to the memories of sleeping next to him at Clemet Summer's place. It had been so warm and safe. She knew the long looks he gave her. Sometimes she had caught Ben looking at her that way. She remembered what Thelma had said; men didn't want a reason to stay warm or safe; they wanted more. Clapping her hand to her forehead, she tried to shut down her thoughts. Ben was like a brother she'd never had— well, not that she could remember. Levi was older and more protective. A provider. Allison sat up, realizing that she'd never asked him how it went at Crocker's. Was he discouraged from having so few pelts to sell? Probably wondering how he could feed both of them? She pulled the roll of bills from her reticule, then tapped her lip. How could she get him to take her money? She glanced over at his things on the bench. Could she sneak the cash into something? No, he would know it was hers. She picked up the brush, calming herself with long strokes of her hair. *Levi claims his peace is from God alone. I wonder what that would feel like.*

"Allison." Levi knocked on the door.

"Yes, I'm ready," She smoothed her hair and carefully tied her bonnet. Opening the door, she sucked in a quick breath. "Levi, you look so different." She always thought him handsome, but he looked so clean...so neat.

"You're looking at me like I'm missing my nose." He ran his hand over his smooth jaw.

She laughed nervously. "Your nose is certainly there, but your curls are gone."

"It all grows back." He wanted to change the subject, starting to feel uncomfortable. "Your bonnet is...nice. It matches your dress."

"You can't begin to know how hard it's been for me to be without one. I'm probably as dark as a plum." She waited for him to contradict her. Instead, there was just awkward silence.

"I feel as if I should bring your mother a gift."

"Why? She doesn't want anything. She likes doing things for people."

"No, more like a hostess gift. If we were invited to your home, I would bring a small gift."

He gave her another blank stare. "Can we just go?" He was obviously still in a sour mood. "Let's just get this over with."

Allison walked out with him, conflicted. Neither one of them had thought this charade would be so difficult.

"Hello, hello!" Laura waved at them. "We picked a table outside since the evening was so beautiful."

Perfect, Levi thought. *As soon as the sun sets, we can go.*

"Mrs. Graham...Laura." Allison stood at the corner of the table. "I can't thank you enough for the lovely things. I was able to take a bath this afternoon and put on these wonderful items. I almost feel like a new woman."

Levi gave her a quick glance.

"You're the most handsome couple ever." Laura smiled. "It's wonderful to see you again, son." She gave Levi a quick wink.

He dropped his hat and ran his hand through his shortened locks. "Glad you like it, Ma."

Once seated, Allison stroked the cotton tablecloth. She stilled; it seemed familiar, and she wanted to keep that feeling.

"It's meatloaf tonight," James said.

Levi nodded. "Looks like we'll have four plates of meatloaf." He restlessly bounced his knees under the table, brushing against Allison's leg. "Sorry." He moved over a bit. "What brings you two to town?" he said, wanting to lead the conversation.

"I'm done with the mine," James said.

"That so?" Levi looked up at his pa.

"Yep, had some pain while breathing. Saw the doc last time we were in town, and he said I needed to get out of the mines. So we prayed about it and this was my last week there. This is a nice time to come to town, so here we are."

Allison squeezed Levi's forearm and leaned in close, whispering. "Did your father just say *doctor*?" He nodded and started to speak, but bit back his words as their meal arrived.

"Let's pray," he said.

At the conclusion of Levi's short prayer, she jerked her hand away from his.

"Are you all right, dear?" Laura asked.

"Yes," she said. "There was a bee." But she glared at Levi when he glanced up from his food. Finally, he realized she was upset about something.

"Could you walk with me a minute?" Allison said.

"Can we walk after we eat?" Levi had no intention of leaving this warm meal.

Allison worked her way off the bench.

"I'll be back," Levi said to his parents.

Once they were out of hearing range, she spun on him. "No doctor. Did you not tell me Ready Springs has no doctor? Please tell me the truth, Levi Graham!"

"I didn't know of any doctor. I'm not privy to what comes and goes in this town. And don't go calling me Levi Graham."

"Did you not hear your father say he saw the doctor last time he was in town? Did he mean this town?"

"I think that's what he meant. Instead of having a fit over it, why didn't you just ask him?"

She turned on her heel to leave as Levi grabbed her upper arm.

"Stop it, Allison." He easily pulled her in. "You're treating me like I lied to you. We're going back to supper. You can ask my pa about the doctor. I have no reason to keep that from you. I don't know this doctor my pa is talking about."

She shook free of his grip, her chin twitching. He prayed she wouldn't cry. Only that could make this night worse.

They mostly ate in silence, their little interruption having put a damper on everyone's conversation. Levi and his father talked about the weather and hunting. Laura commented on the meal and talked about little Miranda, Levi's niece.

"They're expecting another one. Probably by Thanksgiving."

"That's great." Levi nodded.

"We'd love to have you join us for Thanksgiving. Unless you've made arrangements with Allison's family?" Laura asked.

Levi took a large bite of potatoes.

"We would look forward to that," Allison said, filling the gap in conversation.

"Or certainly, invite them also," James piped in.

"Why, yes, that would be wonderful," Laura agreed.

"Thank you, you are so hospitable. Unfortunately…"

"They are too far from here to make it." Levi saved Allison from bumbling. "Ben will be working at the Von Keller's dairy farm. You could send him a post, he might be able to make it."

"Well, good for him," James grinned.

Levi stretched. "It's getting late."

"Don't you want a piece of pie?" his mother asked.

"I think we better turn in early," he said. "We'll be heading home in the morning. We can meet back here for some breakfast."

"All right," Laura said as they all stood up.

Levi rounded the table and hugged his mother. "Goodnight."

"Goodnight, my love, sleep…well," she mumbled, clasping her hand over her mouth. "I just can't believe you're married!"

They walked silently to Room Four and stopped outside.

"Just toss a pillow on the bench." Levi finally broke the awkward silence. "I'll wait out here and check on Patch. You take the bed, go to sleep, and then I'll come in."

"You're going to sleep on the bench?"

He wondered if she might be hinting at something. His mouth went dry.

"I can sleep anywhere," he said slowly.

She watched him a second too long, and something soft flickered in her eyes. "I'm sorry about tonight. I don't think you're a liar."

"I forgive you," he said, locking eyes with hers. "Trust me, I would have brought you here straight away. This town changes every time I come. I'm glad they have someone doctor'n now." He paused, twilight soften her face. "It worked to our advantage. My parents didn't seem to want to ask much about us. They must have known something was wrong."

Allison tilted her head and gave him a small nod. Her smile was inviting, her eyes tender, and she smelled like flowers. Heaven help him, he was going to reach for the door and push her in with him.

"Okay, then." She turned and let herself in, closing the door.

Levi paced around the barn behind Crocker's. He tried to pray. He even brushed down someone's horse, but he couldn't focus. The truth was, he hadn't been able to focus for weeks. Her voice, her smile, her company—even her brave scowls filled him with longing. *Why did my parents have to be here? Lord, what are you doing to me?* He entered the room quietly, then settled on the narrow bench for a long, restless night.

Allison awoke to a gorgeous morning. The window was half open, and the sun cast a bright light on the hardwood floors of her room. Yes, it was her room. Her home. Her grandmother was asleep in the next room, rattling the walls with her familiar snoring. She ran her hands over the brown and cream quilt that had been on her bed for years. The mattress was soft, the pillow too wonderful to move from. She looked up—there was her wardrobe, her dresses. All her things were lined up, in perfect order. *I'm home, my home. Grandmother's home, Uncle…* Allison pushed herself up as she sensed something moving. From the corner of her eye, she saw Uncle Simon suddenly appear from the thick brown curtains. His face was pale and sickly, and he growled from the back of his throat. *What are you doing here?* she screamed, but no sound came from her mouth. Flinging off the bedding, she ran for the door, but he had her by the neck, yanking her back. She opened her mouth to scream again, but only silent air came out. He pulled her by the neck and tried to push her out her window. Thank goodness, it was half closed. He let go with one hand and tried to yank the window up. *Grandmother,* she screamed, yet again no sound would come out. He clasped his hands around her neck and slammed her hard against the glass. She knew she was going to die as he reared back to slam her body once more. This time Allison felt the shards of glass rip through her back as she fell backward…falling…falling…

"Allison, hush. Allison, please wake up." Levi shook her, and she flew up and almost knocked him off the bed.

"What are you doing? Why are you on the bed?" She pushed him back, grabbing for the covers.

"Hold on, these walls are thin. You were crying out so loud, I had to wake you up."

"Oh, my Lord…" She swung her feet to the floor and stood up. "It was my Uncle Simon."

Levi struck a match and lit the oil lamp. "Do you remember something?"

Allison turned her back to him. She was wearing the soft white gown he had seen earlier.

"Look at my back," she whimpered. She pulled loose the soft pink ribbon and the gown fell from her shoulders.

"No," he said. "You must have had a bad dream. Can you just go back to sleep?"

"Please. I need you to look. Do I have cuts and scars on my back?" she choked out.

Levi shook his head, wondering if she was still dreaming. He moved her closer to the light and gently pulled the fabric away from her bare back.

"I...I don't see anything. Your skin is smooth." He averted his eyes as soon as he could.

She turned around and cinched up the gown in the front. "It was a nightmare. A terrible, awful nightmare. My Uncle Simon pushed me out of an upstairs window."

"I'm sorry, Allison. Can you get back in bed?" He pulled the covers back for her. The sooner he could get back to his bench, the better.

"No, Levi." She whimpered, rubbing her eyes. "It wasn't just a nightmare." She sat back in bed and pulled up the covers.

"But it was. You've been asleep." He gently tucked a lock of hair behind her ear.

"No. I mean, I think it was my Uncle Simon who pushed me. But before that, I was in my room at home. It was a wonderful room with a soft bed, the room I grew up in. I lived with my grandmother when I wasn't at school."

Levi sat on the corner of the bed and scratched the back of his head. "You think maybe sleeping here in this soft bed brought on that dream?"

Allison dropped her head, defeated. "I don't think it was just a dream. I think it was real. I think what I saw is from my true life."

"All right, but I still think we should try to go back to sleep."

"What if I can't remember these things in the morning?"

"I'll help you. A grandmother, an uncle, the room." He bent and blew out the light. Being this close to her in her white gown— it was too much. He slumped back to his bench and squeezed his pillow.

⤇⤆

Allison tossed back and forth, and just as Levi closed his eyes, he heard her speaking softly, imploringly.

"I can't do it. I need the light on. I can still see his face. Please, Levi." She sat up.

He got back up and lit the lamp.

"I'm really scared. It was so real. Did I tell you my room was upstairs?"

Levi rubbed his eyes and sat on the end of the bed. "Maybe it was your uncle who pushed you off that ledge when I found you." *This is a bad way to fall back asleep,* he thought. "Do you have any happy memories? Tell me those."

Allison rubbed the crease between her brows and mumbled. "Taking a bath by myself in Sault Creek. You teaching me poker. Miss Thelma's cooking."

He nodded with a half-smile. All those things were from recent days. He thought she would remember others from her past. Maybe she hadn't been as miserable at the cabin as he thought.

"My...my favorite book was one about the Palace of Versailles. There were actually photographs of the inside. Everything covered in gold, the opulence was beyond imagination. The gardens and the fountains..." She looked up, "I could spend hours in that book."

Levi stifled a yawn, "Where was this palace?"

"Outside of Paris." She could tell he wasn't following. "You know, Louie Louis XlV?"

"That explains why you speak French."

"Yes!" Her eyes lit up. "I started speaking French, and some memories started coming back. I also remember..."

"Hey, Allison, you sound better." He knew her excitement could be heard through the thin walls. "In a few hours, the sun will be up, and we can talk some more. Can we go to bed—for now?"

She ignored him, her brows furrowed. "Somehow talking like this feels familiar. In the night....so personal...I seem to...yes...yes...Webster School for Young Women...my roommate was...Suzanne!"

"Shhh," Levi spoke soft and slow. "Please. As long as you don't remember sharing a room or a bed with a man, can we turn out the light?"

Allison pulled her covers tight and kicked his knee off the bed.

"I've only waited for months to have some memories. Go ahead and turn out the light, then."

Levi was being a clod and he knew it, but any minute she was going to remember everything and they would be up all night sorting it out. If she remembered everything, they'd have to start figuring out how to get her home. He had promised—but how long would they be gone? He watched her struggling to sleep, his heart beating like it did just before he pulled the trigger. *Everything's about to change. Why do I feel like I've just been punched in the gut?*

26

Levi awoke the next morning, rubbing his stiff neck. Sleeping on a narrow bench was for the birds. He knew he shouldn't stare, but watching Allison was engaging. One bare foot hung off the bed. He stretched out his leg and tapped the foot with his big toe. She pulled it in and curled up in a ball. Her hair streamed loosely around the pillow, and her hands were pulled up under her chin. A rare sight—Allison at peace. Now he'd seen those perfect legs and beautiful back—did she know what it did to him, how it tormented him?

Allison rolled over and flopped her arms above her head, arching her back with eyes closed. Levi wondered if he shouldn't just run back to Sault Creek as fast as he could. How could his desire for a simple life have gotten so complicated? Maybe he was going to wake up, and this would be his own version of a strange dream.

"What are you doing? Have you been sitting there watching me sleep?" Allison pulled the covers up to her chin.

He shook his head. She didn't deserve an answer. She always judged him wayward without cause.

"Can you be ready in a few minutes?" He grabbed his boots and headed toward the door. "I'm sure my folks have been up since dawn, and they're laughing, wondering why we're so late." He rolled his eyes and swung open the door, slamming it behind him harder than necessary.

Another foul mood—was she up half the night, like I was? Or maybe she's dreading another awkward meal with my parents? Well, her memory's returning for good now. I promised to return her home, but I never expected we'd end up married. What a fine kettle of fish! I wouldn't be surprised if she's planning her escape. Lord, if you can help me get through this morning with patience, it will be to your glory.

Levi found his parents at the little restaurant, and sat while the waitress poured coffee. Laura smiled and looked over his shoulder, waving Allison over to the table. *I should have waited for her.* She looked pretty in her new dress and bonnet, and she nodded at him. He swallowed hard.

"Did you sleep well, Allison?" Laura asked.

"Yes, thank you. The bed was heaven." She snapped her lips together, glancing at Levi as his jaw stiffened.

James stood and held out a chair for Allison. "That's just what Rolf would like to hear. People traveling in and out of Ready Springs want a good night's sleep. Creates more business for him."

A woman wearing a large canvas apron set a platter of eggs and biscuits and a bowl of gravy on the table. Allison ordered coffee, and the family held hands to pray. Levi let go of her hand quickly and held out the eggs to her.

"They look wonderful," she said.

Levi watched out of the corner of his eye as Allison delicately held her fork. *Her small bites wouldn't keep a bird alive. We're so different.* He brushed some falling pine needles off the table. "Clearing his throat, he asked his father, "What are your plans now that you're not at the mine? What did the doctor tell you?"

"He said I needed to get out of the ground. So I'm going to work a couple days a week in the mine store. I know I pushed you toward the mines, but you were right to do it your own way."

Levi swallowed a large bite. What did he just hear? His father saying he was right for going his own way? He felt speechless.

They all glanced at each other with an awkward silence. "You know, son, your ma read her Bible, and I always thought that was nice for her. Good things, those Bible stories, to keep you boys on the straight and narrow. I even sat through a decade of Sunday sermons, most of them I could catch a good nap through," James chuckled.

"But a while back, I had a dream." Something caught in the back of James' throat. "And in this silly dream, I was outside on the porch, sensing a large wind was coming. I could see it, and it made me panic inside. I tried to get the cabin door open, but the pressure of the wind kept me from opening it. I went to bang on the window, and I could see you kids gathered around the table with your ma. The wind was loud, and you couldn't hear me. I needed to get in the house. I knew I was going to be overtaken by the wind and I yelled, and all of a sudden, the wind hit the cabin, took the roof right off. Suddenly your ma and you kids were gone. It happened so fast, I didn't even really see it. You were just all gone. I knew in an instant I was left alone. I sat up from that silly dream with my heart beating out of my chest." James shook his head, chuckling.

"I was so unsettled, I had to get up and get a drink of water. I sat down at the table to catch my breath and looked at your ma's Bible. She had left it open to Amos. I just was going to glance at it for a minute and then this verse…I'll have to read it." He pulled a piece of paper from his pocket. "I had to write it down, listen. Amos 4:13, 'For, lo, He that formeth the mountains, and createth the wind, and declareth unto man what is his thought, that maketh the morning darkness, and treadeth upon the high places of the earth, The LORD, The God of hosts, is His name.' *He createth the wind.* It took my breath away…it really did."

Levi nodded, trying to take in his father's experience.

"I knew instantly that dream was from God. I've been on the outside long enough. I bowed my head right there, in the dawn of the morning. I asked God to forgive me." His voice cracked, and James shook his head.

"I'd been a prideful man. A man who didn't need anything from God. A man who carried more faith in himself than the Almighty."

Levi swallowed, pressing his lips in a thin line. He shot a quick glance at his mother, who gazed at James with love and admiration.

"I don't know what it is," James continued. "I've heard men stronger than I am say they've made their peace with God. I guess I did, too." He pulled out his handkerchief and ran it across his face. "I knew out of my boys, you would understand."

"I think God enjoys coming off the page." Levi locked eyes with his pa. "Thank you for telling me. I know that was a hard thing, but when we go from here…we go together."

"Amen," Laura said softly.

Allison followed Levi down the sidewalk to Crocker's Store, deep in thought. These people had profound faith. She could see herself in James's words—always relying on her own strength. Many an angry teacher at school had called her prideful and arrogant. Allison rubbed her temples; the fitful sleep and emotional morning had caused a headache. Levi turned to approach Room Four.

"I'd like to get these provisions back to Sault Creek." He looked to the ground. "I guess the question is…are you coming with me?"

27

Levi didn't want to hear her answer, but grabbed their things and started to pack. "When I found you, I had no idea if you were even going to live. You looked bad. I didn't know what to do. I still don't know what to do." He pulled hard on the pack buckles and threw it over his shoulder. "So if you have a plan, tell me now. Otherwise, we're heading back to Sault Creek."

"I don't have a plan." She rubbed her forehead. "I hoped you would help me sort out my memories."

"I will." He nodded. "I just didn't know that it would be so soon. I need time to prepare and I...we...have the cabin to think of." He held his breath. Would she go back with him?

"May I stop in for a few personal things at Crocker's before we go?"

He would give her anything if she would return with him. "I have just about this much room on the mule." He held his hands out to make a square. "No china or feather mattresses."

He was rewarded with a small smile.

Allison walked back into Crocker's store and gave a quick nod to a tall bald man with glasses. She scanned the store, thankful Mr. Crocker was nowhere in sight. Last time she was here, she was in a thick fog of confusion and hopefulness. This morning, sudden clarity seemed bestowed to her. Keeping in mind Levi's load requirement, she gathered up as many things as she could. She set them on the counter and asked for a box of tea. She pulled out her money from her reticule and realized there was a huge problem.

"I can't break a twenty dollar bill." The man sneered at her as he looked over his glasses at what was in her hand. "What are you doing caring around that much money?"

"My financial means are none of your business." Allison shot back. She assessed her waiting purchases and remembered Levi had told her to put her things on his account.

"I'm Mrs. Graham." It felt like a lie. "Take away the amount owned from these things and give the balance to Levi Graham's account."

"He's not in the hole that much!" The clerk pulled out a ledger book and flipped open to his page. "I still can't give you change. That would take everything out of my till, lady."

"I know," Allison said. "He'll have a positive balance. When he comes in next, he will have a credit. Do you understand how that works?"

"I know how it works, but nobody around here leaves that kinda money on the books. We're not running a bank here."

"Is there a bank in Ready Springs?"

"No."

"Then it looks like this will have to do. Do you need help subtracting my purchases and his debt?"

"No."

"Wonderful." Allison smiled. "Please go ahead and do that, and I'll want a receipt with the remaining balance to give to my husband. Signed by you, of course."

The clerk glared at her and licked the end of his pencil. She watched over his sums carefully, now delighted she had found a way around Levi not taking her money. This was perfect. The clerk signed the bottom of the receipt and handed it to her.

"You must have been a fine student. Your arithmetic was well done," she said, accepting the paper.

"Thank you." He pushed his glasses up from the end of his nose. "You're really married to Levi Graham?"

"I am." Allison smiled, knowing he was having trouble adding that information up. "Now, I need these things wrapped very tight. I'll hold them together while you tie the string."

Levi thought about the wagon his ma and pa had left in. It was sturdy, and they'd had it for years. He couldn't expect Allison to walk everywhere. He would need to think seriously about at least purchasing a horse. His world had always been fine without one, but things were changing. He thought about the trail they were about to take. A small buggy would probably make it.

"What do you think?" She smiled, stepping off the sidewalk toward him.

"I think something about shopping makes you pleased with yourself."

She held up her compact purchases. "Not over the weight and space requirements, as I promised."

Levi smiled and tied the package to the mule. "After your conversation with Crocker yesterday, I wondered if he would do business with you." He jerked the mule forward and whistled at Patch. He glanced back over his shoulder at her, and she hurried up to walk next to him.

"Truth is, it was another clerk who helped me."

"That's good." He chewed his lip. It seemed as if he was in a different life, walking away with this beautiful young woman.

"I did have to tell him I was your wife."

He grinned, while something flipped deep in his gut. Would she *ever* want more than an agreement? There was no question he wanted more. She could have pitched a fit this morning and insisted they head toward her home. Yet now they were walking side by side down the road. Back home... to his home, his life.

Allison amazed herself. After the excitement and newness of Ready Springs, this last hour of walking in silence was deeply needed. The forest beckoned her back to its tranquility. Levi seemed to need it, too. He often looked over and grinned at her, but said nothing. *When there's peace between us, it's so sweet,* she thought. *Oh, Grandmother, what would you say to all this? And what would you say if you knew what Uncle Simon did to me? Would you believe him or*

me? She pondered her life back in Madison. Could she go back to sipping tea in the dining room, shopping, taking grandmother to lunch at the hotel, the weekly trek to the library? Did she want to return to Mrs. Webster's for a teaching position? Nothing about her past held any appeal. Would she ever feel safe in the same room with Uncle Simon again? Levi always made her feel safe. In all her complaining and feeling like an outsider, these last months had roused her soul like nothing she had ever known.

She watched Levi out of the corner of her eye. *What would it feel like to shake his hand goodbye, to turn away from the depths of those warm brown eyes forever? Not to have him reach for my hand at the table as he prays? Could I ever forget the way he picked me up and carried me for miles? How he rakes his hands through his thick curls when he's frustrated? How it feels to have someone to sleep next to?* A peculiar heat rose up her face.

Levi glanced over as Allison adjusted her bonnet.

"It's almost all shade, if you want to take the bonnet off."

"No, no." She looked away from him, knowing her face was red as a beet.

He brought the mule to a stop. "We need a break for water." He reached for the canteen. "I want to hear what things you've remembered." He poured some water into a cup and handed it to her. Allison took a drink. It wasn't a problem to recite her new memories; the problem was, now what did she want to do?

"Do you want to ride the mule for a while?"

She looked at the poor animal's heavy load. "No, I can keep going. Can we talk at the next stop?"

"Of course."

She didn't mean to keep him wondering. He needed answers. But this time, she needed to gather her wits. She had waited for so long to have some memories, thinking they would set everything right. She sighed; could she trust these new feelings?

"Is everything okay?" he asked.

Allison glanced up from the trail. "Yes, I think so."

"There are some rocks here, to avoid the creek bed mud." Levi held out his hand. He steadied her steps as she walked on the big rocks and he and the mule walked through the mud. When they reached the other side, he kept his hand clutched to hers, and she could feel her insides fluttering.

"Why are you so quiet?" He bumped their hands against her dress.

"Why are you holding my hand?"

He smiled at her. "You go first, and then I'll answer."

"I'm quiet…" She reached with her free hand and scratched her neck. "Because I have so much now to think about. I don't know what to do next." She nodded for him to go.

"I'm holding your hand because I want to help you. With anything you need." His smile was very charming.

She couldn't resist smiling back, but she let go of his hand. "I'm not used to that. I watched your parents. They almost never stopped touching you. Your father patted your back, gripped your neck several times. Your mother squeezed your arm, rubbed your shoulders. If you were near her, she was lovingly touching you. Almost constantly."

"You have my permission to do the same." He laughed and dodged her swatting. "But why aren't you used to it?" His question sobered the mood.

She glanced out to the trees. "My parents passed away when I was a child."

Levi stopped as the mule kept walking. "I'm sorry. No wonder it was hard to remember their names."

"I was raised by my grandmother, my father's mother. From the time I was six, I spent most of the year at Webster's Boarding School for Young Women."

"Where is that?"

"About ten miles outside of Chicago."

"Chicago?" He shook his head. "You're from Chicago?"

"No, I'm from Madison, Wisconsin. I rode the train home at holidays."

Levi breathed in a whistle. "That's a far trek from here. Goodness." He looked up the trail.

"What about your dream last night? You said something about an uncle. You were confused and upset."

"I hope what I remember is correct, but I get terribly frightened when I talk about it. It seems too dreadful to be true. Oh, I don't know." She tried to shake the thoughts away.

"Don't be scared." He reached out and rubbed her back. "That might be enough for today." He moved his hand up and lightly rubbed the back of her neck as they walked side by side. "We'll figure it out together."

"Levi." She moved a step away so he couldn't tickle her ear.

"I was just trying to see a smile. You looked so sad." He held his offending hand up. "I did hear you. You said you're not used to being touched. I'm listening."

❦

After the sun hid low amidst the tall trees, Levi signaled for her to follow him off the trail.

"I know a place to stop for the night over here. It's got a couple of boulders to block anything coming up from the south." Allison followed, fatigue slowing her steps. "Just a bit farther," Levi said.

"Thank you for not picking Clemet Summers' cabin."

"You think sleeping outside is better?" He tied the mule to a tree.

She looked up. "As long as it doesn't rain."

He kicked around a few rocks to repair a broken fire circle, then grabbed twigs and bent to start a fire. "You can pull a blanket free and find some pine needles."

Allison knew if she went down she would never get up. "What can I do to help?"

"Let's eat something from a can—unless you want me to hunt?"

"No, a can is fine." She went to the canvas bags on the mule and pulled out a small, blackened pan, while Levi rolled a large log forward for them to sit on.

"Our cook was Mrs. Clark."

Levi looked up from opening the can and listened.

"She kept house, too. I remember it all now—the house, the people, the town. Like a dream, but one that I know is true."

Stirring the bubbling stew, Levi nodded, deep in thought.

Later, as they finished eating, Allison took a stick and smoothed out the dirt in front of them.

"If Sault Creek is here…" She marked a spot on the dirt with an X. "Where is Madison?"

❧

Levi's contentedness faded. Sitting here in the evening next to her, the last thing he wanted to talk about was how and when she could be on her way. He stood up and tossed the coffee from his cup, then took a deep breath and sat back down. He scribbled out her X. "This is north…Canada." He drew a long line. This is Lake Superior here. Lake Michigan here. Here is Chicago and here would be Madison. You and I, sitting right here on this log are a tiny dot…right here." He barely touched the ground with the stick.

"Oh, my." She saw the obvious problem.

"How do you think you got so far from home?" He threw the stick in the fire.

"My one and only true friend is Suzanne. Her family had invited me to spend the summer in Paris with them. My Uncle Simon was supposed to be taking me to New York to catch a ship, to join up with them."

Levi's brow creased. "And you didn't make it." He stood and paced around their little camp. "If your carriage had flipped or crashed, there would be pieces of it. If something had happened to your uncle, I would have seen buzzards circling him. But why were you left for dead at the bottom of that ravine?"

Allison gazed out to the darkening woods. "If I had to guess, it would be money. My Uncle Simon complained incessantly about my room and board at Webster's. I'm quite sure my grandmother's money covered it, but he always made her feel like she was wasting *his* money. For heaven's sake, I don't even know what his business is. He never explained, and frankly, I never cared. He always treated me as if I was in the way, never a civil word. He drank alcohol like you drink water."

Levi watched her pained expression, wanting to offer comfort.

"I knew something was wrong." Her voice quivered. "I ignored my feelings that he would do me harm. I knew I couldn't trust him. I knew he wouldn't just hand me money for this trip. I think my grandmother knew it, too." She dropped her gaze to the ground, and a small gulp slipped from her throat. "I just wanted it so badly. What a ridiculously naïve woman I am."

❧❧

With charged emotions, Levi wanted to wrap his arms around her, but he remembered her discomfort with touch and gripped his hands together. "I wish I could take away your tears, but I know I can't. The only thing I can promise you is that as long as I'm alive, I won't allow anyone to do you harm."

Allison stood and wiped the tears from her face. "Thank you, Levi." She walked over and took the gray blanket, then kicked a few pine needles into place and laid down. Patch came up and nosed his way into her cozy space. "No, Patch." She gently pushed him away. "I don't want to smell you all night."

The dog returned to Levi and received a good belly scratch. Levi looked over his shoulder and saw that Allison was already sound asleep. *From the beginning, Lord*, he prayed under his breath, *there was something about her.* It was more than feeling sorry for those bumps and bruises. More than a woman who needed rescuing. Like a faith and trust beyond what he'd ever known. God was doing something in his life through her. His pride needed to be crushed. But what about his heart? To love like Jesus was the hardest challenge yet. Only Jesus sacrificed his very life unto death. *Lord,* he whispered, *I have trouble just dying to my plans for the next week.* He shook his head. She looked so calm and peaceful now. *Lord, give her sweet sleep. Dreams of good and not evil, and rest for her mind and soul. Amen.*

Levi could feel it, that hour right before dawn when the cold comes down into the bones. The fire barely smoldered. He inched his body behind her, and pulling his blanket from beneath him, he laid it over her. She stirred, and he heard her whisper, "I'm so cold." Without permission, he pulled her back against himself. His arm came around and found her hands. She fit perfectly, like a bird in a nest, and sleep came on just like the new warmth.

28

Levi had a problem, besides the ache in his shoulder from not moving. He had Patch glued to his backside and Allison glued to his front. There was no Clemet Summers watching, but God and all of creation were. He shook his leg to get Patch to move first. The dog rose his head on cue, but quickly went back down. He tried to hold the blanket steady and remove his arm from Allison. He wondered if just leaping up might be the best way to look innocent. Her eyes began to blink open, and he bumped backward against Patch.

"Patch, get off me." He sat up quickly and left the blanket with Allison, who rolled up and pulled the blanket to her chin.

"Sorry about waking you up. I had Patch pinned next to me." He raked his hand through his short hair.

Wearily, Allison looked back at Patch, who tilted his head and blinked his blameless eyes at her. She held her hand out to Levi for help to stand, then winced when she swallowed. "Coffee."

"We're close," he heard her say behind him. Now familiar with the area around their cabin, she seemed to get a second wind. Even Patch ran ahead, knowing he was finally home.

Letting out a long breath, Levi looked around; everything seemed to be in the condition he had left it. He opened the door for Allison and began to unload the mule. She walked down to the flat rock by the creek, untying her boots and pulling off her stockings. Leaning back, she dropped her feet into the water and closed her eyes. An afternoon breeze pulled stray wisps of hair around her face. Levi couldn't help but stare. They were home. Their home together.

A bit later, Levi had stacked everything he could onto his shelves. He picked up Allison's jacket and reached to hang it on the hook. A piece of paper peeked out of her pocket; he opened it to find the receipt from Crocker's store. His eyes drifted over what she had bought, and he wondered how much he owed.

A credit due? That didn't make sense. A credit due of $11.75 was completely wrong. They had never made such errors in all the years he had been trading there. He saw his old balance and her new balance subtracted from twenty dollars. He shook his head, dropping the paper on the table and glancing out at Allison, resting on the rock. Her reticule lay on the table, and he opened it. There under the hankie and her burgundy gloves was a roll of cash. He pulled it apart to find four twenty dollar bills. She said she had money. She just never said how much. Good heavens…eighty dollars. She could have bought them both horses and a buggy. He'd told her all along he didn't want her money. She purposely went against him. She knew good and well how she felt about her paying for anything. Men provided. Maybe he didn't have a lot, but food and shelter were good enough for most people. *She's like two people. One person can be sweet and kind, the other will do whatever she wants to get her own way.* Just last night, he had been moved by her misfortune. He reached for another burlap bag and unloaded it on the table. His heart was completely swayed by her, and yet he had always desired a pure and honest woman whose life was hidden in Christ. *Her heart is hidden all right, hidden in deception.* He grabbed the paper off the table and shoved it in his pocket.

Levi stayed busy until dark. Allison was glad for the time to rest, but he seemed more distant than she expected. Walking home, they had made small talk on and off throughout the day. He had been friendly. She brushed the crumbs from her bread off the table into her hand. Maybe he had second thoughts about bringing her back to Sault Creek.

She jumped up as he walked by the front door. "I've cut some bread and cheese. Do you want something to eat?"

"No thanks, I'm tired and about to turn in," he said, without looking at her. Something was wrong—what had she said this time? She stepped from the front door and opened the mule pen, where he was throwing hay in the opposite corner.

"Levi, what's wrong? You haven't said two words to me since we've been back." He flung more hay without acknowledging her, and she stepped in closer. "Why are you ignoring me?"

He turned to her. "Allison, get out of this pen before you step in something."

"No." She took a few careful steps. "Not until you tell me what's wrong. What did I do?"

"Just get out of this pen." Even in the twilight, she could see his face fuming.

"No!" Her hands were on her hips. "Just tell me!"

Turning, he stabbed the pitchfork into the dirt. "This is what's wrong." He growled through clenched teeth. "You never do what you're told." He stepped forward, seeming to tower over her. "Did you just take that money and run? Was your uncle chasing you when you fell over that cliff?"

Allison stepped back as if he had struck her.

She knew her mouth gaped open, but there were no words for the cruel words she had just heard. Every kind and noble thing she had admired about Levi disappeared in an instant.

Her knees were about to buckle when she caught the gate and steadied herself. She walked into the cabin and pulled out a chair. Could anyone on this planet have as poor judgment as she did? Maybe this is what happens to children without parents—they spend their whole life looking for people to believe in. She had thought she was going to leave Madison behind and go to Paris. She believed Uncle Simon would take her. *What a fool.* The painful, harsh truth rose from her belly and got trapped in her throat. Her whole body shook, the tears coming forth like a freed dam. *How could anyone be this stupid?*

She dropped her head forward onto the hard table, but then, sensing he might come in at any moment, she rose and bolted the door. The only thing greater than this suffering was thinking he might be watching. *He thinks I stole money from my family?* Shaking, Allison blew out the lamp and lay down on her bed. A feeling of complete abandonment came over her with the dark of the cabin. *I thought he believed me.* Every echo of childhood came back. "That girl is just rebellious... trouble inside and out..." She pulled the blanket over her head and wrapped up in a ball. *If Levi believes horrible things about me, then they must be true.* Every damning voice drummed in her ears. She strained to bury her sobs, but as hard as she tried, her bitter cries kept her awake far into the night.

Levi hurled the pitchfork so hard that it splintered the top fence board. He went over and kicked it, and jumped out of the mule pen. He grabbed the pitchfork and gave it another heave. He ran after it and grabbed it from the ground and threw it again. Nothing worked until he grabbed it and beat it against the tree. The fact that the swing seat Ben had made for Allison got beaten in the process was a sad testament to the war within him. The handle finally splintered in his hand, and he threw it into the woods. He fell down, panting, against the tree.

The next morning, Levi awoke to drips of water coming off the branches and leaves of the tree. It was morning, and it didn't surprise him that he'd fallen asleep at the location of his fit of temper last night. The dark cloud came and hovered over him when he realized it had not all been a bad dream. In his anger, he had destroyed not only his pitchfork but also Allison's precious heart. The light rain was probably God's tears. Was He grieving? God had promised Levi He'd give him the strength to speak with grace, but he had chosen of his own free will to fling his charges against her. Heedless of the drizzle coming down, he bumped his head against the tree. He was damp and cold and had no other option than to beg for her forgiveness. *Oh, please, Lord, prepare this morning.*

Levi knocked and knocked, not surprised that she didn't answer. He warned her he was coming in and easily unlatched the plank from the door. To his surprise, he found the cabin empty. No fire had been built. No lamp had been lit. He ran around the outside of the cabin, calling her name, his heart pounding. He looked up and saw Patch standing at the edge of the woods. *No, not possible. She wouldn't.* Patch paced and circled, just waiting for him to get going.

He wanted to yell out her name, but pressed his lips together. She might take off and hide from him. It just takes one mistake to get lost in the woods. After a few minutes of running, he knelt down on the muddy trail. Hallelujah—it was her boot print. Maybe the light rain wasn't tears, but God's hand of help. He moved his rifle strap to his back and proceeded as quietly as he could. He gave a low whistle to Patch, who returned to stay close to him. The highest probability was that she was going to keep on the trail they had come from. Heading back to Ready Springs made sense. He knew where he could take a steep grade and cut a mile off the trail they had taken. Leaping over a few fallen trees, he ran up the hillside. When his side hitched with pain, he finally slowed down. He grabbed a branch and tried to catch his breath. Just a few more feet to the top, and he might be able to see her walking below.

"Blast it," he huffed. "Where is she?" He scanned back and forth. If she started out at dawn, how much farther ahead could she be?

He usually loved the surge that tracking gave him, but this was the worst version of hunting. It was easy to make miscalculations when he was feeling rash and emotional. To the north, a lazy hawk called.

"There!" He stopped and pointed. "I see her brown jacket. Come on, boy." Heart hammering in his chest, he stopped and leaned against a tree, drawing his hands over the stubble on his face. She was walking slowly, almost dragging. He bit his bottom lip. What was he going to say? Begging was not beneath him. He circled down slowly and watched as she spotted Patch. Her eyes met his, and she rolled them in disdain and kept walking.

"You can follow me all the way back to Ready Springs, Levi, but I'm not going back to Sault Creek." She didn't even look at him as he came up beside her.

"I don't blame you." He went to touch her elbow but decided against it. "I was awful to you. When I found this..." He pulled Crocker's receipt out of his pocket. She didn't look, but kept walking. "I felt like you were betraying me somehow. That you'd done this behind my back." Rain dripped on the ridiculous paper. "That you didn't trust me to provide for you." His voice trailed off, and wadding up the paper, he threw it into the woods. "I tried to calm myself all evening. I actually thought I had."

"Don't strain yourself over it. You won't ever have to consider any of my mistakes again."

He hated that she kept walking without looking at him.

"Oh!" She held her finger up. "Except that one about being married. To think for the rest of your life you made a stupid, impulsive decision that will keep you from ever finding happiness with another. Or maybe for another two bits, you can get an annulment. And if you don't have two bits, maybe Mr. Hardheaded Crocker will give it to you!" She almost lost her balance. "Oh, that's right, you would never use *that* money! Treacherous Allison stole it from her sweet uncle!"

He shook his head at the depth of her anger. "Lord, no, Allison. Please tell me how you got that much money. Tell me right now. I'll believe whatever you say." He grabbed her arm, unable to stand the way she walked on.

"All right, I'll give you credit that because of you I'm alive." Her voice dropped. "The money actually fell from my corset." She chortled painfully. "But it doesn't really matter, because we're done. Don't touch me." She looked down at his grip on her arm. "I'm going home." Tears mixed with rain on her face.

"Okay. If you want to go home, I'll take you."

She looked him straight in the eye. "You're not invited." Jerking her arm free, she continued walking.

Something was crushing his chest. He would never allow… "Then take Patch!" His voice cracked. "Patch, go with Allison!" He tried to shoo the dog forward.

"No, Levi, he's yours." She tried to get Patch to go the other way, but as she kept walking, Patch stayed by her side. "Patch, go back to Levi…Go!" She flung out her arm. Patch sat and looked up at her. She finally looked back down the trail, where Levi hadn't moved.

"Call him back…please. He needs to be with you. You love him." Allison waited, but he just looked at her.

"Levi." She slumped. "I forgive you. Really, I do. I know you're a godly man and you need to hear that. We can part in peace." She waited, her eyes pleading. "And please forgive me. I didn't think the money on your books would upset you so. Crocker's clerk wouldn't make change and so I didn't think anything about leaving the credit to your name." She sighed. "Can you forgive me?"

His eyes locked on hers. The air had resumed its place in his chest, and he walked steadily forward. "Yes, of course."

Patch sat up and happily wagged his tail between them.

"Stay here, Patch," Allison said. "And Levi, please. Don't come to me." She held up her hand. "Don't try to rescue me. I need to rescue myself."

"Allison, please. I want you in my life," he declared. "I want you more than anything. I want you more than an arrangement. I want to take care of you. I want to eat supper across from you…"

She stumbled back a few steps.

"I want to listen to your laugh every day. I want to hold you, and not just your hand."

She shook her head at the ground. "Levi," he heard her whisper. "Don't."

He inched closer. "I want to keep my promise to you. Wherever you want to go, I'll take you."

"And here lies the problem." Her voice shook. "I don't know what I want. I don't trust my decisions. I'm as gullible and fickle as they come." Her shoulders sagged.

"Can you just give yourself some time? You remembered the most things ever, just a few days ago. How can you be sure of your decisions after what you've been through? You haven't had enough time. I said I would help you sort them out, and all I did was get unhinged over something as stupid as money."

"You got upset because you said I never listen."

He loved her correction. "I did, and I'm sorry. Allison, you're so smart, smarter than me. When my pride gets stepped on…I don't know. There's no excuse."

"I'm not smarter than you. I wouldn't have survived a day without you. You have abilities and experience. The very things a girl from an all-girls school doesn't possess an ounce of."

"When I saw you take on Crocker and speak French all at once, your confidence about knocked me into the next county."

She let out a small smile, looking down.

"Do you want to knock me into the next county?" he said softly. "I deserve it." He pinched her finger inside her damp burgundy glove.

"No. I'm just tired and wet. I don't want to go back with you, but you've said some of the sweetest words I've ever heard. I'm the worst case of gullible when it comes to you." Their eyes met, and he thought he saw something warming.

"Fine." She exhaled a weary sigh. "I'll come back. See? I'm already changing my mind, but just until I can figure things out."

For the first time all morning, Levi took a full breath without a sharp squeezing pain.

29

Watching Allison's slow and clumsy steps, Levi realized she must be exhausted.

"Come here, boarding school girl. Remember this?" He bent and swung her arm around his neck and in a quick swoop, captured her in his arms. Surprisingly, there was no resistance, and she dropped her head on his shoulder.

Levi hiked the last mile with her in his arms. Only an hour ago, he had panicked, thinking she was walking away from him. But now she was so yielding. The last steps to the cabin, he wished he could capture these moments forever. He looked down—had she really heard what he confessed? He had just about told her all he was feeling. Carefully, he laid her on the bed.

"You have to get out of these wet clothes." He was thankful for the dry wood stacked in the cabin. Piling the wood in the fireplace, he lit a match. "Hey." He pulled on her jacket sleeve. "Let's get this off."

"No, I'm too cold." She clutched it with her eyes closed.

"The fire is going. Here, take this off." He unbuttoned her jacket and slipped it off her shoulders; she never opened her eyes. Untying her boots, he kicked them under the bed.

"I'm going to throw a blanket over you, so you can slip off your dress. It's wet." Her teeth started to chatter, and he laid a hand on her forehead; she had looked pale all morning. This would be the test of how tired she was. Pulling the blanket back, he began to unbutton her dress, expecting a protest at any moment. Nothing.

For heaven's sake, he would pay for this later. He jerked her dress off and covered her with the blanket while the heat of the fire filled the small cabin.

Levi looked up from his Bible as Allison slept. He'd fixed some food, but he wondered about waking her. He had to let the fire die down and open the door. The late summer rain was quickly replaced by sunshine, and the cabin was plenty warm. He scanned back to some of his favorite verses. "For I know the thoughts that I think toward you, saith the LORD, thoughts of peace, and not of evil, to give you an expected end. Then shall ye call upon me, and ye shall go and pray unto me, and I will hearken unto you. And ye shall seek me, and find me, when ye shall search for me with all your heart." He looked ahead from Jeremiah 29 and decided to close the Bible. His elbows rested on the table, his face in his hands. *Lord, I believe you are a good God. I believe you have wonderful things for me. Father, how I pray I won't mess it up. Help me with my pride and selfishness. Breathe Your words into my life. You are my only hope. Amen.*

Allison rolled to her side, taking the blanket with her, exposing her white undergarments. He rose from the table with a smile and covered her with the blanket. But her hair was damp around her forehead, so he tossed the blanket to the side and poured a glass of water.

"Allison, here, take some water." She barely looked at him, glazed and tired. He supported her head as she tried to drink.

"It's so hot in here! No more fire. No more blankets," she murmured.

Levi picked up the towel and poured some water on it, patting it across her face and neck.

"Thank you. That's lovely." She blinked her tired eyes. "The shelves are all full. The cabin looks different."

Levi helped with another drink.

"My throat hurts when I swallow."

"I think you got a chill from the rain this morning. You've been asleep a couple hours. But you do remember walking back?" he said.

"Yes. But I don't remember taking my clothes off." Blindly, she grabbed at the blanket and threw it back over her legs. "Oh, Levi." She turned away. "I wish you weren't so handsome." Her voice trailed off. "And didn't smell so good." She nestled into her pillow.

"What?" *What in the blue blazes did she just say?* "Allison. What did you say?" He wanted to pull on her shoulder, but he heard her mumble, "Goodnight."

He looked down at his sleeping dog. "Handsome?" He took a sniff of his rust-colored shirt. "Smells good?" He straightened his back a few inches taller. *Maybe some of the heartfelt things I said got in.*

As the sun faded, Levi fed Patch and the mule. He chewed on the corner of his lip, seeing the wet hay on the lean-to bed. *What would she think if I moved inside?* He looked at the cabin and then at the shelf bed. *We are married.* He shook his head and lifted his face to the stars. *Lord, you know I hate it when she judges me corrupt. And I beat my own pitchfork to a pulp because I misjudged her. She didn't balk over the arrangements at Crocker's. If she doesn't like it, she can always tell me to get out.*

Quietly closing the door, he glanced at her sleeping form and laid his blanket out on the floor. It felt amazing to stretch out his legs without hitting a fence board. He had room to pull his arms over his head. This was wonderful. He watched her sleep. Certainly, she wouldn't begrudge him for keeping an eye on her while she was sick. The blanket was back off, but even in the darkness, he could make out her white underthings. Did he dream that she had lowered her white sleeping gown and made him look at her back? Did she understand what kind of problems that created for him? Did she understand what he was thinking the two times she was curled up next to him? He had never felt such desire. But it was more than just wanting to touch her. *I want to keep her. Keep her to myself.* Staring at the dark cabin ceiling, he drew his hands over his face. *That sounds just like what backwoods trappers would say. Only problem is, she isn't some dumb critter.*

Sometime in the night, he sat up with a frantic start. Allison was standing, trying to hold on to the back of a chair, but it tilted and slammed onto the floor. It was still dark, but he was next to her in a moment, holding her by the arms.

"Here, let me help you sit down on the bed. What do you need? Just tell me, I'll help you."

"I'm so hot. I need the door open."

Levi ran his hand across her damp forehead. She was burning up with fever. "This is all my fault." He clenched his jaw, then grabbed some water from the table and brought it to her lips. "Drink." He held it for her until she couldn't swallow and it dribbled down her chest. He remembered something his mother had done when they were burning with fever, and flung open the door.

"Allison, I'm taking you to the creek. It will help you cool off."

"No, please..." she protested, while he easily lifted her into his arms. "Those men will get me."

"No one's going to get you."

"They took your furs, and they want to take me."

"I didn't let them take you then, and I won't let them take you now." He walked carefully in the dark and stepped off the sandy bank into the deeper water. Suddenly her eyes snapped open. "What are you doing? I'm getting all wet."

"Just hold on to me. You're burning up with fever. The cool water will help." He bent his knees to lower her down more.

She sucked in a shocked breath and tucked her head against his neck. Her weight floated, but she clutched her arms tight around him.

"I'm so sorry." He pulled her close. "It's been one thing after another for you."

"Levi..." Her hand came up and touched the nape of his neck. "You're a good man. I think you're the best man I've ever known."

"I'm not good, Allison, only God is good."

"I thought you said God lives in you..." Her voice trailed off.

He smiled and shook his head, looking out into the darkness. Only this girl could make a point while exhausted with sickness.

"I'm freezing." Her body jerked with tremors.

Levi stood up, bearing her weight. Taking careful steps out of the creek, he stopped for a moment on the bank while the water ran down. "It doesn't matter if you ever feel the same about me, but I have to tell you. With all my heart, I love you."

He didn't want a response, but the moment was the most heartfelt, honest one he'd experienced with her yet. He carried her back to the cabin. "Can you go in and change while I wait out here?" He wondered if she was asleep again. He heard a tiny *okay* come from her and lowered her to the threshold. She stood for a moment in the dark, then closed the door. He scanned the dark woods; a combination of embarrassment and relief pulsed in him. It had felt good to say it. Maybe it was a poor decision—but he had told her it didn't matter if she felt the same way. What a lie. It mattered to him like his next breath mattered. He quickly unbuttoned his shirt and wrung the water out of it. *Maybe she didn't hear me. What a coward. Why didn't I wait for a better moment?*

Allison unlatched the door and slumped back into the bed, pulling the blankets up. She couldn't face Levi. He had told her he loved her. She shouldn't be surprised after what he had declared on the trail, but she had wondered then if it was just to get her to come back to Sault Creek. *This is so absurd. Why did I agree to come back to this cabin with him? I shouldn't be in this improper situation.* The compromising minutes were too many to list. Sleeping next to him at Clemet Summer's. The moment she thought he was going to kiss her. Agreeing to a marriage. Sitting on the edge of the bed at Crocker's hotel. The way he rubbed her back, held her hand, carried her, wet bodies against each other… *Oh, for pity sakes, everything was spinning.*

30

Allison was awake when she heard Levi roll up his bedding and put the coffee on. The pounding headache and sore throat had subsided, but she decided it would be better to stay in bed than to face him, even though the thought of coffee and something to eat was about to sway her good sense. She heard him whisper to Patch and open the door to let the dog out. Should she look and see if he had gone out, too? *Oh, this is ridiculous—you can't avoid him forever.*

She turned over to find an empty cabin. Stretching her balled-up limbs, she sat up against the cabin wall. The pressure in her head and neck returned, so she closed her eyes and wondered if she shouldn't just try to go back to sleep. Had she dreamed his tender words? Was her mind playing tricks on her? She remembered putting her hand on the back of his neck and saying something about being a great man. That was all real, wasn't it? Allison rubbed her temples, hearing the door creak.

"Oh." She quickly pulled the blanket around her shoulders.

"You're up." He stopped, studying her. "That's good." He poured her a cup of coffee. "Careful, it's hot." Their eyes locked as he blew lightly into the cup.

"You can just set it on the table," she said.

"Sure. Toast or oatmeal—anything sound good?"

"Doesn't matter, anything would be fine." Allison ran her hand through her hair, realizing she looked disheveled again, while Levi poured water into a pan and grabbed what he needed off the shelf.

Allison breathed slowly, trying to get her heart to slow down. Why did he have this effect on her? Well, facing the facts with him would be better than this tiptoeing around.

"I want to talk about what happened." He turned slightly and gazed at her out of the corner of his eye. If he came too close, she would lose all her nerve. "When we were on the trail, and I agreed to come back here." She let out a breath. That seemed safe enough.

"All right." He turned to stir the oats.

Allison glanced around at her things hung over the chairs, and another familiar wave of weakness hit her. "When you have that finished, could you give me a minute to get dressed?" Being dressed would fortify her nerves.

"Yes, of course." Levi pushed the pan to the back of the small stove and walked out.

Alone, Allison was surprised at how little energy she had. Just getting dressed exhausted her. She combed her hair and pinned the sides back. *What should I say? Do his words of love change my plan? But what about the painful words that made me leave? Every one of those steps was charged with the resolve never to return, and yet here I am.* There was a soft knock at the door.

"Come in." She stayed seated at the table. Levi walked in and pulled his hand through his hair. He looked at the table, the floor, the stove. "You want to eat or talk?"

"Let's eat first."

"Great." He grabbed two bowls and served them each a scoop, then reached for her hand. Allison took it, finding the comfort undeniable. He looked so agreeable, with the softness in his eyes and the break of a small smile. Her gut did a flip, and she closed her eyes. Every sensible thing had left her at the strength and promise of his warmth. She didn't hear a word of his prayer, and she wondered if the dizziness was from sitting up too long. The bites of food brought some relief, and she suddenly knew the most important thing to tell him.

"The night we got into the argument in the mule pen..." she murmured while he nodded. "I've never experienced anything so awful. It was worse than the fall I took, worse than the knot on my head. It was worse than not having a memory." Desperately she hoped that he understood her; it was the most difficult thing she had ever said.

"There was a hateful voice that night." His eyebrows creased. "But it wasn't you, Levi. It was a like an agonizing list of every tormenting thing I could think about myself. There was nothing good, nothing redeemable. Somewhere, somehow I had convinced myself, in spite of everything I've been through, that I was still a good person. But all the dreadful accusations came in like a flood. My life has certainly proved there is no virtue in me." She stared into her warm coffee. "I'm not sure if anyone could understand. I want so desperately for you to help me get back to Madison, but I'm just not sure about anything anymore. I have my memory back, and now I'm worse than ever."

Levi took a deep breath and opened the door wider. The sunlight hit the table.

"What did you think about the dream my pa told us about?" he asked.

"It spoke to me," she said, nodding. "Your father saw himself as an outsider, and it took a dream to open his heart up to what God wanted for him all along."

"Could this be happening to you?"

"Except I didn't have a dream, those voices were real. Real things people have said about me. They're true."

"Maybe some are, maybe some aren't. I don't think it really matters."

"How can you say it doesn't matter?" Allison argued.

"Because Jesus took all our sin on the cross. My pa's, mine, yours, every terrible thing was taken by His death on the cross. We don't have to live with our sin. Trust me on this, my pa was like a person I'd never met before. Something has happened to him. Some kind of load is off his shoulders. Maybe some of those things you heard are true, but you can also be a new person if you want to turn it over to the Lord."

He leaned in a bit. "There is a God who loves you, and believe me, there is an enemy who would squeeze the life out of you by convincing you that you're a terrible person. The truth is, we've all sinned. It's just our choice of what we do with it."

"What do you do?"

"Simple childlike faith. You ask the Lord to come into your heart, to take out the sin and hardness and replace it with a soft and pliable heart."

"And then what?" Allison asked.

Levi shrugged. "Just thank Him for the things He does."

"It's too simple." She shook her head and stared out the door. "I've sat through hours of Bible classes at school. Not one of my teachers had such a simplistic view."

He cleared his throat and sat back.

"I've seen you read your Bible. I'm not saying you don't know what it's about." She didn't want to offend him.

"Every word of those pages is true, and yet people all over the world take it a bit differently. How many different churches did you see in Madison?" he asked.

"Oh, maybe five or ten. My grandmother attended the First Community Church, and now there's another group of people called the Revised Community Church. I don't understand. We never prayed or talked about God the way your family does. You and Ben are the first people I've ever heard talk about God like...He was listening. When you were growing up, did the other people you went to church with talk like your family does?"

Levi nodded. "I believe someone like my pa who thought church was only good for women and children can have a change of heart. Not based on his knowledge, just based on the pure desire to find God."

"I believe that's true," Allison said.

"Is it true for you?" His brows lifted in a question.

"Do I want to find God in a more personal way?" She sucked in a deep breath. "I suppose I do. Do you think it will help with what I told you about?" She scratched the side of her head, hoping he would remember her painful confession.

"If you believe in your heart and confess Jesus as Lord with your mouth, you will be saved." He waited. "Saved. Saved from torment. Saved from doubt and fear. Saved from wondering if your life is worth a bag of beans. Saved for love and joy and peace."

"So back to my other question. How do I go about that?"

Levi reached out his hand. He looked at her and then back at his hand, giving her the smallest smile.

She tilted her head. "Hand holding? Really? Is that in the Bible?"

"No." He smiled and winked, making the air feel sweet and soft around them. "I'll pray something and then you pray, too. Whatever you want."

She gave him a small nod and closed her eyes, feeling his fingers slowly entwine with hers.

"Father, You created this beautiful child, Allison. You knew the day she was born."

She felt a knot in her throat at his comforting words.

"You knew even the harsh things that have come into her life. You know her losses. You know how everything has affected her. And you brought her to this moment. This very day. To come and speak your words to her. Words that should be louder than anything else that comes to her mind. That You, God of all, love her."

This sounds like what Thelma said, Allison thought.

"You love everything about her. So much that you sent Jesus to die on a cross for her so she could have a personal relationship with you. Not of information or distance, but that your heart and her heart would be one. And when those other voices try to speak, I pray that she would hear and believe only You."

How had he had prayed exactly what she needed to hear? She loved the stillness and peace settling over her, and finally, she opened her eyes.

Levi smiled at her. "Now you pray."

"Oh." She felt swept away by his prayer. "Um, God, thank you for helping me. Thank you for saving me. I do believe in You, and I want to know You more than I thought I did before." She knew there was so much more to say, but the right words would not come. "Amen?"

Levi met her eyes. "Yes, amen! Wonderful."

"Is that enough?" She wasn't sure it had worked.

He grabbed both of her hands and pulled them up for a quick kiss. "Just a sincere heart, that's all God looks for." He dropped her hands and stood up. Stretching side to side, facing the outside, he clapped his hands together. "What a beautiful morning!"

31

~~~

Levi loved fishing this part of the creek. A grove of aspen trees danced in the sunlight. He could just watch them and let them lull him to sleep. Sitting down, he leaned back in the tall grass and tucked his fishing pole under his leg. Fishing wasn't his priority today. He felt a hundred emotions as he ran his fingers through his hair. When Allison had said she wanted to talk, he'd just about bet the cabin she was going to put a wall up in front of his declarations. She didn't often let her guard down like that. Surely, she was going to lay out some plan to get back to Madison. His hope had risen and fallen more times than should be allowed. *Is this what all women do? Show a man their sweet smile and then torture him by keeping herself just out of reach? That doesn't seem right. And it's probably a fact that she was asleep when I told her I loved her.* He felt a small tremor against his leg. He sat up and reeled in a tiny blue and silver fish.

"You know how it feels to get pulled at the end of a string." He looked the fish in the eye while it gasped to get back in the water. Taking the hook out, he gently laid the fish back in the shallow stream, where small leaves twinkled back and forth. *Lord, I don't want to complain. I think she wants to know You more. I believe her heart is sincere toward You. I know there's more we should have talked about. I just don't know how to separate what You want and what I want.*

Tell Me what you want. He heard a voice like the light wind through the trees. Setting his pole aside, he put his hands over his face. *I want to be her husband. I want her to be my wife. I want to have a family.* Levi couldn't help but laugh at himself. *You know everything, anyway. I want her to love me the way I love her.* There, that was better. *I want her to be content, happy.* He waited. Just silence. He thought of one of his favorite verses. *With God all things are possible. With God,* he repeated. *I do trust you, Lord. I found out not much is possible with my attempts.*

As the days passed, Levi had many chances to practice staying out of God's way. Allison slowly recovered, more talkative now, with stories of Webster's School, her friends, and her home, but she had yet to bring up his declarations. As much as he was relieved she had recovered from her fever, he was puzzled that she had never mentioned his feelings. A week ago, she had so much turmoil about the kind of person she was and whether anyone would even want her back. *Have those worries lessened? Has God done a restorative work in her?* He should be happy, but the more she talked about her past, the more she sounded as if she was missing her old life. He would not forget his promise; he had been raised to be a man of his word. He said if she would come back with him, he would help her sort everything out and take her wherever she wanted to go. And then what?

Allison covered her mouth and sat down across him for supper. "I still feel like I'm going to cough. The tickle is still there. But then nothing happens." She stirred the potatoes in her soup.

"I'd like to come back in the cabin to sleep," Levi said, eyeing her for a reaction. "The nights are getting colder. Snow has been known to hit, even in early fall."

Allison didn't realize she had stopped eating. "I feel bad. I do." She searched carefully for the right words. "I've taken over your home. This is your place. You shouldn't be sleeping outside."

"I'm used to sleeping outside. You're not." He touched her hand. "Hey, you didn't put me out. I wouldn't have had it any other way."

She kept her eyes down.

"I slept over here." He nodded to the floor next to the shelves. "When you were sick. I wanted to be close if you needed anything."

Allison was clearly aware of what that was like. It just brought back those wanton feelings she had felt at Clemet Summer's cabin.

The tension of longing and comfort battling for a spot in her. The way he held her in the water when she thought she heard him say *I love you*. Her heart began to pound. *I think.*

She stood up. "We should figure out how to get back to Madison. Before the snow flies." She risked looking at him and saw his mouth form a thin line while his eyes turned dark. "That's what we said, right? That if I came back, we would figure something out."

"What does that have to do with me sleeping inside?"

Allison sucked in a large breath. "Because sleeping inside has to do with the cold and inevitable snow coming. Which has to do with how successful we would be, traveling to Madison." For some reason, her hands were flying around with her every word. She clasped them in front of her. "Your stories of last winter, being snowed in. I was listening." She looked up, reading his stoic expression. "Don't look at me like this is a new conversation."

"So you definitely want to get back home? You don't want to stay here with me."

Allison stared back, shrinking inside. He was just setting her up to hurt him. He wanted her to say it. Why wouldn't he just offer to take her? His eyes burned a hole in her, but she would not answer. Instead, she walked stiff-backed out into the cool evening. Something was rising up within her, and she spun around to see him standing on the threshold. "No, I don't want to be here when the snow piles up to the roof. No…I don't." She glared back.

Levi took three long strides and had her by the arm. "I'm not asking about the snow. You know that, good and well." He pulled on her to face him. "Just say it, Allison. You've had a rope around my neck from the moment I met you. You pull, you let go, you pull again, then you let go again."

"I do not!" She shook his arm loose. "How dare you!" She stomped ahead and spun around again. "I didn't even know my family, my town, my life until a few weeks ago. And you want me to say… what? That I love you and will live here forever?" The words flew out so much harsher than she meant, and the impact on his face said it all. He closed his mouth, and his eyes blinked back the heavy dismissal. "Then we need to go our separate ways," he said.

He walked into the tree line.

Unable to sleep, her twisted heart once again condemning her, she rolled the sleeves of her nightgown up. The oil lamp was barely flickering. She knew it was late, but she couldn't bear the darkness. She tried and tried, but couldn't find the answers to all the questions making circles in her head. Could she live here as Levi's wife? Could she bring him back to Madison and introduce him to her grandmother? *Grandmother, this is Levi, my husband.* She tried to rub the tension out of her temples. Could she go back to Madison and forget this place? Forget his love for her? *Love for me.* Those words made her throat tighten with emotion. *He loves me, and all I've done is hurt him. The words I said tonight were a reflection of the person I no longer want to be. He has given up his bed, his food, his family for me. What have I done for him? I've kept him at arm's length. I've taken and taken and showed him no tenderness. I know I'm easily confused. I know I should have...* Allison stood up and opened the door. The night air hit her bare feet and thin nightgown. She took one step outside. *I know I should do something for him. I can't sleep, I can't breathe until I make this right.* She wiped a lone tear from her cheek and walked to the mule pen, the cool air sending a chill up her spine. Swallowing hard, she opened the pen gate. It was only a few careful steps to where he slept, one leg hanging off the hay shelf. "Levi." She touched his leg lightly.

"What?" he gasped. "What's wrong?" He rubbed his eyes and came up on one elbow.

"I want you to come inside," Allison whispered, gripping his arm.

"Why?" He blinked. "Are you sick?"

"No, I'm not sick." She sighed. "I just want you to be inside with me." She pulled on his shirt sleeve.

He sat up. "I can't see you very well. Are you sleepwalking?"

Allison stepped aside as he slid off the shelf and stood before her. "Please," she said, taking his hand. Her heart was beating through her skin as they stepped into the dimly lit cabin.

Levi sucked in a deep breath and took a drink of water. "I'm listening. What is this about?"

Allison feared saying the wrong words. It would ruin everything. She stepped up next to him and carefully took his hand.

Hesitantly, she touched the back of his neck with her other hand. "This is where your curls used to be."

He bristled, taking a step back. "Allison." He took her hand off the back of his neck. She stepped in closer, slipping her arms around his back. Carefully, she leaned her cheek against his shirt, but his body stiffened. Leaning back, she touched his cheek. "I'm sorry, Levi. Can you please forgive me?" She tilted her head to meet his gaze. "I don't want to hurt you anymore. I want to love you."

He looked away, his breath quickening. When he finally looked back, he nodded. "I forgive you." This time when she leaned back into his warmth, he brought his arms around her. Letting out a deep sigh, he dropped his forehead to meet hers.

Just a hint of that small sweet smile was all Levi needed. Her face was so close. A quick kiss wouldn't hurt anything. He watched for every clue he could possibly see in her as he bent to kiss her. Light, soft, and warm—her lips were worth all the risk. Pulling back, he saw her raised chin and her glossy eyes—she was expecting more. She had every chance to move away, and yet she held onto him.

He deepened the next kiss, and she moved against him, returning his kisses with more of her own. Her hands pressed his back, and a hunger like he'd never known took hold as he felt every beautiful curve of her body. He wanted more. He lifted her off the ground. She let out a gasp, and he put her down and stepped back. He should stop. They stared at each other, breathless, waiting. She blinked, then reached up and pulled the ribbon loose on her nightgown. The invitation was overpowering. He worked his hands into her loose hair, holding her still, searching deep into her eyes. "I'm glad we're married," he whispered before he kissed her again. With pure indulgence, he trailed kisses down the side of her neck. She leaned her head back, abandoned to his wishes. Her gown slipped off her shoulders and landed on the floor.

Allison cracked an eye at the sunlight through the window. She had lived in the little cabin long enough to know it was late in the morning. Turning slightly, she realized that her head was resting on Levi's arm. She sucked in a quick breath. It was not a dream. Almost every inch of her skin was touching his. *Oh, for pity sakes.*

The recollection of their intimacy flooded her with mingled love and wonder. *How did he know about those things?*

Patch scratched at the door—was he growling to get in?

"Levi!" A voice boomed and the door rattled. Allison jumped, gripping him. He tried to raise up, but quickly realized she was wrapped around him. They struggled to get free of each other as the door swung open and a giant form filled the opening. Allison cried out as Levi pushed her behind him and grabbed for his clothes.

"Geeze, Levi. Ma said you got married. Ha! I said I'd see it when I believed it. Now I can say I believe it!" The man ran his hand down his thick beard, laughing.

"Junior, do you mind? Do you think you could give us a minute?" Levi barked.

"Oh sure. I've just been riding all morning. Maybe Patch could offer me some coffee," he said as he walked out the cabin door.

"Levi...the door." Allison could barely speak; her heart was beating so hard. She wrapped herself in a cocoon of blankets while Levi pulled on his boots and kicked the door closed. He looked down, shaking his head, at an obvious loss for words. "We'll be outside. Take your time," he mumbled, and let himself out the door.

⌘

Levi finished buttoning his shirt and raked his hands through his hair. Part of him wanted to blacken his brother's eye, the other part of him knew there was something unusual going on.

"Sorry about that, brother. I didn't see anything." Junior shrugged. "Just so you know, once they're pregnant and have a kid, that fun stuff goes away."

Levi ignored this. "Why are you here? Has something happened?"

"Yes and no," Junior said. "Ma thinks Pa's not doing good. Having trouble breathing. She's all worked up and worried that he's dying. I don't think so..." Junior kicked some dirt.

"You don't think he's dying?"

"Well, what do I know? She knows him better than anyone. I think he's made of pure grit. He has some days where he can keep

216

up with small chores, and then some days he sits propped up in bed."

"He's never been one to sit around," Levi said.

"Well, I don't know. She just asked me if I'd come get you. Maybe we can all make our peace with him. Though I doubt that'll ever happen." Junior spat. "But once the snow flies, it might be too hard to come."

Junior didn't seem to know about the change in Pa—a change that Levi had never seen coming, but he doubted his brother would understand.

"We'll come," Levi said.

"Her, too?" Junior nodded toward the cabin. "Can't she stay here? We'll only be a week or so. That way she'll really be glad to see you when you get back." He slugged Levi's shoulder, trying to get him to agree. Levi glanced over to Junior's

horse and the extra mare he'd brought. "She doesn't weigh much. She can ride with me."

"It's your bother, not mine. I hope she can cook through, 'cause I'm starving." James turned and headed back toward the cabin.

32

&c&

Allison's face flushed five shades of red. Even though she was dressed and prepared, as soon as the brothers entered the cabin, she had to get out; after such a rude awakening, she could not muster the ability to be cordial. She mumbled to Levi about gathering something, and he nodded as she slipped out the door. She walked briskly up to the tree line, then far into the woods, finding a stump she could sit on. Leaning her elbows on her knees, she cradled her face. Her mind would not land on what item to be shocked about first. She wrapped her arms around her waist and rocked back and forth.

What came over me? I took him by the hand. I led him into the cabin. I wanted to show him some tenderness after all the things he has put up with. The truth is, I didn't want him to stop. I could have said it at any time. His touch felt passionate…loving…intimate. Then why do I feel so embarrassed and corrupt? She stood up and lifted her face. *What have I done? God, are you even there? I wouldn't blame You if you never looked at me again.* She knew last night had changed everything. *What is Levi thinking? Happy? Shocked? Expecting more? Oh, Lord.*

She covered her mouth. Her first time…it had been like damming Sault Creek, then allowing it to flow free. Her pulse quickened. Later in the night, the second time…was it proper to yield to passion like that? But now—now she wouldn't be alone with Levi. Another brother who had no more manners than a grizzly had come calling.

Allison took her time down by the south end of the creek, securing her hair and splashing cool water over her face. A rustling nearby interrupted her thoughts. "Oh, Levi." She grasped her chest. "You scared me."

"You've been gone awhile." He looked at his feet, shuffling them back and forth. "I wanted to string my brother from a tall branch, but he came here to tell me that my pa's going through something. I guess he's having trouble breathing and my ma wants us to come."

Allison nodded. "Of course." Arms tightly crossed against her chest, she walked with him back toward the cabin, thankful to be talking about anything other than last night. "What do you want to do?"

"James brought another horse." He stopped and lightly brushed her cheek. "We all call him Junior. My brother, not the horse. With his other horse, it won't be like walking to Ready Springs." He looked for her approval.

"You don't want me to stay here?"

"No." He shook his head. "I want you to come with me. The horse can handle both of us."

"Oh." Allison swallowed, aware that more changes were coming.

When they made sight of the cabin, Junior stood out front. "Quit lollygagging, Levi." He held up a rifle. Levi turned to Allison. "Junior and I are going hunting."

"Let's check some of your traps, too," Junior said. Levi reached for his gun.

It was so odd to see him with an older brother. Levi had always been the one to lead. Silently, she waited. Was anyone going to attempt a proper introduction? *Guess not,* Allison walked into the cabin, and Levi followed her in. "I'll cook up whatever we kill. No need to go to any trouble."

She nodded, at a complete loss for words. Glancing at the rumpled bedding from last night, she looked away, blushing.

"Is there anything wrong?"

She gave him a calm but forced smile. "Not a thing."

She started to close the door, but Levi stopped it with his boot. "I'll be back in a couple hours. You'll be here, right?" He leaned in closer.

She wanted to let him squirm, but those soft brown eyes and those dark, thick eyelashes moved her. Memories of his touch from last night sent shivers up her skin. "Yes." She touched his cheek, and his smile was part relief, part enchantment. He left, but reluctantly, glancing over his shoulder at her.

This is the oddest sensation, she thought as the brothers walked away. *I feel almost giddy. Like last night, outside of my senses.* She allowed herself the luxury of staring. Both men were the same height. Same soft brown hair. James was much heavier, though, and with that nasty beard, he looked like some medieval pirate, for pity sakes. He didn't seem to possess the same sincerity Ben and Levi had; he was harder around the edges. Levi was perfect. Perfect in size and strength and...well, goodness, just everything.

It was a day of laundry, cleaning floors, and removal of the ever-present layer of dirt that came in with the open door. A pan of cornbread had been baked and cooled, and a batch of biscuits after that. Hungry, she had eaten four of those herself.

Later in the afternoon, Levi wrung the water out of his shirt and laid it over the pen fence. He was still dripping, so he leaned in the open door. "Hi."

"Hey, you." Allison smiled back.

"Can you hand me the hand crank from the fireplace?"

She grabbed the end, trying to avoid getting black soot on her dress. It was heavy and awkward.

"I've got it." He stepped in and took it from her hand and nodded, walking out.

Looking down at the dirt and grass he had tracked in, she wondered why she suddenly felt like crying. *It's only dirt*, she tried to convince herself. *Just because I've been sappy all day, thinking of him constantly...knowing everything's changed between us...*She reached for the broom, squaring her shoulders. *It doesn't mean I've agreed to live here forever...*

"Allison, we got a few rabbits." Levi leaned back in. "We'll be out here awhile working on them. The plan is to leave in the morning. Can you agree to that?"

"Of course." She chided herself for not remembering his pa was ill, and the brothers wanted to go to him. "I'll be ready." She thought he was about to say something else when Junior walked up and plopped his hand on Levi's head.

"Flint and salt." Junior squeezed his head as Levi moved away from his hand.

"Allison, would you hand me the..." Already moving toward the items, she placed them in his hand.

On a stump in front of the cabin, Allison set out a basket of cornbread and biscuits. Outside, Junior had already chewed one whole cooked rabbit to the bones. Levi had cut up some pieces, and he handed her a plate. She glanced at their system of skinning and cooking and then closely at the brothers. Could she ever get used to this? Hunger over etiquette. Eating trumped conversation.

"How'd ya do trading with Crocker?" Junior said, picking meat from his teeth.

Levi glanced at Allison and then back to Junior. "Not good."

"What happened? Prices falling?" Junior grabbed another piece of cornbread.

"Not really. I didn't have much inventory."

"Oh yeah? Was this your fault?" Junior finally spoke to Allison.

She jerked up, shocked he even knew she was there. "My fault?" Was he trying to goad her?

"The truth is," Levi cut in, "most of my summer's catch was stolen. Two lousy thieves."

"They threatened to kill Patch." Allison thought that sounded important until Junior shook his head at her.

"You didn't even get a shot out? Couldn't at least take one of them down?" Junior asked.

"No." Levi stood and flung the rabbit bones out to the bushes.

"Geeze, Levi, you get married without telling anyone. You had a fire that could have killed ya' and you've been robbed. What are you doing?" Junior demanded, shaking his head.

"Just living, Junior. That's about it."

Allison couldn't figure these brothers out. They sounded harsh with each other, yet she knew all the Grahams were fiercely protective.

"How's Frieda been feeling?" Levi asked.

"How would I know? Every day it changes." Junior shrugged. "You can ask her."

"You okay if it's another girl?" Levi asked.

"It better be a boy. I'll go nuts with two yowling girls in the house."

Levi laughed. "Two little curly-haired girls climbing on you for your attention. "Papa...papa."

"Stop it, Levi," Junior barked. "You're going to give me nightmares." He lowered his plate of scraps down for Patch

Allison remembered Ben and Levi provoking each other, then to fist fighting. Maybe Junior's gruff manners weren't so bad, she tried to convince herself. "I'm going in. I want to make sure I have everything ready for tomorrow." She smiled, halfhearted.

❧❧

Levi watched her walk into the cabin.

"I'll give ya' credit where it is due," Junior said. "She's not hard to look at. But she doesn't look like she belongs out here, either. I hope you know what you're doing. That kind won't be happy until they have everything thus and so. You'll spend all your days making sure her nose don't get bent out of shape."

"Thank you, Junior, for your sound advice on women. I had actually forgotten you were an expert."

"I know more than what's in your pea brain." Junior stood and let out a long burp.

They had worked on the skins late after dark and Levi washed up, the light long gone out in the cabin. His stomach did a flip. He wanted to be in there with her. He didn't want any company. No relatives. No mule pen. How could he have underestimated the satisfaction a wife could bring? Maybe because he never had enough goodwill with her to imagine such a sweet thing. He swallowed past the tightness in his throat and walked up to the cabin. He caught sight of Junior coming around the corner with his bedroll. "Can I bunk on the floor?"

Levi's jaw tensed. "Junior. She doesn't know you. She can be sensitive." He didn't want his brother ruining Allison's recent improved disposition. Junior grumbled some response as he pushed inside and spread out his bedroll.

Allison was sleeping, the covers in perfect arrangement. There really wasn't room for two—yet somehow, that was where he had been with her this very morning. Levi rubbed the whiskers on the underside of his jaw, thinking. He pulled off his boots, glancing at James, already asleep. "Allison," he whispered, shaking her arm.

"What?" She rolled on her back to face him. "Is it time to go?"

"No. I need you to move over." He pulled the covers back.

"No, Levi, we shouldn't." She pulled the covers around her.

"We're not." He slid his leg in until she finally moved over. "My brother's asleep over there." He settled in next to her, as she inched away. "Do I smell bad?" he whispered.

Allison shook her head. "No. I just know I'll never be able to get back to sleep."

"Remember Mr. Summers' cabin?" He turned to find her only a breath away, his heartbeat quickening. "I'll turn and face the table." He moved to his side. "Pretend there are giant spiders on this cabin wall." He took her wrist and pulled her arm onto his chest. She didn't have time to object as she molded into him. The heat was immediate. He intertwined his fingers through hers as he pressed her hand against his chest, feeling her breath rising and falling in unison with his. Once again, the exhilaration of her touch, her hand light against his chest, roused his senses. She let out a deep sigh, the warmth tickling his ear. He was trying to be still, but the heat under her hand was almost burning.

"Good night," Allison whispered.

33

⟨❧⟩

Allison poured the last bit of coffee into their cups. Junior drank it in a couple of gulps and let out a loud huff. "You know how to ride a horse?" he asked.

"No, I've never…of course, I've been around horses, but not actually had any opportunity to ride one."

Junior scratched his beard and walked out, shaking his head. "Let's go!" he yelled.

Allison dropped her fists on her hips. *How can he be so opposite of charming Ben?*

Levi walked in. "Is everything okay? Are you ready?"

Her foot tapped the floor in a fast rhythm. "I think I'm ready. Here are my things." She handed him her bag, and he let it drop, pretending to be unable to lift it.

She smiled. "It's not that bad." Levi smiled back, and there was a sweet moment she thought he might lean in to kiss her. "I need to lock everything up," he said, pulling her back to the present.

Allison walked out, embarrassed to be feeling so giddy again. She stared at the two horses and wondered how this was going to work. Soon, Levi finished and came up beside her. "You can ride in the saddle, but with your skirt, it might be difficult. Or you can ride behind me." He took the reins and stilled the horse. James had mounted his horse and had the mule by the reins. She stared at the saddle and stirrups and pictured her ankles and pantaloons hanging out for the world to see. "I'll try riding behind you."

Levi nodded and swung up into the saddle. Leaning forward, he offered her his arm. "Jump up on three. One, two, three." The horse knew something was wrong and danced in a circle.

"Whoa." Levi held the reins steady as the horse closed in around Allison, her feet reaching for solid ground.

"Let go!" she cried out. Freed, she ran back to the cabin door. Levi swung down and walked over to her.

"Hey. Don't worry." He pulled her wrists away to see her face. "I have another idea. We just need to get you to that stump over there. It'll be easy."

"No, I can't. He doesn't want me riding on him." She bit her lip, pressing into the closed door. "I can't do this. I'm afraid he's going to buck me off."

Levi pushed on the horse to keep him from closing in on her. Junior yelled from the tree line. "Let's go!"

"I'm sorry, Levi. Maybe I should just stay here."

"No. You've overcome so much." He took her with his free hand and led her to the stump by the creek. "This you can do. I'll keep him steady. You're going to have to trust me."

"Why can't I just walk?" Levi had already mounted the horse, and he pulled her to the stump. "See, this is much better. I can pull you—just don't kick into the horse's flanks. Grab my arm and shoulder." He pulled as soon as they made contact.

"Now, grab my waist." Levi urged the horse forward. "That's not too bad, is it?"

Allison reluctantly looked to the ground. How far would she fall? A feeling of dark, ominous fear stuck her. Gripping Levi with all her strength, she mumbled and dropped her face into the back of his shirt.

"I don't want to interrupt your prayers there." He wedged his thumb between his shirt and her grip. "But you're about to crush a few ribs."

Allison let up a bit and concentrated on the trail ahead. Just as her heart started to settle down, he rested his hand on her leg as they descended through a steep patch. How could he be so relaxed? She remembered the conversation they had had when he tried to hold her hand. How foreign that had felt! She shivered, remembering the previous night.

"Are you doing okay back there?" He nudged her.

"Mmm hmm." She was glad he could not read her thoughts.

"You're doing a great job. I knew you could do this." He reached up and arranged his hat. "I know we haven't had much chance to talk," he said glancing at Junior.

"Yes, I've wanted to ask you if you're worried about your father. Does your mother call you home like this often?"

"No, she doesn't. You were at dinner when he talked about seeing the doctor."

"Yes." Allison remembered how uncomfortable that evening was. "But he appeared well. But of course, I don't know how he usually looks."

After a few minutes of silence, Levi shifted in the saddle. Looking out to Junior, then back to her, he cleared his throat. "You broke our deal." He glanced back at her.

"What deal?" Allison loosened her grip on his shirt.

"The deal we agreed to. The deal you accused me of having wrong motives for."

"I didn't accuse you." She cleared her throat. "I just wanted to know what you were expecting."

He took in a deep breath and led the horse around some rocks. "I guess I should have asked *you* what your intentions were." A short laugh escaped his throat.

Allison could feel the heat rising up her neck as she pondered laughing with him. "I guess I should apologize. I didn't keep our deal. It was a mistake, and I won't let it happen again." *Perfect!* Her voice stayed even and matter of fact.

"Oh, no." He twisted in the saddle. "That's not how it works. You broke the deal. It's gone, everything's changed."

"So you're saying a person can't be forgiven and keep a previous promise that they made?" She loved this kind of sparring with him.

"Everyone and anyone who wants to turn from their ways can be forgiven," Levi said.

"Then I…" She knew she was teetering on teasing and making him mad. "I want to turn from my ways."

"Why did you come and get me from the mule pen?" His tone was serious now.

A chill ran up her arm. "I'm going to need a warmer coat."

"Allison." He said her name with gritted teeth and pulled the horse up to a stop.

She contemplated accidentally giving the horse a boot to the flanks. He turned and grabbed her arm. "Why? Did you mean for that to happen? Tell me." He tugged on her arm.

"No. I didn't plan it," she said.

Levi let go of her arm.

"Levi! Why are you stopping?" Junior yelled.

A vein bulged in his neck. Growling under his breath, he urged the horse into a trot. Allison had no choice but to hang on for dear life.

34

After a quick and quiet lunch, Allison started to wonder how long Levi was going to be silent. It was a bit absurd with her sitting behind him, her arms locked around his waist. Once, he pulled her fists loose, trying to stretch away from her. She quickly recovered by tucking her fingers around his belt. It worked better for her not to lean on him, anyway The afternoon was warm, with trees providing some needed shade.

The brothers talked about the terrain, the game to be hunted, and how Junior fared at the mines.

"How did you meet your wife?" Allison asked, tired of being invisible.

"Frieda?" Junior said without looking at her.

"Do you have more than one?" She waited for a laugh, then sighed. No one seemed to appreciate her humor.

"No, of course not." Junior glanced back at her with his usual disregard. "At church. She's the preacher's cousin."

Allison waited, realizing that was all he was going to say. "And what of Levi? Was no one's cousin after him?"

Levi shook his head.

"Why don't you ask him? There were plenty of girls I didn't want he could have chosen from."

Levi let out a curt breath. "Yeah, right." He glanced back at her. "Most wives don't want to know about other girls."

Finally, he was talking. "How many girls would most wives not want to know about?" she teased.

Junior snorted and popped his hat back on his head. "This should be good."

"Junior, you want to make Ma and Pa's by tonight?" Levi said, changing the subject.

Junior held his hand up, blocking the sun. "Yeah, but we need to get riding, and your wife there looks like she's about to fall right off."

Levi pulled the horse to a stop and jumped down. "Move up and put your feet in the stirrups," he said, pulling Allison forward. "Junior, you get that mule moving."

"What are you doing?" Allison wrestled with the fabric of her dress, as Levi adjusted the stirrup length.

"Just keep your feet in the stirrups." He grabbed the saddle and mounted behind her. The horse jumped forward, almost bouncing him off. Before she could protest, Levi wrapped his arms around her and swung the horse into a full gallop.

Levi pointed to the outskirts of their land, but Allison couldn't see anything but trees and more trees. It was dark and cold. How could people live in the snow out here for months and months at a time, with no neighbors, shops, socials? The isolation would be confining. She could make out a small light coming from a cabin. As they approached, she could see that it was much larger than Levi's place, with a large door in the center and two windows on each side, and a small covered porch at the entry. The horses picked up the pace, drawn to their home. Levi jumped down and held the reins tightly as the animals pushed to get into the barn. He reached up for Allison while holding the horse in submission. His arm caught her as she slid down, bumping into his body. He stood unmoving, holding her to him.

"I'm sorry," he whispered. "Something you said earlier got under my skin, but you've been very patient with me." He kissed her temple.

Allison swayed under his strength, tired and close to tears. She lifted her face to his, but her mind would not work.

"Levi, the mule's tied up, I'm heading home." Junior's words broke the moment, and he let go.

"All right, we'll see you tomorrow," Levi said, turning to unload their things.

Laura stepped off the porch and found them, her arms open. "Sweet girl."

Allison moved into her embrace, smelling coffee, cinnamon, and cream. "We're so glad you're here." Laura kissed her check.

Allison tried to discern if something tragic had already happened, but Laura quickly linked arms and led her inside. The cabin was lit up, and the warmth immediately brought a tingling to Allison's skin. There were plates and pottery lined on the open shelves, a nice large black stove with silver handles, and whitewashed cupboards lining both sides. Checkered linens hung from drawers, and padded chairs circled a large rock fireplace. Quilts lined the tops of benches around an old wooden table. *This is Levi's home.* She couldn't ignore the tightness rising in her throat. It looked like a good home. She could see through a cracked door where his father slept, propped up on pillows.

"Oh honey, you look like you're going to cry. Come sit by the fire. You must be exhausted." Laura led Allison by the arm. They both turned to watch Levi enter the front door, and his mother moved away to meet him with a hug. "I'm so thankful you're here." Laura rubbed his back, and Levi returned his mother's embrace.

"Your pa had just been walking around earlier today." Laura led them to the chairs by the fireplace. "That's good, the doc says. I didn't know what to do, son. James didn't think I should send for you. He said it could wait till he's gone to glory." She shrugged. "But I knew you would pray with me for him. And that sounds silly. Pastor and Ruth have been here. I know their prayers are just as wonderful. But you have always carried something special. I don't know what it is. A calm, a comfort. And I know that sounds selfish because your pa is the one suffering. But God just may have a healing for him. Amen?"

Levi reached over and squeezed his mother's arm. "You're not being selfish, Ma. If Pa had a stubbed toe and you wanted me here, I'd be here." He glanced back to his parents' room and took his mother's hand. "Let's pray now. Our Father, we lean upon You in this hour of need. We believe that you can heal and restore. And we believe You have purpose in everything you do."

He paused as his ma whispered, "Why, yes. Give James rest and allow him to draw closer to You in this time. Amen."

Laura opened her eyes and swabbed her face with her hankie again. They both looked at the same time to see that Allison's eyes had not opened from prayer. She was sound asleep

35

There was the most irritating noise in Allison's ear. Her eyes refused to open, but blast it, there it was again. She covered her ears, only to hear whatever it was cry out again. For pity sakes, it sounded like a rooster! Cracking her eyes open, she squinted around in complete disorientation. This blanket was not her blanket. This pillow was not right. The light streaming in wasn't in its usual place.

Pulling her hair off her face, she could smell something amazing. She rose up on one elbow, seeing Levi asleep on his stomach next to her. He had no blanket, just a bare back and brown canvas trousers. Heels up, his bare feet crossed on each other. She laid back down as the rooster went off again. How could he sleep through that?

They were up in a loft of some kind. The log roof slanted down; she reached up, almost touching it. The floor was lined with two or three padded pallets. This must be where Levi and his brothers slept. She thought she heard the front door creak. She sat up and tried to peek over. Her stomach growled, and she wondered where the privy was. Sighing, she looked around; the familiar feeling of being displaced came over her.

Levi rolled over and locked his hands behind his head. His eyes were still closed, so she enjoyed a leisurely opportunity to study him in the light. Tan arms, solid chest, flat belly—now he had crossed his ankles as if he didn't have a care in the world. Her eyes wandered back up and found him awake and watching her. A familiar thickness hung in the air. No one spoke. No one blinked. No one moved. She knew all he wanted was a sign from her that all was well. Her small smile curved upward.

Returning her gaze, he brought his hand up and touched her loose hair. His fingers lingered on her cheek, then traveled down her arm, cuffing her wrist. With a slight tug, her arm buckled, and she fell onto her back. His chest came up over hers, and his leg pinned her underneath him. He smiled and bit his bottom lip. "Hey, Allison," he whispered.

"Your mother…" She tried to squirm out from under him.

"Forget about my ma," he said, eyes narrowing. "Forget about our deal." He drew his finger down her neck. "Forget about it being a mistake…please." His features deepened, and he moved his leg off hers. "I've vowed to help you, and I can't seem to ever get that right. But the truth is, when I think about anything that takes us apart, I can't reconcile it, and I shoot myself in my own foot every time." Sitting up, he wrapped his arms around his knees.

Allison laid still for a few minutes, thinking, moved by his confession and his touch. For pity sakes, it just made him so much more attractive.

"Breakfast," Laura called, making her jump.

Allison followed Levi down the ladder, the only exit from the loft area. It was well-made, but worn. When she reached the floor, she turned to him. "How did I get up there?"

"You fell asleep in that chair." He nodded over at it. "And I carried you."

She tilted her head.

"I'm not saying it was easy." He gave her a quick wink and a smile before he turned to the warm breakfast his mother was setting on the table.

Laura stepped out from her stove with a tray of food. "Levi, would you mind taking this to your pa?"

"No, I don't mind." He tossed a bite of bacon in his mouth before taking the tray from her hands.

James looked up and straightened back against his pillow. "Levi. Didn't expect to see you walking through that door."

Levi set the tray on the side table, thinking Pa sounded weak. "Well, we didn't get much of a visit in Ready Springs. New wife, ya' know." He lifted his eyebrows and pulled a chair over to the bed.

"Is she with you?" James glanced toward the door.

"Yep. She's out there keeping Ma company."

James cracked a grin. "Glad to hear that. Your ma had a bad feeling about the two of you. She thought something might be wrong."

"Hmm." He wasn't surprised by that. "Just adjustments."

"Oh, sure." His pa reached over and patted his hand.

Levi was at a loss. Who was this man? Always in control. Never any emotion. What was that hand pat for?

"You're a good man, Levi, I knew you'd be a good husband." This time his pa squeezed his hand.

Levi blinked as if dust had just flown in his face. "Thanks, Pa." He straightened up and took a deep breath. "Well, let's talk about you. I know something's up. Only time I've seen you in bed is when…let's see, the accident at the mine that crushed your foot."

His dad grimaced. "That was a nasty injury." He brought his foot out of the covers. "Yep, they're still missing."

Levi remembered the day the doctor came and cut the black toes off. He had been so fearful that his pa was going to die.

"Or the time that darn mare threw me off into a tree? I don't know if you were old enough, but I couldn't walk for a couple of days. Probably some broken ribs."

"Yeah, I remember that."

His pa held his chest as he chuckled. "No son, this is different." James' face sobered. "Unless the Lord's got a different plan…well, none of us know." He winced as he sat back. "Since I saw you a few weeks ago, I just can't get these lungs to do their job. The doc's got me on something that helps a bit. I can tell when my clothes hang off me and I can't even hold little Miranda, that it's not good."

Levi hated seeing Pa's chin rise and fall, fighting for control. He nodded at the ground, searching for the right words. "Well, Allison and I can stay. I can help with the chores, and Junior and I can hunt, so we'll get some meat smoked up. Ma and I are praying. Let's just take it a bit at a time."

His pa squeezed his hand even longer. "That sounds like a good plan, but don't spend all your time with Ma and me. New brides need lots of attention."

Levi shook his head. "Ah, first Junior and now you. I'm sure I won't make any more mistakes now that I'm around both of you."

James pressed a pillow to his chest as they shared a laugh.

By the end of the week, Allison had made peace with the dawn-loving rooster, because his harem provided eggs. Lots and lots of eggs. And from the cow in the barn was cream and butter and milk. And from those were the most amazing bread and cake and pies and custards. Laura made it all look so easy. Just as Levi had said, she was a lot like Thelma. She was patient and helpful. She included Allison in everything, and never made her feel as if she was in the way.

Thankfully, it was more comfortable for Allison to answer Laura's personal questions now. *And Levi is different here,* she thought while folding the laundry. *He seems so content.* His steps seemed lighter. He spent time with his father, did countless chores outside, hunted with Patch every day. At night, he was quiet as he lay beside her, sometimes softly rubbing her back. The last time she had seen the weight in his eyes was their first morning here. She tried to remember what was said or unsaid. What had changed? With the obvious lack of privacy, they had fallen back into a cordial place. Allison realized she had stopped folding the laundry and was chewing on her fingernail.

"I saw Levi washing up outside. Why don't you go out there? Ask him to take you for a ride." Laura pulled her shawl off the hook and wrapped Allison in it. "It's not too cold, and you'll have another hour or so till dusk." Laura guided her to the door. "I'll take care of supper, don't rush back." Allison stepped off the porch, obeying her mother-in-law. Levi was around the corner, drying his hands at the outside washstand. Allison watched him; for some reason, it felt imposing to ask him to spend time with her. He probably had other things he wanted to do.

Levi looked up. "Is everything okay?"

"Yes, everything's fine. Except your mother shooed me out of your home."

"She did? It seemed like you two were getting along well."

"We are. To be honest, it's more mothering than I've ever had. She's been so sweet and gracious to me. She said tomorrow we'd work on a new dress."

He nodded at her. "That's good, right?"

She sighed, nervous.

Levi squinted. "Right?"

"She wants us to go be alone for a while."

Levi raised his brows.

"I mean like go for a ride or a walk or something. She pretty much said that we shouldn't come back until supper."

He cracked a grin. "Did you tell her how much you like to ride horses?"

"No."

"I was going to brush down the mare and then take some firewood to an elderly neighbor."

She followed him in, feeling like the barn cat waiting for attention.

"What do you want to do?" He leaned against the barn door and scratched an itch on his back.

"It seems like you have things to do, though I've never met your neighbor."

"Lots of people call her Granny, and we all help out." Levi began to brush the dark brown mare.

Allison stared—his broad back and muscular arms were alluring, and his wavy hair had grown longer. Did he still desire her kisses, her touch? "Your mother even lent me her shawl," she said.

"I noticed."

"She's wonderful. You tried to tell me."

He shot her a quick smile as he came up around the back of the horse. "I'm glad to hear you two have taken to each other."

Allison knew something was coming; for some reason, he wouldn't look her in the eye.

"I'm going to head back to Sault Creek," he said, finally looking up.

"What did you just say?" Allison felt her heart squeeze.

He never stopped brushing the horse. "I'm going tomorrow to Sault Creek, to check on things there."

"Does your mother know about this?"

"No," he said curtly, walking around to face her. "I haven't told my parents. If my ma wants us to be alone, it's to make grandbabies."

She gasped and stepped back.

He laughed, breaking the tension. "It's just for a few days."

"How many days?"

"Maybe a week at the most." He resumed brushing.

Allison sat down on an old stool, dread washing over her. What if he was going to leave her here? What if during those late nights when he and his mother had sat around talking, they had planned all this out? It made sense; he'd been reserved this last week. She watched him, trying to convince herself he would never do that.

"Levi, are you leaving me?"

He slung a loose arm over the mare's back. "Just for a few days."

"Do you want to go back to Sault Creek and live there like you did before? Before you met me?"

He shook his head and kept brushing. "Sometimes I do, and sometimes I don't." He finally quit, untied the horse, and let it loose into the stall. "You know everything's changed."

Allison gazed out the bulky barn doors. "You still have choices. Just like I do," she whispered. The large pine branches slowly bobbed up and down in the evening breeze. Was he regretting their lovemaking? Her chin quivered, and her throat tightened up. Is that why she'd felt so insecure as of late?

"I have to make a decision. I thought the time away would help me pray and find direction." He rubbed his neck.

"What kind of decision? "Allison thought her voice sounded steadier than she felt.

"I saw Junior a couple days ago. He said they need help in the mines. The foreman told him he'd take me for any days I could give. With the money I have, I can buy a horse. With the money I make in a couple months, I can get you to Madison."

Allison exhaled in relief to hear his plan was to get them to Madison. "But why do you need to go to the mines?" she asked. "I have the money." His eyes flashed cold. Of course, he would *never* touch that money. It was like asking him to drink poison. She sighed. "Levi, my grandmother gave me that money. It's like an inheritance. I can do whatever I need to do with it. She would never judge us if it meant getting me back home."

"I'm not concerned with what your grandmother thinks. I still believe something about that money almost got you killed. Something made someone angry enough to leave you for dead. Maybe it wasn't your grandmother's to give, I don't know." He turned, shaking his head.

"Also, I'm worried about my pa." He stopped and pinched the bridge of his nose. "Part of me knows he's not ever getting better. These are the last days I'll have with him. I can't tell you…you can't understand what he was like before. Never a soft word came from his mouth." His expression tightened. "Now he's telling me he thinks I'm a great man. It's like God has flipped his heart around."

Allison hardly remembered her father, but she knew he had been a kind man. She walked to Levi and took his hands. "You *are* a good man. You *are* a great son." Wrapping her arms around his body, she met his gaze. "Maybe Sault Creek was a good place to hide—but maybe that day is over. Maybe we both need to find a home."

❧

He stared at her. "You're supposed to leave your mother and father and cleave to your wife." He pulled her closer as he rested his forehead on hers. Heaven help him, this is how things had started before. "I don't want to be married to you and live at my parents' house."

He kissed her temple. He couldn't help himself; his hands ran up her arms and slowly down her back, pushing the shawl to the ground. His blood pulsed to touch her, to smell her, to have her. Dropping several small kisses on the soft skin of her neck, he undid the buttons on her collar, walking her backward and pressing her against the wall. She let out a tiny cry as he continued kissing her neck. Her hands were pulling at his shirt, his back, and his arms. When he finally got to her mouth, it was as hungry as his. How could this stir even him more than before?

She was breathing as hard as he was, each kiss promising more than the last. He pressed his weight against her, wanting to consume her. Circling his arms around her hips, he lifted her with the intent of finding a soft place.

"Ahh," Allison cried out, twisting from his embrace. She bit her bottom lip and turned to show him a large tear down the back of her blouse.

"What happened?" he said.

She looked over her shoulder. "It was a nail or something," she said, rolling her eyes. "This is embarrassing."

"It's just fabric. I could rip the front and make it even," he said, grinning. He reached out, but she jerked back.

"Levi, don't." She stepped away, watching the mischievous flickers in his eyes. "I'll tell your mother you were ripping my blouse."

"No, you won't." He stepped closer. "You were practically ripping my shirt."

Her mouth dropped open. "That is so… so…" Glancing at the barn door, she turned and ran. She flew around the barn fence and out into the trees.

Levi enjoyed nothing more than a good chase with something he desired. He dodged a bush and ran around behind her, hiding behind a large tree. A short wait provided an opportunity for him to sneak up on her.

A snap of a twig gave him away, and as she took off, he quickly grabbed her arm. He swung her off her feet, squealing and wiggling in his arms. Her laugh and her lovely body moved him. Where could they be alone?

"All right, you win. I've learned running is a bad idea." She squinted, trying to catch her breath.

"You don't say?" He dropped her feet onto the ground. "How do you know?"

"I'll tell you all about it when you get back." She smiled, backing away.

"Oh great…" He rolled his eyes. "I can see how this is going to go."

36

Allison awoke to someone shaking her. "What is it?" she whispered to the darkness.

"Can you come down with me and say goodbye?" Levi said.

"Why are you leaving in the middle of the night?" She tried to get her eyes to focus.

"It's almost dawn," he said.

"Yes, I'll come down." She wrapped the blanket around her shoulders and made her way to the ladder. "Do you have everything? Are you taking Patch?" she whispered as she carefully backed down the ladder.

"Yes." He broke off the corner of a roll and stuffed it into his mouth. There was a bag of food his ma had put together for him last night. He chewed quickly and grabbed it. He opened the door, and they walked out to the front porch. Allison had never seen such faint colors peeking across the ground. He pulled on her blanket and turned her to face him.

"You can go back to bed, I just wanted to have a minute alone." He looked down at her bare feet and smiled. "I love you, and I wanted to tell you that." He grinned, placing a kiss on her lips.

Oh, this man. She wrapped her arms around his waist. "I'm already missing you," she whispered.

"Mmm, you're making this difficult." He pulled his fingers through her soft, loose hair and studied her face. "Be here when I get back."

If he only knew how completely he had won her over. "I will."

Neither one wanted to move. "And you…you don't be rescuing any women falling from cliffs." Allison brushed her fingers lightly through his soft brown hair.

"Trust me on this. One is enough." He captured her hand on his face and kissed her palm. "I'll see you in five or six days."

"Goodbye, Levi." A feeling of desolation swept over her, and she backed away as the tears started to flow. He lifted a quick hand to say goodbye and whistled for Patch. She watched after him as he left, but the bright sun just added to the sting of tears running down her face.

Tiptoeing back to her loft bed, she climbed the ladder and curled up in her blankets. For some reason, the tears would not stop. She reached out and found her hankie. Covering her face, she tried not to let any loud sobs escape. Why such tears? He said he was coming back. She pulled the covers up farther and buried her face in her pillow. Of course he would. It was obvious he was making sure she would be here. Why would he say it if he wasn't planning on coming back?

Her burgundy gloves laid on the wood floor next to the pallet. She eased them on each finger. *Who was that girl with the cream suit yelling at Yvette? Why does it seem like years ago? No one would recognize me now.* Turning to her side, she drew a rattled breath. She hated looking at the place where Levi had last slept. Reaching out her gloved hand, she smoothed the blanket he'd slept under. *How can anything hurt like this? What if something happens to him?* She closed her eyes. *Oh Lord, please watch over him, I ask… Amen.*

Allison could smell coffee. She rolled over, surprised she had fallen back asleep. Unless it was a dream…she realized that her gloves were still on her hands, and Levi was really gone. Her stomach hurt, and her face felt puffy. Lying still, she wondered what Laura would think if she stayed abed all day. She would probably worry. Maybe being busy would help the time go faster, so she pulled her clothes on and headed down the ladder.

"Good morning, love." Laura smiled and set a hot cup of coffee before her.

"Cream and sugar, just for you."

"Thank you." Allison's voice wavered. "How is James?"

"About the same, but you look tired and pale. Are you feeling all right?" Laura brushed a hand down her hair.

"I'm fine, thank you. These flapjacks look wonderful." She stabbed one. "I think I'm just sad to be apart from Levi."

"Well, sure." Laura sat across from her. "It's been such a joy to have you here, but I shouldn't have taken away from your time with him."

"No, no." Allison looked up. "You've been so kind to take us in, and you've gone out of your way to make me feel comfortable. Do you think I should have gone with him?" The thought just rolled out of her mouth.

"I understood that you didn't want to go. It's a hard ride."

Allison studied this dear woman's face. It was creased and imperfect, but so comforting. She had made so many poor judgments, but this face looked like someone she could trust. Desperately wanting to talk to anyone who might understand, she took in a deep breath.

"Well, the truth is, Levi and I do have an unusual marriage."

Laura nodded slowly. That didn't seem to rile her too much.

"I have a strong desire to get back to my home in Madison. Yet Levi loves it here. He's so strong and capable and confident here. I see it. I really do." Allison struggled to find the right words. "And the more we're together, the harder the pull that comes between us." She sighed, taking another gulp of coffee. "That doesn't make sense, I know."

Laura gave her a sweet smile. "Tell me, what do you want for your marriage?"

"Oh! That's just it. I don't know. I mean, I know a woman is supposed to go wherever her husband wants."

"Do you want to live and raise a family at Sault Creek?" Laura asked.

"I don't think so," she whispered. "Do you think Levi would ever want to be away from there?"

"Well," Laura tilted her head in thought. "Levi was raised to believe that a husband should love his wife as Christ loved the church. That brings to my mind a sacrificial love. We know Jesus laid down his life for us. So a good husband will listen to his wife and take her needs into account. It's a lot of responsibility." She nodded at Allison. "But as wives, our charge is to honor and respect our husbands. So as to where to anyone lives, I guess the question is one they both have to ask for God's direction."

That sounded like wise advice, but Allison wasn't sure if it helped or not.

"It tickles me that Ben is off to the Von Keller's to work on their dairy, but he'll be back." Laura grabbed the dirty plates off the table. "He'll circle awhile before he finds the need to settle down, unless one of those daughters catches his eye." Laura smiled and turned to the sink. "Of my boys, Levi was the one who needed his space. Wide open space. I don't know how he would adjust to city life."

Laura had made a realistic point. Taking Levi out of the woods was like a putting Patch in a cage.

A second thought hit her. *What daughters are at the Von Kellers?*

The next morning, Laura came back with James' tray and set it where Allison was finishing her coffee. "What about if we finish up the hem and cuffs on the winter dress for you, and then I can take you over to meet Frieda and Miranda?"

Allison sat up. "Oh, I don't want to take you from James." She wasn't sure about meeting the wife of Levi's burly brother.

"We'll take the wagon, and that way I can drop you off and come back," Laura said as she cleared the table.

"Then you would have to come back and pick me up, though. That sounds like too much to ask."

"Junior can run you back here, or you could just spend the night." Laura pulled the fabric out.

Allison scratched her head, trying to find a way out of this outing.

"Here, you almost have this hem finished." Laura handed the fabric over. "I'm going to go find my button jar. We needed something to close those cuffs with."

Allison contemplated how slowly she could sew. There must be another way to get out of this visit.

Laura pulled the horses and the wagon out front, then looked back into the family cabin. "I think we're ready to go. Allison, can you grab my basket off the table?"

Letting out a long sigh, she grabbed the basket. She didn't want to do this. The horses moved the wagon back a bit, and Allison jumped. "Laura, are you sure about this? Don't we need a man to drive this wagon?"

Laura gave her a smile. "I've done this hundreds of times. Go ahead and put your foot on that step, one on the buckboard, and you're in."

Allison felt a bit of breakfast roll up from her belly. "Can you hold the horses until I get in?"

"Yes, I won't move." Laura stepped down, holding the brown mare by the bridle.

Allison threw the basket in and gripped the buckboard for dear life, then sat down. "Okay, I'm in."

Laura made her way around the other side and grabbed the reins. She pushed the brake free, and Allison held her breath.

The horses jumped forward, and she stiffened. "I didn't realize the wagon had a brake. I must have sounded fearful. I'm sure you've noticed I haven't adjusted to all of this." She gripped her seat.

"All of us women have our own ways to be brave," Laura said.

"Brave?" Allison huffed. "I would never use that word to describe me."

"Why, yes, you are brave. To leave the city and get married. To find love over comfort. To leave your family." Laura steered the horses down the road. "To be brave doesn't mean you have no fears. We all have those. For many, many years I've prayed for Jesus to take my fears. And often He does, but many times He just walks alongside me and asks me to trust Him."

Allison tried to absorb that bit of wisdom. "Levi told me about when Daniel drowned. Maybe you don't want to talk about it, but how could you ever let the others out of your sight after that? I can't imagine what you went through."

Laura placed the reins in one hand and squeezed Allison's hand. "That's a good example of how my fears didn't go completely away. Having Daniel in heaven made it so much more real. And believe me, I grieved like a godless woman, you can ask James."

Laura chuckled. "I'm sure he wondered if I would ever smile again. But I do believe there is a heaven. I don't believe this is all there is. So the Lord somehow comforted me in that He'd already made a place we'd all be together again. And every time the boys left to play or hunt—what should I choose? To let fear steal my life, or trust that even in death, my Father has a plan for that?" Laura nodded. "I'm not saying it's easy."

"Brave," Allison whispered. "*That* is what a brave woman looks like."

"And now I pray for my James. You can imagine how my heart sings with joy at what he shared with you and Levi over dinner that night in Ready Springs. But I want him here. We want to bounce your children on our knees." She smiled.

"Are you worried about being alone?" Allison asked.

"No. I can say that part of my future doesn't bother me. So many years of our marriage we lived in the same cabin, but very much alone. I do a better job of hiding it, but I'm a bit independent. I have James and Frieda, and friends nearby."

Allison watched some birds flitting to from tree to tree. "I would say I've felt alone most of my life, even though I was surrounded by people. I just always felt like I was on the outside." She was surprised that she was able to put such simplicity to her feelings.

"Dear child, you told us the other night about losing your parents so young. Poor little thing."

"You might as well know this." Allison squared her shoulders. "I thought if I attended church services it was all the religion I'd ever need, until I met Levi. At first, I thought he was just strange." She smiled. "He married me, even though I wasn't anything like him. Now knowing you, I'm sure you would wish for a stronger person of faith for him."

"I only wish for a person who'll grow with him. He's not perfect." Laura smiled. "What does your heart say to that?"

"My heart has grown. It has changed. I prayed a prayer with him. He said it needed to be something personal, and I believe it was. In fact, it's helped with feeling alone. To believe there's a God that knows me as a person is quite amazing. To think right now He's watching us and listening to us talk. Thelma goes so far as to say He has great love for us."

"Oh, amen." Laura nodded. "I believe that, too."

Allison realized that the tension was gone from her back. She was able to enjoy the fresh air and smells of the forest. For the first time since she had said goodbye to Levi, the dreariness had lifted. "Thank you for making me come today."

37

The wagon pulled into a side road leading to a house. Allison blinked back the surprise. *They live in a house? Everyone else has thick cabins of logs and mortar, but James and Frieda have a wooden house?* Maybe they were stopping at someone else's home before they got to the real cabin. Suddenly the door flew open, and a curly-haired tyke ran out.

"Gamma, Gamma," the little girl yelled, jumping up and down.

Allison held her breath, hoping the child wouldn't startle the horses. A short and very pregnant woman stepped out after the little girl. Her brown hair was in a tight bun, and she had a warm and welcoming smile.

She reached to help Allison down. "Hello, you must be Allison."

"Yes, thank you for your assistance." She liked having the solid ground under her feet. "Frieda, it's a pleasure to make your acquaintance. And this must be Miranda." The child ran off to jump into her grandmother's arms, and she smiled as Laura picked her up and kissed her head.

"She's a beautiful child," Allison said to Frieda.

Frieda reached in for a hug from Laura. "Can you stay a bit? I have some sandwiches for lunch."

Allison placed her napkin on her plate. "Thank you for lunch. Your home and hospitality are lovely." If it wasn't for the rifle over the door, she would question if Junior really lived here.

Laura had eaten a few bites and hurried away earlier, leaving her at the mercy of the new acquaintance.

The afternoon went along quite pleasantly as Allison and Frieda talked. She enjoyed hearing Frieda's story of becoming part of the Graham family. Frieda had her own strong family and an unwavering strength that she attributed to God's grace. Allison felt at ease, even laughing at some of the ways Frieda described the early days of her marriage to Junior, a bit ashamed that she had placed such low expectations on what Junior's wife must be like.

"But I want to hear more about you," Frieda said. They both turned to see little Miranda walk out, sleepy-eyed, from her nap. "Let me take her to the outhouse, and I'll be right back."

Allison watched them, needing the break to stand. She peeked into the open door of the bedroom and saw a wrought iron bed with a soft white chenille bedspread and a beautiful hand crocheted pillow. She shook her head; she'd been sure it would have been a pallet covered in animal hides. Sweet and simple touches could be found everywhere in this home. She wondered if she should tell Frieda the truth about her and Levi. A pang of guilt struck her, that Laura thought her some brave woman. She hadn't been brave enough to tell Laura the whole truth. Frieda was lovely, but Allison knew that her own life story would make her look like a nitwit.

Frieda peeked in the door. "Do you mind if we visit outside? That's where Miranda likes to play."

"No, that's fine." Allison stepped out to the warm sunshine. "Please show me your garden."

Frieda lifted the gate and pushed it open. Miranda went to grab her little shovel and started digging in the dirt. "Water." She looked wide-eyed at her mother.

"Yes, you can get some water."

Allison reached out and touched Miranda's soft brown curls as she walked by. They felt like fine silk.

Frieda commented on the different vegetables and her luck at getting certain things to grow better than others. Allison wondered if this information was something she would ever use.

"Can I tell you something?" Frieda looked into her eyes, and Allison gave her a slight nod. "You aren't the type of girl I thought Levi would choose."

Allison surprised herself by laughing. "I thought the same thing about you!" She covered her mouth. Both women smiled at each other. "Your home is lovely. Your attention to details. You're so smart…" Allison realized she was just about to offend her. "I mean, Ben and Levi didn't say much about you." Oh, blast, that didn't sound right. "They said you're a wonderful mother." Her face flushed. "Then meeting Junior, I thought…well, it doesn't matter. Meeting you now has been a delight. You're a wonderful hostess."

"Oh, well, thank you. I do wish we had more close neighbors. Junior said something about Levi maybe working in the mines for a while. I'd love to have more family. I'd love for you to meet my sister."

"Well, I'd enjoy that. I'm just not sure where Levi and I are going to end up." Allison shuffled her feet, wondering if she could share her troubles with Frieda.

"Mama." Miranda stood up and showed Frieda her mud cakes. Frieda didn't scold her for the mud all over her smock, but bent her rounded belly down and pretended to eat a bite. "Yum, yum. These are so good. You did a good job, little one." Miranda flashed a proud smile and went back to her mud.

The sweet exchange touched Allison. "You're a good mother."

"Oh, I have my days," Frieda laughed. "Sometimes I lie awake, thinking about how I'll ever manage to get it all done with her and a newborn."

"Thank you for your help with supper." Frieda stirred the beans, and Allison smiled, turning to ask Miranda if she had any books with pictures. The door creaked open, and Junior filled the doorway, just as he had in Sault Creek. Allison blushed, remembering his other dreadful entrance. Luckily, he turned to hang his things on the pegs next to the door. He ran his fingers through his matted hair and turned to give her a faint smile. "Allison."

"Junior."

Frieda came over with a raised face, and he bent down and kissed her on the lips. "It's been the best day." She smiled up at him, rubbing his arms. "Allison is a wonderful addition to the Graham family."

He raised his eyebrows, looking surprised, and Allison stepped back into the parlor. Miranda came around the corner, and Junior reached out and snatched the child up.

"What about your day, sweet pea?" He held her next to his chest, picking dried mud from her hair. "Did you help Mama garden today?"

Allison took another step back. *Who is this man?*

"Cake," Miranda said as she ran her hands down Junior's beard. Junior turned and headed for the table. "Did my ma say anything about Pa?" He grabbed a roll from the table and ate it in two bites. Allison felt like a spectator watching from a window.

"Not much has changed." Frieda set the pot on the table, and Junior set Miranda on a chair with a pillow and went to wash his hands. Frieda and Junior turned to Allison at the same time. "Are you eating supper?" Junior said.

She realized how stupid she must look, standing in the parlor watching them. "Yes, thank you. Where would you like me to sit?"

"In a chair," he smirked.

"Oh, Junior." Frieda smiled at him. "Right here would be fine, Allison." She pulled a chair out. They sat and reached out their hands to one another. Junior's prayer sounded like an echo of Ben and Levi. Frieda, just like Laura, gave her a little squeeze before she released her hand.

Allison took a deep breath. "Thank you for having me to dinner. It smells wonderful, Frieda."

Junior scooped some beans and meat into a little wooden bowl for Miranda. "Blow on it, baby. It's still hot." He set it down while Miranda puffed out the sweetest little breaths into her bowl. Frieda took her little spoon and stirred it around. Junior grabbed another roll and split it in half, dunking it into his bowl. He ate just like his brothers, barely a breath or room for conversation. Allison realized too late they were all eating and she hadn't taken a bite.

"Not hungry?" Junior glanced at her bowl.

She picked up her spoon and began to stir. "I just find eating with the Graham brothers is often…"

"Careful," Junior interrupted, but kept eating.

Allison clamped her mouth shut. She was a guest at this bountiful table and certainly did not have the relationship with Junior that she did with Levi and Ben.

"Stimulating." She thought that word was safe enough.

Frieda snickered and looked down. "Eating isn't the only thing."

Both women covered their mouths to silence the erupting giggles.

Junior shook his head. "Lord, help me."

As if the world had decided to spin in another direction, Allison was sad to be saying goodbye to Frieda. Her day had been anything but dull. A bit unorthodox, in light of her past, but something so personal, so encompassing, stirred her. Scenes from the little family filled her mind: Junior playing blocks on the floor with Miranda. A small fire in the fireplace. The way Frieda cleaned over the wash bowl with Junior stopping to rubbing her back. Miranda flitting around the room, singing her little unintelligible songs. Junior taking her to the outhouse and then helping her into a diaper and nightgown. He still had the temperament of a bear, but she hadn't realized that men could have two sides, as Junior did. And then there was the ease between husband and wife. She'd never seen anything like it. The way they moved through the small home, each helping without words spoken. She felt content just watching them.

"You ready?" Junior interrupted her thoughts.

Allison stood to take her leave. Looking into Frieda's eyes, she said, "Thank you. Today was special." The women embraced.

"You'll have to forgive me. We never got to talk much about you," Frieda said, pulling back. "Let's do a picnic Sunday after church."

"Yes! I hope Levi will be back by then." Allison walked out into the darkness.

Junior disappeared for a moment, and Allison chewed on her bottom lip. When he returned, he was pulling the large horse he had ridden before.

Frieda stepped out behind her and squeezed her elbow. "Junior said you weren't much for riding. But trust me, even with my stubby legs, he's never let me fall. He'll be careful. Right, Junior?" Frieda waited for a response, then pulled on her husband's sleeve.

"Right." He mounted the horse, and Allison wondered if maybe she should just stay the night. He reached down for her and pulled her up behind him. She gripped the bulk of his coat and remembered that she had done this with Levi, and lived.

When they had ridden in silence for a long while, Junior pulled the horse off the road and into the forest.

"Why are we going off the road?" Allison's heart lurched.

"Quicker," he mumbled, the horse straining to go uphill.

"How can you see where you're going?"

"I've ridden this trail a thousand times."

Allison looked down; the trail narrowed as they climbed. Her legs were almost smashed against a tree crowding the trail, and her nerves were starting to fray. She pressed her face into the back of Junior's coat, hoping he wouldn't notice.

She considered the familiarity with this one family. First Levi. Of all the people that could have found her that day, literally saving her life, it was him. What would have happened if those other men that had robbed them had come along? A shudder went up her back. Levi had been so patient and strong. He had fed her and helped her get better in every way. He never treated her like a burden. If anything, he gave his heart to her more than she ever deserved.

Then there was Ben. A smile rose at the thought of him. So helpful and kind. Teasing her and making her smile constantly. He made her feel young and carefree. She had an attachment to Ben, but not a romantic one. Gazing into the darkness, she tried to define the difference. With Levi, it always felt like a force of the wind coming over her, challenging her to sort out her own emotions, pulling her toward him. Could she see them sitting on a little rug with children gathered around? Before today, the answer would have been *no*. But watching Junior and Frieda had changed her mind. They were so humble, yet so rich.

"Hey." Junior wrapped his arm back around her. She sat up, feeling like she was falling.

"You're falling asleep." He turned to look her in the face. "For someone who doesn't like to ride—it might help to hang on to me."

"I'm so sorry." Allison shook her head, trying to wake. "You're not as talkative as Levi or Ben."

"That so? What do you want to talk about?"

She gazed into the dark forest. This would be a test. Her mind circled, searching for a topic. "Tell me what you do at the mine."

"I've done almost every job, but right now I drill into the rock to find core samples." He kicked the horse to pick up the pace.

Allison didn't know what to ask after that. "Is that what your father did before he got sick?"

"No. He built the head frames that go into the mine to hold the walls steady, but he'd done just about every job down there, like me."

"Do you think the mining job is why he's so sick?" She felt him rock back and forth in the saddle.

"Maybe. Everything a man does has a risk. Levi could get shot. A trap through the foot. Infections set in."

That imagery caused her stomach to lurch. "Oh." She swallowed it down. "I think your mother and your wife are simply incredible women."

"Why is that?" he asked.

"Because they…" She didn't have the words. "They…"

"They aren't like you," he suggested.

"No, they're not." She had no trouble giving honor where it was due. "They're strong and confident. They're both so caring and nurturing. I'm a complete stranger, and your mother's done everything possible to make me feel at home. You all are like a knitted blanket, each thread intertwined and connected. I come from none of that. So you're right, I don't hold a candle to them." Her voice wavered a bit, "To none of you, really."

Junior pulled the horse to a stop and shifted in the saddle to look at her. "You're not going to cry or anything, are you?"

She shrunk back at his attempt to see her face. "No. I'm not going to cry." He looked at her a while longer than normal, with the usual Graham sincerity, and Allison had the oddest desire to tug on his long beard. "I'm fine, let's go." She held on as he started the horse forward.

"The best blanket has at least one extra color in it," he said.

"I'm going to take that as a compliment. Coming from you, I'd imagine they're few and far between."

Junior shook his head. "Oh, Lord, I hope Levi knew what he was getting into."

Allison smiled. Maybe he didn't dislike her as much as she once thought.

38

He'd only been four days at the cabin at Sault Creek, but Levi felt the quiet haunting. He rubbed the stubble on his face and flipped the meat sizzling in the pan. This place had once been his refuge. After loading copper and rock on the docks day after day, this cabin was as close to heaven as he'd ever known. How could it have lost all appeal? He had stayed busy enough—surely he would enjoy the solitude he once craved, but now the silence just taunted him. He wondered how Allison fared. Would she be there when he went back? Did he really trust what she said?

He dropped the cooked meat onto the plate and looked at the table. Patch sat nearby, patiently waiting for some scraps. "Thanks for keeping me company, boy. The table seems especially lonely tonight." He bowed his head and said a prayer of thanks, pulling his Bible over to read out loud between bites. It comforted him as he held his hand over the pages and let the truth sink in. He felt as if he had a peace about working in the mines till the snow flew. Then he would have the money to take Allison to Madison and support them until he knew what God wanted after that. As much as he wanted the whole picture, that seemed to be the only step given. He looked around his little cabin. Maybe this place was just for a season? He always figured he would be here forever.

Levi looked at the moon gleaming through the dark. "Let's go pull that last trap by the pond," he said to Patch. It would feel good to fall into his bed tonight, exhausted. He grabbed his rifle and pack and started the four-mile trek. Halfway up a steep dirt rise, he began to sing. *Prone to wander, Lord I feel it, prone to leave the land I love.* He liked to change the words. He pictured Allison standing next to him at the church he was raised in. *Take my heart now, come and seal it, seal it for thy courts above.*

He got to the top and rubbed his burning muscles. An hour later, he had dismantled the trap and thought he heard something. *Must just be Patch chasing something.* Sure enough, he heard the barking, but as he stood and walked toward the sound, he realized it wasn't Patch. He heard the cry and yelp of pain before he saw a wolf shaking Patch by the neck. He grabbed a fallen limb and swung with all his might at the wolf. It jumped back, and Patch scrambled to his feet. The wolf growled and lowered its muzzle to pounce.

Levi held the branch out, looking for something stronger to fend it off. He looked back to his rifle and clenched his teeth. Why had he left it back there? He backed up slowly before he could make out the eyes of one…no…three more wolves coming his way. His heart began to pound, and for a split second, Patch made eye contact. He could barely suck in a breath as Patch went after the closest wolf. It was just what he needed to turn and grab his rifle.

In one smooth motion, he had it up and against his shoulder. A shot rang out, and it dropped the wolf charging him. Patch was tangled in a nasty fight with the other ones. One wolf pulled out enough that he could get a clear shot. It cried out and staggered away. The others looked as if they had Patch pinned down, and he risked another shot. Blood flew in the air as the other two wolves cried out. One dropped in place, the other ran off.

Levi ran to the mass of bloody fur and saw that Patch's eyes were still open. "Oh, Lord, help me, Oh, Lord, help me…" he said over and over as he gently pulled Patch free. The dog's head kept rising and falling, but Levi knew he was in a bad way. He searched the darkness for more evil eyes, but it looked as if that was all of the pack. "I'm going to take care of you, boy. Just hold on. I'm right here…"

Levi built a fire next to the pond and took a closer look at his friend. Some of the puncture wounds had already stopped bleeding, but the one at the dog's neck had made a wide gash. Levi gently held the skin closed and wrapped it with the sleeve he tore off his shirt. Patch's chest rose and fell rapidly, then the breathing dwindled to just a small faint movement. He sat back and ran his hand down his face. How could he be so stupid as to walk into a dark forest without his rifle out? He looked down at the sleeping dog. "I'm so sorry, buddy." Rubbing his hand gently on the dog's head, Levi watched over him for a long time, and when he couldn't hold his head upright, he fell asleep against the pack.

39

Drumming her fingers on the table, Allison looked around. It was too hard to concentrate. Laura was in the bedroom tending to James, and Allison couldn't even focus on reading the Bible. The day had turned cloudy and cool, just like her mood. Her mug of tea was lukewarm and had lost all its comfort. She got up and peered out the window, as if somehow watching for Levi would make him arrive.

"Is it raining?" Laura asked, walking into the room.

"No, I don't see any drops. It's just…when Levi said he'd be gone a week, I thought he'd be back by now. Now it's almost two weeks. Does he do this? I'm wondering if something has happened to him."

Laura came up and rubbed her arm. "If he's not home when he said, there's always a good reason." She gave Allison a motherly nod. "Not all the reasons are bad."

"I suppose that's true. I've just relied on him so much, from the moment I met him." She smiled sheepishly. "And tried my best never to let him know it."

Laura smiled. "I think you're both smart and independent people." She walked toward the kitchen. "I think I'll fry a chicken for after church tomorrow. You let me know if it rains."

Allison dreaded spending the afternoon worrying and staring out a window. "Give me a job, I need to help you."

Allison fastened the last button on the new dress. Laura, a wonderful seamstress, told her over and over how fun it was to be creative with another woman instead of making one more identical man's shirt. Attending the little country church with the Grahams would be a new experience; she wanted to see Frieda and little Miranda, but wondered if she should ask Junior to go check on Levi. Perhaps it was too much to ask. Maybe it should be Laura's idea. She stepped off the last rung of the ladder and noticed Laura was still wearing her work apron.

"I'm not sure if I should leave James this morning," Laura said as she dried her hands on a cloth.

"I understand. You know him better than anyone. I'll stay and help."

"No, no, you look beautiful, all ready for church. Levi had better be careful some other young man doesn't start asking about you." Laura was being kind, but Allison could see that her heart was burdened.

"I can't take your wagon. Really, it's no bother to stay."

"The Strongs come by and get Granny, and they'll take you, too. I know how much Frieda is looking forward to seeing you. The picnic is all ready, and I was hoping you'd ask Junior to have the doctor come by."

"Of course." Allison realized that her desire to get Junior to help her was not as important as the doctor checking on James.

Allison looked past the twin girls across from her in the back of the bumpy wagon. Once again, she found herself in a place of utter insecurity. She didn't know any of these people and didn't want to rely on them. Already noticing people looking at her, she turned away. The wagon finally came to a stop, and Mr. Strong helped her and his daughters from the back. She straightened her dress and looked up to see Rolf Crocker coming her way.

"Oh, for pity sakes." She turned quickly to the girls standing next to her. "Now, tell me your names once again." Turning away from Mr. Crocker, she engaged with them as the store owner walked by to converse with Mr. Strong.

"I'll meet you here after the picnic." She nodded to the sisters and headed for Junior and Frieda. Frieda tugged little Miranda forward and wrapped an arm around Allison. "No Levi yet?" she said.

Her shoulders drooped. "No. He's overdue, and I'm getting worried. And Laura didn't come today. She wants Junior to ask the doctor to come."

"Oh, my." Frieda held her arm out to another woman who strongly resembled her. "Allison. I'd like you to meet my sister, Cory."

"Cordelia to everyone else, but it's wonderful to meet you. Frieda is so pleased to have you as a sister-in-law."

Allison reached out her gloved hand, and Cordelia shook it. "As I am delighted to have her."

"Levi was a much sought-after young man. The more he stayed quiet and aloof," Cordelia laughed, "the more the girls liked him."

Frieda linked her arm through Allison's. "God was saving him for Allison. Cory, if you'll excuse us, Allison has a message for James." The ladies all nodded to one another as they moved apart. Frieda led Miranda and Allison toward a circle of men, including Junior. Suddenly uncomfortable, Allison pulled back. "Let's wait for Junior to be done."

"Don't fret, he won't be mad. You know he's all bark and no bite," Frieda said. Allison didn't want to admit that the sight of all these people unnerved her. She had been so isolated at Sault Creek that it was like she was watching herself in another life. *People are just people.* She tried to calm herself. Had she felt this way moving around in Madison? Sure enough, when Frieda called James over, no one even looked her way.

Frieda touched her husband's arm. "Your ma wants you to bring the doc by."

He looked at Allison. "Right now?"

She bit her bottom lip. "Well, she didn't say that."

"After church?" he said, brows crossed.

"I didn't ask when." She looked at the ground.

"Junior," Frieda said tenderly, "Levi hasn't returned, and they're worried. It's been just the ladies taking care of things. I think we should all go. Can you please go find the doc before the service starts and let the Strongs know we'll be taking Allison home?"

"Yep," he said and walked away.

"You poor thing." Frieda hugged her shoulders. "You're worried about Levi, and now something's happening with James. This has been a lot. You have such a sweet spirit. All this can be so overwhelming."

Allison nodded to Frieda. "Thank you for understanding."

Little Miranda held out a fist full of wildflowers and weeds. "For Papa."

40

∽∾∾

Nothing had changed, but Allison was relieved to be pulling into the Graham property. She had told herself that James was just having a bad day, and that a call to the doctor was normal. Neither Junior nor Frieda spoke much, though, and even little Miranda seemed quiet.

The clouds drifted back over the tall trees, casting a dark shadow on the cabin as the wagon stopped. Junior helped them out and nodded to Frieda to go into the house while he pulled the horses into the barn. They walked in and found the door open to the little bedroom. Laura was sitting in a chair next to James' bed, reading the Bible out loud. Allison and Frieda both stopped and listened. Miranda tugged on her mother's hand, but Frieda told her to be still. Laura's voice was strained and louder than usual. Allison recognized that she was reciting the twenty-third Psalm. The way Laura clutched the Bible to her chest, not needing to see the written words—something was different. As Allison watched Laura rocking and speaking scripture, she felt as if she had entered holy ground. Glancing to Frieda, she saw her sister-in-law's eyes pooling with tears, and her chin trembled.

Junior walked in behind them, standing still and watching. He looked over to Frieda and bent down, gently placing a kiss on her wet cheek, then cleared his throat and moved to his mother's side. Allison didn't realize she was clutching Frieda until Frieda bent down to pick up Miranda. The child laid her head on Frieda's shoulder, and Allison heard her whisper, "Papa is very sick. He can't play today. We have to be quiet so he can take his nap."

Miranda placed her chubby hands on Frieda's cheeks. "Mama cryin'."

They listened as the doctor's carriage rolled up in front.

A few hours later, Allison worked in the kitchen with Frieda while Miranda sat at the table, chewing on a chicken leg. Frieda handed Junior a hot mug of coffee as he scratched his beard and breathed deeply. They all three froze when the doctor came out of the small room. He walked over to Junior. "Son, your pa's a fighter. He doesn't want to go, but I don't think he's going to hang on much longer. It'd be fittin' to have the family come and say their regards."

Junior reached out and shook his hand. "Thanks for coming out today."

"I always wish there was something more I could do," the doctor said as he reached for his coat. "Your ma is a blessed woman. She has three respectable sons and other friends and family. Her grief will be deep, but the folks around here will love and care for her."

Junior nodded stoically. Frieda walked to the door and handed the doctor a basket of food. "Thank you for coming today. Please tell Mrs. Noir we're sorry for interrupting the Sabbath."

Junior took a wet cloth to Miranda's face and hands, but when the little girl began to fuss and pull away, he picked her up.

"Here, give her to me. I think we'll both go lie down in the loft." Frieda said.

Junior came around the table and lifted Miranda over his head, depositing her on the edge of the loft, as Frieda carefully took the steps of the ladder.

When he turned, Allison asked, "Is that how your pa put you boys to bed?" She wished the words back as soon as they left her mouth.

Junior pulled his beard. "Yep." He swallowed hard and walked out the front door.

Sitting in the chair, watching the small flicker in the fireplace, Allison dozed. Sometimes she woke to the sound of Laura crying, and sometimes she heard her mother-in-law praying. After the doctor had left, there had been no more loud declarations coming from the room. Laura hadn't come out all day, and Allison wanted to offer her some tea or maybe a bite of supper. She hesitated, then rose up and went to make the tea. She looked up from the kitchen to see her blankets over Miranda and Frieda. They were sleeping where she and Levi had slept. It was so intimate, this family. Even though the air was thick with grief, there was still just as much love surrounding everything.

Allison approached the door with the cup and saucer. Laura lay next to James, one arm across his chest, stroking his cheek, her eyes closed. In all her days, Allison would never forget this moment. It was excruciating. It was cherished. But it was not hers to interrupt.

❧

Riding up to the dark barn, Levi carefully lowered Patch to the ground. A lone barn cat greeted them, circling in and out of his legs. "Well, you're happy to see me," he said to the cat as he lit a lantern and pulled the horse in to unsaddle him. Throwing a forkful of hay to the horse, he stepped out of the stall, while Patch watched him with hollow eyes. "You're next, buddy." He dipped a pan into a water bucket and brought it down to Patch, then kicked the dust off some feed sacks and made Patch a bed. Brushing the dirt off his hands and pants, he wondered if he should clean up better. He needed to talk himself out of high expectations. *She's been known not to speak to me when she's mad.* He looked down at his condition. *Better test the temperature first.*

Junior's team was in the corral. Probably just visiting late. It would be good to see everyone. Maybe Frieda had made friends with Allison. He walked into the quiet cabin. No one was around. Without a welcome, it felt eerie and solemn. He hung up his jacket, noticing the small fire in the fireplace.

Junior woke, and sat up in the rocking chair. "Levi," he said, rubbing his eyes.

As if a rock had fallen on his head, Levi realized something must be wrong. "It's Pa?"

"The doc was here. He thinks this is it—he won't make it much longer."

"Is Allison here?" Levi swallowed.

Junior's brows rose. "Why wouldn't she be here? She's asleep in the loft."

Levi chided himself, vacillating between joy and dread. "How's Ma?"

Junior rubbed his hands through his thick hair. "I don't know. I can't tell if she's praying or talking to herself. All I can remember is how it destroyed her when Daniel died. I hope you're planning to stay awhile; I can't abide her when she gets crazy. Ahh…that sounded bad. I mean, you were always better at this stuff. She listens to you."

"Did you talk to Pa?" Levi asked.

Junior shook his head. "We got her out of there for a few minutes, and when I sat with him, he was either in pain or asleep. If we're going to make our peace with him, it's going to be up to us, you know?"

Levi peeked in his parents' dark bedroom, his throat constricting. He should never have left. Look what had happened while he was gone.

"Who's that?" Laura whispered.

"It's Levi, Ma. I just got here."

She sat up and stepped to the door, wearing her long white nightgown without her cap. "I thought you were an angel coming to take him." She lightly touched her son's face, and he held her while she cried into his chest.

◈◈◈

Allison was inside the church, where the music had already started. Everyone had their hymnals out—but why weren't they singing? Their mouths were moving, but just a faint small sound was coming out. She wanted to sing along. *Why don't they raise their voices? What kind of church is this?* She thought she knew the song:

Rock of Ages, cleft for me,
Let me hide myself in Thee;
Let the water and the blood
From Thy wounded side which flowed…

She wanted to sing along, but no sound would come out of her mouth. Something was wrong…where was her voice?

Her eyes flashed open, and she drew in a breath. She was just dreaming. But there was singing coming from somewhere in the cabin. Sitting up, she smoothed out her wrinkled dress. She looked around the loft and found she was the only one there. Frieda and Miranda must have already gone down. A wave of foreboding hit her. The singing was coming from the bedroom. Was James gone? Had he passed in the night? Her stomach rolled up—she had no fortitude for this.

While I draw this fleeting breath
When my eyes shall close in death
When I rise to worlds unknown
See Thee on Thy judgment throne
Rock of Ages, cleft for me
Let me hide myself in Thee.

Frieda had a beautiful, clear voice. Allison closed her eyes while the comfort of the words and the image of the family singing over James overpowered her senses.

Just as I am, without one plea
But that thy blood was shed for me
and that thou bidst me come to Thee,
O Lamb of God, I come, I come.

She could hear Junior and Laura joining in.

Just as I am, though tossed about
With many a conflict, many a doubt
Fightings and fears within, without
O Lamb of God, I come, I come.

It felt to her as if God's angels were singing, and she wanted to belong to that holy throng.

Just as I am, thou wilt receive
Wilt welcome, pardon, cleanse, relieve
Because thy promise I believe

O Lamb of God, I come, I come.

This was an ushering in song for James. But each word they confidently sang rushed at her own heart, a feeling similar to that she had felt after praying with Levi—something birthing in her. It was warm and encompassing. It had to be God. She raised her hands and whispered, *I come to You, too.*

Normally, she would never have approached something so intimate, but stepping off the loft ladder, it drew her in, giving her courage to belong, to be accepted as a person of love and faith.

She saw Junior just inside the door. Miranda, with her head on his shoulder, looked up and stuck her little hand out. Allison placed a kiss on that sweet welcoming hand. Junior turned, making room for her to get in. Laura was kneeling at the side of the bed, and Frieda stood just in front of her husband. Allison's eyes suddenly locked on the man sitting on the chair with his head in his hands. She knew those curly locks, the span of those shoulders. A shiver raced up her spine as she gazed from Levi to the ashen face of James Graham. He was gone. He didn't really look like the man she had met. She swallowed back her tears, so glad for the family that Levi was here. Frieda reached over and gently squeezed her arm. *He's gone,* she whispered. Allison nodded, wiping her wet face on her shoulder.

"Would you like me to take Miranda?" she whispered. Frieda didn't answer, but nodded toward Levi. His gaze held hers, and he stood, then took her hand and led her out of the room. In front of the fireplace, he brought her in, closing the distance between them.

"I'm so sorry, Levi," she whispered, bringing her arms around him. He pulled her closer, and his arms went unexpectedly slack. Stepping back, he opened his mouth to speak, but the emotions caught in his throat.

"I..." He ran his hand over his mouth. "I should have been here." His eyes spilled over with tears, and he sucked in a ragged breath. "I didn't think he would go so fast."

Allison grabbed his shirt. "Levi, none of us knew."

"I should have been here." He shook his head.

Is this what grief sounds like? Is this what people say when there are no words? She felt his pain as if it was her own. *There are no answers, no comfort. To come home and find your home will never be the same. His mother is left without anyone.* She gently touched his face. "I love how you love your family." Her head tilted to the side. "And I love you."

Despite the overflow of grief, Levi smiled. "That's good," he said, squinting at her. "The whole time I was gone, I thought of you constantly." He swallowed and looked to his parents' room. "But I never pictured coming home to this."

Junior interrupted their conversation. "I'm going to Ready Springs and get a casket. I'll post something to Ben, but he won't be able to make it in time. Frieda will help Ma…prepare the body. Think he'd want to be buried next to Daniel."

Levi barely nodded.

"I'll tell the neighbors we'll bury him tomorrow." Junior cleared his throat. "Noon. If the reverend is busy, you can say some words."

A noonday wind lightly gusted around Allison as she stood a bit behind Levi, one hand on his back, the other pressed into his right arm. She didn't know if it was appropriate, but it felt right. This time, when *Amazing Grace* broke out, she sang out with passion and love. *An amazing grace saved James, Sr. I'll never forget his dream and how it changed him. Amazing grace to save me from myself, save me from hiding from everything that's good.*

The neighbors and friends all stood around a plain wooden casket that was about to go into the earth. *From dust to dust*, the reverend had said. Their voices swelled.

When we've been there ten thousand years
Bright shining as the sun
We've no less days to sing God's praise
Than when we'd first begun.

"Amen." The reverend closed his Bible to end the service.

Allison stayed planted next to Levi as the folks filed past the family, graciously giving their condolences. She warmed at Levi's desire to introduce her as his wife. Clutching his arm tightly, she watched as the men lowered the casket into the ground and began to shovel the dirt on the wooden box. As Allison listened to the quiet conversations around her, she realized that for the first time in her life, she was in the right place at the right moment.

41

The air nipped Allison's face as she pulled Laura's thick coat around her shoulders and walked into the barn. Patch looked as if he wanted to sit up, but when he saw it was her, he put his head down. She knelt and scratched behind his ears.

"Sorry, it's just me," she murmured. After the story Levi had told, she understood that it was a miracle Patch had lived. Did God know that losing both Patch and his father would be too much for Levi? But then why wouldn't God…she shook her thoughts free. The family was just trying to find their way without James. Asking *why* didn't seem important.

It had been a month since the funeral. People still came almost every day with a load of firewood, some fresh bread, or a casserole. Levi had said there wasn't much they really needed, but it was just the neighbors' way of showing love. He had been getting up before sunrise to meet Junior and head to the mines. She didn't have the heart to tell him that most mornings she woke up to Laura's crying. The door was closed to her room, but Allison could hear her sobs, mixed with prayers. On mornings like this, it was easier to head outside so Laura could have some privacy.

The barn cat rubbed against her legs for attention. *What will Laura do when we head for Madison?* Her heart squeezed, thinking about it. Pulling out the needles and yarn that she'd brought to the barn, Allison worked on a few of the stitches Laura had taught her. She settled back against the water barrel, wondering when she might be able to ask Laura some personal questions.

Midmorning, Allison brought in a basket of eggs while Laura worked on some little items of clothing for the new baby. "Did you help deliver Miranda?" Allison asked.

"I did," Laura nodded.

"What was that like? Had you done it before?"

"Oh, yes, occasionally. The doc travels, so sometimes, the family just asks a neighbor woman or one of their kin. First babies take a while, and I think women are more patient." Laura smoothed out the little flannel smock. "Then the second and third babies come fairly fast."

"Is that because the mother has done it before?"

"Mmm hmm," Laura said. "A woman knows what to expect then. I think we don't fight the pain as much. It seems to go faster."

"I keep thinking about Frieda, with only one more month. She looks like she could deliver anytime." Allison tapped her fingers against the mug, looking for the nerve to say something. "I'd hate to miss it."

"Oh, you're welcome to come along. You two have become such friends, I'm sure she wouldn't mind."

Allison scratched behind her bun, wondering why it felt so tight all of a sudden. "It's just that Levi said we'd be gone to Madison by then."

"Oh, I didn't know."

"Something about the snow flying. Too hard to travel if it gets too deep into winter."

"Well, I guess that makes sense." Laura turned and walked into the kitchen.

Allison felt her stomach drop. Ever since the doctor told James that Laura was lucky to have such good sons, she felt the weight of staying and taking care of her.

"Are you sad that Ben hasn't made it home?" If he would just walk in about now, that might help Laura to let them go.

"Yes, I suppose. By the time I wrote him, his pa was already gone. I said he didn't need to come." Laura sounded tired, shrugging. "It'll be hard for Frieda, not having you here. How long will you visit your family?"

"I don't really know. We don't have much of a plan. It's so far away."

Laura looked down. "I see."

Levi seemed somber. He was never much of a talker, but now he barely finished his supper before he headed out the door to do the chores, with dark circles under his eyes. When Allison asked him how she could be of more help, he commended her for helping his ma, and said it meant a lot to him to picture her here with Laura. They sat and talked for a few minutes each night, and Levi looked as if he was listening, but most often he was falling asleep. He'd get up and kiss her on the cheek and go to bed.

It wasn't anything to be upset about, she told herself. He was still grieving—they all were. Usually, on Sundays, they would head to church. She liked sitting close to him and listening to the teachings. Often, they would discuss the main points on the way home. It was nearing the two months Levi had asked for, and this Sunday she knew she needed to ask about their plans.

"It looks like Frieda is going to hang on a little longer. It'll be sad to miss seeing the baby born," she said as he pounded nails into a large crate.

He looked up, brows raised.

"We…you said we'd head to Madison before the snow flies." He shook his head and flipped the crate over. His silence hung in the air.

"I'll take you." He frowned, raked his fingers through his hair. "I know how important this is to you. You've been very patient." He knelt down and rubbed behind Patch's soft ears, and the dog whimpered. "I'm sorry. I haven't tended to you like I should. My father tried to help me, but I guess I didn't listen."

Allison waited for something from him that would lift her heart up. His words sounded sincere, so why did she still feel like a burden?

42

⁂

The next afternoon, Laura pulled back on the reins when their wagon hit a dip. "They try to get ahead of me sometimes," she said, as Allison gripped the edge of Laura's coat tighter. The warm tears rolled freely down her face.

Laura glanced over. "Are you all right, dear?"

Allison looked down at her burgundy gloves. "I'm so sorry, I must have left my hankie in the loft." She owed Laura an explanation, but Laura did not need to hear the true pain of her heart. "It's just very overwhelming. I didn't know the baby would come this soon. I...I didn't think I would be here. Oh my, that little thing coming out of Frieda's body."

"I wondered if that might be too much for you. It's not a pretty sight, but once you clean them up and count the toes and fingers, you can't help but fall in love." Laura smiled.

"They really are a wonderful little family. I'm so happy for them. Another girl," she said between sniffles.

"I'd love a wagonload of girls, after raising boys," Laura said.

Allison still hadn't had a womanly talk with Laura, but now her admission tugged at Allison's heart. She took in great gulps of air, and the crying started again.

"Oh, dear." Laura held the reins in one hand and rubbed her daughter-in-law's back. "Is there something else? I know you and Levi have been out of sorts. Even though he's my son, I love you like a daughter. If there is anything I can do to help..."

Allison felt Laura's words deep in her cracked soul. "I feel like I'm from a…a… foreign country. I really don't blame Levi." She couldn't control her ragged breath. "He doesn't belong in the city. And I'm not sure I belong here." There, at least she got that out. She hated feeling like a child again, lying alone in her dormitory room. But at home in Madison, she'd always felt bored and lonesome, strangely longing for school. Allison's chin quivered, and she buried her face in her hands. She felt Laura's hand again, trying to rub away the ache of years adrift.

৵৽৶

Levi quickly let go of Allison's hand after the prayer at supper. He wanted to hear about Junior's and Frieda's new baby. He filled his plate, listening to his mother tell about the new little one. Allison looked down at the potato pie without picking up her fork. He tried to ignore her obvious distress.

She swiped a tear from her cheek. "Excuse me," she said as she let herself off the bench.

Levi glanced at her, and then back to his mother. He felt exhausted by the last weeks; he'd said he would take her, what now? His mother scowled at him. "I've tried." He shook his head. "There's nothing to say, or do. I'm sure it was just from watching the baby come." He shoved a forkful in his mouth as Allison disappeared into the loft.

"Since you don't know for sure," his mother practically growled, "get up there and find out. She's been crying all day." Laura didn't speak this harshly often, and Levi took note.

He dropped his fork and stood. "Yes, ma'am."

He approached the ladder, wishing he could at least have had the benefit of a good meal in his belly. Allison was curled in a ball, with a blanket over her body. He sat and looked around—he hated it when she cried. He noticed her hands were covered with her burgundy gloves. "Are you cold?" was the only thing that came to mind.

She shook her head as he lightly ran his finger down her gloves. "These bring you comfort, I'd guess." She nodded.

"Do you want to come back and eat some supper?" Blast it— that came from the condition of his stomach.

"No," she murmured.

"Did you get to hold the baby?" he asked.

She finally looked at him with a sad smile. "No, I was afraid I'd drop her."

He let out a small laugh. "You wouldn't have dropped her." He brushed a tear from her cheek, and they both froze at the familiar tenderness.

Allison's pale face shrank back. "I heard your mother tell you to come to me." She sat up and sucked in a large breath. "I wanted to think of something to say to you. To tell you how I miss you. To tell you I was wrong to press you to go from here. I…I was so small when I lost my parents…"

Levi tried to follow her ramblings.

"…and I can't understand what it is to be part of a family. Not like your family. The way you love and respect your mother. Then I was wishing Ben was here, and…"

Levi looked away. *What does Ben have to do with anything? Does she miss him, too?* "You want Ben to take you to Madison?" He regretted his words as soon as they left his mouth.

"No!" she said with a twisted face. "To help your mother while we're gone." She dropped her head in defeat. "How do we speak and never hear each other?"

The long silence was uncomfortable; they heard Laura closing the door to her bedroom.

Allison sat up taller. "Levi, I love your mother. I'd wish more than anything that her future would be as wonderful as she is. She's so strong and kind, and even in the valley of grief she's shown me more love than I've ever known." She closed her eyes and stilled her irregular breaths. "Now, I think I need her."

He knew she couldn't say that about him. "I never meant for things to happen…to be here. I know you don't believe this." He rubbed his hand down his jaw. "I guess I'm going to prove it to you. I get paid this Friday, so be ready, because I'll be taking you to Madison."

Levi watched in disbelief as Allison shook her head. *Why isn't she smiling? Maybe even thanking me? Isn't this all she's ever wanted?* Junior's words of warning came back to him. "This kind you can never please."

It was a cold, dreary ride to Ready Springs. Allison looked at the familiar store and hotel, and grimaced at the church building. She already missed the Graham's cabin, already missed their little country church. Levi held his arm out for her to dismount in front of the stable. He unloaded their pack and led the horse to the corral. Laura was gracious to give her the warm jacket that she had been borrowing. The knitted scarf was also a gift. Her stomach flipped as Levi paid for his horse to be boarded, recalling Uncle Simon doing the same thing. He gave her a half smile as he took her arm. "Let's get some coffee and food. If the weather holds, the stage should be here in an hour."

They walked quietly to the little outdoor café. Most of the tables were gone, but there were two tables inside the building that housed the kitchen. The woman who had served them before set some cups down. "How about eggs and pancakes?" she asked while pouring the hot coffee. Levi nodded. Within minutes, the woman generously filled their plates. For a rare moment, Levi gazed at Allison, wanting something—maybe their simple little prayer before a meal.

"I see your pack there." The woman interrupted the moment. "You two trying to catch the stage?"

"Yes, ma'am." Levi nodded and started eating.

Allison was glad for the distraction. She had fought tears most of the way here, and wondered if she could eat with all the knots in her throat.

"I get the grub ready for them. Most weeks they've been on time."

Allison nodded and smiled weakly as she ate. She wondered how Laura was feeling in the cabin, alone. Her chin began to quiver, thinking of the time they had spent together. Now Laura had no one. Saying goodbye had turned her heart inside out. She set down her fork and caught the tears with her napkin. Levi cleared his throat as the woman poured more coffee.

"We can go—or you can go by yourself—into Crocker's. You have that credit on his books." He sounded calm. "You might as well get whatever you need."

Allison had always wanted Levi to have that money. "Please use it for some things for your mother when you get back," she whispered. "Fabric, yarn, certainly a coat." She looked down at the one Laura had given her.

Get back? He studied her a moment, then glanced away.

Levi helped Allison enter the stagecoach, then sat across from her. There was a small window to look out and fresh cold air to breathe, but after hours of rocking and jerking, Allison's stomach rebelled. *Oh, why, did I eat that breakfast?*

"Do you know when the next stop is?" she asked.

"Potato Patch." She looked uncomfortable, but that was hardly unusual. He watched her gulp ragged breaths, wishing he could help, but knowing once again that there was nothing he could do. He sighed, looking out the other window. *How much help do you receive?* he heard in a whisper. He closed his eyes; the Lord was speaking. *I don't receive much.* He knew the truth of God's conviction. *I guess you put two opposites together who suffer from the same disease.* He wondered if there was any hope for him. He'd been called independent all his years. And setting his mind like flint to keep everything under his control, God had put this person in his life who he could not control—not for one minute. He almost laughed out loud. She had never molded into what he thought he wanted, but he loved her fiercely.

She was swallowing hard, struggling to keep her stomach down. Compassion rose like a warm fire in him. This bumpy stage was the last place he thought God would show up. Reaching over, he touched her arm.

"Father, please help Allison. Calm her stomach, calm her nerves. Please, Lord, help her." *And please help me. I'm back at your feet. Please take this stone from my heart.* He whispered, content to see her frail smile.

Maybe it was the prayer, maybe it was the flatter roads, but Allison made it more easily through the last stage stop for the day. Her entire body had never been so grateful. Levi explained that the next leg of the trip would be on a small steamer across Lake Michigan. They walked along the wooden sidewalk, and with each step, she smelled a hundred new smells. Wondering if she would remember this place, she watched as people crossed the wide dirt streets. Nothing looked familiar. Levi led the way up some steps to the double doors of a hotel. They entered a lobby and noticed a dining area to the left.

"We need a room for the night," Levi said to the man standing behind the tall podium. Allison was grateful to hear they had a room available. She felt a surge of expectancy. It had been so long...Levi headed to the right, then dropped the pack and put the key in the door, nodding for her to go first. She saw a large bed with a red flowered bedspread. She walked to the window to look out into the street, while Levi dropped the heavy pack into the chair. He looked around, rubbing his hand through his hair. Reaching out to feel the bed, she looked up. "It's feather, not straw." She wondered if he was going to try to sleep in a chair again. "We can share it," she said.

"All right." He nodded, hanging up his jacket and reaching for hers. "Can we just eat supper here, downstairs?" he asked.

"That would be fine." Allison was relieved that the nausea had passed. "Thank you for praying for me today. I'm dreading the boat ride. I don't think they'll let me out to walk around on land when I need to." She gave him a small smile.

"No, they won't," he grinned back.

Heaven help her, his soft brown eyes were so warm.

"You're staring," he said. They both laughed.

"Shall we go, then?" She nodded toward the door.

Allison savored her beef and vegetables, but her delight was in watching people. Young and old, well-dressed and homespun. She and Levi were somewhere in the middle. For pity sakes, how she had changed. She used to judge everyone by how they dressed— now she wondered if they were good folk. *Do those children in the little dining room have good families? What makes that couple seem so happy?* Being happy was more important than a trunk full of fancy dresses. She wondered—would Levi stay and meet her grandmother? Would he care about where she had lived?

"Would you like some pie?" he asked.

"No, I'm too full." She pushed her plate away and caught a yawn in her hand. "And tired."

Levi stood, setting some money on the table, then reaching to pull her chair out. Such a simple gesture—but it filled Allison with tenderness. His hand was light on her back as they climbed the stairs; she had missed his touch very badly. He stood closer than usual as he unlocked their door, and Allison thought he smelled wonderful. They stepped inside and closed the door, and Levi rubbed his face. "Maybe I should go for a walk while you go to bed." He didn't really wait for an answer, but headed back toward the door.

Allison grabbed his hand. "Don't go."

His eyes held the strangest mixture of desire and hesitancy.

Giving him a small tug toward her, she whispered, "I want you to stay."

Moving to the bed, she untied her boots. At the other side of the bed, Levi began to undress. She couldn't ignore her racing pulse—she wanted to be with him again. *Will he take me in his arms? It's been months. So many things have changed.*

Walking to the pack, she pulled out her nightgown. Strangely shy, she slipped it over her head and dropped her clothes. He had already gotten into bed and blown out the small lamp. Slipping between the sheets, she laid back. The bed was pure luxury, and the silence was as thick as the wonderful pillow. "This bed is like being in a dream," she whispered, and turned, reaching her arm across his warm bare chest.

He turned to face her and brought his hand to rest on her waist. "I'm sorry I've been so distracted." He pulled at her long gown until their legs could intertwine. She rose on her knees and shrugged it off, loving the freedom of being alone with him in their own world. She lowered herself closer and closer, finding him once again.

43

Levi awoke at dawn, his body perfectly molded to his wife. He tried to hold still, but he opened his eyes. Why did she feel different? Tenderly, he stroked her belly, thinking that her body had changed since he'd last seen her unclothed. His mind whirled, and he suddenly pulled his arm back and sat up on one elbow.

Allison rolled onto her back, trying to recover her sheet. She cracked open an eye. "Staring again?"

He opened his mouth to speak, and then closed it quickly.

She yawned and reached up to touch his face. "Please, can we just stay here forever?"

Levi didn't answer, but instead asked, "Are you pregnant?"

She sat up, clutching the corner of the sheet. "Why? Why are you asking that?"

He rubbed his face again. "Do you know how a woman gets pregnant?"

"Yes, I know. And just because of last night doesn't mean…"

"No, no," Levi interrupted. "Not last night." He paused. "From Sault Creek. Months ago."

"Levi." She shook her head. "I…I…doubt…"

He took her arm. "I swear to you, I'm not making this up. I had my hand on your belly. Think about it. Don't get upset. But you feel different. Your stomach is …wider."

He realized too late that was the worst thing to say. She shoved him back with all her might.

"How dare you! My stomach is wider! Oh…I have never!" Heat flushed her face. "I've sat at your mother's table for over two months. So condemn me for enjoying the best food I've ever had! Anything was better than living off varmints from Sault Creek. Haven't you ever known anyone who has gained weight?" She gripped the sheet. "My grandmother carried her weight in the middle, some folks just do."

"Except I haven't been in bed with your grandmother, but I have with you." His eyes were wide, his jaw set.

She puffed out a breath as she slid off the bed and reached for her clothes. "I think I would know." She turned, glaring. "I was going to ask your mother a few questions."

"Like what?" In one swift movement, he pulled her back down onto the bed and held her tight. "Listen to me, before we both say things we'll regret." He felt her arms and body go lax. "All I want to know is…are you keeping this from me?"

The sound of rain pelted on the window, but she never took her eyes from his. "No, Levi," she sighed. "I would have to know it was true for me to keep it from you."

"Oh, for pity sakes, is it going to rain all day?" Allison shook her head at the wet window. Levi had only spoken a few words over their breakfast. They both decided he should run to the station in the rain. She didn't need to get soaked just to get to the dock for their boat tickets, so she paced, finally stopping to gaze into the mirror hanging on the wall. Had she gained that much weight? Her face didn't look fuller. If anything, it looked more drawn than she remembered. She lifted the hair that swept over her forehead. *Is Levi right? I've had nothing but stomach problems, accidents, and wild food for months. No wonder my ladies' days have been irregular.* She thought about Frieda's prolonged labor, and a shudder ran up her back. She knew how babies were made. If they continued the intimacies from last night, she might very well be pregnant soon—if she wasn't already.

The key turned, and Levi walked in, shrugging off his wet coat. "It's good news and bad news." He pulled an envelope from his pocket. "The good news is I got our tickets and a small berth for the trip. The bad news is the weather is looking uncertain, and they're worried about the late fall storms. I guess they lost a ship this time last year. All the cargo, crew, and passengers, somewhere on the bottom of Lake Michigan."

Allison tried to ignore that last bit of information. She would be getting on that boat, no matter what. "When do we board?"

"We don't, if this storm doesn't pass over."

"But you said they sold you tickets."

"Yes, and they're loading the ship with cargo as we speak, but no passengers until they're sure the weather will calm down."

Allison walked to the window. Not a hint of blue sky anywhere. The old feelings of needing to get her way started to rise up. "I'm sure it'll be fine. They don't stop these ships every time it rains."

"True." Levi stood next to her. "But I'm not taking any risk with you or the…" He cleared his throat. "…trip. I used to work on the docks. I've seen waves that would sink this hotel. I've seen frozen waves. That lake is dangerous."

"Can be dangerous," she corrected him.

Pulling down the corners of his mouth, he turned her from the window. She watched him suspiciously. He took her hand and nervously kneaded it. He locked his eyes on hers and flashed a small smile. Bending down on one knee, he took his free hand and pulled something from his pocket.

She jerked back. "What in the world?"

"Allison, I've been a poor example of how a beautiful woman like you needs to be courted. To be treated. But from the moment I met you, well, from the moment I knew you were going to live, I've been completely drawn to you. I've been overwhelmed with wanting to protect you and care for you. I've never felt this way in my life. Ever." He swallowed.

"Most of my attempts drove you further from me. But you have to know the truth. I…I desire to be a loving husband. I can't survive without you. Well, I can. I just don't want to." He took a quick breath.

"I will always love God more than you, but I believe He will help me do better, by you…by us. I love you more than my life…the one that I thought I needed. This isn't sounding the way I wanted." He swallowed hard. "I'll see you home and stay there…if you'll have me." He stilled, eyes locked on hers.

"Oh, Levi…" She pulled him up from the floor and clung tightly to him. She ran her fingers through his hair, and he easily lifted her off her feet. When it was good, it was so good. "Yes, I want you, too," she whispered in his ear. "I'll wear that ring with great affection and devotion to you."

Levi remembered the ring was still caught on his pinkie. "Sounds like this is for you, then." He set her to her feet and took her left hand.

She trembled as he put it on her finger. It was a bit loose, but holding it up in the air, she whispered, "Thank you."

The cold of the ship's metal fixtures seeped through the burgundy gloves, freezing Allison's hands. How could one day go from delightful to damnation? She sat on the bottom bunk and cling to the pole with all her might, but nothing, absolutely nothing could bring calm to her body. The steamer had sailed on time, but with all the pitching up and down, her stomach constantly heaved. Her head pounded and her back ached, and waves of feverish sweat kept rolling over her. She couldn't remember if Levi had promised for better or for worse all those months ago in Ready Springs. Well, now he'd seen her at her worst. She reached for the old bucket and tucked it between her knees. Her head fell forward as the heaving began again. If she didn't have her arm wrapped around the pole, she would have fallen head first onto the floor.

Levi patted a wet handkerchief across her forehead. "Here, let me have the bucket. Can you try to lie down?"

"No, I tried while you were out eating supper," she moaned.

He tucked some loose hair behind her ear. "I wish there was something I could do. Do you want anything?"

"I want off this ship," she whimpered. "I want land. Even your land would be fine."

"I might hold you to that," he said under his breath.

"I want Patch. Poor Patch, we never should have left him behind." She repositioned her face against the cold pole. "Oh, please God, make it stop."

"Just try this, for a few minutes. I have the bucket right here. Just try to close your eyes." He pulled her prone onto the bunk, and exhaustion lapsed into unconsciousness.

A loud slam rang hard against the boat. Levi looked up with concern, but Allison didn't move. She had finally found reprieve—for a few minutes, anyway.

Somewhere in the middle of the night, he jumped down from his bunk. *Was that another hard slam against the boat?* It was dark and cold, and he checked to see that Allison was asleep. With the blankets holding her in, he was relieved to find her free of the seasickness. Truth be told, the rocking had even gotten to him. Falling asleep was the only respite from the churning of his belly.

"Porridge served. Last door on the left," someone said from the hallway. Gray light streamed through the small porthole. The rain was still falling in sheets, the boat rocking from side to side.

"Allison." He rubbed her arm. "Are you hungry? What can I get you?"

She groaned and pushed his hand away. "Sleep," she croaked out.

"I'll be back shortly." The cold hit him as he opened the door. There was no movement in the hallway; everyone was likely stricken with seasickness. He climbed up a set of stairs and walked into the galley area. A few sailors sat holding their bowls and mugs. The cook nodded to him, and he sat down. The porridge was hot, and for a few minutes, it did the trick. Then men were talking low and secretively, and when Levi took his last bite he finally asked, "Is this vessel going to make it?"

44

❧❧

"If your name is Jonah, we'd advise you to jump." One of the sailors cackled at Levi, slapping his buddy on the back.

He realized they were making light of his question; he had probably offended them by suggesting the ship wouldn't make it. Nodding his goodbyes, he headed up another set of stairs to the deck, the rain cold and stinging his face. The air was so dark and gray it was hard to tell what were clouds and what were waves. He hung on to the doorframe, trying to steady himself, but the ship bucked like a new horse. He reminded himself it was only a lake, but quite the mad lake it was. He felt the water seeping into his boots and turned back to their cabin.

Shaking the water from his jacket, he reentered their tiny cabin to find Allison back at her familiar post-hugging posture.

"Did you talk to the captain?" she said, trying to hold herself steady. "Is the storm going away? Ever?"

Levi sat next to her, rubbing her back. "No, just some deckhands eating breakfast. They didn't seem too worried. They were joking about it, actually."

The steamer moaned around them. "Those sounds are scaring me."

He placed a kiss on her pale cheek. "Tell me about your home. What's the first thing we should do when we get there?"

"*If* we get there." Her eyes rolled. "I've been thinking about how to approach my grandmother. I'll probably speak to Mrs.

Clark, the housekeeper. She makes the most wonderful scones." She whimpered, gripping her stomach. "The bucket, please."

Levi was relieved that Allison was able to doze on and off throughout the day, but he was feeling like an animal caught in one of his traps. When he could tell she was fast asleep, he went up top for some fresh air. The water now covered the steps and seeped into his trousers. The wind howled. He heard curses coming from the landing and saw the deckhands struggling with the crates that were trying to break free from their ropes. Another man sped past him, sliding into the workers. "We're taking on water. The crack is worse than we thought!" he yelled. "Get the lifeboats ready! Get the passengers ready!"

"What!" Levi lunged at him and caught his arm as he tried to pass. "These waves will sink a smaller boat!"

"It's all we got!" The man yelled at Levi over the wind, gripping him to steady himself. "You seem strong enough. It's going to take every man to manage the lifeboats. You'll need to row straight into the wind! You'll hit land, I promise! Can you help us?"

"Yes, of course!" Levi yelled back. *Oh God, we need you far more than anything I can do,* he muttered as he followed to help.

The seven people in front of Allison had already jumped or fallen into the reeling lifeboat. She gripped Levi with everything she had. "I can't do this!" she cried into his ear.

"You can and you will!" He pulled her along to the edge. The ship sprayed a new layer of water on her. "When he reaches out, you let go and get in that lifeboat! Do you hear me? Don't hesitate! Get ready." He was about to pick her up if she didn't move quickly enough. The ship rocked up and down on cue, and a man reached out to grab Allison. Levi held her free arm and felt his grip slip down her forearm to her hand as the lifeboat fell off the wave. Hanging off the edge, he fought to straighten up. He could see she had safely made it into the lifeboat, and looked down at something in his hand. Her wedding band. He must have pulled it right off her finger. A rogue wave came up from nowhere and hit him clean in the face as he went flying backward. He tried to find his feet, and realized the ring was gone. Crawling and searching over the water-covered deck, he looked up just in time to see a large crate thundering toward him.

"Levi!" Allison screamed over and over above the wind. An older man pulled on her sleeve until she fell down onto the hard seat. "Shut up! Do you really think he can hear you?" She bit into the sleeve of Laura's coat, certain she was going to drown along with these other poor souls clinging together. Why God, oh, why didn't he jump in after her?

Right before darkness enveloped them, Allison heard a woman shout, "Lighthouse!" She didn't care. It couldn't possibly be real. The screeching of the wind and the numbing, wet cold had addled her brain. Conscious or unconscious, nothing was real.

It was light. Painful, but light. Was this heaven? Did heaven look like the nurse's room at Webster's' School for Young Women? Taking a deep breath, Allison decided that this was certainly some dream. Her whole head spun with visions of Ben pushing her under the tree, Patch coming into the water while she bathed, hands folded in prayer on a small plank table, looking into Levi's soft, warm eyes...

"Hello, dear," a familiar voice said. "Try to open your eyes, will you?"

Allison's mind would not cooperate. "Mrs. Webster, are you real?" she croaked, her mouth parched.

"Yes, Allison, I'm real. You're back at school. Do you remember how you got here?"

She tried to put the pieces in place, but the strain was too difficult. "No."

"Oh, dear." Mrs. Webster pulled up a chair and sat close. "We've had a terrible storm here. You were in it, out on Lake Michigan, poor dear."

"Yes. I remember that." Allison swallowed. "I'm so thankful to be off that boat. But how did I get here?" Dizziness assaulted her as she attempted to sit up.

"It's somewhat of a long story. Our Mr. Stewart was at the docks for another pickup. Listening to the people talk about the fate of your vessel. Someone knew that you were asking for Webster's School and he remembered you and…"

"I was asking for Webster's School? I don't remember that. Oh, no…" Allison rubbed her forehead. *What if I lost my memory again?*

"I don't know what else you said, but maybe this was just the closest place to bring you." Mrs. Webster squeezed her hand, trying to still her.

"The good news is that the doctor came by. He said you'll be fine—possibly you're just dehydrated. We've been giving you sips of water."

"Levi!" Tears pooled in her eyes. "Was there any sign of Levi?"

"Who is Levi, dear?" Mrs. Webster asked.

"My husband." Allison reached for Mrs. Webster's arm, and something rolled over her like a phantom wave. "We got separated. He was supposed to get on the lifeboat, but he never did. Do you know about the ship? Did it go down? Has anyone seen the others that didn't get on the boat?" She gasped for air.

"I'm so sorry, dear. I don't know. You can imagine what a shock it was to see you after all these months."

Allison noticed her crumpled clothes draped over a chair, her burgundy gloves sitting on them. She sucked in a ragged breath. "Does my grandmother or my uncle know I'm here?"

Mrs. Webster rose and straightened the pillow behind her back. "Your grandmother has passed, dear. Months ago."

Allison stared at her. "What?"

"'I'm sorry, dear, I assumed you knew."

She sank back into the pillow and covered her face with her hands. "Oh please, God. Please don't leave me. I can't be alone."

"I won't leave you, dear. We'll sort this all out. Please take a few more sips of water." Mrs. Webster held the cup to her lips, but Allison turned her body into the pillow, burying her face. Mrs. Webster rubbed her back as she drifted into a fitful sleep.

"It's too much to bear." Allison whimpered in the middle of the night. She could still see Levi hanging over the boat, drenched, holding out his hand. The pain in his face would be her last memory of him. "Levi, I'm so sorry," she whispered, weeping. "I'm so sorry. It's all my fault. If I had never insisted on going to Paris, if you had never been on the trail that day, if I had never pressed you for this trip, if I had never fallen in love…oh God, why?"

Allison spent the week in bed, listening to the rhythms of her old school—the timely bells, the familiar sounds of girls talking in the hallways. The noises were like numbing medication. Mrs. Webster came by every morning, noon, and night to try to coax her into eating. Allison would appease her, in hopes that she would just leave her alone. Alone, where she could fall asleep dreaming of Sault Creek. Some days, she wondered if she had just dreamed it all. Where was the ring Levi gave her? She wished every night that she could just sink into darkness. It surrounded her anyway—why didn't it just entomb her and be done with it?

"You should at least be walking the halls," the doctor told her that afternoon. He scowled at Mrs. Webster. "She needs to get out of bed. She is no longer dehydrated, and should be quite well soon."

Mrs. Webster drew in a long, tired breath and looked to Allison, seeming to ask permission from her to speak. "She is suffering from family loss," Mrs. Webster said to the doctor.

"I see," he said, preparing to leave.

"Wait," Allison said weakly, as he neared the door. "May I see the doctor alone?"

"Certainly." Mrs. Webster left, closing the door behind her.

Allison chewed her bottom lip to keep it from quivering. She felt as if she had swallowed glass. "Could you tell me…" The words kept getting caught. "…if I am with child?"

"Certainly." The doctor put his bag back down and asked her a few questions. She laid perfectly still as he pressed her belly. She didn't know if she could comprehend the outcome, whatever he said.

"I'd say you're about four months along. Now, I'm sorry to hear of your loss, but you have a baby to think about. They come into the world in much more dire straits than yours."

45

Mrs. Webster kindly brought new clothes and offered to have Yvette help Allison with bathing. "No, thank you. I can do it." Allison smiled. An hour later, she walked down the hallway to Mrs. Webster's office. Softly knocking on the large wooden door, she knew it was time to tell her the entire story.

Mrs. Webster touched Allison's hair, trying to find words. "I can't imagine the state of confusion you have been living with, yet I see in your eyes that there was a lovely, though complicated love story intertwined. You thought Paris was your adventure, yet I can't help thinking about God's plans." Mrs. Webster finally smiled, putting Allison at ease. "I have one other piece of news, though I was afraid to bring it up before. Now it may bring you comfort."

Allison breathed in a bit of courage. "Go ahead."

"Your Uncle Simon was sent to prison. He had many investors that he couldn't pay back, but to think of being so desperate as to harm another family member, to do what he did to you…"

"Do you think he harmed my grandmother?"

"No, I don't." Mrs. Webster said. "I received a lovely letter from Mrs. Clark. She was by your grandmother's side until the end. It sounded like a natural passing. And your home has gone to the bank."

Allison told herself to breathe. A sudden spinning encompassed her.

"Everything I so longed to see is all gone, and I've had to assume the worst about Levi."

Mrs. Webster took in a breath. "I don't want to say this, dear, this being your hour of need, but as I pray for you each night, I feel we are just a temporary stop. You carry such strength, Allison. I saw it in you as a child. As much as I want to wrap you in safety and keep you, I know that's not what is best for you. God has made your will strong, your stubborn determination for something greater than this school. I've known it all along."

"Thank you for saying that, Mrs. Webster. I'm sure you have many young girls who need your time and attention. I will always be eternally grateful for your help in my recovery."

"That doesn't mean you are not to visit and write." Mrs. Webster rose and wrapped her arms around her.

"I will be happy to share my—*our*—future as it unfolds."

Allison clutched her burgundy gloves as the carriage approached the docks of Chicago.

"Which port, ma'am?" she heard the driver call.

"I'm not sure. I'm one of the survivors from the big storm weeks ago. Do you know where that dock is located?"

"I'd check in with the port authority. The building ahead with the red sign."

Allison thanked him and climbed out. The freezing wind came up off the lake, threatening to numb her resolve. Her body swayed at the memory of that horrific trip. She stepped into the office and took a seat. The line wasn't long, but she needed a moment to gather herself. When she got her heart to slow down, she approached the man behind the counter. "I was wondering if you could help me. I was on the lifeboat that came in during that storm a few weeks ago. My husband and I were separated. He never got on the lifeboat." She swallowed hard. "Could you tell me what happened to that vessel?"

"Ah yes, the Montreal. It made it in, after all. It's a miracle they didn't get swamped."

"What about the crew? The others that were still on the boat?"

"I wouldn't know, ma'am. The crew probably went to find work. That vessel will be in repairs for weeks."

Allison went back to her empty seat. She should be rejoicing. Levi may have made it back alive, but where should she look for him? Did he go on to Madison? Did he try to find her? Would someone have a record of her going on to Webster's? Was he still in Chicago? For the first time, she gently placed her hand over her growing belly. *We have to find him, he's all we have.*

She spent two nights at the Park View Hotel. The city was still under construction, and the noise kept her from being able to think. The truth was, she didn't know what to do next. She rose early and gathered her few things. The hotel clerk helped her with a carriage to the train station. It was time to go on to Madison. Maybe Levi was there.

Allison gripped the case she had bought to hold a few of her new things. Stepping off the train to the familiar landing, she had forgotten how bitter the cold could be. She looked around, hopeful, yet fully aware that no one was here to pick her up. Thank goodness, not much had changed, though. She walked the three blocks to the hotel, stopping to watch a boy and his dog pass by on the other side. The sight pulled at her insides. She exhaled cold air and entered the hotel, scanning the lobby and each face. Something dropped in her gut. *What a ninny I am. Levi isn't going to be sitting there waiting for me.* She paid for her room and slowly took the stairs; the depression she had been pushing against weighted each step. Finally closing the door to her room, she collapsed onto the bed.

Each day of the next week, Allison visited her grandmother's grave, but she left with more loss. It was a simple cross with the name *Kent*, not even a proper headstone. No flowers—there were none to be found in early winter. She walked by her once-stately home, wondering what had happened to Burch and Mrs. Clark. She peeked in the windows and saw that it was empty. The bank must have sold whatever they could to eliminate some of Uncle Simon's debt. Later in the afternoon, she walked to where Mrs. Clark's daughter had done some sewing. The young woman she knew wasn't there, and though the other seamstresses were polite, it just made Allison feel more melancholy.

Allison entered the mercantile to get out of the cold. It was clean and tidy, nothing like the smells and sights of Crocker's. She walked around, listlessly fingering the beautiful things. What would be appropriate for her grandmother's headstone? Maybe a figurine, or something more personal. As she pulled on her gloves, she knew what to do. She walked back to the cemetery. An icy rain had begun to fall. She quickly pulled off her gloves and laid them at the foot of the cheerless marker. This was her personal tribute to her grandmother, her own way to show her love.

❧⟡❧

Levi awoke in the barn near the church. The elderly pastor had felt sorry for him and allowed him to stay there. At least it was dry and warm, and the reverend's wife had left him a tray of food. Holding a slice of bread, he tried to pray. He cut it short today, tired of repeating himself. He cracked the hardboiled egg and downed the simple food, then rested his face in his palms. *God, I know You said You would never forsake me, but I have no strength left. I'm out of ideas. What should I do?* He stood and decided he might as well leave Madison. She wasn't here. He'd looked, he'd asked. The only thing he'd found, with the help of the pastor was a gravesite, a wooden cross with the last name of *Kent.* It could be Allison's grandmother. He buttoned up his jacket and looked toward the cemetery. One last time he'd say his goodbyes and try to think of what to do next.

Approaching the grave marker, he squinted at something unusual, then stepped closer and picked up a pair of burgundy gloves. Her gloves. Tattered and worn, but he would know them anywhere. He threw his head back and yelled, "Thank You! Oh, a thousand times thank you!"

❧⟡❧

Allison finished her breakfast and sighed, thinking about finding a place to live. The hotel wasn't the best way to hold on to her money. She wanted to ask the clerk, but he looked busy, so she decided to take a short walk and come back later when he was free. She knew of a boarding house not far from the cemetery; she liked the idea of being close to her grandmother. As she approached the cemetery, she saw through the picket fence that a man was standing next to her grandmother's grave marker.

Surely her mind was playing a cruel trick. That curly brown hair looked so much like Levi's. She ran toward the fence, yelling,

"Levi!" Flying across the grounds, she jumped into his arms. "Is it you? Is it you?" She pulled back from his kisses to see his face. "How…how…"

"Yes, it's me. I've been here for weeks, searching, looking, praying…" He leaned away, still holding her, looking into her eyes. "But today I found these!" He held up her worn burgundy gloves. "I can't believe it. I love you…I love you so much." His kisses ran up her neck and onto her lips.

She pulled back. "I lost the ring you gave me."

He touched her forehead with his. "I don't care," he chuckled, out of breath. "You're here, we're married, and that's all I care about." Pressing another kiss to her lips, he laughed. "And I'll get you another."

Four months later

"Levi, I want you to get right up behind her shoulders," Laura said. "Allison, look at me. Look at me, dear!"

"Never again!" Allison screamed. "I will never have another baby! Never!"

"This is it! I can see the head!" Laura exclaimed. "Stay with me. With the next contraction…here it comes! Push! Push! Yes! You're doing it! Keep pushing! Yes, Jesus! We have a baby! It's a little boy!"

Levi dozed on and off through the night. It was too overwhelming to be lying next to Allison and their son, Daniel. She had loved the idea of naming him Daniel, after his brother in heaven. He was perfect.

The morning light broke through the window of their small home as Allison gazed at their new babe.

"Isn't he amazing?" She touched the baby's soft face.

"And you are, too." Levi gave her a wink.

"When I thought you had died on the lake…when I was at Webster's School…"

Levi nodded.

"When the doctor told me I was pregnant, it was the only reason I got out of bed. I had a reason to live. Every fiber in me wanted to have your baby."

"Our baby." He smiled.

"It's so strange how everything I thought I had to have has faded. I wanted to find my *real* life in Madison." She paused. "Oh, Levi." She looked up, surprised, "I did."

He leaned in and inhaled the new scent of his son. Nothing had ever filled his being so much as the two of them, snuggled close to him. He reached in and touched the baby's little nose. "New day, new life."

"It was so hard to say goodbye to your ma," Allison said as they walked back into their home. "I'm glad she was able to make arrangements to come and take care of us as soon as we wrote about the baby coming." She laid baby Daniel in his cradle. "When you see her traveling back home, do you think of going back? Do you want to go get Patch? Are you sure about staying in Madison?"

"Yes, I'm sure." The corner of his mouth turned up. "Besides, you said you would *never...*" He imitated her high scream. "...get on a boat!"

She swatted his arm for making fun of her.

He took the opportunity to grab her arms and draw her up against him. "But that other part, about *never* having another baby. That part we need to talk about."

"I never said that." She gave him a sly frown.

"Good. I must have misheard you." Levi looked down to the sleeping baby and back to Allison. "God has given me more than I could even think or imagine. Being your husband, Daniel's pa, starting the hunting guide business, helping Pastor Johnson with some of the teaching...who ever would have thought that after all those winters alone, preaching to Patch, that God was leading me to teach the Bible to real people?"

"You're good at it. Look what you did to save my soul." She smiled.

"I did more to ruin it, but God has redeemed us both. All our mistakes, all our stubborn areas and memory losses..."

Allison dropped her chin, eyeing him. "Trust me, both of us still have a way to go." She gazed at Levi's deep brown eyes, and a powerful wave of certainty filled her heart. Merciful Lord, how she'd longed for this deep sense of belonging.

"I'm so thankful," she whispered, leaning in to kiss the baby's soft curls.

CLOSING NOTE:

The Mighty One series: *Burgundy Gloves, Broken Chain,* and *Black Coat* intertwine two families in the late 1800s. Both families face similar tragedies, yet each copes with their grief and loss completely differently.

Burgundy Gloves introduces you to Laura Graham. She is a composite of every believing woman who lives her faith out mostly alone. You know these women today, just as I do; maybe you are one. Silent courage radiates as they attend church alone, pray alone, believe alone, all the while standing in the gap for their children and grandchildren, neighbors and other family. Their strength does not come from a man standing beside them, but from the One who lives inside. If this is you, well done, beautiful one. The Father has seen the longing of your heart. He has seen how you choose Him, regardless if anyone else does. You are so important, so valuable.

Charm can be deceiving, and beauty fades away. But a woman who honors the Lord deserves to be praised. Show her respect, praise her in public for what she has done. Proverbs 31:3031 CEV

Amen to that!

AUTHOR'S NOTE:

I have lived for over twenty-five years in one of the hottest areas of California. I'm the mother of a bunch of active kids who spent hours upon hours in the backyard swimming pool, leaving me housebound. Our desk and computer sat facing the window that overlooked the pool. One day, I was digging through an old cosmetic case that had been with my grandmother's things, and I came upon a pair of soft burgundy gloves. As I pulled them on, I wondered about the wear and tear on the fingertips. Certainly, my grandmother wore them in the 1930s 40s. But what wore them down? Did they ever wipe a tear? Who gave them to her? Did they travel anywhere before they came to her lovely hands? They had survived fairly well. I tend to get completely sentimental over weird things, so one hot afternoon I thought, *what kind of story would the mother of wet, wild children, with a computer facing the back yard* like *to tell?*

Grandma holding my mom. Darn those black and white photos. Could she be wearing the burgundy gloves?

Jesus walked on this earth telling stories: "There was a certain man who fell among thieves..."

Good stories have a way of defusing the commotion of our brains, allowing the simple conflict and emotions of others to speak to our own souls. Jesus didn't come to demonstrate facts. Facts seldom move the heart. He spoke stories that touch, reveal, and encourage.

My hope is always that you, the reader, have escaped to another era, where healing happens, truth wins, and true love prevails.

Julia

Julia David

I invite you to join me at juliadwrites.com for more fun tidbits, release dates for future books and great prize giveaways!

THE VOYAGE
Inspired me

Speak, even if your voice is trembling
Please, you've been quiet for so long
Believe, it'll be worth the risk you're taking

You're afraid, but you can hear adventure calling
There's a rush of adrenaline to your bones
What you make of this moment changes everything

What if the path you choose becomes a road
The ground you take becomes a home
The wind is high, but the pressure's off
I'll send the rain wherever we end up
Wherever we end up

Set your sights, sailing far beyond familiar
In the rising tide, you'll find the rhythm of your heart
And lift your head, now the wind and waves don't matter

What if the path you choose becomes a road
The ground you take becomes a home
The wind is high, but the pressure's off
I'll send the rain wherever we end up
Wherever we end up

I am the wind in your sails
I am the wind in your sails

Julia David

I am the wind in your sails

The Voyage (Official Lyric Video) // Brave New World // Amanda Cook ...

https://www.youtube.com/watch?v=Jd3vuxpMKUM

Next in The Mighty Ones Series
BROKEN CHAIN

Ben Graham wakes up behind bars. A long walk in humility lands him on the Von Keller dairy farm with another distraction named Nadine Von Keller. The perfect opportunity comes to rescue the Von Kellers older daughter from a life-threatening mission. Finally a chance to do the honorable thing. With a broken chain in his hand, will his past repeat its self or point to his future?

Another clean inspirational romance with a dash of steam.

Find it at Amazon:

https://www.amazon.com/BrokenChainMightyOneBookebook/dp/B079B17L2Y

www.ingramcontent.com/pod-product-compliance
Lightning Source LLC
Chambersburg PA
CBHW030314200626
46816CB00006BA/1785